After the Flood

Memoirs of a Tyrant King

Larry Culliford

Contents

Also by Larry Culliford

Fiction

The Red Chairs Mystery

Non-fiction

Love, Healing & Happiness
Much Ado about Something
The Big Book of Wisdom

In The Guardroom

Feeble light from dusty wall lanterns reveals the bare room in which, on wooden floorboards, stands a scarred and greasy oak table with benches either side. A similar light source illuminates the sombre faces of two people on duty, a man and a woman. Both are wearing rough, dark uniforms with no insignia.

"It's time... Go and finish him off." The man speaks with firm authority.

"No. You... Why not you?"

A two-foot length of cheese wire lies curled but lifeless before the woman, who is seated. Handles at either end make it an efficient garrotte. Silence.

The woman again, with her argument. "You're stronger."

The man's dismissive riposte. "He's a feeble old bastard. You'll be fine."

More silence. Another plea from the woman. "You hated that shitty tyrant. Don't you want to do him in?"

Dense, like cigar smoke, the matter rests heavily upon them, impossible to ignore but acrid, unpleasant. Soon the woman shrugs in submission. His face betraying no sign, the man smiles inwardly, sensing victory.

"Ladies first," he says, not bothering to conceal a leery, lop-sided grin this time.

"You're a real gent," the woman responds sarcastically, fully aware that the irony would be ignored. "There's no need to do me any favours... But, honestly, I wouldn't want to mess it up."

Solidly built, she is barely forty, and her chances of failure seem minimal.

"I've seen you finish off an old rooster with your bare hands," he says. "This won't be different."

"But I'm not hungry now," she replies. The power of necessity in lean times has given her strength; however she feels weaker now, less determined, as it dawns on her finally that the battle is lost. He's as resolute mentally as he is strong physically. They might as well have been arm-wrestling, as she clearly has no chance at all.

"It's midnight," he says; then repeated, "It's time."

Standing wearily, the woman picks up the weapon, drawing apart the handles, pulling taught the wire to test its strength, as she walks towards the door.

"Maybe I'll go down in history," she says, clutching at something positive to alleviate the foreboding fluttering in her breast. "That'll be something, won't it?"

"You'll never have to buy yourself a drink again, I promise."

The man raises his voice, as his comrade sets off on her deadly mission, meaning to sound encouraging, to reassure her; but, as he silently takes another garrotte from the drawer under the table, moving to stand behind the still-open door, he knows his promise would be kept.

One

I am very old, ancient, almost at the age when, like previous monarchs, I could send myself a congratulatory telegram from this 'Palace' I live in; if telegrams still existed. I have survived these many years, and achieved a great deal, being the King of southern Britain's island rump for decades. After the flood, and the riots, someone had to take charge... *Tyrannosaurus Rex*... Fierce and fearless; the most magnificent of dinosaurs whose Latin name, as I learnt at school, means 'tyrant king of all the lizards'. Ha Ha Ha! That is me! Or it was...

Nowadays I sleep a great deal. Asleep, I usually dream: sweet, sexy dreams, of Carol, my long lost love; but also troubled dreams, nightmares, about the past. Last night, for example, as so often, I woke in a sweat, certain I was dying, my life forfeit. Coming to, lying there in the total silence; no voices, no hum of machinery; I remembered vividly that desperate gun battle in Lalibela when, outnumbered by ferocious insurgents, a dear mate saved my life, but only by surrendering his. And I remember the first time I took a man's life. How could I ever forget?

Some of the army lads took their broken dreams, flashbacks, startle responses and terrifying rages to psychologists, some of whom told some of them to get it all out; to make themselves remember, little by little, and work towards exorcising their demons by writing it down in make-believe letters maybe or journals. Perhaps that's what will help me now; but, on account of my arthritic claw cramping up far too quickly, I won't be using paper and pen. I can only dictate the stuff. The story's pretty unique.

T. Rex...There's a definite sense in which I identify with and glory in that bygone monster's superlative power; and the irony is not lost on me that it shares a name with one of my mother's favourite rock groups. A young girl at the height of the flower power era, she'd been to see them with her folks at the Albert Hall, the warm-up band for Donovan, a gentle balladeer of great renown whose lilting voice contrasted massively to the destined to die young, shock-haired, boy-man, Marc Bolan's distinctive throaty warbling on tracks like 'Debora' and 'Children of the Revolution'. Charlie played those tracks over and over on the tape-deck in the van when we were boys.

Mother's true name, that she detested, was Charlotte. It always reminded her, she said, of a sickly Russian pudding. Nor did she countenance 'Ma' or 'Mum', much less 'Mummy', for she was a free spirit, Charlie. "Having a label is boring", she used to say, as if to emphasize her individuality; and to make the point, I suppose, we twins were seldom given separate identities. It was always just "You Kids". I learned a lot about double-standards from our mother.

Father's name was Henry, but that appellation too was seldom used. He was always called 'H' as in 'Aich'.

"I'm H without an h," he used to say, having adopted this curiously apt amalgam of 'ache' and 'itch', sometimes also insisting on the superior aspirated version, 'Haitch'.

"Haitch-you", we would say to his back when he'd upset us or, once again, let us down.

It's such a pity that all the great stretches of shoreline beaches were wiped out by the flood, because so many fine memories of such magical places remain etched on my ageing brain. When Raul and I were young, Charlie took us to the beach all the time. One summer, for instance, H and Charlie were getting on well. Somehow, they must have come into a bit of money because they'd bought an old camper-van, and we hurtled around the country from beach to beach, music festival to music festival, political rally to political rally. They were lefties, crypto-commies faintly allied to the Workers Revolutionary Party; and they just loved the rock bands of the era like Ten Years After. H boasted that he once hitched a ride in Ric Lee's Roller, but I doubt it was true. Anyway, Alvin Lee was the real musician. What a voice! Ric was okay, but he was only the drummer.

My father loved blues-rock especially. He played "I'm Going Home" repeatedly in the passion-wagon that hot year... Although, of course, we never actually did go home. For a while, as far as two shallow, irresponsible people could be, they were serious political groupies, hapless children of the revolution indeed; professed Trotsky followers. How else did I get to be called Fidel and my brother Raul? We were the Castro brothers, and our folks thought that was cool. But they were mayflies, forever short on endurance, relentless in their search for good times.

Legend has it that they met at the Isle of Wight festival one year. Bob Dylan was singing 'Blowin' in the Wind' when, close to the stage, as Charlie remembered it, their eyes met and it was love at first sight. H's version was cruder.

"She was swaying topless to the music, Man. It was instant. I just fell in love with those tits." Typical H!

He had no backbone, our Pa, no fibre. Born into middle-class money, he had a privileged education, won a place at Oxford's Exeter College to read politics, then favoured Exeter University and economics instead.

"It was my Exeter exit strategy," he used to boast. "My way out... I

4

didn't want all the hassle, to be honest, all that posh pressure."

How glib he sounded, but then honesty was not a quality H had in particular abundance; and how things might have been different; but the die was firmly cast. In the first year of study, he learned enough armchair Marxism to poison him against his father, Ralph, the 'fat-cat capitalist', to whom he owed everything; so he soon became a virtual dropout without, of course, giving up either his parental allowance or his student grant. H the hippie-with-a-cause that excused him from any and all responsibilities. Also, naturally, like everyone in those days, he regularly smoked a ton of marijuana.

Although her background was poorer, Charlie told a similar tale. Her father died young from a Hodgkin's lymphoma, whatever that was; some fancy kind of cancer; so her mother returned to work as a nurse. Charlie thought of doing the same, but multiple dreary hospital visits to her dying father, not to mention her mother's endless disgusting tales of sluice-room duties, put her off. She applied for teacher training instead, started the course, then went to the Isle of Wight, met H, and let him talk her out of it. What a waste!

They were a feckless couple; convinced when they had children that they were grown up, but they really couldn't be bothered to act genuinely as parents, except in a jokey, sporadic and half-hearted way.

"If there'd been one of you, okay", Charlie used to say in the early days, "But twins! That was asking too much".

As if it was God's fault she couldn't be bothered to manage, or H's maybe for providing twice the required number of sperms. Their lives had to be fun, full of energy and excitement. If we got neglected food-wise, clothing-wise, education-wise, love-wise, do I care? Looking back from this distance, not at all. But if I'm going to record stuff accurately, it does all need to be said.

I dreamed about a coffin the other night; 'six bits of wood'. I know death is coming, so this is my last chance to give an account of it all: the pandemics, climate change, the great flood and all the devastation that's happened; not simply to try and stop the nightmares, and certainly not to make excuses, just to explain, to tell the whole amazing, pitiful story before my ancient ticker finally stops beating and it's too damn late. Will anybody ever listen to it, transcribe or read it? That doesn't seem to be the point. It's giving me something to think about and do as the days drag by, that's one thing. It's a project. Also, despite the painful stuff, much will be a genuine pleasure to recall.

That summer was typical. It was a vagabond life. Ralph had long since given up on his only son, reducing his allowance to a pittance, and we were always either on the move, or H and Charlie were stoned, immobile, in a dream. Most of the time for Raul and me, sadly, that dream was our nightmare. We were often bored. We had no friends, only each other; and the truth is; being non-identical twins with completely different interests; we were not particularly compatible. Our temperaments were forever at odds. Whenever there was nothing to do, we ended up arguing, often fighting.

"Peace, Man!" H would say in that stoned whisper of his, while rolling another huge joint.

Charlie, less patient, would more than likely simply yell at us to "Shut-the-fuck-up!"

Sometimes she would whisk us off in search of ice-cream and pacification. More often, she would simply pull us apart, stick one of us in the front part of the camper van and the other in the back; but that didn't work. The cardboard partition, H's typical botched-job handiwork, was flimsy. We could still shout at each other, maybe reach through and pull each other's hair. In the end, she usually gave up; and so eventually did we. If anyone ever says "I-Spy" to me, even now, my fists automatically clench. I really hated that game, and don't let me hear the word 'Monopoly' either.

The only good times were at the beach. H was great at finding little out-of-the-way places, beautiful sandy coves where we would be entirely alone. He had a little pair of faded khaki shorts, ripped in places, and wore a red bandana round his throat. I can see him still in my mind's eye, the strangely fond image of a trim, nut-brown body strutting up and down the shoreline, book in hand, shouting lines from Rilke or 'Das Kapital' at the waves, spittle streaking his ragged moustache, long hair streaming out behind him in the wind.

Charlie, child of nature, was always topless, and often wore nothing at all on those beaches. She was elemental, a blonde-headed, golden-skinned waif, dancing in and out of the surf. They were happy, the two of them, and that was good for us. Quite often, they would tell us to stay down the beach while they returned to give the camper van's suspension a full-scale rockabilly work-out. Loud music; Ten Years After naturally, Pink Floyd, The Doors, Jefferson Airplane, or occasionally the exquisite, lilting Rodrigo Guitar Concerto; magic sounds wafting across the sands as the creaky VW bounced rhythmically up and down to their feverish lovemaking. Even at night, almost every night as we pretended sleep, Charlie's high-pitched sighs and H's regular grunting told of the inexhaustible passion they had for each other. To us, of course, it was pitiful.

Raul was happiest with the rock pools and their myriad little creatures flitting about in dappled sunlight, but it was the sand I loved, fashioning wet sand into structures. I had an old biscuit tin full of plastic soldiers, field guns, tanks and other military knick-knacks. My joy was to build a fort with a moat and people it with defenders and attackers, playing out the siege and bombardment, men storming the ramparts, then the ensuing pitched battle on the battlements and in the castle yard. I could spend hours locked in concentration, until nature – the rising tide – would bring my play to a close, demolishing my creative efforts with irresistible force as I scrabbled about gathering up that precious cache of warriors and their accoutrements. Who said war couldn't be creative? Sometimes H or Charlie would call me away, long before these final scenes. Passion spent, they were hungry, wanting burgers or fish and chips, and I would be disappointed. Perhaps it's not so strange, given what's happened, that I should so often feel triumph in the midst of death and destruction. I always took delight in disaster.

Two

We argued a lot in later years too, my twin brother and I. He often accused me in all seriousness of being a monster; that I deluded myself about being a nice guy. University educated, and fancying himself as a psychologist, he insisted my problem was that I couldn't tolerate either shame or guilt, and therefore avoided experiencing them at all costs. These were two emotions he called essential in a well-rounded, sociable human being. He charged me with shielding myself from them by becoming angry whenever these unwanted feelings threatened, especially when I felt accused of wrongdoing by others. Anger was my personal default position, he said, which gave me the false but comforting sensation of being right in my actions and attitudes, and 'in the right' in my arguments. I felt strong when I was angry, making me see others as weak.

He talked a lot of rubbish, my brother; but, if all this does happen to be true, I'm not complaining. I know I get angry, but it has made me strong, and I do get things right a lot of the time. How else could I have become king?

Anyway, the endless weeks of that high summer eventually wore on towards autumn. "I'm Going Home" began to sound more like a possibility. Charlie and H began bickering. The money was running out, and this was a sure-fire guarantee to set them on edge.

"Something'll turn up," H kept repeating with a grin, like a latter-day Micawber on speed; but his faux-optimism could never achieve calm over Charlie's interminable fretting. She wore him down, I guess, and mid-September found us back in the cramped flat we were renting in Tooting that year.

H had sub-let the place for the summer to a bunch of foreign students, in London for a language course. They'd gone, but predictably had left the place in a total mess; rancid milk in the fridge, dog food scattered all over the kitchen floor, ripped curtains, broken blinds, all kinds of stuff missing. Charlie, showing some gumption for once, took charge. H, of course, headed right out to the pub. Raul and I did the chores, and the next day we had to go back to the crappy school up the road where, fair-skinned, albeit suntanned, we definitely formed a racial minority, and punch-ups in break time were the routine order of the day. Luckily, I was tough. Raul, on the other hand, regularly took a beating.

We had already missed a couple of weeks, I seem to remember. Cliques had formed and set by then, so the two of us were on our own.

Brighter than me, or maybe just more dedicated to the studious life, my little brother was put in the A stream, while I was in the B; so we could not even get together, gang up and support each other, except one time when, after school, I came across three teenagers giving Raul a right pasting in the local park. Unlike me, he had not yet reached puberty, and was defenceless. If I say that one of his cowardly assailants went home with a black eye, and the other two had to visit the hospital for stitches, I'm giving an accurate picture, for I carried a sharp knife in those days, and was handy with it even then.

Raul was always smaller than me and, although he would prefer to be thought of as 'sensitive', he was weaker and somewhat timid with it. That's why I always think of him as my "little" brother although, strictly-speaking, he was the older by seventeen minutes according to Charlie. Nevertheless, might was definitely right in the jungle of our childhood; and, though I would never stand by and let anyone else batter seven bells out of him, there were occasions when I had to let him know who was boss between us two. Not that it was much fun. He never put up much of a fight, not until later anyway, but I'm getting ahead of the story.

As we went back to school that year, Charlie found part-time work in a nearby confectioners; which was truly handy, because nearly every day she brought back packets of Smarties and Mars Bars that she'd 'liberated', according to the crackpot wisdom of that hackneyed old Communist dictum she and H used to go by: *"From each according to their ability; for each according to their need".* To our advantage, she was an accomplished and opportunist kind of thief, always on the lookout for low-risk profit. Putting the welfare of her children before upholding the letter of the law in such situations seemed like virtue to her; and we desperately needed those Maltesers, Man! Who could doubt it? H and Charlie needed sweets too, especially chocolate bars. Mary-Jane gave them the munchies.

Soon after our return, H disappeared again with the van. A week later we had a post-card from Kent. He was picking hops. The harvest would take about three weeks and the money was reasonable, even if the conditions were dreadful. In the event, six weeks went by before he actually returned, and then only briefly.

As I pieced the story together from Charlie, with a few more details from H later, the night after we got back from the West Country, a friend of his from his student days, Mark, came to visit. Another college friend, Victor, was the son of a hop farmer. It was the season, and they were looking for a replacement picker at short notice. The inducement Mark offered was a hefty chunk of hashish, top-grade Moroccan Gold. H would only be able to pay for it if he took the hop-picking assignment. That was the catch, but I don't suppose he thought twice before signing up.

Some years later, before I joined the army, I too tried hop-picking, only to discover that it's no barrel of laughs. The grind starts before dawn and continues until after dark six days a week, almost fourteen hours hard graft every day. I think H said they knocked off early on Saturdays, but could do a voluntary morning overtime shift on Sunday for double pay. At least when I went, the accommodation was comfortable and welcoming. The hop-pickers H joined were billeted in a huge, windswept old barn with bunk beds and only basic washing amenities. Their day began with a porridge breakfast and a cold walk through narrow lanes flanked by dew-lined shrubbery to the hop fields. 'Lunch', in the form of sandwiches and a hot drink, tea or Bovril, was delivered at 9.00 am. 'Dinner' back at the barn at noon was usually hot soup and bread. 'Tea' at 3.00 pm, also delivered to the field, meant more sandwiches and another drink. Finally, a big 'Supper' at trestle tables in the barn ended the day, usually something like rabbit stew or chicken and leek pie with heaps of potatoes, greens and carrots. There was nothing to stop them going drinking after that, but the gang of eight were busted by then, with only sleep on their minds.

I wonder how many beer drinkers ever knew what hops actually look like and how they're harvested. The fruit are not fleshy like plums or strawberries. They are pale green leafy nests, one or two inches long, hanging down from vines draped over strong wire netting held up by tall wooden poles in long rows. These are quite unlike grape vines; you can't simply walk along them and cut off ripe bunches of fruit. With hops, you have to take down a ten or twelve foot length of vine from which dozens of hop florets are shooting; and, to do this efficiently, a tractor is driven slowly down each row, pulling a specially adapted trailer, on which two 'pickers' perched either side at the front, with a 'cutter' stationed above on the 'crow's nest', a small platform atop a removable ladder that was temporarily fixed at the back-end of the trailer. Another cutter would walk ahead to sever the lower end of each of the four vines surrounding each pole on either side of the tractor-line. The pickers, as they passed, had to grab the dangling vines and wrap them between two staves, while the cutter leaned forward with a sharp knife to release the same vines at the top, allowing them to fall into the trailer bed.

When the space has been filled, everyone jumps off. The crow's nest is taken down. The tractor then shoots off to the barn where the dryer and threshing machine are situated. Eventually, the dried hops are bagged up mechanically in massive brown sacks for transport to the brewery. Meanwhile, the crow's nest is swiftly hoisted up and positioned at the back of the next tractor-trailer combo, and off we all go again. Except I couldn't hack it for long, and gave up after three days.

Hop vines are vulnerable to insects feeding voraciously on their leaves, so the big drawback is that large quantities of sulphur-based insecticides are used. As you cut the vines and load them into the trailers, there's no way of avoiding a liberal dose of sulphurous dust getting everywhere. It is fairly harmless to the skin, but penetrates deep into your eye sockets. During the day, there is not much of a noticeable effect. I remember we used to blink a lot more than normal, that's all. But, when you close your eyes at night, your eyeballs are totally aflame. It's like having red hot chilli-peppers stuffed right into your skull; and eyewash doesn't help. You just have to put up with the twin fire-bombs boring into your brain night after night until you fall asleep. Luckily, exhausted as we were, this didn't usually take long; but the whole thing was hellish so, on the fourth morning, I simply refused to get off the mattress. I hated the glutinous porridge too, as it happens, so it wasn't hard to convince myself at the time that I'd no such great need of the experience.

Back in the day, pissing off was not a viable option for H. I can see him trying out the Moroccan magic as a remedy, only to discover it making his eyes more sensitive and smart even worse. Not being much of a drug purist, he probably tried boozing as well; but you can't do that every night and keep getting up at dawn. Finally, it was Mark who gave him the cure, snow-white powder for H to sniff up his nostrils: cocaine. H was hooked in a heartbeat.

They should have tried dissolving the coke and using it as eye drops. One of Sigmund Freud's lesser-known gifts to humanity, it turns out, very useful for the eye surgeons of his day, was the discovery that cocaine drops can be used as a local anaesthetic. H must have injected it eventually, though, because whatever actually took place down on the hop farm, he suddenly became Mark's poodle, forever following him around, hungry for the next dose of snow. And that spelled curtains for us all.

Three

When the hop harvest was over, H followed Mark back to London from Kent. All the money he'd earned went on drugs, of course: cocaine when Mark could supply it; later heroin, not as effective but, H always said, the next best thing. Whenever he was off his head, you could hear him obsessively repeating, "H is for Horse," over and over again. Other times he'd amuse himself by clapping his hands in your face, suddenly yelling out, "Smack!" And that was it, smack down went our fortunes. The three of us had no chance.

When H came back to Tooting, he was a mess; but he couldn't see it. Mark was dosing him up. He felt fine, so why shouldn't everyone else be? Then, about three weeks later, there was a bad patch. He needed a bigger dollop, so one evening he tried to hit on Charlie for cash and they had a big row, stormier than any I remember; and this one, for a change, did not end with them getting stoned together and bonking; probably because H had switched the fullness of his passion away from Charlie onto coke and heroin by then... But he was desperate, you could tell. The flat being a tad too small for Raul and me to hide anywhere from the noise or the kerfuffle, we were blessed with front row, ring-side seats at the ensuing marital meltdown. Raul cried, but no-one took any notice. Me, on the other hand, I found the whole spectacle strangely thrilling. Charlie was snarling like a she-tiger at one point, and cussing fit to bust. It was like being at the circus; but eventually I too realised this was serious and began to get scared.

H usually stood his ground during arguments. When a stalemate was eventually reached, they would normally both back down; but this time, as Charlie grew more confident, H's gruff shouts turned increasingly towards whining. He began sounding increasingly pathetic. When, finally, she yelled at him to bloody well get out, he just did. To our amazement, H got up, went out through the door and more or less out of our lives. I ran after him into the street, but he ignored my cries to come back, just slunk away, head bowed. He'd sold the van, of course. We were penniless.

I am not a cry-baby, but I do admit that was the one time I shed a couple of tears for a minute. It was frightening. Charlie was crying too as she put us to bed, and so of course was Raul, who even went back to sucking his thumb for comfort, just like when he was six. Possibly the sight of his infantile relapse helped me pull myself together and stop blubbing, but I was still gripped by shock and a kind of empty numbness. I remember also a slight feeling of panic when I woke up in the night, remembering what had happened; but I needn't have worried. The crisis was bringing hidden strengths out in Charlie, a mother at bay about to show some real grit. Having at last discovered her backbone, she was up early the following day, bustling around preparing our school lunches then getting herself all dolled up. Lying awake during the night, she had devised a workable plan.

Drawing on her mother's example, too proud to live on welfare, she knew that, without qualifications, she was never going to make ends meet and give the three of us a decent life. While H was busy getting lost in the hell-realm of his junkie habit, she decided firmly that we would not be part of a wasteful sacrifice to the gods of substance abuse. Charlie had made up her mind to call on the one person wealthy enough to make our lives liveable, H's dad.

After making excuses to Mrs Reid, her boss at the sweetshop, and walking us to school; looking her absolute best in as handsome an outfit as her present wardrobe allowed; Charlie made her way to the imposing town-house in St John's Wood belonging to Ralph Manning, our grandfather. As I imagine it, he was probably surprised by his visitor, but not at all by her mission. They had only met a few times previously. He was a widower, with no obvious interest in family. The rumour was that his wife, Gertrude, a shy and retiring kind of person, had simply given up and died in the face of his relentless indifference. Like his Dickensian namesake, the avaricious Ralph Nickleby, his only real interest was business, laying up treasure upon the earth. Charlie, undaunted, somehow managed nevertheless to talk her way in to see him, sitting in state at a desk laden with paperwork in his plush, dimly-lit study.

"I have come about your grandchildren," she told our intended benefactor, whose stern expression never faltered as she described our new circumstances as succinctly as possible. "Henry has left us, and I'm here to ask what you can do for little Fidel and Raul."

Grandpa Ralph remained silent for a full minute, then told her to return in a week, giving him time to consider the situation. Always highly cautious about disbursing money, I imagine he wanted to make enquiries. And it occurs to me that H had probably already tried to get a sizeable amount off him, so he may have already been wise to everything by the time of Charlie's return visit. As per his instructions, I should add, we were to come along too; so, on a bright sunny day, squeaky-clean in school uniforms, shoes uncharacteristically shiny, Raul and me followed Charlie into the great house to hear him proclaim our fate. This was our first visit to the mansion, and I remember being struck by how gloomy the place felt. No sunbeam seemed ever to penetrate the dim edifice, and no ray of good humour either.

It had been different when Granny Gertrude was alive. The couple lived in comfortable splendour near Wimbledon Common then, in the house where, even if he never actually grew up, H had at least spent his childhood. Our grandfather was seldom at home, naturally, which suited H; who would only visit when his father was at his London office; and I remember how Granny used to give us home-made lemonade and send us out to play in their spacious garden while she tried persuading her son to visit more often. Charlie was sweet with her, but Granny must have known H went there only when he needed cash. Anyway, she died and that was that. No more cream buns for tea, the treat we always looked forward to. She died and, as far as I could tell, nobody mourned. Her funeral was, I think, the first time I ever saw Ralph; not that he took any notice of me or Raul. His face could have been made of alabaster for all the life it showed; his eyes glazed over with... with what? I don't think it could have been grief. More likely it was just bored resignation.

And here he was again; not tall, but a corpulent and imposing figure, formally attired in a well-tailored dark suit and some kind of old-fashioned light-grey silk cravat. Living in the mausoleum he had bought for himself closer to town within a few weeks of that funeral, surrounding himself with servants who knew how to keep silent, he was continuing with what he knew and seemed to love best, accumulating stacks of money. The front door was closed behind us by some silent wraith, and we were whisked swiftly up to the study on the first floor, where he not so much greeted us as turned away towards his well-laden bookshelves while the three of us sat in pre-arranged chairs before his highly polished desk. Charlie perched in the middle.

To interrupt the semi-circular symmetry, I quickly pushed the heavy mahogany chair back an inch or two. The carpet softened the sound, but something was audible in that still and stifling room, a faint noise that brought Grandpa Ralph back to life. Turning suddenly, drawing himself up to his full height before leaning forward, resting well-manicured fingertips on the desktop, he instructed me to return the errant item of furniture to its original place, and continued speaking as if giving orders.

"Charlotte," he started. Mother flinched, unaccustomed to the formality behind this address. "Charlotte, in response to your application for assistance, I have this to say... Please listen carefully."

He paused, like a schoolmaster intent on assuring himself of our fullest attention, before resuming in doom-laden tones.

"Until they leave school or university, these boys will be educated at my expense; as long as they apply themselves and I continue to receive satisfactory reports from their teachers. Rent will also be taken care of on a suitable property for you to reside in, one I have already selected from my own portfolio, where conveniently on my instructions the current tenants are due to vacate at the end of this month. These children will thus have a secure home to return to at half-term and during the school vacation periods. You will also receive an allowance to cover their necessities, food and clothing and such like."

When he paused again, I stole a glance at Charlie, who seemed a little stunned and appeared to be holding her breath. Was she content? I wasn't. What was he going on about? Half-term and school vacations? I didn't fancy going to a boarding school; and I didn't think Charlie would have wanted the three of us separated, so I was hoping for some sign of protest from her, but she just sat there; and worse was to come.

"There is no need to thank me for this," Ralph added in smug tones, "But there is one absolute condition upon which I insist... That the boys' names be changed. This one," he said, pointing at Raul, "Will be Paul." Then, barely glancing in my direction, he continued, "The other will be Frederick, or 'Freddie'... Is that clear?"

"Freddie! You must be bloody joking," I shrieked. It came out of me as an angry, sarcastic kind of laugh; but Charlie told me at once to be quiet, then traitorously tried to apologise.

"It's a shock, Sir." (She actually called him 'Sir'.) "Fid... Fidel... I mean Freddie... He doesn't mean to be rude. We're all extremely grateful... Aren't we, Paul?"

My brother nodded, and that was that! Full capitulation from my turncoat mother; and no further words were spoken, except Ralph quietly informing Charlie that he would be in contact again through his lawyers. Soon we were back on the street, heading for the bus stop. My dear twin, the acquiescent little creep, hadn't made a peep the whole time.

"So... What do you think, Raul, my love?" Charlie asked him as we waited for a Number 19. "How will you like being Paul from now on?"

"I think it'll be okay," he said meekly. "I don't think I'll get teased about it so much at school."

So it was left to me to lead the revolution, a protest group of one. Unfortunately, though, there was not the ghost of a chance of any successful rebellion from me, however determined I felt.

Charlie fixed it with Mrs Reid to have more time off later that week as she trundled us into town, to this huge department store near

Oxford Street, with a long list of necessary purchases for our forthcoming removal to the educational boarding establishment of our Grandfather's exquisitely Dickensian selection: 'Torville House' in West Sussex. 'Torment House', I called it; but, strangely, I was already wondering if maybe things could turn out alright. Charlie said the school had a tuck shop, and we would be getting regular pocket money; which information set me thinking that there would be other snobby kids around with cash for the taking. Grandfather Ralph wasn't the only one in the family more than keen to get rich.

Four

There has been no harvesting of hops or brewing of beer for decades now; a great pity, because all this reminiscing is making me thirsty. A few pints of Doom Bar or Hophead would not go amiss at the present moment. Neither, of course, is there any wine; the cellars are empty, and such spirits to be had are undrinkable rotgut from makeshift distilleries.

At least I'm still 'Keeper of the Keys', thankfully, and have access to a precious if dwindling supply of vintage malt whisky... *Usque-baugh,* 'the water of life'; wonderful stuff! Last evening, I went foraging for a bottle of the peaty golden elixir that is Lagavulin from the blessed Isle of Islay, most of which, peat bogs especially, disappeared long years ago beneath the waves of the North Sea, a genuine cause for lament.

Torville House, billed as a 'Preparatory School for Boys'; like this equally labyrinthine so-called 'Palace' building I've occupied these last many years; was situated near the top of a Channel-facing slope of the South Downs. Surrounded by playing fields, farmland and woodland, as well as open chalk grassland, it was 'preparatory' in the sense of preparing boys by the age of thirteen for moving on to Torville School, a minor public school, occupying somewhat larger premises and grounds about a mile away.

We did not have to endure for too long that somewhat pathetic preppy establishment because me and Raul (or Paul, who I had started calling 'Praul' - as in 'prowl around' - or just plain 'P'), were already twelve when we went there. Most of the male teachers were either ancient and desiccated, or young and irredeemably sissy. The two women teachers were also both fossilized, and the most masculine member of staff in my eyes was the school matron, Miss Rudge. Naturally, the other boys were drips of the first order. Teasing them, taking their money at brag and poker, even beating them up, was so unbearably easy as to be no fun at all.

Two things were taken very seriously there: lessons and sport. In the latter, I excelled, being fast on my feet and fearless on the field. It was disconcerting to discover that rugby, rather than football, was the winter game, but I soon learned the unparalleled satisfaction of launching myself at the legs of opposing ball-carriers (and, I admit, occasionally at some unfortunates who were not actually in possession of the oval object), bringing them to earth with a terrific thud, and using the trick of aiming low, just above the ankles, and clinging on tight. That way I would avoid getting hurt; no more, anyway, than just a few bruises here and there. Equally pleasing was to dodge such tackles, weaving at pace through the defence and over the line to score a try. By the end of the first term, my prowess was being acclaimed throughout the school as we won match after match against the traditional enemies, other prep schools on the rota.

In class, however, never having acquired the knack of learning, I was rather less successful. My form teacher, Mr Wright, off-puttingly passive on initial acquaintance, but a man I eventually came to admire, advised me early that, in order to gain access to Torville, or any decent public school, I would need to pass the Common Entrance examination the following summer. My initial plan, of course, was to fail it comprehensively. That would put paid to my grandfather's ability to manipulate my fate as he saw fit; but for once I listened to P as he explained how rotten life would be in the long run were I to pass up this, as he put it, 'great gift' of an education.

With hindsight, I see now that I did have a reasonable brain all along, but failed to make proper use of it because, impatient to be outdoors and active, I was always bored in class. Nothing anyone tried to teach me seemed in the slightest bit exciting, or even remotely relevant to the life I expected to lead; but, between them, Mr Wright and P got me thinking.

The unavoidable subjects were English, Maths, Latin and French. Optional additional subjects, of which we had to take a minimum of two, included Classical Greek, Spanish, Russian, History, Geography, Science, Scripture, and Art. The problem for both me and Prowl was that neither had been taught either Latin or French before. Gifted with intelligence, P's solution was to go for them anyway, as well as Geography, Science and Scripture. Mr Wright thought I should just pick three of the extra subjects to go with English and Maths, which seemed like as good a plan as any. Languages were beyond me, so I plumped for what seemed easiest: History, Scripture, and Art.

As luck would have it, I could do maths. It came to me fairly naturally, even algebra. And something from the years of English classes I'd sat through at the South West London Primary seems to have seeped into my consciousness somehow; utterly disinterested though I remember being, especially by even the thought of grammar and syntax. I couldn't tell you now, by the way, the difference between those two arcane mysteries; and probably couldn't then; but I did seem to know enough of the subject to scrape by.

As for the new subjects, well I did know some history and had at least heard of the Bible, so was not completely overwhelmed. As it turned out, they were both about stories; so all I had to do was listen to the narratives in class, and usually write a short essay later, covering the main points in my own words. At first I got into hot water for copying great chunks from the textbooks. Mr Wright said that was 'plagiarism', so at least I learned one new word; and I learned another when he described my grammar, syntax and spelling as 'quirky'. He meant freakish, a word I could spell; but 'quirky' always came out how it sounded, as a 'k' and a 'w' then 'erky' like in 'jerky'.

Afterwards I found a way of simplifying the same textbook material, and learned another word from Mr Wright too, 'paraphrasing'; but, luckily, he didn't seem to mind me doing that. As for Art with Mr Prendergast, it was just mucking about with paint and stuff, drawing - which I learnt to do quite well - making things called 'collages' by sticking odd stuff onto paper with glue, also little pottery items. It was an absolute gas the whole time.

So, there I was, much to my surprise, as happy as a pig in shit after the first few weeks of acclimatisation; and if the school food hadn't been so meagre in amount and bland to the taste buds, I would have been totally content. There was the religion to contend with, of course. The school boasted Church of England credentials, and I wasn't keen on going to chapel every morning, but it was only for twenty minutes on weekdays, and I did like some of the hymns we got to sing: 'Onward Christian Soldiers', 'The Royal Banners Forward Go', etcetera.

Despite all the scripture classes, I never really fell for the God bit; but I did find these military anthems stirred the blood. 'Fight the Good Fight'' was one of my favourites.

"Fight the good fight with all thy might...
Run the straight race...
Cast care aside...
Faint not nor fear!"

These became some of my watchwords as I too faced battles of one kind or another later on; and I'm not talking here about the rugby pitch. Sunday services were a bit harder to take, especially the draggy sermons, but as the rest of the day was free when they were over, it was bearable.

Another good thing that came my way at Torville House arrived in the colossal shape of Big Al, who arrived the day after P and me. Even at twelve, in the throes of puberty already and badly needing a shave, Alan Firkin was massive, a great asset in the rugby scrum; but poor Al was a touch gormless and clumsy, a simple oaf of a boy who, I mistakenly thought at the time, would probably grow into a simple oaf of a man. And 'Firkin', which means 'small barrel', a name that half-suited him but which gave him so much trouble from crude-minded numbskulls throughout life, was not even truly his. He seldom spoke of it but, having been abandoned at birth by his natural mother, he'd been adopted; and only after sojourns in several children's homes and numerous failed foster placements had the elderly, childless Firkins finally taken pity on him at the age of six or seven. This benign couple tried sending him to local schools, near where they lived in South London, but institutions didn't suit Al. He always rebelled against them, and kept returning home where he felt safer. If the teachers ever tried to prevent him from leaving, he'd kick up such a fuss that he'd require physical restraint; and, as time went on, he grew too big to handle, often causing damage to furniture. When he head-butted a teacher in a fit of pique, it was the school authorities that sent him home, permanently this time, unforgiving that poor Miss Stocker's broken nose would never look quite right again.

What could they do? Ada and George Firkin organized a private tutor for Al, a robust ex-army type, unlikely to brook any nonsense; but that arrangement lasted only a week. The soldier expected full military-style obedience, with which Al found it impossible to comply. He was the immovable object against which the Major utterly failed to muster any kind of irresistible force.

"I'm wasting my time," he told the Firkins, who paid him anyway up to the end of the month.

After he marched away down the street, Al simply languished at home, increasingly silent, irritable and threatening.

Soon after, old man Firkin, never strong, responded to the mounting tension by having a stroke that left him speechless and half-paralysed; so Al was finally shipped off to Torville House from where, typically, he tried running away three times in the first week. He had a problem, though, having limited funds and lacking the necessary knowledge and experience (of train and bus services, for example), so he never got far. By the time I started taking notice of the likeable goof, all the spirit had drained out of him, and he spent his free time wandering listlessly around in a dream. That he needed someone sympathetic to guide him was obvious so, for that reason, when he started gravitating towards me, I made no attempts to push him away.

It's true, I was a leader even then. I've always been at the forefront of things. But Big Al was probably the first person I was to lead deliberately; unless you count Prowl, of course, which I don't because he so seldom did what I said. Al was biddable, obedient and loyal because, unlike the Major, I took the trouble to befriend him, offering advice rather than instruction. I particularly liked that he was grateful. I'm not sure that, other than the elderly Firkins, anyone had ever shown him kindness before, kindness and a tiny smidge of respect. It was not my intention to make him my slave or stooge; but treating him well, I must admit, was hardly due entirely to love and compassion on my part, for I could already foresee the many ways in which, once he shrugged off the lethargy of despair that engulfed him, Al could be useful to me.

In truth, he was a gentle kind of giant. Once he regained his equilibrium, nothing bothered him much, and his great round face burst often into smiles. In fact, whenever he was down in the dumps, I had the happy knack of always jump starting him out of it.

For instance, if I came across him feeling gloomy, one trick was to sidle up close and whisper, "Why are pirates called pirates?" And he would bellow the answer: "Because they Aaaarrrgh!" It never failed. Nevertheless, like the irascible Blackbeard of old legend, I did teach him to act fierce when needed; and that because, I've found, there are two ways to gain a person's cooperation: by bribery or by intimidation; and it's the latter that usually works best. Al's intimidating size and muscle power came in handy when coercion was required to further my fond aims and ambitions. He could put the terror into anyone's heart if he tried; probably even in mine.

What kind of aims and ambitions does a twelve or thirteen year old have? I can assure you that in those early days of my collaboration with Al, there was nothing very well planned; but I did like asserting myself over others, and generally getting things to go my way. Isn't everyone like that, deep down? Because we're all built that way, there's no shame in it in my book. Anyway, by the end of that first term, I was pleased to have Al as my sidekick; and we would surely both have been heartily amazed if told then that it would stay that way until one of us died; but, mostly, it did.

Five

Having no idea they could be so exciting, the scripture lessons at Torville House were a pleasant surprise. You expect to hear about battles in history class, of course, but it was great to read of them in the bible as well. There were some serious conflicts in those old testament days, lots of betrayals and infamy. One tale in particular caught my attention. It was about Jacob's daughter, Dinah, being royally raped by a dude called 'The Schemer', whose father was a Prince. Once he's done the evil deed, the story goes, this rascal finds he's rather taken with the girl. Overwhelmed by conscience, a fatal mistake in my book, he wants to marry her; so the deal goes like this:

"Okay, it's a good match," Jacob and his men say, "You can have the wedding; but only if you and all your men get circumcised first, according to our religion."

Well, who would agree to that? Crazy! But they did... And it was a shocking mistake.

You have to say, all things considered, that Jacob's mob were the better schemers; fooling with the Prince's men all along. A couple of days later, when those poor guys were still feeling pretty sore where it really counts if you're just about to get married; at a significant disadvantage, then, if you happen to be attacked by bloodthirsty invaders; Jacob's sons entered the city and massacred the lot, including The Schemer and his father. After this, not yet satisfied, they went on a bit of a plunder spree, carrying off not only all the goods and animals, but all the young wives, and their children too. It was a total victory; although I would have liked to know what the sadly abused Dinah thought about it all, and whether she considered that her honour had been truly restored. Anyway, once their kid sister had been avenged in such cruel and merciless fashion, unsurprisingly, Jacob and his family were not popular in those whereabouts, and had to nip off sharply somewhere else.

It is a wicked story; and it wasn't the only one I liked from the Old Testicle. There were tons; like when Joshua sent his two spies into Jericho to lodge with a sex worker called Rahab, who hid them and later helped them escape. She was a tart with a heart alright, that girl! I wonder what the three of them really got up to during the night. The bible is regrettably silent on that.

There were many likeable stories, too, about King David. The best known, of course, is how, while still a shepherd boy, he bumped off the Philistine giant, Goliath, with a pebble from a slingshot. What a lucky strike! Later, when he was king, he turned out by no means a saint, jumping on Bathsheba, making her pregnant while she was still married to Uriah, one of his bravest soldiers. Trying to get himself out of this ugly fix, David, a bit of a schemer himself, had his rival called back from the battlefront, where they were still fighting the Philistines, fully expecting the sex-starved fellow to go straight home and get into bed with his wife. David was thinking, of course, that she could easily later claim, when it arrived, that the new kid had to be his, Uriah's; although, as I see it, unless his arithmetic was as bad as Big Al's, this dodge could not have worked; but Uriah did not go home that night, or the next two nights either. (Who knows? Maybe he had a girlfriend somewhere else), So David tried something different. He sent Uriah back to the war carrying a sealed letter for his general, which told that officer to place the unsuspecting cuckold where the fighting was hardest, pretty much making sure he got neutralised, which is what happened. In no time at all, the widow Bathsheba was living with David the King, and later gave birth to his son. I'm inclined to believe it happened. Could anyone make up a great story like that? I'm not sure... Although, come to think of it, someone probably did.

'Embellish'; that's another word Mr Wright taught me. It means improving or elaborating a narrative by adding fictional details. Sometimes the stories from history are embellished by historians, usually in favour of whoever comes out on top. It's natural isn't it? Enemies have their reputations blackened while heroes are created and praised. It all adds to the appeal. As a boy who fought so many skirmishes and pitched battles with my toy army on golden beaches, I adored the many glorious tales of warfare I came across in lessons. The bible gave sparse details of the actual fighting, but the history teacher, Mr Phillips, sometimes spent a whole lesson on one battle, drawing maps and diagrams of troop movements across the blackboard to show us what happened and how luck - maybe with the terrain or the weather - so often played a part. If it wasn't for a break in the stormy weather on D-Day in June 1944, for example, he told us, we could all have been speaking in German.

One of my favourites was the battle of Agincourt. It's well known because of Shakespeare, who definitely embellished the story of King Henry the Fifth for his play; but it was actually fought on St Crispin's Day, the 25th of October, in the year 1415. Crispin was a French shoemaker who, with his brother Crispinian, was beheaded by a Roman Emperor for being Christians over a thousand years earlier; and the battle was part of the Hundred Years War between England and France, which had started in 1337 and didn't finish until 1453; which means, as even Big Al could tell you, that it lasted for more than a hundred years.

The English had won battles at Crécy in 1346 and Poitiers in 1356, but the war dragged on indecisively, and there had been a prolonged lull in hostilities until Henry, who was claiming the French throne, launched another military campaign after yet another round of failed negotiations, during which he had even offered to marry a French princess. The sticking point, however, had been the money. He was seeking a dowry of two million crowns from the French King. Nice! But when offered only a fraction of that amount, he used it as the pretext to invade. Together with 12,000 soldiers, he crossed the Channel and besieged the port of Harfleur, eventually taking the town, although not before his mighty army was reduced, mainly by sickness, to somewhere near 8,500 men, the remnant affected considerably too by both hunger and fatigue.

Things were not looking good. It was late in the year, but rather than simply retreat to England by sea, Henry pushed boldly north towards his preferred embarkation port of Calais, covering over 200 miles in a meandering route to Agincourt where the French army was waiting. The longbow men in the party, about 7,000 of them, many suffering dysentery, were pretty knackered by the time they got there, still 45 miles short of their safe destination. With nowhere to go and massively outnumbered, they were obliged simply to fight.

The French had mustered 10,000 men-at-arms, 5,000 footmen and crossbow archers, plus an additional 10,000 so-called 'varlets' or armed servants, and they also had a small, elite cavalry section. The whole predicament could have turned nasty, but the Brits were in luck. They met the opposing army in fields confined into a narrow space between two patches of dense woodland. The English and Welsh archers; with men-at-arms and knights several ranks deep, shoulder to shoulder in the centre between them; took to the slopes either side, where they prepared defensive positions, driving sharpened stakes angled into the ground to stand behind. The fields had recently been ploughed and were thick with mud so, when the French advanced, the poor boogers got totally stuck.

Imagine what it was like for a French lord, wearing full plate armour that weighed masses, having to plod several hundred yards up a gradient through the softened landscape towards the enemy. Soon, you become so tightly packed with your comrades that there's barely room to swing your sword. Suddenly, then, long before you even get close, a daunting shower of literally thousands of arrows, minute by minute, come raining down on you. Lowering your visor for protection means you can no longer see clearly while, in front, your fellow men-at-arms, some already bogged down to their knees, are falling breathlessly over one another and beginning to pile up, some dying through suffocation, while those behind continue pushing forward... And there is no escape on either side!

This was the nightmare scenario before they even reached the English army front line, ranged menacingly ahead of them; and it was all about to get worse.

Trying to help those on foot, the French cavalry charged towards the English archers on the flanks, only to find that their horses couldn't penetrate the barricade of stakes. Forced to turn away, they immediately became new targets for the British longbow men, the attack on the helpless animals' unprotected flesh causing the hapless creatures to stampede back and sideways in the direction of their own infantry, trampling many and further churning up the glutinous terrain.

When some of the French men-at-arms did finally reach the English front line, archers simply turned towards them, firing at almost point-blank range, causing much greater mayhem; then, once their arrows were spent, they dropped their bows and attacked using swords and hatchets, some of them even wielding the mallets they had used to drive in their stakes.

The fighting lasted three hours and resulted in total massacre; the French losing over 6,000 men, with many also taken prisoner. The English and Welsh casualties, in contrast, were few. By the middle of November, crossing at Calais as planned, Henry was back in England with most of his army intact.

It was the hundred years war that gave us the V-Sign to mean something rude; knowledge of which became useful to me at the school in the necessary education of a boy by the name of Randy Blenkinsopp the Third, a 'Blinking Soppy Turd' if ever there was one, who was from Poughkeepsie; somewhere in America where Randy is just a name that doesn't mean sex-mad or horny, like it does here.

This particular turd's father worked for one of the big American car companies as 'Corporate Vice-President (Europe)', an elevated position his son never stopped bragging about; and his mother was a Vanderbilt, although this cut no ice with Al or me, having no clue either one of us who the Vanderbilt family might be. All we could see was a big-headed Yank who needed pulling down to size.

"Why do you guys call this a 'Public School', when it's obviously not?" He challenged from time to time. "It's a private school, Dummies!"

Luckily, he was awful at poker. You could read him like a comic book, having a playful little smirk on his face when he drew a half-decent hand. And every time he lost, he gave me the sign with his middle finger, like they do over there.

"Furr...koff, Castro!" he used to drawl like a Texan, or "Furr... kyu, Commie bastard. You just got lucky is all."

I hated him.

"Fuck You too!"

I always returned his venom, giving like for like, but flicking him a proper British V-sign every time; so that eventually he asked me, "Why do you Limeys always do that?" So I told him about the French warriors of the Hundred Years War, who both hated and feared the British archers so much that, whenever they captured one, they cut off the index and middle finger of his right hand, the two fingers needed to draw back the deadly bowstring. And that's why, whenever longbow men faced the French in battle, they raised their hands waggling those two fingers aloft as a great taunt: "Here are our fingers and we're keeping them, so get stuffed."

I loved that story; and even the turd-faced American liked it enough to use our version once in a while. Unfortunately, though, he started improving at poker.

Six

Batteries... Batteries... Batteries! What can you do? There's a supply in the stockroom still, but half are completely dud, and most of the others store only enough juice for a few minutes' work. I shall soon have to look for one of those old portable typewriters somewhere. On the other hand, even if such a thing remains in existence, hitting the keys with my wayward arthritic fingers would take forever.

I remember the messy fountain pens we had to use at school. I wrote hundreds of essays at Torville House. It wasn't so bad there, and learning so much history and a bit of scripture, I began feeling confident about the common entrance exam; but there was a problem with Al. I wanted him to stay at my side but, as things stood, he was never going to pass. He liked Art, but he was clumsy and found it hard to acquire any of the required techniques or skills; until, that is, Mr Prendergast had a brainwave and presented him with one of the early digital cameras. Then, Big Al was off, developing a real flair for nature subjects, which meant that on free Sunday afternoons he usually went into the countryside, happily snapping away at the immense vistas and fields full of cattle and sheep. He took close-ups and telephoto images of things like the foliage, wildflowers, fungi and birds. One of his most creative pictures featured a colourful squadron of painted lady butterflies; wearing their camouflage colours of orange, black and white; flitting around on a dark-brown cow pat with a couple of dung beetles in a tussle to one side. Seeing that, and hearing Mr P giving him unstinting praise as a result, I was really proud of my pal. Perhaps he would scrape through the art exam with a pass; but what about English, maths and the rest? It was going to be a struggle. Unsuspecting, however, and in a strange sort of way, luck turned out on our side.

Winning at cards is great, but to really enjoy it, you need somewhere to spend the cash, plus something agreeable to spend it on. Whenever a decent-sized stash accumulated, I used to take Al and buzz off down the school drive, onto the public footpath that led across the downs, to the local village where, of course, there were shops. It was quite a trek, taking about half-an-hour (longer if Al had his camera with him), and it was quite steep on the way back; but it was a worthwhile hike, if only for the bit of excitement that came with breaking school rules. Mostly, we bought sweets. I was too young yet to be interested in booze, cigarettes or girlie magazines, but Charlie's petty pilfering from the confectioners when we were little had given me a decidedly sweet tooth.

One day we set off rather late, after rugby practice. This was great, because it was growing dark and we were less likely to be spotted; but it wasn't so great because we had limited time to get back before supper. I told Al he had to leave the Canon behind, and for once he didn't complain; even though he insisted it was good enough to take pictures in low light conditions. We got to the shops, filled our pockets with goodies, paid for most of it, and made our way back in quick enough time, laughing breathlessly as we emerged from the path back onto the school driveway.

It was pretty dark by then, but there were lights every thirty yards or so, and we weren't alert or quick-thinking enough to dodge round them and seek out the dark patches. Even if we had, we would probably have been caught anyway because, just as we reached the school's back entrance, out came the headmaster's Volvo, headlights blazing, catching us in its unforgiving glare.

"What's this then?" Asked Fizzle, after winding down his window. "Where have you two been?"

"Just out for a walk, Mr Fitzjohn," I said, trying to sound innocent.

"Get in the back!" He ordered without hesitation.

Old Fitz, the headmaster, turned the big old car in a half-circle and drove round the back of the school to his private entrance where he ordered us to get out and follow him inside. Once upstairs in his study, he made us empty our pockets. Then he told me to wait outside while he beat Al. I could hear each stroke through the door while my brave friend remained silent, and knew I too would be getting six strokes across the buttocks.

Fitz was a tall, thin man, a onetime cricketer with a strong arm who favoured a thin, whippy cane like the one Charlie Chaplin's tramp twirls around as he walks off down the road in the final scene of his movies. I'd been beaten by him before, and it hurt. But somehow, too, it wasn't so bad, like a badge of honour among the other kids. You need to have been beaten a couple of times to earn any kind of respect.

Fitz was by no means a sadist. You could tell he really thought that, by teaching you a lesson in obedience, he was doing you a lasting favour. Well, in this instance, he truly was because, as I bent over the back of a chair in front of his desk, preparing myself for the onslaught, I caught sight of a large envelope with the Common Entrance logo on the front. Sure enough, when I made my way back there that night, long after lights out, the beam of my torch revealed, inside same envelope, the following week's Common Entrance exam papers for English, French and maths.

Demonstrating both the same alertness to opportunity and

problem-solving ability that was to stand me in such good stead as life with all its challenges proceeded, I had been blessed with the intelligence to bring Al's Canon with me. Click, click, click was all it took to make sure we were both going to pass. It's true I had to write the answers on small sheets of paper for Al to carry with him and copy in the exam, impressing upon him the vital importance of taking care not to get caught. I also thought it wise to build in a few mistakes, so as to avoid suspicions about his unexpected and near-miraculous brilliance; but it worked, and after a nervous three-week wait, we finally got the results we desired; both being accepted at the big school for the following September. Loads of others graduated to Torville School at the same time, but Soppy wasn't among them.

Sometime In June, during an evening 'prep' session; which is when about fifty boys sit about pretending to take an interest in after-class studies under the watchful, eye of one of the junior teachers unfortunate enough to draw the short straw that day; Randy Three was unexpectedly called out of the room. Eunice; who was Fitz's secretary and quite possibly the only decent looking woman on campus, but hidden and hardly ever seen outside the head's office; came along to fetch him. His mother had arrived unannounced; and what follows goes to show that all the money in the world won't protect you from misery.

We were jogging along together almost as friends by this time, a sufficient degree of mutual respect having sprung up between us, and I watched closely as he left the room and reappeared outside the window a few moments later, walking along one of the paths between some flower beds in front of the building, side by side with a tall, willowy woman dressed in a full-length, navy dress, with a tight jacket of the same dark colour, a deep crimson scarf at the neck over a white silk blouse, her eyes obscured by dark glasses and face shadowed by a broad-brimmed hat of the same colour as the scarf. It looked almost as if his Mom was in mourning.

After a while, strolling between the long row of garden seats, they sat, framed vividly by the vibrant colour of surrounding plants, lit artistically from the west by the dimming sun. The mother put out a hand, as I watched, letting it rest on Randy's arm. Whether she wanted to comfort or restrain him I couldn't tell, but I could see she was talking in great earnest, more at him than to him.

She had prepared her short speech, it seemed. Once delivered, they were both then silent for an age. Finally, he must have asked her a question, which she answered in a word. Briefly, then, there were fireworks as Randy stood abruptly, shouted some emotion-filled riposte, pointed his finger at her then waved his arms in despair, before turning and running back towards the building.

His rage was obvious, so intense that I half expected him to flick her a V-sign as well; but there wouldn't have been any point. Unruffled, like an iceberg, she sat still while even my heart quickened at the scene; then, slowly, she rose too, tried waving him back, even called faintly for him to return, taking a few paces in his direction; then she shrugged, faced about, and walked away across the lawn. She had given up on him, or decided to let time heal whatever trauma she had inflicted. Either way, moments later, a chauffeur-driven Rolls transported its enigmatic passenger in smooth near-silence, down the driveway and off into the evening gloom.

Something drastic had happened. I wanted desperately to find out what it was; but Soppy didn't return to the prep room, and I simply had to wait, wondering at first if perhaps his father had died; but then why was he so angry? And I'd seen his father once, a man in his fifties who looked pretty fit; which is what was later revealed to be at the heart of the problem. Randolph Blenkinsopp II had more life in him than his wife could continue to satisfy, therefore he'd found a new girlfriend. I suppose he thought it logical; and, in consequence, he was seeking divorce. Mrs B had been obliged to come and tell her son that she was returning to America in short order, and that he was going back there too. No wonder Randy felt betrayed. With a little help from friends like me, he'd really begun to settle into the Limey way of life, as he called it. He genuinely wanted to stay.

"Bollocks and two fingers to all that shit!" he said the next day, telling me all about it. "Poughkeepsie High School is the pits."

I said not to worry. His mother would surely enrol him in a fancy private school before he could say "Agincourt", but he was still miserable; and I told him to write once he got there, but he never did. That poor boy was always going to be a misfit, wherever he was; too Yankee for us, and much too English for them. Sometimes, I wonder how his life ended up.

Seven

Big Al and I found ourselves in Marlborough. Not the town in Wiltshire, but one of eight subdivisions or 'houses' at Torville School, all named for male British heroes. The headmaster decided to split us up, and I wasn't sorry when brother Prowl was allocated to Wellington. The other houses were Haig, Montgomery, Churchill, Nelson, Wolfe and Clive, people whose reputations mostly wither under close scrutiny, but there you go.

Unquestioning patriotism was paramount in that place. Robert Clive, known as 'Clive of India', for instance, was a ruthless, self-centred, bad-tempered shocker of a bloke, responsible almost single-handedly for bringing poverty, starvation, misery and death to countless native people in his relentless quest for personal wealth and glory. Although it had no legal right to muster fighting men, he led the army of the East India Trading Company in a successful series of defensive and offensive encounters on the Indian subcontinent, most notably at Plessey in 1757. The company's activities, military and commercial, while destroying native allegiances and government, enriched the home country enormously through epic-scale plundering, preparing the way for the addition of India to the British Empire. One of the largest and purest diamonds ever, once the property of a subsequently deposed maharajah, even found its way into the British monarch's gold crown, along with rubies, pearls, sapphires and emeralds from a similar source. Nice pickings indeed!

Marlborough House was named after one of my personal heroes, John Churchill, who became the first Duke of Marlborough in 1702. Also ruthlessly ambitious, but not as unpleasantly so as Clive, he was Commander-in-Chief of the British forces during the so-called 'War of the Spanish Succession' against the French, fought not in Spain as you might expect but in the Netherlands and Belgium between 1701 and 1711. These hostilities followed the death of Charles II of Spain in November 1700, a king who had no children, therefore leaving rival claimants to the throne; one backed by Louis XIV of France, and the other by Leopold I, the Holy Roman Emperor based in Vienna. The British formed an important part of the Grand Alliance of countries supporting Leopold.

The problem was Vienna's vulnerability. Its capture by the French would have been bad news, so Marlborough and his brother, General Charles Churchill, marched over 20,000 men south-eastward from near Cologne to cut off their advance. The army's journey, travelling at a maximum of seven miles a day, was one of more than three hundred miles, brilliantly described later by John Churchill's equally ambitious, illustrious and ebullient descendant, Winston, as, "A scarlet caterpillar, upon which all eyes were at once fixed, crawling steadfastly day by day across the map of Europe, dragging the whole war with it."

They were heading for the River Danube, where Marlborough's first success involved the taking of Schellenberg, a town and fortress protecting a vital river crossing. Then, needing the security of a second crossing, the bulk of the troops were moved twenty miles south-west along the river, much closer to the enemy.

On 13th August 1704, the Grand Alliance and Franco-Bavarian armies opposed each other near the modest village of Blenheim. The battlefield was more than three miles wide. The British on the left, close to the Danube where a stream filtered towards it, found themselves in marshy terrain and, much like the French at Agincourt, could have become dangerously bogged down. However, their luck held. Using makeshift bridges and other devices, they were able successfully to cross the boggy brook at the critical moment.

Marlborough and his allies were outnumbered, but attacked valiantly and repeatedly despite tremendous early losses. Such was their ferocity and determination that one of the French generals was soon panicked into making a fatal error of judgement, ordering his reserve battalions into the village of Blenheim to fortify troops already there, with the result that they were so tightly packed in as to make manoeuvring impossible. They couldn't even fire their weapons, they were so crowded together, let alone receive or carry out orders.

Marlborough spotted the opportunity presented by the situation and swiftly profited, allocating just five thousand of his men to corral and so neutralise twice as many of the enemy. The previous discrepancy in numbers was effectively nullified, leaving the remainder of the allied army to fight and overwhelm the remainder of the opposition.

Nevertheless, the battle, which had started at around 10 in the morning, was still in the balance by 3 in the afternoon, when the French almost made a breakthrough in the centre. They were thwarted only by Marlborough's quick-thinking, summoning help from allies on the right flank.

About an hour later there was a pause in the hostilities, allowing time for much-needed reorganisation, while large contingents of the enemy remained besieged in Blenheim and another village, Oberglau. By early evening, cavalry charges and artillery fire got things moving successfully again against the tiring French. Many died where they fought, and there was an eventual chaotic retreat. Over three thousand French horsemen plunged into the Danube, while numerous others were dispatched by the pursuing cavalry.

Even then, the battle was not done. French soldiers penned in at Blenheim continued to resist. Despite being attacked on three sides, they fought valiantly back, inflicting considerable losses on the British troops. Only at 9 o'clock did they finally agree to parlay, and 10,000 of their best infantry, seeing their fellows so roundly defeated elsewhere in the field, agreed to lay down their arms. A total of 27,000 French soldiers were killed, wounded or captured.

In recognition of his great victory, a few months later, Queen Anne awarded Woodstock Park to Marlborough, plus the enormous sum of £24,000 with which to build 'a suitable house', which of course became Blenheim Palace. The remarkable success, however, was not sufficient to decide the war. France remained too powerful. Although Marlborough went on to defeat them again throughout the Netherlands in battles at Ramillies in 1706, Oudenarde in 1708, and Malplaquet in 1709, it never became strategically possible to actually invade France and march on Paris, as he must have wished. Politics took over, and the British eventually made peace with France in 1711.

My great hero, who never fought a losing battle, died after a series of strokes at the age of 72 in 1722, without doubt one of the finest soldiers Britain has ever seen. How dreadful, then, that the boys of Marlborough House in my day were known as 'Fag-ends' throughout the school; the insult arising when billboards started carrying larger-than-life images of a cowboy on horseback. 'Marlboro Country' was portrayed as the idyllic backdrop to the pernicious habit of smoking. 'Fags' was the current slang for cigarettes (only in America was it a derogatory term for gay men), and 'fag-ends' meant cigarette butts; hence our shamefully undeserved and inappropriate nickname, the use of which against us at least ensured we were brutally determined when it came to sporting and other contests against our fellow pupils at school, especially against the oiks in Wellington, like my brother.

These unfortunates were always called either 'Booties', because of the Duke's famous footwear, or 'Uglies' by inversion (because 'Booties' = 'Beauties'). Fags and Uglies were bitter rivals, especially on the rugby pitch; but, against all the other houses, we were top dogs together, not comrades exactly, but holding at least a smidgen of mutual respect.

There may be some truth about human nature buried in this kind of compatible rivalry, don't you think? We spurred each other on to greater heights of achievement while duelling, as it were, to the death. I wouldn't be where I am now, it's fair to say, if I hadn't paid close attention to such matters throughout my life. Building temporary alliances with natural enemies for short-term mutual benefit became an essential part of my strategy.

During the summer months before I went to Torville, my balls dropped, as nature intended, and my voice began to deepen. I had not yet started shaving, but all kinds of hormones were definitely kicking in. Sadly, though, here I was in an all-boys institution. What kind of sadist dreamed up that torture? With four more years in that place, the possibility of fulfilling my masculine destiny seemed unlikely.

It wasn't as if a lively boy like me had a choice whether to think about sex or not. All kinds of awkwardly timed, impossible to conceal hard-ons, messy nocturnal embarrassments and such; all these things happened, whether I wanted them or not. There was no inboard regulator or off-switch, and only one kind of relief available: solitary, unnecessary to describe in detail, usually occurring in a locked toilet somewhere in a quiet corner of school with the help of Dude, High Time, Fling, Parade, Hustler, Rapture, New Directions, or, for quality, either Penthouse or Playboy.

Auto-eroticism is said to be the most common form of sexual activity by far, and that was certainly the case for captive adolescents like me. I remember, age thirteen, the first time I held in my hand the glossy colour photo of a topless pin-up in a nudie magazine. It was like a religious experience! I can still bring the image to mind, a lithe young blonde lying beside a sunlit swimming pool wearing only her bikini bottom and an alluring smile. She looked so gorgeous. I was confused, excited and happy all at once. There would never be any doubt about my sexual orientation being totally 'hetero', even if I didn't understand the terminology at that stage. But I was confused, because I couldn't see any way to get from here, stuck in school, to there, lying beside that stunning chick next to the similarly inviting swimming pool, into either or preferably both of which I was dying to take a dive. Regrettably, of course, I was right. It took a long while to attain blissful satisfaction like that.

I did fall in love at Torville, if only remotely, so to speak. For a long time I did not even know the girl's name, which turned out to be Helen. Mr Holland was in charge of the kitchens and everything to do with catering at the school. Neatly dressed in a dark grey suit and sombre tie, he would always take up a rigid, perpendicular stance throughout meals at his regular station by the kitchen entrance to the dining hall, unfussily supervising the feeding of more than five hundred hungry kids. Helen was his granddaughter.

In fact, she was one of Dutch's two granddaughters. Her older sister, Mary, had been serving tables for a year or two already when

Helen started. Both were very pretty; but, whereas Mary was bold and brooked no flirtatious nonsense from the older boys, Helen was shy. She blushed a lot, especially when she first started; but she also seemed fascinated by the scene in the hall, often standing half-inside the doorway whenever she had nothing else on hand to dish out or clear away, peering timidly out at our uniform-clad, somewhat regimented bodies and pale, frequently spotty faces as we sat and ate. I used to stare back, trying to make a connection, rapidly besotted with her perfect little face, a sculpted oval porcelain picture with lovely, slightly puckered pink lips, sparkling violet eyes, the whole neatly framed by a sea of lustrous dark hair.

It was my bad luck that she was responsible for Wellington and Churchill tables, at the far end of hall near the kitchens. Only rarely did she ever come close to Marlborough or Wolfe at the back, and if she did, would always dart away again quickly. She would point at things and gesture meaningfully when necessary for her work, but I never heard her speak. I even wondered for a time if she was mute. How many other boys were captivated by the vision of her, I do not know, but few could have felt the same degree of passion as me. It wasn't lust exactly. It was a deeper and more chivalrous feeling than that. I felt a kind of need to protect her.

I was, at that young age, also incredibly hesitant. I thought of writing Helen a note and trying to pass it to her. But, what would I say? More than once I decided to wait for her as she went home after the evening meal, loitering near the kitchen exit; but she never came out alone, only with her sister or old Dutch himself. And then I was too late. She had gone.

"Catering school... She started last week," Mary told me, when I eventually plucked up the courage to ask. "Was she something to you, then? She never said."

I'm sure I blushed, but luckily didn't have to say anything. Disinterested, Mary turned away without waiting for a reply. I can't remember how long it took me to get over the disappointment, but I do remember the next would-be target of my affections who, funnily enough, was also called Helen, a girl I met at a rare, well-chaperoned dance organised with the rather posh, nearby South Downs Boarding School for Girls. Something clicked between us, and she agreed to meet me in the town for a coffee one Sunday afternoon, but I was destined to be disappointed because, as I soon discovered, the only true target and recipient of her passion was a pony, her favourite. The piebald she loved was called Daydream.

There were a few other girls to gawk at, encountered in much the same way, such as when a bunch of them were recruited for walk-on parts in the annual school play; but I suspect that, like most teenage girls from that social milieu in that era, they were brainwashed into virtue. Some even accused me of being 'dirty', as they put it, should I so much as ask for a kiss, or tried to fondle their blossoming busts. As they pined only, it seemed, for pop stars or youthful military men, attempts at flirtation always turned out to be hopeless.

My chances appeared better when I met someone called Catherine, the sister of my Marlborough housemate Richard. His family, the Squires, were a caring bunch, if somewhat staid and traditional. Richard's father had been educated at the school years earlier and had then become a stockbroker, so the family were pretty well off. His mother had been a nurse. In addition to Richard and Catherine, there were two younger boys, already enrolled at Torville House, and a tiny baby sister. I got to know them when the whole mob descended on school sports days and similar events from time to time. Richard was half-a-year younger than me, which would have made Catherine just six or nine months my senior. Although her face was a little plain, she had a fine figure already; and it was encouraging the first time Richard introduced me when she appeared really friendly. The smattering of conversation we had on that occasion ensued probably because she was terminally bored with the cricket match between the school and an Old Boys eleven that we were supposed to be watching; but it was a start. I liked her and she seemed to like me, so no surprise that I began fantasizing about being with her that night.

Cathy had wanted to know a bit about me, so I made up a lot of stuff about H being a seafaring man who was always regaling us with wild tales of faraway places. I fibbed that Charlie had been a celebrated beauty queen. I also told her loads she didn't need to know about Marlborough; the soldier, I mean, not the house; and in return she told me that she was at a private school for girls, like SDBSG, with a similarly strict regime. Its reputation was so wonderful world-wide, she said, that its girls were never allowed to forget it, having to uphold it rigorously at all times in public. She clearly found it too agonisingly repressive, a bit of a joke in fact, having to behave unrelentingly in such a prim and proper manner; so it was natural to interpret this hopefully, as an indication that she might be willing to join me in some rebellious activity, a prurient spot of intimacy and adventure of an essentially reproductive nature, for example, which was why I got Richard to invite me to the family home as soon as he possibly could.

Fortunately, Mrs Squires took a shine to me at the cricket, and insisted I join the family for their picnic in the tea interval, so everything was soon arranged for me to visit them at home at half-term. I must have been at least sixteen by then. Despite H's lack of stature, I had grown fairly tall. Charlie's grandfather had, by all accounts, been a giant of a man. Also, I was strong, muscular, and not too bad looking. The drawback though, of course, was that I had never so much as kissed a girl, my inexperience meaning that, however reluctant I am to admit it, I really got nowhere with Catherine. In the first place, when I visited, it was hard to get away from Richard and be alone with her. In the second, she seemed more distant than at the cricket match, polite but less friendly, excusing herself by saying she needed time alone during the weekend to revise for upcoming exams.

On the final Sunday, we were due back at school for chapel in the evening. I felt the opportunity slipping by so, during the afternoon, I told Richard I was going to pack my things, but instead made my way to Cathy's bedroom, knocked on the door and barged in. She was sitting at a small table covered with books, one of which she held in her hands. Looking up suddenly, I could tell she was more than a bit shocked by my abrupt entrance. Then, when she sussed the purpose of my intrusion, showed even greater alarm. Ignoring the warning signals, though, as I had made up my mind to do, I simply blurted out that I fancied her and thought of her as the most fantastic person, and continued wittering on about her good looks, fine figure and whatnot until she stopped me with a genuinely horrified look. As I paused for breath, she pointed to the books she was using to study, and said simply, "You have to go now. I've so much work to get on with!"

Crestfallen, I simply stood there until, moments later, taking pity on me, she explained. "You're sweet, Freddie! But you mustn't think of me like that... I already have a boyfriend..."

Trying to let me down gently, I suppose, she said he was doing officer training at Dartmouth College; and so, obviously, he was years older than me. I don't think I really believed her. It would have been easy to make up. Anyway, I left and went back to school feeling like a right chump, pretty sure I'd never get to have sex... Happily, though, I was completely wrong about that.

Eight

Catherine telling me to piss off out of her bedroom was particularly deflating. A happier side of life at Torville for me was provided by the ACF, the Army Cadet Force. Normally I rejected discipline. If there was a rule and I couldn't see the point of it, I'd make it my business to subvert it, and that was true at first with the army cadets as much as anything. Each Wednesday afternoon, every member of the school lined up in military uniform on the big central square to do drill. 'Eyes right... Eyes forward... Left turn... Quick march... Right wheel... Right wheel... Right wheel... Halt! Stand at ease... Stand easy.' Over and over again. I think it was hypnotic. That's the only explanation I can give, because otherwise it was moronic, repetitive, and could have been so boring. But, somehow, I came to love it, the orderliness of it. The biggest drawback was the kit.

We had two uniforms: fatigues, which were like grey-green dungarees for regular use, and mustard-brown battledress for the big parades. The smarter uniform was coarse and itchy, also too hot to wear on a summer's day. Worse than all that, it had to be perfectly presented, which meant gleaming brasses, brilliantly burnished black boots, and webbing properly spruced up with blanco, a foul, runny, khaki-coloured paste to be applied to our belts and other bits of kit then allowed to dry.

I never knew whether to clean the belt and stuff first, and risk getting black, hard-to-disguise, Brasso stains on the webbing later, or go for the brass and risk getting blanco all over the buckle when I started on the belt. It was a nightmare, at least until I managed to persuade a boy called Pipkin to do it for me every week. I can't remember whether I paid him or threatened him with a bashing but, either way, he usually got the job done.

We were also issued a rifle each, World War One relics, the famous Lee Enfield 303, which we had to learn to clean. In fact, we never took them completely apart. As they were so old, they probably would never have gone back together again. All we did was clean out the barrel using wadding and a 'pull-through', a long piece of cord with one weighted end and a loop at the other in which to affix the wadding. Holding the rifle vertically, the weight dropped down through the barrel with the cord, so that, when the wadding was in place, all you had to do was pull it through; hence the name. With so many dunces involved, the ACF couldn't afford to be subtle.

Unless you volunteered for more drill, after marching around the square for half an hour or so, we'd be put to some other activity - as signallers, using walkie-talkies, for example, or engineers, trying to construct a pulley system. We were all also trained to use the rifles, and eventually to take marksman tests. Because there was only room for eight of us at a time at the indoor range, little groups were forever coming and going for their turn, and the afternoon air was constantly disturbed by bursts of shooting at intervals. Since I'd inherited H's air rifle when he left, an item of no interest at all to my pacifist sibling, I was already Deadeye Dick with that weapon, and soon had the Marksman badge for Matron to sew on my battledress.

As far as I remember, I got badges for everything, and one happy day my Lance Corporal's stripes and lanyard too; which meant I was now the one giving the drill orders on the square, a privilege I instantly found mighty appealing. I was a born leader alright. There were the two genuine army officers; Major Northwood, the geography teacher, who took parade most Wednesdays, and old Colonel Parker, the physics teacher, a relic from a bomb disposal unit; who still looked permanently nervous, as if a device was about to explode nearby, and who only turned up for the biggest parades. By my last year in school, under these superannuated military men, I had become the senior NCO; the Non-Commissioned Officer in charge of the whole cadet force; a role that, as things turned out, gave me inestimable experience.

Also helpful were some of the skills we learned as cadets. On what were called 'Field Days' once a term, and at army camp once a year, we practised map-reading, communication, fire-lighting, cooking and other essential camping skills, like how to keep stuff dry and the use of a tin opener. I even mastered a smattering of Morse code. Taking loaded ACF rifles to shoot pheasant or rabbits was forbidden, unfortunately, although we were once allowed to catch a few fish. I also learned the value, the necessity even, of teamwork.

The first four-day summer camp I went on took place in the Brecon Beacons. The Major was in charge, and there were about forty of us. The journey to get there in hired coaches, especially the last part meandering through Welsh countryside, where all you could see was hedges either side of the road, seemed to take forever. Our sandwiches long gone, we were all starving by the time we arrived; but first, of course, we had to line up in formation and march about for a bit, before being allocated in groups of ten to our barrack huts. With astonishing originality, the groups were labelled A, B, C and D. I was in B group. Prowl wasn't there, incidentally. He was excused by virtue of suffering from hay fever and asthma; but this was one time I really didn't envy him. Big Al missed out too, much to his disappointment, stuck in bed at home on account of getting chicken pox at the wrong time, poor lad!

Anyway, it didn't take long to set out our kit in the approved manner by our beds, but we were then treated to a comprehensive lecture from the NCO attached to the school's assigned barracks. The other schools presumably had similar martinets of their own to keep them in line. This lecture was about a number of things, including how to make the bed properly, when we would get up ('reveille'), where the mess hall was, how we were to keep silent during meals, at which someone would always say grace before we would be allowed to sit down, and all kinds of other stuff like that.

Many of us, too tired to bother, forgot most of it instantly, which is where teamwork first came in. Pimple-faced Timothy Pipkin, astonishingly, actually listened and was then able to remember it all, which is how we managed to find the mess hall not too much later and ahead of everyone else, taking up station (at attention behind our chairs, as instructed) at the table nearest the serving hatch, certain to get our food before the others, so we thought; wrongly, as it turned out because we were served last. The principle would have been correct, except the army always does things backwards. It was an important lesson: work out what to expect, and that was the one thing certain not to happen.

It took an age for the whole gang of amateur soldiers to find their way to that meal. The Torville mob were restless. We couldn't help muttering to ourselves, complaining until the NCO appeared and warned us to shut it or we'd be going hungry. Eventually, the entire party assembled, in walked the officers and we all stiffened to attention. When all was silent, the padre, wearing a dog collar with his uniform, suddenly proclaimed in a booming voice, "Jesus wept... Thank God... Sit down!" This was the grace.

He was obliged by orders from above, I discovered; orders from the army, I mean, not God; to read at least one verse of scripture before giving thanks. A wise man, he must have been, to understand so perfectly our need for rapid access to sustenance at that time. "Jesus wept." That was the shortest verse in the bible.

After a reasonably satisfying meal of bangers, eggs, chips and beans, washed down with a filthy-tasting grey liquid supposed to be tea, we were naturally ready for sleep. It was late and dark outside, but bed was not yet on the agenda. We were sent back to barracks at the double, there to change swiftly into fatigues for a night exercise. An older lad called Singh was given charge of our ten-man platoon. He had been issued with a map, a compass, a torch and a set of instructions that he read out as the army truck we were in took us up into the great hills that were the Beacons. We were given 90 minutes to complete a circuit on foot between four designated compass points: A, B, C and D. Our school and one other was involved in the exercise. We'd been the unfortunate ones first on the roster for it. Others would be doing the same thing on different nights through the week.

We'd been told to keep silent. Singh had been instructed to use the torch only when essential to look at the map, but was indecisive, and seemed to have trouble telling his left from his right. They should have put me in charge. As well as being incapable of reading a map, our hapless leader failed to maintain order and keep the rest of us quiet. It was a miserable situation, and we were all complaining again, with no-one able to work out whether to set off uphill to the right or downhill to the left, until Pipkin had a brainwave. "Let's stay here and watch for a few minutes," he suggested sensibly, "And keep our eyes open for torchlight."

The genius fellow had worked out that, to complete a circuit, it doesn't matter if you go clockwise or anticlockwise; also that other groups had probably been given different starting points around the circuit. Assuming we were at Point A, their torch flashes were most likely to give away the locations of B, C and D. Five minutes later and we were off. I'm sure, too, that we would have been the first group back by quite a margin, if it weren't for an unfortunate mishap.

We were carrying backpacks with nothing much in them except water, a small ground-sheet, and a couple of army-issue bricks to add weight. When, about half-way round, we took a short break so that Singh and Pipkin could consult the map and get their bearings, other members of the platoon took the opportunity to dump their backpacks and sit on the ground. Needing relief, I decided to move a short way off the path to empty my bladder. There was no moon and dense cloud cover, so I couldn't see anything; which is my excuse for tripping over somebody's pack and tumbling down the slope, giving my ankle a nasty twist in the process. I couldn't help crying out, at which point Singh shone the torch in my direction, but I was behind bushes, out of sight, trying to stand up and falling again with renewed pain in my ankle. The injury was obviously not slight, so they all had to carry me back.

There's an old wisdom story from the East somewhere that comes to mind as I remember all this. One day, a farmer discovers a handsome and healthy white stallion on his land. He doesn't know where it came from, but it's tame enough to be led into his stables. Hearing about this, a neighbour congratulates the farmer on his luck, but the wise fellow says, "Let's wait and see!" A couple of days later, the stallion disappears. When, this time, the neighbour commiserates, the farmer again simply says, "Let's wait and see!" A few more days go by and the stallion re-appears, accompanied now by a beautiful mare. Even better, the mare is heavily pregnant. "What wonderful luck again!" the neighbour says. "Let's wait and see!" replies the farmer once more.

When the farmer's son tries to ride the stallion, he is thrown off and breaks his leg. The neighbour thinks that's bad luck too. The farmer's not so sure. A war breaks out, and soon the army is looking for conscripts. However, because he is walking on crutches, the young man is exempted. In other words, what looks at first like misfortune, often turns out to be a blessing in disguise... and vice-versa, of course. In this case, my wrenched ankle excused me from further unpleasantness at the camp, and I was sent home by train. My comrades all thought I was lucky, and wanted to exchange places with me; but the truth is, I felt disappointed. Army life was seeping into my blood.

Nine

Last evening, to savour it at leisure, as is my wont, I took a tumbler of whisky onto the balcony. There was a break in the drizzling rain that seems to be a constant feature these days, although the cool air still seemed damp as I managed to get one of the armchairs onto the decking and sat there, looking up at the sky, taking the occasional refreshing sip. After a while, my eyes accustomed to the gloom, a break in the clouds appeared. There was no moon, but I could make out a few faint stars. Then, suddenly, a fireball erupted, careering right across the heavens, followed by a lengthy cascade of sparks.

There are people alive now, a majority I suspect, who have never used a smart phone or experienced the internet, the 'World Wide Web', as it used to be called. That's not so strange for me, of course. I was born when such things were only just being invented. However, people soon came to depend on them heavily. Increasing numbers of earth-orbiting satellites went up, three-thousand or more by the end; and even now some are still coming down, the big ones in fireballs, the smaller ones shattered into debris, tumbling earthward in scintillating showers, night after night. It is beautiful in a way; but is also a reminder of the untold death and destruction that occurred long ago, on which I do not yet wish to dwell. Much happier memories come first.

The rebuff from Cathy Squires hurt, but it did not take me long to emerge from the despondency. For example, we had a great ACF Field Day at a military barracks near Aldershot, where I renewed my marksman award using the Army's latest self-loading rifle, accurate (in my hands anyway) up to three hundred metres. We also got to shoot hand-held machine guns at targets no more than thirty metres away. I truly coveted that weapon, I won't deny it; and really did not want to give it back at the end of the day.

Soon enough, not long after my seventeenth birthday, the summer holidays arrived. About a week after term ended, one hot, sunny Saturday morning, I was loafing about the kitchen in my shorts and flip-flops when Charlie came to say she was taking brother P for his cello lesson; then they were going into town to buy him some shoes. I wouldn't go because I didn't have the patience for music lessons; nor did I need Charlie to choose my shoes, always insisting firmly on buying them for myself. After a few minor bust-ups over it in the past, Charlie acquiesced. She would advance me the money, as long as I promised to give her the receipt later for Grandpa Ralph. Her main concern, naturally, was keeping our benefactor happy.

I went outside to wave them away, so as to be quite sure they'd left. In the event, this meant standing around for a while because Mum was busy chatting to the neighbour, her friend Carol, who was out there in the adjacent driveway cleaning her tiny, shiny, little yellow Fiat. I wasn't really listening, thinking they'd just be talking about the weather or other boring stuff, but then heard a remark from Carol about how much the boys had grown and how well they looked. P, already sat in the car, took no notice, but looking up quickly I saw Carol smiling while glancing approvingly in my direction.

Wondering what signals she was intending to send, I decided to avoid showing any reaction, although it's true that I may have coloured a little. Whatever minor embarrassment might have arisen was happily, in any case, short-lived as P called out, tapping his watch, and Charlie immediately took the hint. Moments later, they set off, with me watching closely until the car entered traffic at the far end of the road.

I was excited, turning back towards the house, for this was a moment I'd been waiting for, an hour or more of freedom to peruse the latest edition of Penthouse, acquired days earlier after getting off the school train at Victoria, where I had tucked it safely out of sight into my backpack before catching the tube out to the leafy suburbs of Colliers Wood.

In a heady mixture of guilt, shame and excitation, fetching the precious object from its place of concealment in my bedroom, I made my way quickly to the bottom of the garden where, beside Charlie's vegetable patch, there stood a summer house, a kind of glorified shed that I liked to use as a bolthole for certain activities when I could count on being left alone and undisturbed on occasions such as this. It was a cosy enough private space. Sunlight streaming in and a pleasant breeze wafting through, I propped the door open and sat facing inwards in the old comfy chair that was there. Pulling my shorts to my knees, I allowed my eyes to feast eagerly on the centrefold for a while before turning to a highly informative article, graphically describing variations of oral sex while discussing their merits and drawbacks.

I was soon totally immersed, oblivious to anything other than the erotica in front of me and the erection between my legs, when a deep, sexy voice, unmistakeably Carol's, took me by surprise.

"It looks like you might need some help with that, Freddie," she said.

Later Carol claimed that, having finished cleaning the car, she'd only entered our garden to collect a few courgettes, accepting an earlier offer from Charlie. She even had with her, as I recall, a sharp knife to cut them and bowl to put them in; but I often wondered later if that was just a pretext for approaching me in the shed. No matter; and no matter that I felt badly caught out, because in no time Carol had drawn near, put one hand on my thigh, knelt beside me and, gripping the shaft with her other hand, placed her lips around the bulging head of my manhood.

The pages of Penthouse slipping from my grasp to the floor, her head moving rhythmically up and down, I was swiftly transported to ecstasy; although, I admit, much too soon, for Carol had suddenly to release her hold and sit back as a large amount of tacky ejaculate spurted up, catching the side of her face, showering over her wonderful, gleaming, copper-coloured hair, which, like the brilliant yellow car, had clearly been given a thorough wash earlier in the day.

"Now I'm going to have to take another shower," she said, apparently unfazed, dabbing herself with a couple of the man-size tissues I had to hand. "And perhaps you'd like to help me, Young Man!"

I was feeling a tad sheepish, embarrassed that my shorts as I pulled them back up were soiled too; but did not need any persuading. Carol gave me a peck on the cheek for encouragement, suggesting I collect fresh clothes from the house and join her in a couple of minutes. I had been in her house before, but only in the kitchen, reached through a mirror-image side entrance opposite our back door. The houses were near-identical so, having cleaned myself up a bit at home, I had no problem finding my way. When Carol met me upstairs, with a damp face flannel in hand, she had obviously been making good too.

Our neighbour was a handsome, fiery kind of woman, about the same age as Charlie, with a full, even generous figure, bright eyes in an attractive, welcoming face, well-creased from smiling, with fetching dimples in the cheeks. She was still wearing a short skirt, but the blouse had gone, revealing a beautiful pair of full-sized breasts straining against the thin fabric of her brassiere.

"Why don't we rest a little before we have that shower?" she said, ushering me backwards into the master bedroom, where a very large bed awaited. Face to face with this desirable woman, and my destiny, I remember I started to tremble, not from fear but excitement.

"Give me a hand with this, please, Freddie!"

At that moment, her silky voice saying my name was genuinely the most sexy I'd ever heard. Carol turned slowly to reveal the fastening at her back; and, surprisingly perhaps, I didn't fumble. It was easily done. The bra was off and there was me, staring in rapture at those twin marvels, the deep pink areolae and darker, proudly-standing nipples. I wanted to touch them, of course, swallow them whole possibly, but had no time to think as Carol, pushing me gently until I fell back on the big bed, attended to my buckle and zipper, deftly removing every last stitch I had on.

"Impressive," she said, wide-eyed, looking down at my privates. "Now, Freddie, there's something I'd like to show you."

Swiftly removing her skirt and panties, this magnificent woman hopped naked onto the bed. Arranging a couple of pillows against the head-board, she then sat back against them, her legs wide apart, beckoning me closer, saying we'd both benefit if I learned a few things before 'John Thomas', as she fondly referred to my pecker, was ready for a personal, private and intimate introduction to her 'Lady Jane'.

She said not to be afraid; but I wasn't, certain I was in kind, gentle and experienced hands. As I knelt instinctively down in full view of her curly, lustrous, golden-red bush, Carol drew my head even closer, pausing to carefully, with both hands, draw the soft flesh apart, like a curtain, to reveal the satiny, coral pink sheen of her love canal. I'd seen Charlie naked, of course, on the beach and such when we were young, but never anything remotely as wondrous as this.

"These are the labia," she said. "The lips... And this," she added, putting two fingers firmly inside, moving them slowly back and forth by way of demonstration, "Is the holy of female holies... The vagina."

She was right to assume my ignorance. I knew something from biology classes, of course, the names of certain things, like those she was showing me; but this would clearly not be a good time to interrupt my glamorous teacher. Shifting my weight to move a little nearer, I felt a distinct thrill as proud 'John Thomas', finally closed in on his goal.

"Don't get too excited," said Carol, mindful no doubt of my untimely explosion earlier. "There's more to teach you first."

"That's easier said than done," I was thinking, highly aroused; but nature is merciful, and I did seem to have slightly better control for round two; which was just as well as Carol, using both hands again, was drawing her labial curtains further back to reveal a small, fleshy kind of hooded protuberance.

"That," she said, "Is my clitoris... It's like a tiny penis women have, very sensitive, to give us pleasure. When stimulated, it grows too... See?"

I did see. Her little pink bud expanded gradually as I watched Carol's fingers at work.

"Here..." she said. "You touch it... Gently please!"

She took my hand to place my fingers on the spot, drawing them slowly back and forth, moving her pelvis rhythmically side to side all the while. Nostrils flared, breathing more heavily; she was becoming excited as well.

"Would you like to kiss it?" she asked. "Kiss it, suck it, lick it, tickle it. Women like all of those things, as long as you're not too rough."

So I manoeuvred to bend forward, then cautiously stuck out my tongue. This area of Carol's groin was quite moist now. The pink lining of her vagina, and the rubbery bud of her clitoris, tasted slightly salty, or rather, strangely salty and sweet at the same time. Shedding my reserve, intoxicated by the new experience, I was soon sucking away as Carol found my hand again to lead it on towards Lady Jane, wanting me to pleasure her with my fingers inside. The rotating motion of her hips grew faster and, glancing up, I could see she had started fondling her own nipples one after the other, giving out little moans of satisfaction, working towards a crescendo; and soon her whole body gave a tiny shudder as the peak moment approached; but Carol wasn't yet ready.

Her self-control was remarkable. On the point of orgasm, she had no problem at all putting the brakes on. Resting her hands on my head and pushing it back slightly, she took control of me too.

"That was lovely," she said when I sat back on my haunches, just a little deflated. "You're a quick learner, Freddie; but we don't want to end it too quickly, do we? We can have plenty more fun."

She got up to fetch us both a glass of water, and to give us both time to simmer down. Then she made me lie down where she had been; my head supported by a pillow and my legs stretched out; as she sat astride my thighs, taking most of her own weight on her knees, in perfect proximity for me to feast my eyes on her; on her face, her torso, her magnificent boobs, which she seemed happy now to let me fondle and kiss to my heart's content. It's hard to describe the degree of pleasure I took from lovingly handling the soft flesh and firm nipples which, as she lent forward to encourage me, I took greedily between my lips one by one. After several enjoyable minutes of this delightful activity, though, Carol realised that 'John Thomas' had reared up again, and was beginning to throb; whereupon she called another halt to proceedings.

"He's eager, isn't he?" she said, sitting back and looking down, "But I want to try something to calm him a little, to help make the pleasure last. Is that okay?"

I could only nod as she leaned forward again to place her thumbs and forefingers, fore and back, at the base of what she called the 'glans', the bulbous end of my organ shaped like a military helmet. Gradually increasing pressure, causing my heavily engorged prick to wilt visibly, she said this was called the 'squeeze technique' for reducing erections, before releasing her hold moments later when I was already down at half-cock.

47

"That can be done as often as we like," she added, before asking, "What do you think?"

I wasn't sure what to say. The procedure seemed to challenge a fellow's masculinity; but it was painless, and I could see how useful it would be to prolong our love-making. Also, I had not subsided completely and was pretty much still primed for some action, which was just as well because the longed-for moment was fast approaching. Carol was building up steam.

"What goes down must come up," she was saying with a grin, leaning forward, reviving my passions further with her lips in place of her hands.

The desired effect was achieved speedily then; so, moving fully astride me, with careful aim and moving slowly, Carol planted herself upon my eagerly upright pole, engaging it with her love passage, lowering herself until 'John Thomas' and 'Lady Jane' were joined right to the hilt.

Remaining totally motionless for several moments allowed me time to appreciate that heavenly sensation to the full. Then Carol began raising and lowering herself, little by little, while also rocking gently both forwards and backwards. Once or twice, she stopped moving, leaning forward to kiss me on the mouth, our eager tongues entwined, the wondrous weight of her breasts delightfully brushing my chest until, of course, I was soon close to bursting again.

"Hold on!" I whispered.

We used the squeeze method again; taking the edge off my tension just as effectively as before. Carol climbed nimbly aboard again afterwards, riding the saddle of my thighs, firmly gripping my manhood, until I needed another break, and we went through the sequence again.

This happened perhaps three or four times. I lost count. It always worked, and each time my teacher-lover grew more excited, as her powerful pelvic muscles gripped my love-machine tighter, to the extent that she was soon grunting in a sexy way, giving out deep animalistic noises, low-pitched moaning accompanied by occasional high-pitched squeals. From below, I was instinctively increasing both the rate and depth of my thrusting. Sometimes, Carol would stop and lean away, as if to operate a kind of squeeze technique on herself, reducing friction on that little miracle, her clitoris, so that we could remain clasped, delightfully motionless, holding off momentarily the great climax yet to arrive.

Finally, when I was once more ready to pop, Carol spoke in an urgent whispering, "I'm going to come... Quickly... Can we turn over?"

I'm not sure how we managed that tricky manoeuvre without

disengaging, but we did, necessarily sweeping the pillows out of the way. On top of her now, I could feel a big difference in both the force I could apply and the speed with which I could move up and down; my gargantuan inflamed cock now deep inside her treasure house, now withdrawn again; long, fast, penetrating thrusts precisely matched to Carol's repetitive pelvic motion back and forth. So highly lubricated was she by now that friction was minimal, allowing me longer to savour the dance-like coupling in which we were so energetically engaged, but still sufficiently present as to bring us closer and closer to the inevitable triumphant culmination of our effort.

A staccato series of tiny shudders passed quickly through Carol's body, and then another, greater and longer one, emanating, it seemed to me, from the very spot where we were joined. At the same time, an unforgettable sound emerged, a great outbreath of joy, pain, and I don't know what.

"I'm coming", she breathed ecstatically, as we climaxed together in an almighty, prolonged, volcanic eruption of sexual energy, leaving us spent eventual.y; smiling, sweat-soaked, and completely content.

For a long while, many minutes, we lay together. Ignorant of the protocol, if there was any, I left a very relaxed John Thomas inside Lady Jane's welcome harbour. Reading my mind, at one point, Carol assured me there was no risk of her getting pregnant, as her tubes had been tied after the birth of her daughter; and soon after this, we began kissing again. It seemed so natural. I felt her breasts and noticed her nipples standing proud once more, then I began to respond. Not expecting John Thomas capable of repeating his performance just yet, Carol spoke of having a shower; but I suggested we wait a while, taking her hand and leading it down to witness the phoenix of my rising manhood.

Before long, we were passionately making love; and there was no need for the squeeze technique this time. We just worked away steadily, taking our time, to another mind-blowing climax. When it was over, lying side by side, both smiling away as if we'd won the lottery, Carol kept saying, "You're amazing! I can't believe it... You are simply amazing."

She was amazing too. We were amazing together! So, our wonderful love affair had begun.

Ten

Big Al's story about losing his virginity was equally astonishing, but I did not hear about it until long after our schooldays, when we were both in the army. Even with my help, the GCE exams proved too big a barrier for my cerebrally challenged friend, for there was to be no repeat of the luck we'd had over the Common Entrance. He did manage, somewhat miraculously, to pass 'O Level' art when he was sixteen, but that was all, comprehensively flunking the other subjects, lamenting later that he hadn't even understood a good many of the questions.

Old George Firkin's health was in sharp decline during that summer I got together with Carol, so Al spent July and August at a residential crammer in Croydon; a grim place where nothing happened for him but lessons in English, maths, history and the dreaded Latin; preparing for examination resits back at school in the autumn, three of which he managed to fail badly again. The surprise was a scrape-through pass in maths, achieved, he later told me, by luckily revising two of the questions that came up the evening before the test. He might have passed English, he said, but his spelling, as always, let him down.

A decision had to be made about whether he should stay on for further resits a year later; an idea Mr Ash, the headmaster, was dead against, saying he'd be better off as an apprentice somewhere, learning a trade; but Ada Firkin was adamant. With her husband so sick, she would not countenance Al living back at home. Finally, it was Mr Prendergast who saved the day. Having taken quite a shine to Al, he agreed that the big lad could spend as much time as he liked in the art school during term time. It helped my pal's cause that he was useful on the rugby pitch too.

It's not hard to imagine the misery in the Firkin household as George eked out his final days. Al returned from the short winter break quite disconsolate as we sat together over cups of tea and leftover Christmas cake.

"He keeps having mini-strokes," my glum friend told me tearfully, spluttering his words out. "Can't speak at all now... Has to be fed... Awful to watch!"

"Tell me about him, Al," I found myself asking. "You've never really spoken about them before, your parents."

Al wiped his eyes and blew his big nose before answering, telling me what he could. Later, accompanying Al to the February funeral, giving him a bit of support, I pieced together more details from the eulogy. I remember Ada answering a few questions afterwards too. Their story was quite impressive.

George was a small man, measuring only a couple of inches above five foot. Ada, in contrast, was tall for a woman in those hungry days, towering six or seven inches above him. Was the difference in altitude the seed of their mutual attraction? Who knows!

When they met, George was working as a travelling salesman for a menswear company; a good job to be holding onto during those pre-war years, an occupation which involved lengthy train journeys on Mondays; to Yorkshire or Cornwall maybe; always hefting two great suitcases of samples, no easy feat for a short man. Meanwhile, Ada was helping run her step-mother's little grocery in the daytime, while also working an evening shift as a barmaid at the White Horse twice a week, a welcoming hostelry in Greenwich, which happened to be George's local, and always his first port of call when he returned on Fridays from his trips selling trousers, neckties and shirts.

He liked getting together with chums from his youth, many of them workers in the nearby docks and shipyards, enjoying the male camaraderie and cheery, irreverent banter of the place. Unlike his friends, though, George drank only modestly. He liked beer, but had reduced his intake after a couple of times getting pickled and starting fights with longshoremen twice his size. Drink made him fiercely pugnacious. The first time, he took a great pasting. The second time, his burly opponent with a fist on his forehead simply held him harmlessly at arm's length as he flailed away with both arms. It was comical; but for George it had been humiliating beyond bearing, hence his decision to moderate his alcohol consumption.

There was another difference, too, between him and his mates; many of them were already married. Despite feeling confident enough among the lads, cocky even, George was painfully shy with young women.

Ada noticed him, of course, as the weeks went by; and he must have picked her out as someone he'd like to get close to; but somehow Friday evenings would pass and he would trundle off to his bachelor digs alone, having spoken to her only matter-of-factly, if at all, when it was his turn to buy a round of ale.

Four years his senior, Ada had already been married; not for long, but for long enough to fall pregnant. Sadly, though, she was widowed and miscarried soon after when her husband, Jack, came off his motorbike one winter day, sliding across black ice into the path of an oncoming truck. Unwilling to show weakness, Ada appeared on the outside to take the double tragedy in her stride, but it must have left

51

deep scars. By the time George was growing interested in her, she was decidedly against any thought of marrying again.

It doesn't sound promising, does it? Makes you wonder if we ever come to know and understand ourselves properly. So, what happened to change things? Possibly it might have been the conversation George had with another barmaid, in another pub, and on a different night of the week.

His work took him to Harrogate and, having that day secured a particularly good order for the company, he made his way to the Star Inn for a celebratory pint of the local brew. There, the landlady, Freda Maple, a matronly person of mature years and much experience of life, having few customers that Thursday evening, decided a natter with George might be a rewarding way to pass the time, and so engaged him in prolonged conversation by asking personal questions right and left without shame or hesitation, cajoling him along with plenteous smiles, winks, nods, nudges and such-like, drawing him into revealing his intimate thoughts to the point where, unlike his usual taciturn self with strangers, he freely started mentioning Ada and the designs he might have had on her if he could only summon up the requisite courage.

"Get her out on her own!" This was Freda's considered advice. "Don't try chatting her up in the pub in front of all the other customers while she's working... That won't do... Meet her before she gets there, or talk to her on the way home."

To George, this seemed to make sense.

"It won't matter what you say," Freda carried on. "If she's interested, she'll help you along, right enough."

The following evening, back in Greenwich, George made a confident decision. Visiting the White Horse as usual, he left the pub shortly before closing time, but did not go home. Happily, the night was warm as he lingered about the vicinity, waiting as patiently as he could and as nervous as one might expect until, half an hour later, Ada, after helping to clear up, finally left her workplace. Waving goodbye to the landlord locking up, she turned towards the bus stop about twenty paces away. Half way there, though, a figure stepped alongside, stopping her short. The street light, beaming down on their faces, showed that she had been properly startled. George was surprisingly calm.

"Hello!" Was all he said, attempting an intimate tone.

"Hello," she replied, her voice rather shrill, and louder than she intended. "What do you want then?"

George paused and swallowed hard. "Would you like to go to the pictures with me sometime?" he said softly. "Maybe tomorrow?"

He was almost whispering, but these words rang loud in Ada's ears. Without suspecting it, he had already reached his goal, for she simply nodded, amazed at the intensity of joy welling up in her heart. Scarcely daring to hope, George took his prize by the hand and, in the gentlest of voices, breathing as much poetry into her name as he could, intoned the single word, "Ada..."

It had been a wild experiment on his part, rehearsed in private but with no guarantee of success. To his delight, evidently pleased that he knew her name, she responded likewise with, "George..."

When the bus came, they sat together; and alighted together too, so that he would know where she lived, in the flat above the grocery, the address from which he would collect her the following evening. Her step-mother was waiting inside.

"Who was that you were lingering with on the doorstep?" she said as Ada was hanging up her coat.

"That's George Firkin," Ada replied nonchalantly. "You may have to get used to him, Mother... I don't think he's going away."

War was on the horizon at this time, so the couple wasted no time getting married, and with the minimum of fuss; after which she moved into the rooms he was renting in a terraced house near the hospital, St Alphege's. As before, George carried on travelling, and Ada continued to help her step-mother; although, married now, she did not return to the pub. Secretly, she started thinking about getting pregnant again and having a baby. It was what she wanted, a baby to be a mother to; but it was not an ideal moment.

The war came. The Dunkirk fiasco and remarkable evacuation happened. Things began to look grim. Men volunteered for the services. Women signed on as nurses; and then conscription began, which meant uniforms had to be made and distributed, which in turn meant a switch for George's employers. Government contracts took over the need for salesmen to travel, so George was out of a job.

As patriotic as the next man, he volunteered for army service, only to be informed - none too politely - that his stature was lacking. He was too short, in other words, or, "Do you really think things have got so bad that the army's taking little runts like you?" as one of the more objectionable recruiting officers said rudely. "Why not bugger off and join the navy?"

"I don't think he should have spoken to you like that, George," said Ada when he told her; but his response was good-natured. " Love," he said cheerily, "They really don't know what they're missing!"

Weeks later, George was called up to the army anyway, and sent to Yorkshire for training. Eventually, he and his troop were shipped off to Singapore, while Ada went to work in a munitions factory, somehow surviving the blitz, despite the surrounding docklands being heavily targeted by Luftwaffe raids. One of her half-sisters took over the grocery, making sure all the family had plenty to eat while others were tightening belts, which was a particular blessing for Ada. Her work being heavy at times, she was ravenously hungry on a daily basis. With time, her big frame developed strong muscles, and she put on additional bulk, so she was soon as solid and strong as an ox.

In February 1942, after the Japanese took Singapore, news about the largest surrender in British history was suppressed at home for fear of damaging morale. Ada found out only that George was a prisoner of war, and there was no further word, either from or about him for over three years. She felt sure she would know in her heart somehow if he had succumbed, so harboured both hope and fear tightly in her breast. Mostly, she kept herself numb.

George, it eventually transpired, had been made to work on the death railway from Thailand into Burma, suffering untold cruelty, sickness and deprivation at Hellfire Pass and such places. Very robust by the end of his training on the Yorkshire Moors at the start of hostilities, there had been just enough grit and determination left in him to survive the unspeakable ravages at the hands of his Japanese captors. When he returned home, though, after enduring so much, he was broken in body and spirit.

Ada knew of other women who had given up on their men, found replacements, unable to endure the wait and uncertainty, but she remained steadfast in her embattled optimism without giving in to despair. Her reward, after so many months, was a curt note from the Ministry. Rangoon had been liberated; and the war in the East was finally over after the first atomic bombs were dropped on Hiroshima and Nagasaki, bringing about the Japanese surrender. Over seven thousand prisoners had died on the Burma railway, but now George and surviving comrades were being shipped home. The official letter, now in her hand, said she would be notified of his arrival.

After the troop ship docked at Southampton, returning soldiers were put on a train to London. Ada therefore prepared herself to meet George at Victoria Station. She was working in a local laundry now, and had been granted the day off. She was fussing in front of a mirror when she suddenly sat down on the bed and started sobbing in dismay. "What a fright I look," she was thinking.

As if scales had dropped from her eyes, she realised what George was about to witness: a deterioration in her appearance that he would surely find devastating. Some of her hard-won muscle had turned already to fat. Her clothes, no longer fitting, stretched over ugly bulges everywhere. Her hair was dry, badly cut, and now contained numerous strands of grey. Her hands were red. The skin of her face was pale and pasty, but applying make-up only made her look more ridiculous. The conclusion was unavoidable, "Don't I just look like a clown?"

Reflecting on her dismal appearance, full of trepidation, she gave little thought to how her husband might be after their long separation. Once at the station, seeing the train pull slowly in towards the buffers, she began feeling more optimistic as men still in uniform began to alight and make their way towards the barrier where she stood, expectant.

Ada scanned every face quickly, checking each against her memory of George. There were scores of them, mostly thin, heavily lined, bald-headed or fully grey, some marching upright but many walking slowly, bowed over, none of them resembling her husband. As the stream slowed to a trickle, she took out the telegram to confirm that she had the right time, and was scrutinising it again several minutes later when a diminutive old man in ill-fitting civilian clothing, lost and feeble, sidled by.

"Ada..." this phantom of a man barely whispered.

It was George. She had failed to recognise him, so broken down did he seem, like a lost child. The irony made itself felt. Hadn't she always wanted a child?

Eleven

They never did have children of their own, George and Ada. They must have tried, but George's health was never the best. Besides, Ada had her hands full, looking after him in the beginning. She also had to make some kind of living, because her husband couldn't yet work. After a time at the laundry, she was promoted to floor supervisor. Her stepmother had died, as had her half-sisters; Sally a random victim of one of Hitler's doodlebug flying bombs, Rachel with tuberculosis. Fortunately, once the grocery shop was sold, Ada's legacy was enough for a good down-payment on a modest terraced house in Raynes Park; and this is where George would remain day after day.

He seldom spoke. Whenever he did, it was to say, "I'm alright now," but she worried about him all the time nevertheless. Hour after hour, he simply sat in the kitchen, where it was warmest. She had to coax him to eat and drink. He showed no interest in reading or listening to the wireless, although she left it on sometimes. She could only wonder what was going on in his mind. The nights were worst. He cried out often in his sleep, tossed and turned about; sometimes she even found him sleepwalking downstairs. He was jumpy all the time, as if waiting for a beating or some other unspeakable punishment. To her, it seemed like he was still stuck back in that camp.

The laundry being close by, Ada could slip home two or even three times a day to keep an eye on George and coax him to eat. In the summer, she would lead him into the small patch of garden at the back of the house, and settle him in a deck chair; but usually on her return later, he would have retreated to the safety of the building. Quite often, he took himself back to bed. For many months, nothing changed; then, one day, when she came home to check on him at lunch time, he was gone.

George's disappearance put the poor woman into an immediate panic, forcing her into the street to look for him, calling on those neighbours still at home to ask if anyone had spotted her errant husband, walking up and down nearby streets and alleyways, going gradually further afield until she eventually reached the Police Station, where she felt she must ask for help, but where no-one could be spared to organise a search.

"Think about where he might have gone," a kindly Sergeant suggested. "Where do you think he'll feel safe?"

It was a warm day. Perhaps that was what had enticed him out. A gentle, cooling breeze was blowing; and it made her think that George would have wanted space, open countryside. They had enjoyed a couple of weekend rambles together in the early days of their marriage. George was a pretty good hiker. "Maybe he's up on the Common," was all she could think.

Wimbledon Common covers a large area. As Ada trod the pathways across it, she thought her task might prove impossible, and that George might in any case have already made his way home. Mulling it over, though, she decided there was nothing to do, except simply to carry on looking.

It was hours later, as dusk was falling and the temperature dropping, that she came finally to a clearing besides one of the ponds. Taking a step forward, she let out a small, almost silent sigh of relief; for there he was, alone, sitting on an overturned log at the water's edge, gazing contentedly down at a robin flitting here and there, rooting about for insects and grubs. Approaching quietly, she sat down beside him, gently so as not to disturb the evening's peace.

"Hello, Love!" he said calmly. "I've been making friends with this bird."

She took his hand and gave an affectionate squeeze. The silence enveloped them.

"I had a little bird for a time in the camp," George continued after a while. "Made a little cage for him... Colourful little creature! I never did find out what kind it was, but he kept me company while I had him... Reckon it must have been him that kept me sane..."

It was a turning point in her husband's recovery. Ada had a small aviary installed in the garden, and George spent more and more time outside with his birds; finches mainly; silently building up the courage to gradually venture forth into everyday society once again, gradually making progress to the point that, a year or so later, he was able to apply for a job with the old clothing firm, not as a travelling salesman this time but in the office. Perhaps it was charity that made the directors sanction it; a reward for his sterling service to the company before the war; and it was only part-time at the beginning; but huge explosions from little atoms do blossom, and by the time the couple thought of adoption, to fulfil as best they could Ada's dream of motherhood, George was in charge of a section and once more working full time.

They were turned down at first, of course. Their age and George's history of infirmity were against them; but they were allowed to be short-term foster parents for some of the more troubled, older children; always boys, never girls. George had a tendency to be lenient with them, letting them get away with all manner of mischief, but Ada was firm; and this double-act was the key to their obvious success. Al was the third boy they fostered. Nobody else had come close to taming his wild, angry ways, but the five-year-old calmed down enough with them for the social workers to take notice and, after six months, the adoption went through. The two-bedroom home seemed too small for three so, with George again earning a fair salary, the family were able to move to a bigger house further out, near West Byfleet. Another, bigger aviary was installed in the garden, which ran down to a screen of conifers bordering the nearby golf course, and Ada set about planting roses.

In the summer after old George died, Ada hatched a plan for the seventeen-year-old Al to spend time in America. She'd heard about a student programme linked to summer camps, and promptly enrolled her boy who, despite being on the point of leaving education, was still eligible to join the British Schools North America Club. BriSNAC arranged air travel, visas, and camp placements at subsidized rates. Ada's brainwave led to Al spending three months in the USA, having a fantastic adventure.

After the plane from Gatwick landed at Kennedy, dumping its excitable load of adolescents, they were quickly processed through Immigration and herded onto buses for the drive to the city, where they were accommodated for three nights in a massive, scruffily-ageing hotel; and where they were put agonisingly through something called 'orientation'. It seemed strange to Al, remembering fragments of both Latin and geography, that to travel three thousand miles to the West should result in a course of 'Easternisation'. I would have explained this reversal as 'seemingly absurd and contradictory', thus a perfect example of 'paradox', which was another word Mr Wright had once taught me.

The kids were given a walking tour of the city, went right around Manhattan on a boat trip, and reached the top of a sky-scraper, although Al forgot which one. They learned usefully, if confusingly, that chips were called 'fries', and crisps were called 'chips'; torches were 'flashlights'; trousers were 'pants', the 'boot' of a car was the 'trunk', petrol was 'gasoline' or 'gas', and they were instructed to walk on the 'sidewalk', not the pavement, which would have proved dangerous as 'pavement' in America means the middle of the road. Al couldn't remember much more; except not to ask a City cop for the time, after one hapless teenager did so and was rebuffed by a huffy, gun-toting officer's curt reply: "What do you think I am? A goddam information bureau... Get outa here!" He did remember the interviews.

The youngsters had not yet been allocated to their camps. The first interview, in a small room off the cavernous lobby of the poorly-styled 'Majestic', on the third morning after his arrival, was with two hard-bitten US Camping Association officials in identical pants, shirts and blazers; one allegedly male, the other allegedly female. This was to determine the suitability of each candidate and agree a placement. Unfortunately, Al was told, most camps had started a week earlier, as schools in America broke up sooner than in England, and there were few places remaining.

He was asked about his experience of summer camps; so Al told them about the cadet force at school, and the camp in Brecon he went to the year after me; but the tough-looking woman said, frowning, that it sounded too military, and maybe he was too tall.

"We don't want you frightening the little campers," she explained.

"I think they were looking for excuses," Al told me. "I was expecting to be a camp counsellor. You know, someone leading the smaller kids in their groups. But they didn't want me for that... I think they treated me pretty rough."

At the end, when the other British teenagers had all been seen, he was told there were no suitable placements for him in USCA camps at that time; but he was assured nevertheless not to worry. They had an arrangement with another organisation that was affiliated to several private summer camps: Camp America Plus. He was to have an interview at CAP headquarters early that afternoon.

"It's only five blocks," the skinny fellow told him, handing him a slip of paper with a name and address on it. "You've plenty of time to walk up there. Mr Centrella will be waiting."

As usual, it was hot and humid in the city that July. Al was toting the ungainly, army-type khaki knapsack Ada had bought him for the trip after reading the BriSNAC guidelines; so, not surprisingly, he was red-faced, dry-mouthed and sweaty by the time he finally arrived at the Third Avenue sky-scraper and took the lift, or rather the 'elevator', to the 19th floor, the home of Camp America Plus. When the doors opened, though, he felt sure he'd made a mistake, because in front of him was an enormous office filled with empty desks, light shining brightly from the acres of glass window on three sides. Blinking, he couldn't see any people, but he did soon hear his name being called.

In the far right corner, at the only occupied desk; one laden with telephones, a mountain of paperwork and an empty pizza delivery box; sitting in a reclining office chair, swivelled in his direction, all of fifty feet away, was Joseph Centrella, beckoning and calling to Al.

"Leave your bag over there!"

Al went over and sat down where 'JC', as he liked being called, indicated with a stubby forefinger. The man's chubby face seemed friendly. He was about sixty, with tousled grey hair, a rumpled, faded tartan, or rather 'plaid', shirt, equally faded blue jeans and bare feet.

"Where is everybody?" Al asked.

"I am everybody right now," he was told. "Everyone else left already..."

Joe Centrella explained that he'd been running CAP for ten years, but that it took up only two or three weeks of his time each summer. He didn't run any camps. He was just a broker, a human resourcer of sorts. He had a huge office because he'd found it cheaper to hire for a short time than a smaller one, which he would have had to take for a much longer duration. He ran it with three others, but had let them go that morning, because there was so little work remaining that year.

Joe, in a particularly sociable mood, was in no apparent hurry to get on with fixing Al's need for employment.

"Haven't had anyone to talk to all day," he said, smiling.

Joe told Al he was some kind of lawyer, and that he spent every winter in Florida, except the year he went to the Bahamas, which he didn't like so much. His three sons had been to summer camps, but were all grown up now. One was in Geneva, high up in the World Health Organisation. The other two were both in California, one raking in cash as a rock band manager and entrepreneur (pronounced 'enter-pren-yure'), and the youngest running a surf school.

"He's just a bum... Never grew up," JC told Al. "But, tell the truth, he's the one I love best."

On he went, rambling for more than half-an-hour before finally getting to the point.

"I'm waiting for a call back," he said. "This camp owner needs someone. Somebody got sick at his camp and needs replacing. I left him a message about you."

Al asked for a drink of water and was given an ice-cold coke from a miniature freeze-box under the desk. He was given a chocolate bar too. The phone rang loudly on the desk as he began to unwrap it. J C picked up the receiver, listened for a few moments, said "Yes... His name's Alan," listened some more and said, "Got it!"

"Okay," he told Al finally. "You're in luck!"

My friend had to get on the subway heading North-West, stopping at a station out of the city on the raised section of track in the open air. Going down to street level, he was to wait at the intersection, where the camp owner, Dan Minsky, would be waiting for him at around four-thirty. Al said he followed the instructions, but when he got there, he could not see Minsky, and nobody approached him.

Confused, he noticed a much bigger intersection only a short block away, a highway with four lanes of traffic in each direction; so Al made his way there, thinking this must be where he should be. Unfortunately, no-one was waiting for him in that spot either. In fact, the traffic moved through the lights in such numbers and so quickly that no vehicle could have stopped anyway without causing a major pile-up. By the time Al realised he was mistaken, it was already just after five.

Back at the subway intersection, he was in a right fluster, thinking he had little money, no work, knew nobody, and did not know where he could or should go if he had missed his ride to the camp. Turning this way and that, looking around everywhere, he was definitely beginning to panic and squirm inwardly when an elderly black woman poked him sharply in the arm.

"Are you Alan?" she said. "Somebody yonder is calling."

It was Minsky, leaning back against a slightly battered, cream-coloured Cadillac, one of the biggest cars Al had ever seen, parked illegally against a fire hydrant on the opposite side of the street.

"It was like a boat on wheels," he said later.

Feeling total relief, he made his way across to apologise.

"Don't worry, Alan!" Minsky said. "I just got here... Put your bag in the trunk."

After he had done so, Al went round to the car's near-side.

"I think I'd better do the driving, don't you?"

It was Minsky again, indicating without much subtlety that his new employee had forgotten he was in America, and was about to get in the driver's side of the vehicle. Al, red-faced and flustered, grew miserably apologetic all over again; but Minsky was fine. He didn't take any notice.

On the ride, 'Uncle Dan' told him they were headed for the Catskill mountains, a playground for New Yorkers, also a little about camp routine and what would be expected of him. One of the four camp waiters had left two days earlier, after a sudden family bereavement.

"Where there's death, there's hope!", Minsky quipped. "That's what I always say. It's how you got the job... Don't worry! You'll soon pick it up."

The car seemed to float, sideways as well as up and down, on its slack suspension, so that after about an hour, Al began feeling seasick. Fortunately, they then made a stop, pulling into a gas station with a diner, where Uncle Dan bought hamburgers and fries with milk shakes for both of them. After they'd eaten, Al was told to sit tight or take a walk for twenty minutes; Minsky explaining that he was going to take a power nap on the back seat of the Caddy, which he did.

"I've never seen anything like it," Al told me. "I followed him to get a book from my backpack in the boot. One minute he was walking about with his eyes open. The next he was fast asleep, just like that."

He gave a flick of the fingers to illustrate.

"Then, as far as I could tell, exactly twenty minutes later, he opened his eyes, sat up, got out of the car and called me over. Seconds later, we were on our way again... It was amazing!"

It was late by the time they reached Diamond Lake Camp. The younger campers were already in their bunks in their cabins as Uncle Dan parked the car and led Al into his office where the lights were already blazing. A thin young man, with a shock of dark hair emerging from a tightly-tied red bandanna, got up from behind the desk as they entered.

"Skip... This is Al!" Minsky waved a hand between the two. "Al... This is Skip Morgan! Skipper's pretty much in charge around here. He'll show you around."

Skip's name, it turned out, did not signify that he was a ship's captain. It really was what the twenty-two year old was called. He'd been coming to the camp every summer since he was about six; had been a counsellor for two years, and head counsellor for two more. He was also related in some way to Minsky, who perhaps truly was his uncle. Without asking him any questions, or saying much at all, Skip took Big Al back out into the gloom to show him where he would sleep.

Twelve

It was a short walk from the office to the waiters' hut, which was somewhat similar to a large garden shed, much less luxurious than the log cabins occupied by the fee-paying campers. Placed well away from those little palaces, it was out of sight down a slope, adjacent to nearby trees of the encroaching forest. There were no windows, and only a weak light bulb hanging on a cord from the ceiling. Three bunk beds arranged inside made it cramped, especially for a tall fellow like Al, who's additional problem was having to bend his knees to fit into the short bunk; but the 'Bimmies', as the waiters were known throughout the camp, apart from sleeping, were not expected to spend much time in this den.

They were widely treated as dehumanised minions; their days consisting of getting up at six o'clock; taking a shower in the outdoor facility, which had a concrete base and a screen around it at midriff height, the water being pumped cold, direct from the lake; dressing quickly and making their way uphill to the kitchen and dining-hall complex to lay tables, four tables of nine places each, then into the kitchen where Cook and her assistant, another bimmy, Pete, prepared all the food.

The waiters served the campers at the same tables during each meal, cleared away, and helped stash dishes in the industrial sized washing-up machines after, then went back to their hut area for a lengthy break before repeating the process at both lunch and supper time. The only alteration to the schedule was on Wednesdays, when campers were shipped out en masse by bus for some kind of excursion, taking packed lunches prepared earlier by Cook and the bimmies. This gave Al and the guys their only time off in the week; but they still had to turn up and lay tables for supper, serve food and clear away. It wasn't much of a break.

On that first day, Skip turned up early to make sure Al was awake, guiding him through the routine by helping serve the kids at his designated tables, all of whom he seemed to know by name. Al got the middle group, ten to thirteen-year-olds, two tables each of girls and boys, eight campers and one counsellor per table.

"The girls were awful," I remember Al telling me. "Spoilt brats! The boys just fought with each other; and the girls were always on my case, demanding this, demanding that... More cutlery, more food... 'Al, Al, Al', they went, over and over, never satisfied." He sighed.

"The worst was when it was pancakes for breakfast. Cook always cooked extra, but there was competition between me and the others to get them and bring them out from the kitchen. I was usually too slow; and when I failed to deliver, the cry always went up: 'No tips... No tips... No tips!' At first I didn't know what that meant."

It was Skip who explained that he was getting paid for being a waiter, but not much, well below the statutory minimum wage. The shortfall, however, would be made up by gratuities from the campers on the last day of camp. Every day, though, these tips were under threat from among the greediest and least mannered of his charges. Al tried learning how to cope from his peers.

The other waiters were Nate 'Spiderman' Wills, whose nickname came not because he was a super hero, but on account of his strange fondness for eight-legged creatures and their webs after he was seen protecting a great hairy one from a broom in his corner of the hut; Billy Judd, known as 'misery' because he hardly ever stopped smiling; who, moreover, when you called him that, seemed to smile even more; and Albert Crocker, who was called either 'Einstein' or 'The Professor'. Al's given name was 'The Hulk'.

Nate, a small, wiry, nervous creature, was always on the move, a nature-lover, happy in his free time to go rambling through the woods or by the lake. Billy was quiet, a contented soul ambling his way through life without asking any favours. Alby Crocker, in contrast to the other two, was neat and fastidious in habits and demeanour. These three occupied the lower bunks in the hut. Unlike the messy jumble of clothing and possessions of the others, Einstein's was tidy, everything stashed neatly away in tins, boxes, packets, bags, sundry other containers of different sizes, and a small suitcase. But Billy, by far, had the best collection of music.

After breakfast, Skip took Al on a brief tour of the camp; mostly, it seemed, to be warned about what was off-limits to bimmies. The lake itself, sparkling in the sunlight, was tear-drop shaped, the top over half-a-mile away to the north-west. Its belly was where they stood by the jetty and roped-off swimming area.

"You're not allowed to swim without a Diamond Lake certificate of proficiency," Skip told Al. "You lucked out though... Most people got those in the first week, so we're not running the test any more."

Feeling the water and finding it icy, Al didn't mind this too much. A small group of campers, having gingerly entered the lake as he and Skip approached, were already rushing back out, screeching and dripping wet, hunting urgently for their towels, most having turned a purplish shade of blue from their cold bath, the boys in particular looking highly distressed. A bigger disappointment for Al involved being forbidden to use any of the canoes, despite a flotilla of over thirty tied nearby, and obviously ready to go.

"I would have loved that," Al told me, "But never did get the chance... Only once!"

The view across the lake was of a majestic tree-covered hillside, part of the rather diminutive Catskills. Diamond Lake was up a long unpaved driveway off a minor highway, several miles from the nearest town, Roscoe, so it was peaceful in the camp, where the dining hall and administration buildings faced each other across a large, flattened earth compound, some of it grass-covered in various sized patches, a place used for roll call, softball games and such by the campers. Either side, in tidy rows, were the sixteen main cabins, inside each of which a single bed for the counsellor was flanked by four bunks for campers, the same group who sat and ate together at table during meals. These cabins were completely off limits to Al too. Forbidden from using any of the camp's equipment, or joining in any recreational activities, it was left to the bimmies to amuse themselves during their morning and afternoon breaks. Music played a vital part in their recreation; as did marijuana.

Al did not remember a single day of rain during his summer at the camp; only occasional downpours during the night, beating down hard and noisily on the roof of the hut, inches above him, lying awake in his bunk. Clouds drifted by, but the daytimes were filled with plenty of sunshine. Following the lead of the others, Al would strip to his shorts and sunbathe for hours, forgoing though the strange reflector panels that Billy and Nate held up to their throats as they sat hour after hour with the aim of perfecting their tans, oblivious, he thought, to the perils of melanomas and other deadly forms of skin cancer.

The studious Professor was more cautious, seldom discarding long pants and a lightweight long-sleeve cotton shirt, preferring to sit in shade, reading a serious book about astronomy maybe, or computer science. Al tried reading too. He had a couple of paperbacks, stories of derring-do by a favourite author, Philip McCutchan, like 'Drums Along the Khyber' and the naval thriller 'Dangerous Waters'; but, even though full of excitement, they couldn't hold his attention throughout the long periods of idleness. For the most part, he daydreamed and listened to music.

The other bimmies, including Pete from the kitchen, seemed to prefer light, cheerful songs from Charlie and H's era, by American singers and bands like Crosby, Still, Nash and Young, Love, Judy Collins, Joni Mitchell, Don McLean, and the Irishman, Van Morrison; but also darker tracks from Frank Zappa, Jefferson Airplane and The Doors. *"Father, I'm going to kill you.... Mother, I'm going to... Aaaagh!"* Al soon grew hugely fond of all this kind of stuff.

As for the drugs, it soon became clear that everyone was using the dried leaves of the cannabis plant, 'grass', or its resin, 'hash', even some of the youngest campers, no older than six. Faced with this, though, Al made up his mind not to indulge; which his new chums instantly took up as a challenge. Pete tried to explain how harmless Mary-Jane was, and how pleasant the experience could be. Either grass or crumbs of resin could be hand-rolled into a tobacco cigarette; but Al, who's airways had tightened up alarmingly when he first tried smoking at home, leaving him wheezing, breathless and scared, refused point blank to give this method a try, despite even the cautious Professor urging him on.

"Okay," said Pete to the others in the face of Al's intransigence, "I'll get Jerry on the case. My brother's sure to persuade him, if anyone can."

Jerry Garcia, who referred to himself as 'The Thankful Living' rather than 'The Grateful Dead', to distinguish himself from the infamous member of that band of the same name, was also a kind of bimmy in the camp. Three years older than the seventeen-year-old Pete, he was in charge of the busy laundry (overactive, he would complain, because of too many bedwetting boys), and it was he who should have occupied the sixth bunk bed in the hut with them all; but Jerry had a car, an ageing maroon-coloured Pontiac, that he had driven up from Brooklyn towing a small caravan, which was now parked behind the Admin cabins, in which Uncle Dan allowed him to sleep, also to cater for himself. The vehicle came in useful, it turned out too, for Jerry's essential trips back to the city every two or three weeks, so that the laundryman turned dealer could replenish the camp's supply of intoxicants.

"I thought he'd be a monster when I heard about him," Al told me, "But he was really nice; Spanish-looking, with a little upper lip mo above a black shaggy goatee beard and a big smile. I liked him. We soon became friends."

Like Skip, Jerry had been through the camp year after year, and kept coming back every summer. Unlike Skip, for whom camp traditions were sacrosanct, Jerry was a born subversive, refreshingly honest about the camp's failings: the money-grabbing ethos of Uncle Dan; the consequences of the enforced shoestring budget on the infrastructure; leaking roofs, flaking paintwork, and antiquated washing machines being among Jerry's particular bugbears, also the dire quality of the five-member adult staff, lazy, self-centred men and women without exception in his view. Once you got Jerry started on such a topic, his ranting would run on forever; but his mood was kindly and cheerful with Al when they met on his third day at the lake.

They chatted a while to get acquainted, then Jerry broached the delicate subject uppermost in his mind.

"I hear you can't take tobacco," he said, thinking this was Al's only objection to becoming a pothead. "Don't worry! There's other ways of getting it into your system."

Jerry showed him a cylinder, six or seven inches long, about a quarter-inch in diameter, explaining how it was taken from one of the cardboard coat-hanger tubes they use to avoid unwanted crease-marks in America. With a sharp penknife, he cut out a half-inch section quite close to one end, fitting then into the gap he'd made a piece of copper gauze prepared earlier, poking it gently with his finger so that it sank in the middle, creating a shallow bowl. Next, he taped the gauze in place and covered the end of the tube with the same insulating tape; then he took a match-box sized chunk of hash from a pocket, lit a flame and warmed one corner, from which he was easily able to crumble a little into the bowl he had just manufactured. Raising the open end of the tube to his lips, "This is how you do it," he said.

Jerry lit another match, held it close over the morsel of hash in the bowl and inhaled sharply, keeping the breath in his lungs for as long as he could, the nugget glowing brightly for a moment, as he did so, before fading out to gray ash.

"That's all there is to it," Jerry, his eyes twinkling now, said to Al. "How about you have a try?"

Nevertheless, Al was adamant. He didn't like the idea of it; an unknown foreign substance in his lungs. However, Jerry was not one to quit. He went away, but he would return day after day until Al's resolve gave way and he did finally agree to swallow a small piece of the resin one afternoon with some chocolate, rather than smoke it. He was delighted however two hours later to find that nothing whatever had occurred.

"It didn't affect me at all!" he triumphantly told Jerry, who was there to assess the effects; but the laundryman wasn't worried.

"It sometimes happens," he said. "You should try it again."

Al had, by now, witnessed the effects of cannabis on the other bimmies and a few of even the quite young campers. Truth to tell, he could not see any evidence of harm happening. Everyone just seemed to become mellow in mood at first and then cheerful, often laughing a lot. The only bad thing, he thought, was the so-called 'munchies'. As I also remembered from my parents' highs in the past, Mary-Jane made people crave sweet things, particularly chocolate bars. They couldn't get enough of them.

Al did eventually try ingesting the resin a second time, simply swallowing some of the bitter tasting, firm, dark, clay-like material;

but with the same result.

"It's another dud," he declared.

"You're resisting," Jerry told him. "Try once more... You have to!"

And he did; although he insisted again after a couple of hours that nothing was happening; until, that was, Nate pointed out the smile all over his face.

"After that," said Al, "I couldn't stop myself laughing. I was gone!"

Somehow, he got through serving at supper, but was still giggling hours later as he got into bed.

"What was so funny?" I asked him.

"I just kept thinking of Elaine," he replied, clearly embarrassed; and that was all he would say.

When Skip was showing him round on that first morning, they looked in on Uncle Dan in the Admin block, took a peek at the laundry building behind it, then went over to the sanatorium, the health centre, which was the operational base for the two 'Camp Mothers', Jeanette and Elaine. Inside the door was a waiting area, then an office, and next to it a treatment room that doubled up for physical examinations. A couple of young campers were sitting around waiting their turn. One said she had a headache; the other sported an ugly gash near his ankle that was still oozing blood.

"We're busy," came a deep voice from the treatment room, after Skip put his head round the door. "Send him back after lunch!"

"That's Elaine," Skip explained. "You have to have a physical. Everyone does when they first get here... Uncle Dan's rules! She said to come back later. And don't forget Alan, please! You don't want to mess with Elaine..."

The only woman he had caught sight of, darting between the office and the waiting area, was Jeanette, a mousy blonde in her mid-thirties, thin, with an off-putting squint so you couldn't tell if she was looking at you or not. The kids in the camp called her 'Cross', short for 'Cross-eyes'; but cross was an accurate description too of the irritable mood she often carried about, like a storm cloud ready to burst. Only Jerry, it seemed, appreciated her charms, and did so in a way that earned him another unflattering sobriquet. He was known as the 'Camp Mother-fucker'. Al laughed when telling me all about that.

When he returned in the afternoon, Elaine was alone in the clinic. A stocky woman in her early forties, with cropped dark hair and plain, unsmiling features, she was wearing a buttoned-up white coat that hugged her contours much too tightly to flatter. Sitting at a desk in the office when he went in, she had a business-like clipboard in front of her. When Al was seated, she proceeded to read out, in a monotonous voice, a series of questions about his medical history: measles, mumps, vaccinations; eating, sleeping, urinary and bowel habits; allergies; smoking and drinking, drug use, medication, etcetera. Satisfied eventually, she told him to go next door and strip to his underwear.

First she measured his height and weight, took his temperature and blood pressure, then got him to lie on the couch; lowered, he assumed, for some of the smaller kids' use. Elaine shone a light in his eyes, pinched his ear lobe, stuck a stethoscope on his chest, got him to sit up so she could listen at the back, prodded his stomach when he lay back again, then pulled away his underpants and started crudely fondling his testicles.

"We just have to check your equipment, you know," she said by way of explanation; adding, to Al's astonishment, "You know, you have a very big penis. You know?"

"She was always saying 'You know'," Al explained, unnecessarily. This was many years later.

"Anyway, all the while she was stroking it, Freddie," he went on, "I was getting aroused; but she didn't stop. It was embarrassing! You know me... I hadn't even touched a girl until then."

This was just the beginning. With one hand, Elaine undid some buttons on the white coat, revealing herself to be naked below the waist underneath. Then, when Al's prick was fully distended, she suddenly clambered aboard; this giant leap of unethical behaviour catching Al quite by surprise, as she continued writhing like a manic serpent while holding him down, leaning with her fists on his shoulders.

"She was strong," Al explained. "My legs were dangling over the end of the couch. I couldn't get any purchase... I couldn't shove her off, even if I'd wanted to..."

"Did you want to?" I asked.

"I'm not sure," he replied with a lop-sided grin. "It all happened so fast."

Moments later, their somewhat brutal coupling was over; an affectionless encounter that may have satisfied one participant, but left my friend breathless and confused. He'd lost his virginity, and was glad about that part, but was also left feeling unclean; somewhat used and abused.

Strangely, perhaps, he could not bring himself to complain, or even tell anybody. He assumed that would get him in trouble; that he might lose his job and be sent packing. This was Elaine's hold over him; so perhaps it is not so surprising that, when summoned by her to the health centre for a repeat 'physical' every week, he meekly went along with the practice.

"Eventually, I did get her to slow down a bit, so we could enjoy it some more," Al said, "But there was never much conversation."

We had both been seduced by older women, but our experiences were utterly different. What I had with Carol was special; in fact, it seemed to me, almost sacred.

Thirteen

Al found himself entranced by the night skies at Diamond Lake. The location was so remote from the light pollution of towns and cities that the heavens were utterly clear. On hot days, the bimmies would drag their mattresses off the bunks to sleep on the ground by the hut. Tired, they would fall asleep instantly; but Al remembers waking, hours later, when it was fully dark, looking up, listening to the soft breathing and occasional snores of his comrades, totally absorbed in the stunning vistas above. On moonless nights especially, there seemed to be trillions of stars.

It was Alby, the Professor, who kindly pointed out the constellations and visible planets, also the blip of the International Space Station (the one that crashed and burned so spectacularly years later) as it passed across the skyscape at regular intervals; so Al's vocabulary and knowledge of astronomy gradually improved. He was rightly proud of himself.

Once he'd got the hang of the routine, those first weeks seemed idyllic. One Wednesday, he, Pete and Billy piled with Jerry into the Pontiac for a trip to town. They spent the time in Monticello eating hamburgers, drinking beer and playing pool. Al did explore a little, taking a look around the main street area; but other than buying another couple of paperbacks, did not find it particularly exciting. When offered the same trip again another week, he decided against; a decision explained also by the high tension that had arisen between the waiters in the interval.

About five weeks into the camp, at breakfast one day, Al discovered he did not have enough cutlery or crockery to set up all four tables. Naturally, the kids gave him a hard time about it, so he went in early to set up for lunch, finding Nate there ahead of him with the same idea, grabbing hold of the full complement of kit before the others arrived. To Al, this seemed like a great solution. Nevertheless, by the start of the meal, several items had gone missing again. He went back early that evening as well, set up his tables properly, then waited to see what would happen. First, Billy came and got organised, apparently unconcerned that there was a small shortfall; then Einstein arrived, laid knives, forks, spoons, plastic beakers and side plates as usual; and when he ran out, calmly helped himself to those he needed from Nate's tables while Nate was taking a leak.

This kind of thing went on for a couple of days; laying your tables, then stealing from others while backs were turned; the situation getting gradually worse, until the bimmies were openly bickering with each other in the hopeless attempt to field a full complement of utensils for their tables. The squabbles escalated; and back at the hut one time a fist-fight broke out between Billy and Nate, the only time Al saw Billy upset. He and the Professor broke it up, Al's size and strength coming in handy to keep the combatants apart, before what started as a scuffle deteriorated into something more serious.

It was the Prof who identified the problem.

"It's not us," he said, when everyone was calm again. "We're not to blame... It's the kids. The campers are the ones taking all the knives, cups, plates, anything, back to their cabins. They're a bunch of thieves, and we need to tell Uncle Dan."

So they formed a small delegation and went to the office, expecting a lukewarm reception at best, only to be pleasantly surprised. The camp owner grasped the situation right away; said they should have come earlier; then he called Skip, loading him, Al and Billy into the Caddy for a trip to the local supermarket. By supper, they had enough of the replenished stock to furbish an extra five tables, and all the friction between the lads disappeared. How much human conflict runs along similar lines? People are friendly, then things start running out - fuel, energy, food, water, medicine, safe space in which to live, whatever - and everyone else is a rival. Aggressive instincts kick in. We saw plenty of that in Africa, and in the aftermath of the flood. Friends became enemies overnight!

When Diamond Lake Camp closed at the end of the season, Al stayed on in America. Through BriSNAC, Ada had paid for a thirty-day Greyhound Bus pass that he could use to go anywhere; so from New York City he went up to Canada, taking in Montreal, Toronto and Niagara Falls, before heading back into the States, crossing the border into Michigan as dawn was breaking after sleeping on the bus through the night.

We met up in a pub near Waterloo Station, soon after he got back from the adventure. It was going to be strange returning to Torville without him and, as Ada had arranged for him to work on a farm in Herefordshire; her plan to turn him into a dairyman; this would be the last time we'd see each other for a while.

Al told me that when the Greyhound stopped at the US Border Patrol centre, the driver took everyone's passports and went inside, then came back to return the documents of Canadians and Americans only.

"You go inside... Take your bag!" he said to Al, who was still feeling sleepy. The bus would wait.

The man in uniform behind a counter opened Al's bag and

rummaged around inside before drawing out a small packet of white powder.

"What's this?" He asked, clearly suspicious that it might be heroin or cocaine.

Al, in his daze, guilty-looking no doubt, could not at first find the words; and was only able to watch aghast as the officer licked the tip of his pinky-finger, plunged it into the stuff, withdrew and immediately licked it again, coated with what looked like snow.

Finally, Al found his voice as the disgruntled customs man grimaced and spat quickly sideways.

"Washing powder," said Al. "I use it for washing my clothes."

Maybe because it was a parting gift from laundryman Jerry, Al himself hadn't been totally sure. With the officer giving him a hard stare, he thought he was going to be arrested.

"Get outta here!" the man said, chucking Al's passport down on the counter. Al didn't need telling twice.

"He was bad, that Jerry," my friend told me, still laughing about the incident. "Let me tell you about the party we had..."

A few days before camp broke up, Jerry organised a celebration for bimmies and a few of the counsellors. Edwina, the cook, who was usually called 'Cook' or 'Cookie', possibly the sanest person in the camp, a benign, wise, wrinkle-faced, sixty-year-old who seemed to spend all the hours of all her days in the kitchen; who never seemed to change out of the same rumpled blouse, pants and sneakers outfit, topped at work by drab brown overalls; suspecting nothing, gave Jerry permission to bake a pretty large sponge cake, which was going to be his way of using up the appreciable lump of hashish still in his possession.

Al, who had avoided pot for the most part since his near-interminable fit of the giggles, did not discover this cake's intoxicating powers until it was too late. The lads had clubbed together for beer and other alcoholic delights, which would have been plenty for Al. Cook also supplied sausages, chunks of chicken, potatoes for baking, hamburger buns and other foodstuffs. Jerry's plan involved temporarily 'liberating' five canoes, paddling them across the lake, and having a barbecue in a clearing over there.

This was Al's only time on the water, he reminded me and, sadly, it turned out to be just a one-way affair. The gang set off after supper, fairly quickly made landfall and got a fire burning. It doesn't sound as if much of the meat was adequately cooked, though, and the potatoes certainly didn't have time to bake properly, but these folk weren't going to let that spoil the fun. Al remembers drinking a few beers, eating a lot of cake because he was hungry, and then settling down with a bottle of Southern Comfort one of the others had brought along.

"I'll never drink Southern Comfort again as long as I live," Al told me that day in The Globe. "It's so sweet... Rots your gut... And it did my head in proper!"

The hashish baked into the cake, combined with the strong booze, made him drowsy, so Al fell asleep on a mossy patch of ground. When he woke up, all was quiet. There was a half-moon; and the fire's dying embers emitted a soft glow, making enough light to see that he'd been abandoned by the others, marooned even. The canoes had all gone. It was four in the morning, and he was due to set tables by seven... The stuff of nightmares!

Standing up, he noticed one more body lying there, on the other side of the fire. Nate was fast asleep. When Al woke his bimmy-buddy, he discovered by having it shone into his eyes, that Nate luckily had with him a flashlight. There was no path. The two had to struggle about a mile and a half through the forest's undergrowth and thick scrub, leaving their bare flesh scratched and cut in places, requiring conspicuously bright red mercurochrome treatment from Jeanette, who opened the clinic room early for business that day. Badly hung over, too, they were the laughing stock of the campers. "No Tips... No Tips!" The cry went up over again.

But this was no joke for Al, who needed funds if he was going to spend another month in America, ready cash for accommodation and food. If he didn't get any tips, he was obviously going to struggle. If possible, too, knowing that farm labourers don't earn much, he wanted to take at least some money home. However, when he approached Skip on the subject, the head counsellor was equivocal.

"I'll do my best for you," he was told, but Skip's tone was not reassuring. "You could try talking to Minsky."

After explaining his need for cash to see him through the rest of his stay, Al asked Uncle Dan for a decent-sized loan, promising to pay it back after returning to England. He didn't truly expect a result, but it seemed worth making the request; and in a way, it did work in his favour. Dan called in Skip and all the other counsellors to insist on the camp's tradition of generosity.

"These kids can all afford it," he reminded them. "Their folks are wealthy or they wouldn't be here. Go and collect at least a few bucks off each one of them, Skip, and bring the money here. I'll make the distribution later."

So Al got tips aplenty... Plus an unexpected bonus! On the final morning, about to board Jerry's Pontiac along with Pete and Billy for the ride back to the Big Apple, he was surprised by Elaine strolling towards him, hands deep in the side pockets of the white coat she was always wearing. Silently, she passed him a cash-filled envelope, turning away quickly before he could respond. Was it guilt money or a sign of appreciation? Al never knew.

"She was an enigma, that woman," he said mournfully to me once, years after. "I guess she fucked me up, Freddie... Fucked me royally, and in more ways than one!"

He was flush with money, so I took the opportunity to suggest he buy the next round. As things turned out, he hadn't needed as much dosh as he first imagined. To cover the distances, he often took night buses, sleeping in recliner seats and making use of the on-board toilets, so there was less need to spend on hotels. One of the few times he did pay for a room, in San Francisco, an earthquake woke him in the night.

"It was bloody scary," Al admitted. "This heavy old wardrobe against the wall started swaying back and forth. I felt sure it would topple over with me underneath; but before I could get out of the juddering bed, everything calmed down. The whole thing lasted about twenty seconds, I'd say. The wardrobe shifted six inches away from the corner. Even though it was empty, I couldn't shove it back... It just shows how powerful those earthquakes can be. I'd hate getting caught in one bigger."

Al went to the Grand Canyon, Disneyland at Anaheim, and Yellowstone Park in Wyoming, where he watched the geyser 'Old Faithful' spout impressively to great height as she does every hour or so. Back East at the end of his stay, he travelled through the New England states to Boston and back to New York for his flight. He travelled so quickly, and moved on so frequently, that he doesn't seem to have absorbed much detail.

"It was great, though!" he said. "The people I met on the buses were so friendly... But I'm really glad to be home!"

Fourteen

I'm still thinking about that same unforgettable summer when Carol and I first got together for the first of our tumultuous couplings. I look down on the sorry, shrivelled state of my once proud manhood, and it does me so much good to remember those wonderful times. Some might say I was taken advantage of by Carol; as Al had been by Elaine at Diamond Lake; that she was the perpetrator of a form of sexual abuse, but I would argue vehemently against that interpretation. In the first place, I'd reached the legal age of consent. Secondly, I was an eager, more than willing partner. Thirdly, you can hardly say I came to any real harm; quite the opposite. Carol taught me a great deal; and my confidence grew steadily as our relationship progressed.

The morning after Carol and I had sex, Charlie set about making one of her terrific curried soups and sent me to gather courgettes. Naturally, I cunningly picked too many, then slyly suggested, while keeping quiet about what had actually happened, that I run the surplus over to Carol, muttering that she had expressed a desire for them the day before, while cleaning her little car.

"I've been thinking about you all morning," Carol said as I entered her kitchen via the back door.

I handed her the vegetables. Holding up the largest, she laughed. "And guess what? This reminds me precisely of what I've been thinking about... How is the Honourable John Thomas today?"

She was wearing a bright red pair of tight-fitting shorts, with a yellow, light cotton top and no bra. Naturally, then, the aforementioned JT was soon feeling playful, standing up, ready-primed for action, if a little tender from previous exertions.

"You'd better take a look at him," I responded, unzipping my blue jeans. "He definitely needs care and attention right now."

Needing no further prompting, Carol led me swiftly towards the couch in the front room, where we remained delightfully employed for the best part of an hour. When we were satisfied, at least temporarily, she took a well-worn paperback from a bookcase, *Lady Chatterley's Lover*, a horny tale about a poor toff whose precious nuts were injured during the First World War, as a result of which sad eventuality he was no longer capable of making love to his beautiful young wife, Constance; who then goes off for an extended fling with his gamekeeper, Mellors; the very man who invents such poetic names for their sex parts: his 'John Thomas' and her 'Lady Jane'.

Carol lent me the book so I could read it at home. Although I was not usually interested in reading books, I did like this one; struck by the childlike affection and joy between the not-so-ill-matched couple, the servant and his lady. To shield it from prying eyes, I remember putting it into the bag I'd carried the courgettes in; but I needn't have worried. Charlie was away to the shops for more curry powder; and, in his room, Prowl's head was stuck in his stamp collection, an occupation that, to my amazement, would occupy him happily, silently and serenely for many hours at a time. Carol and I definitely didn't want Charlie to discover that we'd become lovers; but I could foresee problems from that squeaky-clean blabbermouth P and his powerful antennae for stuff to make trouble with for me.

It was good that, in her job as a carer in a nearby nursing home, Carol worked shifts, for it meant she was often around during the day. While we'd been away at boarding school all these years, with Grandpa Ralph's financial help Charlie had pulled up her socks and completed accountancy school. Now she worked at a job that involved a thirty-minute commute each way and regular nine-to-five hours. As P had chess club every Thursday afternoon lasting three hours, including the bus ride, that became a regular date for Carol and me. Sometimes my twin also went to spend a day with his friend Henry, which gave us other opportunities; but, of course, it was never enough.

Our appetites for sex with each other were so strong that we began thinking of other ways to come together (and I do mean *come together*) in secret. One involved Nicky, a black Labrador dog belonging to a widow lady, Mrs Masterson, who lived across the street. Instead of saying, "Let's have a quickie!" Carol used to whisper to me jokingly sometimes, "How about a Nicky?" It worked like this. A gate at the end of all the gardens in that road led directly to a service alley for waste bin collections and such. I would collect the dog from his grateful owner, unable any longer to exercise him herself, march him up the street towards the park, double back along the lane until I reached Carol's gate, enter, make my way up the gradient through the garden, reaching my goal and getting into the house unseen through the French windows. Afterwards, I would reverse my steps and take the dog back to Mrs M.

Ricky was a fine accomplice. He never barked or gave the game away. Carol kept dog food in the kitchen, where the animal lay languid on a soft rug while we went upstairs for raw sex. It was the perfect solution; or it was, that is, until P spotted me from his bedroom window one afternoon as I strolled with Ricky back down Carol's garden path.

"What were you doing at Carol's place?" he challenged me

immediately on my return.

I told him I'd gone to fix a dripping tap.

"You never doing anything like that around here," he countered accusingly.

There was no need to respond, so I shrugged, knowing I'd got away with it that time; but I also knew that Prowl, once alerted, would stay watchful. If he was at home, the Ricky ruse would always carry risk, so we had to think of something else. The easiest way was simply to nip across the driveway between the two back doors when no-one was looking. The only problem was my need for an excuse to leave the house for the time I was going to be absent; so I took up cross-country running.

I was bored by cricket at school. Running was one of the sanctioned alternatives, which I had already taken up, as well as some track and field events, giving me the excuse to say I was going for training runs during the holidays, kitting up in the mornings before Carol set off for a late shift, in the afternoons when she came back from an early one, and even last thing, as it began to get dark, if I simply couldn't wait any longer. No-one was ever surprised when I came home covered in sweat.

To help time my visits, we had a simple code. If Carol was home and available, she put a red cloth in the kitchen window. On the rare occasions when she was busy, or maybe someone else had called round to see her and I couldn't go, she'd put a blue one out. This way, John Thomas and Lady Jane managed to find and excite each other three or four times a week... But I should have known that we couldn't keep the secret forever.

The thing is, I grew slightly careless with regard to concealment and P, prowling about, spotted me coming and going from Carol's place once or twice more. Growing firm in his suspicions, the filthy sneak said he'd tell Charlie, so I had to threaten him with an almighty beating. I was still concerned he would blab, though, so Carol suggested being nice to my dear little brother, using the carrot method rather than the stick; after which I started taking him places he wanted to go every week, like the movies or an adventure park. I'm not sure he enjoyed my company that much, but he seldom went out by himself, too introverted and timid. He hated the Imperial War Museum, which I loved visiting, so we ended up doing boring expeditions to various dull museums about things like transport and his favourite, natural history. The Science Museum was okay, but don't talk to me about stamps. I hate the things; tedious little scraps of coloured paper you couldn't even use any more to send letters. Anyway, it kept the little tell-tale happy; and Charlie was so delighted about the arrangement, she didn't hesitate to give us the money... Until, that was, she, too, began smelling a rat.

"Why are you being so nice to Paul all of a sudden?" she asked one day.

"Well!" I said. "He is my brother."

But she wasn't convinced and must have spoken to P, who may not have given the game away completely, but must have hinted at something suspicious about me not always being where I said I was; so my dear mother came home from work early one day and surprised me as I returned to our kitchen, heading for the shower, after a particularly energetic love-making session next door.

"I should have guessed sooner," she said with astonishing calm. I can smell sex on you, Freddie. You've been sleeping with Carol..."

It wasn't even a question; and I blushed so hard, there was absolutely no point denying it. Even though, strictly speaking, sleeping was hardly on the agenda while we were together; but this was no time to quibble.

"Go and shower!" Charlie instructed. "We shall talk later about this."

The next amazing thing, while I was upstairs, was that Charlie went boldly across the shared driveway to speak to Carol herself. I so wish I knew what they said to each other, but it obviously wasn't the blazing row I imagined. Nor was Charlie angry with me. I was fully expecting her to be furious with us both, but she seemed, if anything, miraculously relaxed about the situation. Later on, with P banished to his room, we had the required conversation.

Charlie started by telling me about the free-love era of her young days, of how she met H when she was still in her teens, and how they had definitely not considered it necessary to ask for anyone's approval or permission to become lovers. They were just following nature, she said; and after speaking to Carol, she felt sure I was being suitably looked after.

"You're in a safe pair of hands, my boy!" was how she put it.

"Quite literally, at times," I thought, suppressing a snigger; and you could be excused from thinking, based on Charlie's calm tone of voice, that it was cookery or knitting Carol was teaching me. My mother wasn't bothered at all; insisting that Carol was honourable in her way and wouldn't hurt me if it could be avoided, but that pain would probably follow. The relationship would run its course and come to an end, possibly before I was ready; so she advised me earnestly to make the most of it now, while being prepared for change - either in my feelings or, more likely, in Carol's - later on.

These were wise words. I'd been wondering what would happen

when I went back to school in September; and had already sometimes been experiencing pangs of jealousy when lying in bed thinking of Carol, such a cheerful, attractive and voluptuously sexy human being, almost certain to be seeing other men. It was irrational and based only on my inexperience and insecurity, I half knew it; but it was hard to disregard those sneaky emotions, and I suffered such torment as a result.

I need not have worried. I eventually accepted that Carol had no other lovers; and Charlie was about to make it much easier for us to get together, even paying for us to spend a weekend in a big fancy hotel on the south coast; although, I confess, apart from one afternoon strolling along the beach, we hardly saw anything of whatever was going on outside our room. Sleeping the night through together, after having to tear myself away from her side so many times previously, was quite simply divine.

This delightful excursion, gave Carol the idea of paying me visits, after I went back to Torville. I had much of the day free on Sundays; and, in addition to the longer half-term holiday, there were several 'exeats' each term when boarders were allowed a Saturday night away from school. Having booked herself into an elegant, 'bijou' seaside hotel in a town far enough away to minimise the risk of meeting anyone who might recognise me, Carol would motor down to Sussex in the little yellow Fiat. There we would enjoy whatever time we had together in the usual way; so nothing drastic changed until I came home at Christmas, except perhaps once, the time she still had the last of her period. However indelicate, I'll mention the episode because it did turn out to be pivotal. One Saturday, having collected me from the end of the school driveway where I waited, to prepare me for disappointment, Carol mentioned in the car that she had not yet finished menstruating. There would be no actual sex, she said, but we could still kiss and cuddle. Feeling sure we'd find ways around the problem, I wasn't upset in the least.

Carol was embarrassed so, to put off the awkward moment, we strolled along the seafront and laughed ourselves silly trying to play Crazy Golf, then went to a pub for fish and chips. I recall the calm sea and the warm, sunny evening as we sat in the beer garden while Carol lingered over another glass of wine, then another. I'd not seen her this vulnerable before. As the sun was setting, we went up to the room, had a playful shower together, and snuggled up in the bed. Something felt different. Carol, wearing a formidably proper, long, pink, cotton nightie, seemed somewhat passive lying beside me. I sensed that she wanted to talk.

To begin, she asked about school, about my studies and my friends, rugby matches and things like that; safe subjects; and, as we talked, the atmosphere in the room became increasingly intimate. In my turn, I asked Carol about her work; but she didn't want to discuss it. I could see there was something else on her mind, so just waited. I held her close and we had a little kiss, then lay there peacefully; until finally she asked if she could tell me something. It was going to be a confession; something she had never told anyone before, neither her ex-husband when they were married, nor even Gabi, her daughter.

Instinctively, I simply held her tighter, knowing she wouldn't stop now.

"I was abused for years by my father," she told me, and gently started to cry.

This man she trusted implicitly had come into her room at night when she was twelve or thirteen. He took off his clothes before climbing in beside her, and this became a regular occurrence. Her father was never rough with her, and only penetrated her once, taking her virginity, content mostly to lie beside her, caress her budding breasts, and rub his bloated sex organ against her young body until he was satisfied.

"Don't tell your mother," he would say each time, leaving her ashamed, but also confused, because sexually aroused and excited herself.

"The thing is," Carol explained, "I really loved my Dad... I worshipped him as a child. What he did was wrong. I know that. He could have been locked up if I'd told anyone but, from some kind of love or loyalty or fear, I never could. In the hospice years later, when he was dying of cancer, he tried to say he was sorry... sorry for ruining my life. But I never thought there was anything to forgive; or, rather, there was. What he did was wrong... But I always had forgiven him, right from the first time. He couldn't help it, you see."

Her mother had been viciously cold-hearted towards her husband after Carol was born, as if having a child was such a painful and shameful experience that she never wanted the risk of getting pregnant again. After that, the couple never made love, leaving her father frustrated.

"I was ashamed," Carol continued. "I felt awful, but also I sort of loved and craved the attention he gave me. I was so mixed up... Still am in a way! When I had sex with my husband, and sometimes when we're together, shocking though it is, I can't help thinking about my father, about the times he came to be with me in the night."

When she finished speaking, with nothing to say, I carried on holding her tight as she lay in my arms, crying great sobs, until they gradually subsided and I could hear again the sound of the waves lapping against the shoreline, and occasional calls of the seagulls, still foraging for scraps below the window.

Quiet now, it was a different Carol who turned her head to look at me, eyes still glinting, her burden lighter.

"Thank you for listening," she whispered gratefully, swivelling her body into mine.

We enjoyed a lingering kiss; after which the nightie soon disappeared as our passions again began rising.

"Are you sure you want to?" Carol's question was loaded.

She was asking if I still wanted to make love, knowing now about the incest at the hand of her father... Also, did I want sex while she still oozed menstrual fluid? But, despite these taboos and imponderables, I knew what I both wanted and she needed: action rather than words. As slowly and tenderly as possible, I set about transporting us both to where questions need not apply. That she had trusted me with her secret bonded us together, I felt. There was love between us now; and that felt wonderful, because whatever might happen, the most magical part surely would last forever.

Fifteen

I don't remember exactly when, but at some point the powerful nations began shooting down redundant satellites, using them for target practice. The Russians were first; then, when China started invading Taiwan, the Americans retaliated, but instead of risking a nuclear conflagration on the surface of the planet, they brought down a dozen or so Chinese military satellites instead, disrupting their communication systems in the process, with the desired effect of impeding all prospects of invasion.

Unfortunately, the less desirable effects, which could have been foreseen, proved devastating to us all. Smash any object in space and its remaining components, large and small fragments both, continue to ricochet around like pinballs in some grand, chaotic, cosmic game, hurtling at vast speeds, ripping asunder anything that gets in their way. Some of the debris wafted harmlessly away into deep space, and some fell to earth or got burned up re-entering the atmosphere, hence the starry light shows from time to time. But much of the garbage remained as space junk, deadly shrapnel forever lurking up there in the dark, a dynamic trap reeking havoc for decades to come.

The space stations were immediately evacuated. *Tiangong*, the Heavenly Palace' of the Chinese, survived superficially intact but unsafe and unusable, their incomplete second station abandoned altogether. The International Space Station, two hundred and fifty miles up, was completely obliterated; whether deliberately by a global power or accidentally from a wreckage collision, I couldn't say. Countless other pieces of celestial hardware bit the stardust too over the next days and weeks, so we all suffered; a process that continues even now. Vital observations of the earth from space were no longer possible, and GPS signals were lost; as well as the ability to transmit messages and communicate directly through smart-phones. All in all, losing many of the relay satellites, the internet was badly affected. Military, political priorities took precedence, leaving ordinary civilian communications in trouble. The shares of all the social media platforms took stark tumbles as stock markets everywhere crashed. It was like a dark age descended in one fell swoop; and this was only the start of the global techno-catastrophe leading up to the flood.

Be that as it may, after the weekend in the seafront hotel, Carol and I became increasingly like actual friends rather than just enthusiastic sex-partners, meaning we spent as much time sitting in conversation, talking and listening to each other, as we did having the other, raunchier kind of intercourse in bed. I remember, for example, her telling me about her ex-husband, Dennis, who was a self-conscious, mild-mannered Scot from Fife. He'd been a boy golf champion who turned professional. After a spell with a golf academy near Glasgow, he came south to find fortune as a junior staff member at one of the prestige south London clubs. Carol, then training as a nurse at Kingston Hospital, met him one night at a dance.

"I was pretty wild in those days," she confessed. "Looking back, I'm sure I was desperately searching for someone to make me feel special, like my father had, someone to take his place... But, no-one ever did... Or could, really."

She was over-sexed, she said, sleeping with anybody who looked with kind, or even simply lecherous, intent in her direction, often ending up with complete strangers when she got tipsy at a dance or party. There was no shortage of offers. In those days, she told me, women were expected to be on the pill, and young men considered nurses fair game, an easy lay for the price of a couple of rum and cokes.

"Because of the shift system on the wards," she said, "Some of us were always available; so any word of a party would go round the nurses' home like wildfire."

"I went to them all," she added, "Even when I'd been on duty and hadn't slept the night before. I loved the sex, you see, and went for all I could get. The problem was... I didn't like most of the men."

Dennis was shy, she told me, different from the others. A friend from the golf club had taken him to the dance, then gone off with his other mates, leaving Dennis nursing a pint of lager, standing awkwardly on the sidelines of the big hall. Carol soon spotted him, while typically scanning the room, trying unconsciously to identify her next father substitute to take for a lover. How surprised he must have been when this exceptional, flirtatious, good-time filly sidled up to say Hello.

"He was a bit slow," she told me. "I had to ask *him* for a dance, then practically had to twist his arm off to buy us a drink."

Her plan at the dance was to find someone to take to a house party afterwards, so she invited Dennis to this event where things could develop more cosily. The second gathering, a noisy one, was in a big Victorian house where a bunch of nurses were living together and sharing expenses. At the top, an otherwise unoccupied bedroom was known as the B Room... 'B' for bonking. When a couple wanted intimacy without being disturbed, they switched an airplane-style 'occupied/free' sign on the door, which lit up in the kitchen and elsewhere too, so people could tell whenever it became available.

Chatting up Dennis, getting him gradually to unwind, Carol kept her eyes on that sign.

"He was so tense," she said.

They had a little kiss. She arranged for her bra-less breasts to rub up against his shirt front when they danced. They had a couple more glasses of wine; and when the light turned green, Carol made sure they were the first pair on their way up the stairs.

"It was a bit comical," she said. "Dennis had never done it before, so I had to show him everything. He was so embarrassed. At one point I thought he was going to get dressed again and bolt. Luckily, lust won the day..."

But, perhaps they weren't so lucky, for it was not a good match.

"He was so serious, and I was just a fun-loving girl," Carol explained.

And the worst luck of all, being hopeless at remembering her daily pill, she quickly managed to get herself pregnant.

"All the other girls were having terminations at the time," she said. 'One of my friends told me the procedure was no more bother than having your hair done, and took about as long; but I didn't believe her... You'd be taking a life away..."

"I did think about it for a while," she continued, "But I knew I'd always have regretted an abortion, so couldn't go through with it. On the other hand, I do wonder if I made a mistake telling Dennis. I should've known he'd insist on doing the honourable thing."

They were married without fuss, fifteen weeks before the baby was born, and moved into a tiny apartment in Surbiton. "Suburbitan", she called it, a kind of deadly dull underworld of a place. Carol gave up her training to look after the little girl. Dennis was paid a pittance; they had barely enough to live on; and Carol began to go crazy.

"He was a decent man, Dennis," she told me. "He still is. But, craving excitement rather than stability, that's not what I needed at the time. As the baby grew up, I played every trick on him in the book. I was deceitful about money. I was unfaithful so many times. All the same, he always forgave me; and, of course, he would never agree to divorce."

"What happened?" I was curious. "What made you split up in the end?"

"Well, when Gabrielle was about ten," she replied, "Denny was offered the job of head professional at a club near Edinburgh. It wasn't a top club or anything, but this was a dream opportunity, so off he went. I stayed behind so that Gabi could finish her school year, pretending I'd follow him later... But that was never going to happen. I put Gabs on the train by herself that summer. She was very grown up at that age. Although he wasn't happy about it, Dennis met her at the station, as we had arranged on the phone the night before. Discussing the situation, I made sure he agreed that she would return to me in the autumn. Gabs took additional briefer trips north at Christmas, also sometimes at Easter; and that was the pattern we sank into. Once or twice he came down so that he could accompany her on the journey, but we never met face to face. Finally, after we'd been apart for three years, I filed for divorce, which went through without a hiccup. Unfortunately, though, about a year later I had a solicitor's letter announcing that Dennis wanted full-time custody. Gabi was an impressionable child, it said, and I was an unsuitable person for her to be living with. This was a hint, I thought, without spelling it out, at my promiscuous former lifestyle. The evidence given against me was that I had been perfectly content to put a ten-year-old girl on a train for a 400-mile trip without any kind of an escort. What kind of mother would do that?"

We were sitting at her kitchen table. The sun, peeking from behind low clouds, suddenly lit up her sorrowful face.

"I couldn't argue," she said, "But I was shocked. Gabi, by then, was my life. And this was just typical of Dennis's thinking; that I was, and would always be, much too much of a floozy to take proper parental responsibility for her."

"I remember asking Gabi what she wanted," Carol continued. "She told me, 'I love you both Mum... In an ideal world, I'd want you and Dad to get together again, but I do know that's unlikely'. Then she told me Dennis had met someone who had come to him for golf lessons, a young widow called Sue. Gabi thought they would get married soon."

"I still didn't know what she wanted," Carol continued. "But, then, as you can imagine, neither really did she. She was only young, and it was unfair of me to ask, I realised; so I decided I had to speak to Dennis again and put my cards on the table."

"I told him on the phone that I'd grown up a bit since we separated. I had given up working as an Enrolled Nurse and started at the care home, where the work was lighter and the shifts more regular. I had dated once or twice but nothing had come if it. I hadn't had a boyfriend... By which I meant sex... for over two years. I don't know if he believed me. There was no reason why he should. But something of my new sincerity must have got through. I insisted that I was devoted to Gabi and would do everything I could at all times to protect her from bad influences, while at the same time balancing this with allowing her a good measure of freedom. This is the tightrope parents with teenagers must walk constantly, I told him. Was he ready for that?"

"Actually, at first, our daughter was not a problem," she went on. "He'd seen her close up during her many visits north, and he probably knew that; but I think he did still pause for a moment. Maybe he wanted some time alone together with Sue as well. He agreed, too, that it would be better not to interrupt Gabi's schooling; if only because the Scottish educational system differed so much from what she was used to. So, in the end, we compromised, agreeing a delay until she was older. I was so pleased; but then, within a couple of years, she and I had our big bust-up."

I remembered that Gabi was no longer living with Carol at the time when we'd moved in next door. I had seen her a few times over the years, when she visited for a few days in school holidays, a flaming redhead with a slim figure, three or four years older than me, completely disinterested in young boys. We had barely ever spoken, in fact, much less become friends.

According to Carol, her daughter's character changed completely when she was about fourteen. Attending the local comprehensive, she had started mixing with much older kids, wearing make-up and sassy clothes, staying out late and the rest. It seemed like normal experimental teenage behaviour to me, but it triggered something in Carol, seeing her daughter behave provocatively towards the opposite sex when still so young; just as she had, of course.

In addition to her job at the care home, Carol was having to do bar work; two or three evenings a week at The Three Tuns pub, earning the money needed to get by. Dennis's contribution towards Gabi's upkeep helped, but Carol had taken over the mortgage, and her monthly repayments to the bank remained pretty steep. Her life in those lonely days was undoubtedly tense and demanding, so when she was really tired one night, growing anxious about her daughter; possibly also envious that the young folk were out and about, having a good time when she wasn't; a storm blew up when Gabi came home smelling of alcohol. Carol lost her temper and the two had a blazing, no-holds-barred row.

It was the first of several fierce, eyeball-to-eyeball confrontations, the culmination of which was Gabi asking her father if she could stay on with him at the end of the next summer break. Married to Sue by now, and with her unqualified support, he was only too pleased to say yes.

"It broke me up," Carol told me tearfully. "I hated her going, but it was probably the best for both of us. I'd become really stressed, working too hard, worrying all the time about money. Something had to give. Dennis was doing well for himself. He'd entered a few professional tournaments on one of the minor tours and chalked up a couple of wins. The prize money wasn't that great, I gather; but the success helped him move to a more exclusive club, where the annual retainer was higher, and he could charge more for lessons. He also ran a profitable golf shop for club members, some of whom spent pretty freely, making a point of getting fitted out with all the latest golf clubs and kit, so he was comfortable financially."

"He even sent me a lump sum to pay off part of the mortgage at one stage," she said. "Gabs must have told him my problems. He didn't have to, but that's the kind of person he is."

All this detail was preliminary to an announcement, which came as a bit of a shock to me; Carol was off to Scotland for Christmas. She'd been describing all this because she wanted me to understand the decisions she'd made and how things came to be as they were. She and Dennis were largely reconciled, to the point where he and Sue had invited Carol to be part of their family Christmas celebrations. A university student in Edinburgh now, Gabi would be there of course, as would Edward and Sam, her two young half-brothers, plus Sue's father and Dennis's Mum. Obviously, given the circumstances, I couldn't go with Carol but I would sorely miss her as well.

Reading my thoughts, she told me I could trust her; that she wouldn't be having a fling with another man at a party; and that promiscuity was a thing of her past. She was over all that. Then she gave me another book to read, an English translation of Flaubert's 'Madame Bovary'.

"That book helped me understand myself," she said, smiling. "Perhaps I'll be able to explain it when I get back."

I must have been looking particularly disconsolate. Did she really think I'd like a 350-page book, instead of enjoying her company?

"It'll only be four days," she said, pouting in sympathy to lower my aggrieved sense of abandonment. "We've been apart for much longer than that before."

So I bravely said I could take it; but the whole thing put me in a grumpy mood, which would lead to unfortunate results.

Sixteen

Carol's absence, and my resulting irritability, were definite factors giving rise to what happened on Boxing Day that year, but there was more to it than that.

The punch-up between Paul and me was weird, particularly because I had definitely not tried to provoke him. It was raining outside. I was happily about to set up one of the war games from my high quality collection that reproduced actual battles with many pieces on either side; like the collection I had from the American Civil War: Antietam, Fredericksburg, Bull Run, Gettysburg, Stones River and others that I was working my way steadily through. These games each took hours to play, spread over several days. At school, I could usually find an opponent, but at home I had to play both sides because P was never interested.

With the games came a subscription to a monthly magazine which; other than Playboy and similarly illustrated literary delights; was the only kind of reading material that held my interest for any length of time. There was a series of articles about the first Gulf War in the December issue; so, as usual, I was giving this priority; which is how I came to be absorbed in reading the magazine, rather than Flaubert, sitting on the throne in the bathroom, when Prowl came banging on the door.

Charlie had already gone to work. P said he needed to pee, so I invited him succinctly to bugger off to the downstairs loo; but he was soon back, banging on the door again, saying he needed to brush his teeth and take a shower. There was something to get to; another cello lesson, chess class, poetry circle or something; and for once he was not only impatient but aggressive with it. I couldn't be bothered with him.

"Hurry up!" He kept yelling, while trying, so it seemed, to bust the door down.

Contrarily, of course, the more he carried on, the greater grew my determination to thwart him and stay put. It was only a few minutes, I'm sure, but when I did finally emerge, he went totally bonkers, attacking and punching me in the face, then kneeing me so hard in the nuts that I doubled over in pain, at which point he jumped on my back, pushed me to the ground, got my neck in a stranglehold, and began squeezing with a vengeance.

P was shorter than me, lighter than me, and weaker than me, but I don't think anyone, before or since, has overpowered me so completely, not ever in my life. Displaying truly demonic strength, he really meant business; and I was helpless, feeling faint almost immediately. No blood was getting through to my brain. I was fading fast. It felt surprisingly peaceful.

What stopped the boy, my brother, I don't know. Probably, when my body went limp, he realised what was happening and simply desisted. As far as I was concerned, the whole incident was unexpected and inexplicable, but P did eventually calm down enough to get off me and walk away, retreating into the bathroom. I recovered fairly quickly, of course, escaping back to my room where I locked the door. Afterwards, strangely, we never spoke of it again; and nothing was ever said to Charlie about it; but I did mention it to Carol a few days later, when she was back from the north.

"What could have possessed him?" I wondered aloud, sitting in her kitchen while she busied about in the cupboards. "He's never exploded like that before."

"What a shock!" she replied sympathetically over her shoulder. "Maybe he's envious of what's going on between you and me."

"I don't think so," I replied truthfully. "That secret was blown months ago. He does make a few sarcastic remarks from time to time, but doesn't really seem to care much either way."

"Has anything else been happening at home?"

My first response to Carol's insightful question was to say "Nothing special," but then I remembered what Charlie told us weeks earlier, during the previous half-term. Grandpa Ralph had broken his habitual silence to inform her that H was suffering from severe liver disease and other complications of excessive drinking and drug-taking. He was dying, in fact, and had been asking to see us.

My reaction was to refuse. H had been gone so long that I didn't know him, and didn't want to know him; but Charlie and P had trotted along, first to his death-bed, where they found him comatose; and then, a few weeks later, to the crematorium. (Prowl got a day off school, so I was tempted to go too, but stayed away all the same.) On their return, my brother's mood was low, but nothing much was said and we carried on as if nothing had happened at all.

When I told her, Carol stopped what she was doing and sat down beside me.

"That's your answer!" she said.

She thought P had been bottling up his grief, and that the confrontation between us had triggered its release; but I was doubtful.

"Why would he be so angry?" I said. "I don't get it... And why would he take it out on me?"

"I'm not a psychologist," she said, "But I've seen a lot of people die in the care home... I've seen how grief affects people differently... And

I've seen plenty of people get angry, violently so on occasion, as a result. Sometimes, on rare occasions, they even try taking it out on us, and we're only trying to help."

This was one of those times when we were content just to talk. Some other things had occurred in the previous few days that I had gone to discuss with her, but this was interesting.

"It may seem strange," Carol told me, "But I've noticed that, during the angry phase of grieving, people usually pick on someone they feel pretty safe with. Someone they can count on to react and sort of validate their feelings, and maybe someone they rely on not deliberately to try and make them feel worse. It's not a conscious thing, of course. You are natural rivals, as siblings, but Paul also looks up to you, you know... Since your father left, you've been a kind of parent-by-proxy. Remember how he trotted round after you like a lamb last summer when you were being nice to him? Then, after Charlie gave us her blessing, you hardly spent any time with him... He's probably disappointed deep down."

Me... A 'poxy' parent, more like, than a proxy one, a substitute! I had to think about that.

H's death hadn't affected me at all. I'd written him off years ago. So Carol's explanation about P being in a rage about it seemed rather far-fetched at first. Later on, though, it did seem more plausible and I came to accept it. Whatever the reason for his dudgeon, thankfully P did get through it in the end. He even gave me what he called a 'New Year present', a Swiss army penknife. Charlie said it should have been boxing gloves, a pair for each of us. We had a good laugh about that.

That morning, I also wanted to find out if Carol's feelings towards me had changed. The conversation about Paul (as he now insisted I call him, following the bust-up; not 'P', and certainly not 'Prowl') had been reassuring, but something had happened that could easily have upset our cosy relationship.

When Carol set off for Edinburgh just before Christmas, Charlie agreed to ferry her to the airport so, when she was due back, I asked mother if I could come along to Heathrow. We were expecting Carol to be alone, of course, but there she was emerging from the arrivals area with a stunning, tall redhead in tow... Her daughter, Gabrielle.

In the car as we returned home, Carol sat in the front with Charlie, leaving us young ones somewhat awkwardly placed side by side in the back. At the airport, I'd wanted to give Carol a big hug and a kiss, but felt inhibited under the circumstances, our salutation turning into a rather distant, hands-on-shoulders embrace and a brief peck on the cheek before Carol introduced we members of the younger generation to each other. Dutifully, I stuck out my hand but, to my surprise, Gabi stepped up and gave me a huge hug, resting her freckled cheek against mine for long enough to feel her warmth and smell the alluring fragrance she was wearing.

"I already know you, Freddie," she said, smiling. "Don't you remember me? I once threw your football back over the fence when you were little... I'd say we were old friends."

Although not actually recalling the occasion, I was happy enough to accept Gabi's word. It could have happened. Paul and I were always kicking footballs and hitting tennis balls over that fence.

"Did you have a good flight?" Charlie chimed in, setting the conversation in train for the rest of the journey as the two women chatted away like they'd been parted for months rather than just a few days.

Paul came out to say Hi, when we got home; and Gabi made a big fuss of him too, which he liked; then mother and daughter disappeared inside without me speaking privately to Carol at all. How long was Gabi staying? I was eager to know. More importantly, when could I see Carol on her own again? But I would have to be patient.

The next day, mother and daughter went to London on a shopping expedition. In the evening, thankfully, they popped across to us for a drink, and Carol found a way undetected to whisper fondness in my ear, squeezing my hand and cheekily patting my bum.

"Don't worry," she said. "I'll soon sort something out."

So I felt better, and was delighted when Charlie suggested a 'Safari Supper' for New Year's Eve. We'd provide a first course in our house, and Carol would cook a big chicken for a main course in theirs. Paul, would make do with fish; and we'd all share a huge chocolate cheesecake to follow.

I had thoughts of a quickie with Carol in the garden shed the next day, but that was a daft idea. There was no chance we'd get away with it undetected; and I was sure Carol would not want Gabi discovering our still supposedly secret affair. It would have been a frustrating wait, but Charlie made sure I was fully occupied.

I had started driving lessons, so we put the L-plates on the car, and she asked me to drive her around the neighbourhood while she sat in the passenger side directing me. Eventually we arrived at the supermarket where she wanted to get some supplies. It could have gone better. My general impatience was not conducive to silky gear-changes, moderating our speed, or stopping smoothly; but somehow we made it back home in one piece. Charlie then told me to go over and check on Mrs Masterson and Nicky the dog, to see if there was anything they needed; which I should have done before we went to the store because, of course, she did need both dog food and milk.

Rather than go back to the mall, Charlie suggested I try the convenience store down the road, and to bring back a couple of bottles of sparkling wine too; which is how I came to have my first drink of the day... Also my second and third!

I will admit that, since meeting her at the airport, I'd been thinking a bit about Gabi. She was taller than Carol, almost my height. She was thinner, too, of course, but shapely in the right places. She smiled a lot and seemed at ease with herself; and the short-cut flaming head of hair surrounding her sweetly freckled face gave her added appeal in my eager eyes. At the same time, I felt ashamed of such prurient feelings for my girlfriend's daughter, gripped by a kind of incest taboo that I experienced as foolish but undeniable. The way I coped was by reassuring myself that no way could anything possibly happen between Gabi and me. How could it?

The safari supper started out perfectly fine. Carol and Gabs joined us for Charlie's smoked salmon and prawns dish, which all agreed was a great success, perhaps because there was plenty of wine to wash it down. Even Paul had half a glass before reverting to lemonade, Prosecco making him dizzy.

"That's the whole point of it, Love," Charlie told him. "Alcohol loosens your inhibitions... You're supposed to feel a little bit woozy."

But that was enough for Paul. Just like he never ate meat, I don't think he ever touched drink again for the rest of his life. Not so me, though... I'd been drinking beer, and occasionally wine with Carol, for months, if not years; and I liked getting mildly drunk; so, by the time we went next door, I was increasingly merry. My tongue ran away with me somewhat, and I remember making saucy comments, toasting the comeliness of our hostesses... Both of them!

Carol called the main course, 'Coq au Vin', emphasizing the 'Coq' and saying that we needed red wine to go with it, unscrewing the cap on a bottle of merlot, which I remember because it reminded me of Merlin, the wizard; also because of its truly magical properties; enabling normally tongue-tied adolescents like me to wax lyrical and humorous on a whole host of unlikely subjects. I was having a whale of a time.

After the cheesecake, we were going to take coffee and liqueurs in the next room, watching the end-of-year festivities on the television; but Paul chose that moment to say he was feeling sick. I don't think Charlie was ready to leave but, as it was already fairly late, she decided to shepherd him home.

"You can stay after midnight," she told me. "See the New Year in... It'll be nice."

Feeling mellow, rather than totally intoxicated, I did not need persuading.

Sitting in the living-room with Carol and Gabi, utterly content, I wondered what would come next. We chatted a bit, laughed at the silly folk on the telly, and sang along karaoke-style with a couple of songs, but were then silenced, slightly dismayed, as the telephone suddenly rang. Out in the hallway, Carol took the handset, from where, having silenced the TV, Gabi and I heard her say, "Oh dear! Yes. I'll come right away... Please call me a taxi. Okay?"

It was Mrs Dodds, the care home manager. One of the elderly residents had fallen and an ambulance sent for. Only one other member of staff was on duty, so Carol was going to have to escort poor Mrs Blakemore to the hospital, staying with her until she was either settled in or returned to the home. As Kitty Blakemore's favourite carer, Carol was the obvious choice. Fortunately, she had not drunk as much as the rest of us, but she still did not want to drive. Before the taxi came, she changed into her uniform; and, in a trice, she was gone, leaving Gabi and me on our own together. It took a moment for us to adjust to this new situation.

"More coffee?" she said. "Or a brandy, maybe?"

We were both standing up after waving goodbye at the window. The sound of the telly remained muted. Gabs was wearing jeans and a tight-fitting sweater that emphasized the pleasantly jutting twin-peaks of her breasts; little Alpine hills besides her mother's rather larger Andes mountains maybe, but delightful for all that. Perhaps she noticed me ogling them tipsily. Whatever it was, she caught on quickly.

"Mum said how good you've been to Mrs Masterson," she said, catching me by surprise, "Taking Nicky for walks and such...I don't suppose he's had many outings lately."

She must have been teasing. I didn't think her mother would really have divulged such details of our sex-life, and how we'd tried to conceal it, but I couldn't easily read her expression. Poker-faced, Gabi handed me a shot of cognac from the drinks cabinet in the corner then, as I sat down on the couch, came close and stood between my knees, looking down with obvious intent to ask if I'd help her with something.

"Okay," I said as nonchalantly as I could, for I was wondering wildly what might be coming next.

"I've got a ball to go to soon at Uni," Gabi explained, "Yesterday, when we went shopping, I bought two ball gowns. Now I'm not sure which one to wear and which one to take back for a refund. I'd love to know what you think... Would you mind?"

Of course I didn't mind. When she disappeared upstairs, I was expecting her to return carrying the two items to show me; but she obviously thought that, to give my best judgement, I needed to see her actually wearing them. Sipping the fiery drink, I sat back on the couch; and had closed my eyes, feeling dreamy, when a gorgeous apparition re-entered the room.

Gabi was wearing a full-length, traditional, strapless ball gown in a kind of cherry colour that on Charlie, for example, would have looked magnificent. She did look great, in a way; but, unfortunately, her ginger complexion resulted in clashing hues that disqualified much of her beauty. As she twirled around a couple of times for my benefit, disappointment must have showed in my features. I didn't say a word before she understood my reaction.

"Alright," she said. "This one doesn't work. Thanks... So, let's try the other one. I'm just worried that it will be too cold at this time of year."

Gabi retreated upstairs again, but moments later, there was a call. Having trouble with the fastener, she wanted me up there to help.

"Right away!" I yelled, put the brandy snifter down with due care, stood up a little unsteadily, advanced manfully towards the hallway and began climbing the stairs.

The vision that soon greeted me, inside Gabi's bedroom, was perfection. Her second dress was emerald green, ideal for setting off the glow of her hair and freckles; but I had to agree that it was rather cool attire for a winter event, being backless, and having a collar from which, at the front, the satiny fabric fell away in two folds, one covering each breast, reaching downward to the waist and a full-length skirt.

The clasp behind the collar was proving awkward, Gabi explained, as she turned her back so that I could get at and fasten it. The temptation to plunge my hands beneath those folds and cup those two breasts was almost irresistible but, the job quickly done, there was no chance to fulfil the fantasy as she stepped away.

"What do you think, Freddie?" she said, adopting a glamorous pose, throwing an airy, darker-green woollen shawl across her shoulders, heightening the dramatic effect.

"Gorgeous... Utterly gorgeous, Gabi!" I replied with complete honesty. "Breathtaking! Someone's going to be a very lucky man."

"Alastair Mackay, who has asked me to the ball," she insisted to my amazement, "Is a bighead and a bore... But he is also astonishingly rich. And you're right... He's so wrapped up in himself, he does *not* know how lucky he is."

"I wouldn't mind taking his place," I was bold enough to reply.

"Well, anyway," she shrugged, "You have been a big help... Now undo this again, please. I'd better get it back on its hanger."

Gabi turned around and stepped back towards me so that, as I was raising my hands to her neckline, her taught buttocks made contact with something equally firm about my personal anatomy, rising unbidden through animal instincts, fuelled no doubt too by alcoholic disinhibition. In an instant, the fastener now loose, this prime specimen of young womanhood turned round. Letting the garment's folds fall, she put her arms around my neck and kissed me full on the lips, her little tongue darting forwards to arouse me further, the warmth of her bosom against my chest, natural animal desire instantly drowning all possible threats of shame or taboo. I should have wondered what Carol might think, but was too tipsy, right then, and much too raunchy to care.

Our hands were exploring each other, and I finally attained the smooth nipple-tipped mounds of my desire as Gabi ventured further south, deftly unbuckling my belt on her way. In seconds, as I was peeling away my shirt, I was naked from the waist down as well,

"Hello there, John Thomas!", said Gabi, gleefully addressing my standing member. "I've been hoping to meet you someday."

I did not have time to wonder at this most astonishing revelation, that Carol had shared such intimate details about me with Gabi, because she was taking off her dress and folding it quickly, while I lay back on the single bed. Soon, she climbed up and began fondling my scrotum, caressing firmly my manhood with eager fingers, and bending to lick clean a single pearl of fluid emerging out of the spout, before taking me whole deep into her throat, back and forth as I watched, running my fingers through her hair. Soon, judging the moment perfectly, she rose up, straddling my thighs with her knees, and impaled her love canal to the hilt upon my unbending equipment, riding me furiously, her cute breasts whipping up and down in my face.

"Oh! Oh! Oh... John Thomas!" she breathed as a climax rapidly approached. "Come on Baby... Come on! Yes! Yes! Yesss..."

We stayed like this a short while until, as she leaned forward, I knew I had to take charge. Grasping her wrists and heaving, I managed to flip the pair of us neatly over, giving me the advantage of more powerful thrust as she kicked off the bed-sheets and wrapped her legs round my middle. Unlike her mother's more guttural moaning, Gabi's voice was rising to a high-pitched keening sound, more like someone in pain or in the throes of grief rather than pleasure, its thrilling effect spurring me on. With a final mighty plunge from me, we were carried simultaneously into blissful orgasms, collapsing finally... sweaty, exhausted, and strangely pleased with ourselves.

Time passed. I may have slept. Eventually, though, I grew faintly aware of night sounds; a train in the distance, then what would have been fireworks; because, of course, it must have turned midnight. But neither Gabi nor I had heard the returning Carol who, when I looked towards the door, was standing there, holding my discarded, half-full brandy glass in one hand, looking on.

"I'm glad you two have made friends," she said with no trace of irony. "Both the people I love best in the world..."

She was holding up the glass, as if to say "Cheers". I remember smiling before falling asleep once again.

Seventeen

After Gabi had returned to Scotland, Carol told me about New Year's Eve: how the taxi driver said she was exceptionally lucky to get a ride; that it was only because Laura Dodds' niece was working the switchboard; how she found a distressed Mrs Blakemore waiting unattended in A & E before being assessed, then went with her to X-ray to hold her hand; how midnight came and went in a flurry of clinical activity but little celebration; how someone then came to say the old lady had a broken femur, and was being kept in for surgery the following day; also how she was not fortunate enough to get a second taxi ride home, but that an ambulance driver had taken pity on her and given her a lift to the corner at the end of the road, from where she had walked briskly home.

"Which explains why we didn't hear you," I said.

"You had other things on your mind," Carol giggled. "Both of you!"

She was very understanding.

I had woken up beside Gabi on the first of January, desperate for a leak as the morning light filtered through the curtains; and I was making my way back after flushing the toilet when Carol called out.

"Is that you, Lover Boy?" Her voice a little husky.

So I went into her room instead of Gabi's.

"It is me," I admitted, standing beside the bed.

"Hop in then," she replied, throwing back the covers by way of invitation.

How could I possibly refuse? We were both sleepy, and at first just cuddled up together, dozing pleasantly. I might have drifted off once more; but then woke to hear the toilet flushing again. Soon after that, Gabs clambered in with us; at which juncture, naturally, one thing led to another; and we three began making love.

At first, lying on my back between these two gorgeous women, mother and daughter, I felt bashful, uncertain who to turn towards and what exactly to do; but Gabs was wide awake, and began stroking John Thomas, pointing out his responsiveness to her Mum.

"I'm not one to let a proud wonder of nature like that go to waste, Gabi. Are you?" Carol said, leaning across to repeat what she had done on our first encounter, back in the garden shed.

More experienced, happily, I avoided disgracing myself by coming too quickly this time. Our one and only threesome had begun. Truthfully, though, it was not a great success. I gave it everything. John Thomas gave it everything; but it was hard to do justice to the situation and satisfy both lovers. The experiment was interesting nevertheless, if only to compare the two women: Gabi's love trap encircled by a fringe of bright, neatly shaven, reddish hair, against the full, luxuriant foliage of Carol's sweet, copper-bronze bush; her freckled skin and taut, smallish, rosy-tipped breasts against her mother's darker complexion and full, weightier, brown-nippled pair; Gabi's love pocket tight and smooth, Carol's looser on entry, but satisfying through the wonderfully controlled use of her well-practiced pelvic muscles, milking me like a farmer's wife squeezing the sensitive udders of her favourite cow, extracting the maximum in milk and mutual pleasure; the younger woman more energetic, almost impatient, quick to a sudden, explosive climax; the other more restrained, pacing the action, building gradually towards a lingering finale, coming in lubricious, sweat-drenched wave after wave. I hopped back and forwards between them, losing track of time, until I could last out no longer.

And so it was that, days later, Carol and I are sitting in her kitchen together, chatting about brother Paul's uncharacteristic homicidal outburst, with me still worried that she might feel a lot less of me for succumbing to temptation with her daughter. When I finally found the courage to broach the delicate subject, though, she was great... Simply told me, "Relax, Love... There's no harm done at all!"

"If you truly love someone," she explained, "You don't want to own them. You just want them to be happy... And I love both of you".

"Gabi is a little like I was at her age," she continued. "She enjoys sex. But she's much more mature than I used to be. She's in control of herself in a way that I never was... I told you, didn't I? In those days I was rampant!"

"Fortunately," she added, "I've changed."

She asked if I'd managed to read the book she'd given me, 'Madame Bovary'. I said I'd looked at it; which was true. I'd looked at the cover, but sadly hadn't actually opened it, my 'War Games' taking priority.

"What's so special about it?" I asked.

She told me then that Flaubert's novel had helped her change her ways, and had done so by helping her understand herself better, in particular about why she'd been so desperate for men and for sex.

"Soon after Dennis went back to Scotland, and I was at a low ebb, there was an article in a women's magazine that made me curious about the story, so I bought the book," she said. "Emma Bovary had trouble controlling her sex-drive too."

The French novel, she explained, is about the teenage daughter of a prosperous farmer, whose mother died when she was quite young. Whenever Charles Bovary calls to treat her father, she flirts with this recently-widowed country doctor, who is completely enchanted. She thinks herself in love; and eventually agrees to marry him, but soon finds him dull and is unhappy at the lacklustre routine of their lives together. She is, in contrast, transfixed by the finery and manners of the highborn people they meet while attending a banquet and ball at a neighbouring manor house. The occasion seems full of excitement and romance; but her husband seems right out of place.

Growing increasingly irritated with Charles, Emma becomes capricious and hard to please, in time insisting that they move from Tostes, a village, to Yonville, a country town; where, she imagines, there will be more opportunities to experience fun, laughter and thrills. A man called Leon comes into the picture, and is soon utterly smitten with the coquettish Emma. However, by this stage, she has become pregnant. Hoping for a son, when she gives birth to a daughter, disappointment strikes, and she fails to bond with the little one, who is therefore put out to nurse with a carpenter's wife.

Leon hesitates to declare his passion; while Emma, completely wrapped up in herself, wonders about love, which she now believes should strike and engulf her like a hurricane with thunder and lightning, snatching away her will-power, turning her life upside-down.

"I was a bit like that when I was a teenager," Carol told me, "Full of fantasies, and definitely looking for something totally momentous in my relationships with men".

In the article about the book, there was a suggestion that Emma Bovary responded to the early loss of her mother by seeking to replace maternal nurturing with much more attention from her father. Unconsciously, she had developed a strategy that made full use of flirtatious gestures and a coy childlike manner, which was, of course, successful. Such playfully enticing behaviour is highly appealing in a young girl; but, the article said, when the girl reaches puberty, instead of motherly affection, her sexualised signals start attracting a very different kind of masculine attention. Deep-down, she wants kindness and maternal security. Instead she finds herself offered insincere flattery and short-lived episodes of passion in which, as seducer, she in turn becomes prey.

Carol had to go over it again before I began to understand what this meant. A girl wants a Mum, and gets mothering from her Dad by acting cheeky, 'a right little madam', as Charlie would have said. Later, her signals are misinterpreted by men as come-on signs, causing them to think of her as inviting sex; then she either rebuffs them and gets a reputation as a prick-teaser, or she goes along with it and makes a bad-name for herself as an easy-lay. This is what Carol had risked, although the birth-control culture at the time was more favourable and forgiving than in the 1850s when Flaubert was writing.

"Can you see how like Emma I was?" Carol asked. "My mother didn't die, but she was a frozen-hearted woman, who never showed anyone any affection. I always wondered why my Dad had married her. He never said, but I expect she trapped him into getting her pregnant, and then her father insisting on a shotgun wedding, otherwise I wouldn't be here... Anyway, I ended up marrying Dennis; who was completely safe and protective, like a mother figure; just as Emma had married Charles. And then, like her, I found myself stuck in a deadly dull marriage, longing for a way out. Luckily, unlike her, I was delighted when my daughter was born and loved her dearly, but once she was off to school every day, my life seemed empty again... And the thing is, I always liked sex. I wasn't afraid of it, like some girls... My father had seen to that, I suppose."

Emma Bovary, may not have been afraid of sex, but she did nothing to encourage Leon, preferring to indulge in nothing more than a fantasy relationship, seeking solitude to revel in his image, rather than the flesh and blood reality. Disappointed, no doubt, Leon departs for Paris to further his education; but his place is immediately taken by another.

Thirty-four year old Rodolphe is a hard-hearted, free-spirited, cunning man, with much experience of women. When he meets Emma, finding her attractive, he immediately plans a seduction; which he carries out when, with poor old unsuspecting Charles's blessing, the two go riding together. This time, she does respond passionately, quickly becoming intoxicated with this man and their illicit liaison, to the extent of pestering him for attention, even daring to visit him at home, with the inevitable result that her possessiveness begins to upset him, and he becomes much less eager for her company.

At the same time, at the mercy of an unscrupulous merchant, through buying expensive presents for Rodolphe, Emma has gone into debt. As well as being unfaithful in love, she has started deceiving her husband over money. Her solution is to run away with her new man who, when she pleads with him, appears to agree to the plan. Nevertheless, on the eve of their departure, he writes to say he's backing out, adding a cowardly lie, that he does not want to ruin her life.

"Be brave, Emma!" he writes; but far from bravery, after a fit of rage, she falls flat to the floor in a faint, takes to her bed; presenting a mystery to her doctor-husband, and the local chemist; only to stay there incapacitated for a full forty-three days.

According to the magazine article, this was a 'psychosomatic' reaction; the mind influencing the body; a hysterical defence against the shame, rage and confusion eating away at her soul, a means of unconsciously protecting her from further foolhardy destructive behaviour, while also inviting sympathy from those around her, especially from her hapless husband. She suffers relapses; notably when she is reminded of Rodolphe, and a flight into religion as she experiences a glorious vision of God surrounded by saints and angels with wings of flame; but she does eventually get better.

"Thank goodness I never got anything like that bad," Carol commented as she told me how the story unfolded. "If Dennis and I hadn't split up, though, I can't say how things might have turned out."

To aid Emma's recovery, Charles takes her on a trip to the opera in the city, Rouen, but 'No good deed goes unpunished', as they say, and here she meets Leon again, a bolder man than before, and her passion for him is soon reignited. Without shame, she returns alone to Rouen to meet with him for a three-day tryst; and then persuades her unfortunate husband to pay for piano lessons, giving her an alibi, and the opportunity to spend time with her lover every week. The book says, "From now on, her existence becomes nothing but a tissue of lies". Worse; the family gets more into debt.

"Well, I didn't have piano lessons," Carol told me, "But I did tell Dennis I was going to the gym an awful lot more than was true... And we were careful never to spend more than we earned, so that was okay."

But things were not okay with Emma. Her relationship with Leon grew ever more dependent and demanding. He inevitably failed to satisfy her extravagant needs, making her even more bossy towards him, an attitude which naturally he resents. Their passions cooling, as Flaubert puts it, "She rediscovers in adultery all the banality of marriage."

"What can she do now?" Intrigued by the tale, I was beginning to wonder.

Matters deteriorated, of course. The bailiffs are called, and Emma tries desperately to borrow money to pay them off. Leon is financially poor and cannot help. Others refuse her. A lawyer she visits offers her money for sex, a proposition which, horrified, she rejects; although then, swallowing her pride, she looks up her former heart-throb Rodolphe and suggests something similar: if he pays her, she will become his mistress again; but again she is roundly rebuffed.

Hopeless and, as ever, impulsive, Emma visits the chemist and, knowing where the deadly white powder is kept, opening a drawer, crams poison into her mouth. Arsenic leads to a fatal result within hours. Suicide has claimed her life.

"I cried," Carol told me, "When I read that part... I really felt for her. You couldn't say any of it was her fault, could you? That's just the way she was made."

After reading the book, Carol had looked at the article again.

"I'd just finished with a bloke I met at the gym," she said. "Nothing serious, you know... Casual sex a few times, fun but not going anywhere... I just knew it was the right time for me to stop screwing around and change my ways. Emma's story taught me a lot. She was a victim of her own sexuality; and I didn't want to be like that. There were offers, of course, lots of them; but saying no to them felt empowering, made me feel strong. At first, I was afraid I'd be lonely; but it didn't turn out like that. I discovered I enjoyed my own company. Also, because I could be more natural with people; not seeing other women as jealous rivals all the time, or men as potential sex partners; I was much more relaxed and happy... And people responded to that. I made a lot of new friends.

"I suppose you had a bit of a relapse, then, when I came along," I blurted out, tactless as usual.

"You know what, Freddie?" she said, giving my hand an affectionate squeeze. "You were different... I don't know what made me go after you down the garden that day, but it wasn't the same as before... No way! It was like some kind of great cosmic message deep within me to follow you; a compulsion that could not be ignored."

"We were meant to be, you mean?" I said, smiling.

"Yes, my Love... We truly were meant to be!"

Meant to *be* we were; but sadly not meant to *last*. Carol died much too young, like Emma Bovary, even though neither in debt nor despair. Within three years of that conversation, she was gone. I was heartbroken, naturally; and it was all the more painful because I couldn't go to her funeral. Carol's death acted as more than a simple shock to my emotional system. I certainly changed after that. My world fell completely apart. If I had not already been in the army, with duties to perform, I cannot say what might have happened.

During the period we were seeing each other, the successful worldwide vaccination programme had allowed people to more or less recover from the first pandemic; but nothing stays the same for long, does it? In those days, climate change was definitely on the international agenda, but it still amounted mostly to talk, and only minimal action aimed at reducing global warming. Things were still heating up, and catastrophic weather events had become pretty routine. When it arrived, the second virus, 'Covid 2-27', a completely new entity, rather than a variant of the old one, took most people by surprise, particularly because it was so deadly. Quadruple Covid-19 vaccination plus boosters every year offered but marginal protection. The new Co-27 vaccines took many months to arrive; by which time over a billion people had died, almost one-tenth of humanity, a genuine decimation of the world's population.

As before, lessons unlearned, to make way for the tidal wave of sick younger people, hospitals rapidly decanted elderly folk into nursing homes, like *Home Lea*, many such patients already infected. Full protective equipment was in short supply once again; but even if there had been enough, Carol would not have stood much of a chance. Alive and vibrant one minute, the love of my life was gone within days. Ironically, Mrs Blakemore, closing in on her ninety-ninth birthday, was one of the survivors. Cats have many lives, they say. No wonder she was called Kitty!

Lockdown and social distancing came back in force with a vengeance; so funerals and cremations went ahead without ceremony, and were sparsely attended. Not so much miserable, I was furiously angry at missing Carol's. Some vital part of me seemed to have perished with her, taking all joy and sunshine out of life. There was no more satisfaction in my dull everyday existence, and I needed a new reason to be alive. In my head I knew that loads of people were suffering at least as badly as me. However, hurting badly, I desperately wanted to blame somebody, punish somebody, get busy and take my revenge on someone... But, of course, this was shadow boxing. Who exactly could be blamed? No-one. You can't get angry with a virus; punch it, put it in an arm-lock, throw it to the floor and spit on it; can you? So maybe that's when hate took me over. I wasn't fully conscious of it then; but I think that's when I started hating everyone who seemed happy, in fact every single person still drawing breath... And there was plenty of scope for revenge.

Eighteen

Paul's aggressive outburst that Christmas following H's death marked a surprising change in my twin brother. He started going to church.

We weren't against religion in our family, but those things were simply never deemed relevant. Granny Gertrude must have insisted H and Charlie had us Christened when we were babies, and of course there was chapel and scripture classes with Miss Warner at school; but it never sank in with me as anything real. It was just ancient history; and until then I assumed Paul thought the same. Nevertheless, St Nicholas church was only a couple of streets away from our house, and that's where he started going.

An ugly brick building set back from the road, surrounded by a poorly kept graveyard, St Nick's was easy to ignore and walk past. Even on Sundays, nothing much seemed to be happening there; but they did have a big signboard outside that was always advertising something called 'Alpha Groups', which I assumed had something to do with addictions, like AA or Gamblers Anonymous, but which were actually evening courses introducing people to Christianity. An evening meal was served, according to Paul, people got to know each other, and then they talked about Jesus.

After he'd completed one Alpha course, he immediately started another, and soon Paul himself could not stop talking about God and religion. "Jesus this... Jesus that...!" On and on he went; until I told him to shut up with his saintly claptrap and shove it up what H used to call his 'fundamental orifice' (in other words, his arse) where the sun don't shine. Normally, the boy would have got angry and argued back, but this time he just smiled, exuding so much Christian patience and forgiveness, it made me sick. That's how I knew he'd definitely been transformed... Hallelujah!

Charlie went with him to a service one Sunday. When P stayed behind to put away hymn books and talk to the vicar, it allowed me to get her honest opinion when she came home on her own. Unsurprisingly, she said the service was dull. The church was nearly empty, populated mostly by old people, except for Paul and one or two others. She said she quite liked singing the hymns, but the sermon was all about giving more money to help the restoration fund, and giving time as a volunteer.

"They are looking for cleaners and flower arrangers, also someone to be an assistant warden," she said. "I expect they'll ask Paul to do something like that."

In other words, like everywhere else in our greedy, materialist world, the church authorities wanted what they could get out of people. How hypocritical, I thought, was that?

Paul must eventually have seen it too; but it only made him go deeper on a kind of lifelong spiritual quest. In the meantime I kept trying to provoke him, arguing that science had disproved the possibility of water holding the weight of anyone walking on it, unless of course it was frozen, which wasn't likely in Galilee. I also liked to joke about being able to turn wine into water myself, just by drinking it, while scoffing at the idea that some ancient beardie in a long robe could perform that same particular trick in reverse. As for raising the dead! The man Lazarus must have been alive all along, in some kind of coma maybe. But Brother Paul wasn't fazed. Talking to me calmly, like I was some ignorant peasant, he said that what Christians worship is a mystery, a mystery to be explored and experienced rather than explained away. Belonging is more important to many people, he said, than belief. He insisted, too, that instead of dismissing the Holy Spirit as a fantasy, religious people aim genuinely to feel it in some way as a force or guide in their own lives, and that there were tried and tested ways of seeking this experience - through worship, prayer, studying scripture, acts of service and kindness to others, things like that. It all seemed so boring to me.

The church did eventually lose him; but not before some helpful fellow seeker advised him to try meditation; so off he went in search of a guru, a master of stillness to teach him the art; all a complete waste of time if you ask me. Why would a sane person sit completely still, in silence, for twenty minutes twice a day? If that isn't boring, what is? Paul even agreed with me that "on the surface" that's what it appears to be, a big load of nothing happening.

"So, what *is* the point then?" I asked him.

Instead of giving me a straight answer, he suggested I go with him to the Buddhist monastery where the monks were teaching him.

"They can explain it much better than me," he said.

But I didn't want to do that, thinking, "Better just let him carry on, I suppose."

So Paul set up a little altar in his bedroom with a candle on it, some foul-smelling incense sticks, a crucifix and a small Buddha figure. Sometimes he'd pick a flower from the garden and set it there in a little vase too. He had a Tibetan hand-bell, and a special mat with a round cushion a few inches high where he sat cross-legged for his twice daily sessions. Charlie encouraged it, to my surprise. She'd tried mindfulness groups and said it involved a similar kind of mind-training practice. I said I'd rather go out for a jog in the park.

"Off you go then!" she smiled cheekily at me, knowing I'd do no such thing. Carol was still taking up most of my time.

"Are you a Buddhist or a Christian?" I demanded of my brother one day, trying my best to put him on the spot.

"Like you," he said, "I'm a Christian."

"What do you mean, like me?" I was rather shocked at the suggestion.

"You were baptised a Christian on the same day as me, when we were little," he replied. "That's not something you can undo..."

"No, no, no!" I assured him. "I'm an atheist."

But, truthfully, I was disconcerted for a moment and needed to counter-attack.

"So, how come you worship the Buddha as well?"

"I don't," he said disarmingly straightaway. "I don't *worship* the Buddha. I simply acknowledge him as a great spiritual guide and teacher. In many ways, finding out about Buddhism is making me a better Christian. I understand more each day what it means to follow Jesus' teachings. When you really understand them, they are simply about love and kindness."

But I didn't get that at all.

"Then why all these wars, the Crusades and such; conflict everywhere today still in the name of religion?" I demanded again. "And how come Christian missionaries went to the Americas, to Africa and the East to help subdue native peoples, corrupt and enslave them? Surely that was from greed and a hunger for power, rather than love, don't you think?'

He tried to explain something about mature and immature followers of religion; that people don't start wise and knowledgeable; they have to grow and develop as life goes along, gaining experience, often through hardship. He said it's the same with whole nations, and with most religious organisations, that they get things wrong, become corrupted by authoritarian influences and powerful, self-centred leadership, and tend to see differences as threats; until, that is, they wise up and discover that human beings are basically all the same, 'of one kind' - hence the importance of 'kindness'. We all, he insisted, have the same basic needs and desires for safety and protection, water, food and shelter, for love and affection, and for a reason to live.

Paul made a lot of this point, and kept returning to it. *"Everyone's blood is red; everyone's tears are salty,"* he used to say, quoting a Russian proverb; and always insisted that people do eventually learn to benefit themselves, and everyone else at the same time, by learning to live harmoniously not only with each other but also with nature.

It was a big speech of which this is only a summary, but he hadn't yet finished.

"How else do you think we got into such a mess everywhere?" he said, talking about the parlous state of modern civilisation, the pitch of his voice rising slightly. "Back in the day, science trumped mystery... But how clever was that? And in the resulting secular society, all that counts, it seems, is profit, productivity, property and possessions; so-called 'success' in worldly terms (abject failure, though, he would say, in spiritual terms). People's ambitions are fixed on the kind of goals that can only lead to rampant consumerism, the rape of the earth, eco-destruction, massive pollution, climate change and the rest."

Even with all his new-found calm, Paul tended to get visibly excited with this argument, having become a proper little social critic along the way; and as a result I loved provoking him; so this was a discussion we returned to over and over until the day my poor deluded brother's life came to its premature end.

In this perpetual debate we had going, I always took the Darwinian view that you had to be strong and look after your own, on account of only the fittest survive; but Paul tried to tell me I'd got Darwin's ideas wrong. Rather than being toughest, he said, the old evolutionist had meant 'fittest' in the sense of being 'most suited' to a given environment. It wasn't the same. Might, then, was not necessarily right.

Paul used to say, in fact, that global warming owed much to the aggressive military-industrial ambitions of the great powers, who couldn't stop themselves inventing, making, and then of course selling ever more destructive weaponry to all and sundry, to anyone prepared to consider using their extraordinary firepower, like kids playing Cowboys and Indians. They made their billions by stressing the necessity of building up a nation's 'defence' (the best form of which, inevitably, is always attack), and would stoop even to inventing pretexts for wars and invasions, like in Iraq years ago and that monumental bluff given out about Saddam having weapons of mass destruction, which he didn't. And what a great wheeze subsequently: taking advantage of the opportunity to claim 'generously' to be spending millions of dollars rebuilding the country they had barely finished smashing up, while hypocritically awarding the lion's share of contracts to companies from the USA, so that all those millions of dollars could stay locked safely away in the economy of the aggressor, with mighty little of it actually benefitting the tragically bereft families and individuals left behind, thousands of whom became refugees, further adding massively to the totality of human pain and suffering.

There was no stopping Paul when he got started on to this subject. As far as I could tell, though, he exaggerated everything. Forever more studious, intelligent and knowledgeable than me, I couldn't always keep up with him, but having heard his ideas so many times over the years, I think I've got the gist of what he said. To be sure, though, he never persuaded me. In the early days, I'd even say he had a hard time convincing himself, but he did later influence many others, which became quite a problem for me.

"To reverse climate change," he used to say, "People must alter more comprehensively than just in terms of behaviour. They... We, I should say... need a wholehearted kind of transformation, a sea-change in our basic attitudes, aims and ambitions."

He said that people needed to become altogether wiser and more spiritual, respecting and behaving kindly towards one-another, and that we absolutely must learn to treat this fragile planet as sacred, forming the firm intention to give up fossil fuels, for example, eat less meat, recycle everything, use less plastic, reduce our carbon footprints in one way and another; but he also took the view that none of this would succeed without a new level of responsibility in people for their thoughts and intentions, their words and actions; for what they do and say... also, critically, for what they don't do and remain silent about.

"People must grow much more wise and mature." That was his view in a nutshell.

My brother was always big on wisdom. He thought it the answer to everything. People who deliberately became wisdom-seekers, he thought, and set an open example for others, could truly work towards saving the world; people, in other words, who prized above all else values like honesty, humility, frugality, kindness, patience and tolerance, stuff like that...

"Can you imagine what would happen to the economy if all advertising, business and politics suddenly became totally honest?" I was thinking. "There would be absolute chaos."

"So what's going to happen?" I asked, my voice doubtless betraying deep scepticism. "Is God just going to wave his magic wand over the earth and make it happen?"

"You can scoff," he replied, as I recall, "But things are already changing. Think about young people growing up with this threat hanging over them. They know their parents' and grandparents' generations aren't up to it. And they really know how to connect with each other across the globe..."

This, of course, was before all the satellites came tumbling down, a time when social media still ruled the airwaves. I was thinking about voicing an objection; that the schoolkids involved would soon become adults needing a job and an income to feed their families, like their parents had to so as to provide for them so handsomely, and that they wouldn't for long therefore have the luxury of their superior points of view. Not everyone could work in the eco-sustainability industry. But Paul had the religious bit back between his teeth and just went rabbiting on, dredging up this time some more weird stuff from the Old Testament.

"Okay," he said. "So you want to know about God taking a hand... There are precedents... The great Old Testament flood, for instance, survived only by Noah, his family, and all the animals they crowded into his ark."

Paul told me then that, in the Book of Jonah (the same guy who, in unlikely circumstances, found himself swallowed up and later spat out by a whale), there is a story about the ancient city of Nineveh, where northern Iraq is now, and about its people who were widely known for their wickedness. When he got fed up with them, in a fit of anger, God sent the whale-victim to give them a warning: the city would be overthrown in forty days. The people reacted with lamentation, the full works apparently. They were grief-stricken and sorry. Treating the threat of doom as an ultimatum, the king of the city ordered everyone to turn instantly away from their evil ways and give up all thought of violence... And when they obeyed (as if they would, really)... Bingo! God changed his mind and let them off. What a relief!

Before I could protest at how ridiculous all this sounded, aware I was getting ready to pounce, Paul continued rapidly.

"Let me finish," he said. " The Book of Daniel has something as well."

Daniel was the prophet who, supposedly protected by God, somehow escaped the lion's den when several of those magnificent fierce animals all lost their appetites at once and stayed clear of him. Paul said that this prophet delivered a similar doom-laden warning about, *"A time of anguish, such as has never occurred since nations first came into existence."* On this occasion, though, there was a twist to the tale, for Daniel added, *"At that time your people shall be delivered."*

I didn't like it. I didn't like the Christian belief that only Christians were going to be saved, whatever that might mean; but when I said so, my smart-ass brother corrected me by saying that the people concerned had been Jews, not Christians. Jesus hadn't been born yet in the time of Daniel. Which, of course, I knew, but had forgotten in the heat of the moment.

"Stop splitting hairs!" I yelled back at him. (I could get excited too.) "That's the trouble with all the religions, as far as I can see... They claim exclusive knowledge. 'We know the way to salvation and everyone else has it wrong...' It's too much!"

To his credit, Paul held up a hand in surrender, kind of agreeing with me.

"I think you're right in a way," he said. "The time for that damaging kind of one-upmanship in religion has long passed..."

He said one of the monks teaching him had likened the different religions to the separate, but connected, trunks and branches of a great tree, which shared common spiritual roots; that the different beliefs and practices were based on the same fundamental truths.

The same teacher had also described world faiths as being like the different spokes of a wagon wheel radiating from a single point, holding the whole thing together, giving it strength. All the great traditions, he said, aim back towards this mysteriously unified and unifying truth at the centre. While growing increasingly wise and knowledgeable about their own religion, a person naturally therefore moves closer to the wheel's hub, and closer at the same time to all other religious people travelling on different paths with the same basic goal.

"Everyone's soul, whether they heed it or not, is passionately bent on seeking the endpoint, which some refer to as enlightenment, as if making for home," he said, "And each soul has its own unique path to tread on the way".

He was parroting his teachers, and I was still trying to absorb all this, make some kind of sense of it, because all the talk about 'souls' made me edgy. But Paul suddenly changed tack and stuck in another sly counter-punch.

"Don't forget, by the way," he said, "That there are also atheists and other non-religious people consumed by secular beliefs who are equally dead sure *they* have it right, and that everyone else is misguided... What do you think about that?"

It was all too much. I could tell he was pointing those words directly at people like me, trying to make me ashamed, and nothing less than a hypocrite, by accusing other non-believers of exactly what I was guilty of myself; but then he surprised me again.

"It's nobody's fault, thinking that way," he continued, not sounding in the least accusative or judgemental, letting me off the hook as abruptly as he had snagged me on it. "Through no deliberate fault of their own, that's how most people have been conditioned, by the secular pressures of society and its educational institutions, by science being revered and elevated to the pinnacle of the human value system... But there's a flaw there somewhere. It's led us to think we can and should be controlling nature; that there's a scientific explanation for everything, and therefore a scientific solution to every problem... But isn't that surely just make-believe?"

Naturally, I did not agree.

"Where would we be, for example, without science to provide effective vaccines against the coronavirus?" I asked in rebuttal.

But Paul accused me of missing his point, explaining that he was trying to say that the scientific worldview was too mechanical, that it tended to see human beings as objects, like so many billiard balls bumping into one another all the time, rather than sensitive, flesh and blood kinfolk, capable of both fellow-feeling and a degree of independent decision-making.

In return I said that, as far as I knew, that's what the sciences of psychology, anthropology and sociology were all about, but he dismissed that line of thought with a wave of his hand. He argued that proponents of those subjects, by 'objectifying' their observations, were making the identical mistake. He was clearly impatient to get back to his precious topic of religion again.

"You must admit," he resumed, "That we are living in a 'time of anguish', as Daniel put it, with a catastrophic increase in natural disasters linked to global warming; and that this, with the pandemic, is already causing much painful suffering among the world's population, threatening unrestrained destruction and massive loss of life."

He did have a point, I thought, but couldn't bring myself to agree or concede anything.

"I admit," he went on, in the face of my silence, "That in a secular society, talk about God intervening in favour of humanity cuts little ice... So, rather than 'good' and 'evil', how about thinking in terms of 'wise' and 'foolish', or if that sounds awkward, maybe 'ignorant'; also less in terms of a God who responds to human behaviour with either 'vengeance' or 'mercy', but more in terms of global eco-systems that respond to wise or foolish choices about reducing fossil fuel use, protecting rainforests and so on? How does that sound?"

To me, it did not sound good. When the chips were down, people looked after themselves and their own kind. It wasn't a question of wisdom, just survival. But, as ever, Paul wanted the last word.

"It will go disastrously way beyond what we have now," he said. "If people don't stand together, everyone working for the common good, no-one will escape the apocalypse. I really mean it! (He was getting excited again.) Listen to the words of Saint Paul: *'Brothers and sisters, be careful how you live, not as unwise people but as wise'*..."

"Of course," he managed a little light-heartedness, "Worldwide spiritual transformation might take just a bit longer than forty days!"

Maybe it would have helped, back then, if everyone *had* suddenly begun thinking and behaving like saints when the warning signs were still in the air, but it wasn't going to happen. As a result, Armageddon has come and gone for all who were alive on the planet at that time, and we are still living through the tragic aftermath. Come to think of it, I may well now be the sole survivor in these parts... But, of course, unlike others, I have grown ancient. And that's only true because I was crowned ruler, Tyrannosaurus Rex, king of all I survey.

Nineteen

By the time he reached twenty, I must duly concede, my twin brother Paul had grown into quite a handsome fellow. He used to be tiny compared to me, but had now undergone a late growth spurt and was almost as tall. Still lean, his thin face, strong jaw line, soft floppy brown hair and piercing blue eyes (mine are brown) gave him an appealing appearance, offset slightly by the blemish that was his marginally up-tilted nose. As he might have admitted himself, this ski-jump proboscis, without making him ugly, certainly detracted from perfection. Offsetting such a minor flaw, his calm demeanour (most of the time), a kind of good-humoured stillness that he carried about with him, the product no doubt of countless hours of meditation, seemed to imbue him with an other-worldly trustworthiness and charm that you might even call charisma; but that was not the full sum of his gifts, for his arguments had grown more persuasive.

From school, where he concentrated on Latin, Greek, English Literature, German and French, my astonishingly clever brother had gained a place at one of Cambridge's smaller, friendlier colleges, choosing there though to ditch languages in favour of something original: a three-year degree course that combined philosophy with psychology.

A new professor, Julian Eckhart-Smith (formerly of the University of Stockholm; hence his nickname, 'JESUS'), had recently set up the programme, which crucially (according to Paul) included a daily routine of so-called 'wisdom exercises', among which meditation was key. The students met in a lecture hall at 8 o'clock every weekday to sit in silence with their esteemed leader for twenty minutes; then spent the remainder of the hour scribbling away in their notebooks, or on their tablet computers, 'journaling' about their deepest experiences during the preceding 24 hours, including about their dreams. This 'reflective practice' was supposed to hasten the arrival of wisdom.

Sometimes, in small groups, they would go on nature rambles together and visit sacred sites; Glastonbury one time, for example, or the National Memorial Arboretum. They'd watch selected films, attend theatre and opera performances, and always reflect and write on them later. Paul was particularly moved, he told me, by a two-day visit to the death camp at Auschwitz. The mystics-in-waiting would also read, reflect on and discuss mountains of what Paul called 'wisdom material', which included scripture from all the world religions, top quality literature, refined poetry and, it goes without saying, both classic and up-to-date textbooks of psychology and philosophy.

The heart of the course was guided by the work of a French philosopher, Pierre Hadot, whose influential book 'Philosophy as a Way of Life', published back in the 1990s, spoke of a philosopher being *'in love with wisdom'* for, to quote, *'He knows that the normal natural state of men should be wisdom; for wisdom is nothing more than the vision of things as they are, the vision of the cosmos as it is in the light of reason; and wisdom is also nothing more than the mode of being and living that should correspond to this vision'.*

I've got that word perfect because Paul insisted on writing it out for me. You can see why he found it appealing.

Hadot took his cue from the ancient schools of Greek philosophy. *'In antiquity,'* he wrote, *'The philosopher regarded himself as a philosopher, not because he developed a philosophical discourse, but because he* lived *philosophically... All the schools believed in the freedom of the will, thanks to which people have the possibility to modify, improve, and realize themselves.'*

This is what Eckhart-Smith and his pupils were attempting; in marked contrast to the more usually prevailing abstract, theoretical, and impractical style of academic philosophy found in university departments everywhere in the West at the time.

"But what exactly is wisdom?" I asked Paul on one occasion.

"It's tricky," he admitted, "Here's a definition to use as a starting point: *'Wisdom is the knowledge of how to be and behave for the best, for all concerned, in any given situation'.* In other words, it's about how to live well."

But I didn't follow; so, when I expressed my confusion, he tried to clarify things.

"Okay," he said. "Wisdom is not objective, intellectual knowledge, like the knowledge gained through scientific enquiry. It is rather a subjective and intuitive kind of knowledge, gained from practice and experience... You just *know* a course of action is right, without necessarily knowing why."

This was sounding like gobbledegook, and when I still looked puzzled he continued by trying to help me understand the distinction between *knowing* something and, more simply, knowing *about* that thing.

"For example," he said, "Take clay... People tend to know about clay, the nature of its substance, what it is; but only an expert potter, from experience and skill acquired through learning about and actually working it, can properly be said to 'know' clay and so be able, almost as if it were living matter, an extension of his or her personality, to use it and create a distinctive object; a simple bowl perhaps, useful and beautiful, both."

"This distinction between merely knowing *about* and really *knowing*, regarding not just things but people too, is important," he said. "Eckhart-Smith describes this as the essence of wisdom. Both sides of the brain are involved: the rational left and the intuitive right. He says there's a *law* of wisdom; just like there are laws of science."

According to Paul's professorial wizard, the law of wisdom states that it depends on a person experiencing, in a deep and transformative way, the most profound sense of connection with the universe as a sacred unified whole. It depends on having a vision of wholeness, in other words, according to which the affected individual feels seamlessly linked to the totality, and through it to every other person on the planet (including those who have died and those future generations still to come). At the same time, in the throes of such an epiphany, you similarly feel a profound personal connection with nature, with everything living, even with inanimate matter like mountains, rivers and oceans.

"Wholeness and holiness are linked," Paul asserted. "Think of it," he added. "Every atom of all our bodies was formed among the stars!"

This, I have to say, remained way over my head at the time; but fortunately I kept one or two of his famous journals, which I have since read numerous times.

"It's a mystical experience, right enough," Paul continued, unaware that he'd totally bamboozled me already. "But not that unusual. Research on children shows convincingly that we all have a degree of spiritual awareness when we are young, feelings of humility, awe and wonder, a sense of seamless connection to a higher being or intelligence (whether we call it 'God' or not), and an unbreakable link to other people and to nature, the glorious experience of knowing ourselves to be an integral part of something much greater than ourselves. Mostly, though, we lose this sense of spiritual consciousness when we go to school, where all these fabulous insights are constantly challenged, ignored and belittled, overwhelmed by rationality, materialism and secular conditioning."

He was so passionate. Even now, many years on, and with so much that has happened in between, I can still clearly picture his shiny pink face, unbridled enthusiasm illuminating those youthful features. Despite our differences, in a strange way, I felt proud of him.

"I think it's commendable," he carried on breathlessly, "That so many high schools, and even primary schools, are introducing meditation or mindfulness practice, what some prefer to call 'stilling', into the daily curriculum. It's good, because it has already been proven to improve children's learning ability and creativity, their self-confidence, also the harmony with which they interact in the classroom. Teachers say they love how calm and focused their pupils become when using, even for just a few minutes a day, a simple method that costs nothing. I'm sure it'll help at least some young people retain into adulthood a priceless degree of holistic vision and spiritual awareness."

Funnily enough, I do remember when I was at school sitting still and in silence in a darkened room for long periods; but this was not meditation... It was punishment for misbehaviour. There was I, stuck in detention after yet another petty misdemeanour, while my mates were enjoying themselves playing sport, or more likely in the school tuck shop, without me. Humiliating it was, I agree; but not in a good way at all!

"Don't you remember ever being infused with a tremendous feeling of awe, delight and majesty when you were young? Just stunned into admiration by the natural world?" Paul continued, unaware of the negativity running through my brain. "Isn't there anything that stands out in your mind?"

Only when I was in bed with Carol, I remember thinking.

"You know... On the beach, maybe?"

A little wistfully, Paul began reminiscing about our family holidays in Cornwall with Charlie and H.

"I used to get this terrific sense of joy and satisfaction, for example, marvelling at all the little creatures in those beguiling rock pools and such. Did nothing like that ever happen to you?"

"But that's just kids' stuff," I thought. "It's all very well poncing about with your mates on fancy outings and things like that; but, 'Get Real!' That's just not how the world works."

Paul's psycho-philosophy seemed more like a new-age cult adventure type of thing than a serious and sober academic pursuit, but what did I know? It certainly made my brother happy.

"So where is your God in all this?" I asked, hoping to peg him back a bit as there didn't seem to be a deity in this new scheme he was proposing.

"Good question!" He replied quickly. "In Christianity, God is a Trinity, as you know: Father, Son and Holy Spirit... Let's start there."

With all his erudition, my brother reminded me sometimes of Mr Wright at Torville Prep who loved teaching people the meaning of words. This time it was both 'holy' and 'spirit'. According to Paul, as he had already mentioned, holiness was related in the ancient Sanskrit language to words for 'wholeness', 'holistic', and 'healing'; so, to 'heal' someone, rather than just curing their symptoms; as in the rather mechanistic model of modern medicine; actually meant making them

117

whole again, whole in body, mind and spirit. 'Spirit', he then told me, came from the Latin word *spiritus* meaning 'breath' or 'wind', something invisible, vital to life, capable of moving objects (and people) around, and so acting as a kind of guide.

"You don't necessarily experience it," he explained, "Because it's like being in a hot air balloon. The spirit-wind propels the balloon along; but, as you are travelling with it, at the exact same pace, the only way to notice its effect is to look around at the scenery you're moving past, at the ripples it causes on the surface of a lake below, or at the beautiful wave-forms running through a field of ripening wheat. If you don't take note of what this breath-wind is doing in your vicinity, and within your body, mind and soul, of course, you may not be aware of it at all."

The 'Holy Spirit', he said, emphasizing 'holy', could be understood then as a kind of invisible, sacred and inviolable life force or energy, reflecting the seamless *totality* of creation. It is an indescribable mystery that anyone can tap into and experience by means of a natural kind of intuition. We are all connected to it, he insisted, indeed we are part of it; and so to better experience its power, and the wisdom it contains, we do well to engage in wisdom exercises, not least religious practices and rituals like worship and undertaking pilgrimages, also like offering ourselves in service, volunteering to benefit the poor and suffering.

I grew fidgety when Paul started talking about religion again. Noticing the change in my demeanour, and to encourage me I suppose, he quickly added that there are comparable secular wisdom exercises, like engaging with the arts and with nature in various ways, indulging in creative pursuits, volunteering for public duties, even going to music festivals to share in a naturally joyful common humanity. The list, he reported, was endless.

"So God, in the form of this Holy Spirit of yours, is like the Force in Star Wars," I suggested. "Is that what you're getting at?"

"Well, yes... In a way," he admitted. "Although I don't like the idea much, because it's really nothing special. You don't have to be Luke Skywalker or Princess Leia. In childhood, almost everyone feels the force, the sacred wind-breath-spirit, so to speak, and many adults train themselves to re-establish the connection later, as we are attempting with the Professor."

"Okay," I replied, ready to move on, "But how about God the Father? How come that almighty personage can be so cruel, making so many innocent people suffer terribly, especially children?"

"That's a tough one, you're right," Paul said, giving a sigh. " And, to answer it best, I'm going to have to start with the objective, scientific viewpoint. Think about this... If you have a body with a functioning nervous system, you will inevitably experience physical pain. It goes with the territory... Can't be helped! Similarly, if you have a brain, a mind, and are conscious, you will feel emotional pain. It's completely unavoidable, just an inbuilt part of being a living, breathing human. We are made that way, by God if you like, because it couldn't really be otherwise."

"But that's a bit of a cop-out, don't you think?" I blurted out. "It doesn't say why little kids get terrible diseases and either die young or, maybe worse, get left with lifelong disabilities."

"Well, in a way, it does," he said. "Disease and decay, dementia, for example, and death too, are inevitable aspects of life. Wisdom says we have no choice but to accept them. Let me tell you an ancient true story."

In India, two and a half thousand years ago, a woman had a baby that died of a fever; but she refused to believe he was gone. Half-mad, she heard about a great teacher with the power to work miracles and heal people. It wasn't Jesus, of course; it was the Buddha, a former prince who had left his palace many years earlier in search of enlightenment, someone who may never actually have performed any miracles. Anyway, the woman didn't know that and set off to find him on foot, travelling for many days, carrying her deceased infant child. The Fully Awakened One, as the Buddha was sometimes called, when he saw the woman with her tragic burden, and heard her asking him to heal the boy, instead of sending her away, said it would take a special medicine made from mustard seeds, and she would have to collect those seeds from villagers living nearby.

"But be sure," he told her, "To take seeds only from householders living where none of their relatives has died within the last two or three years. Only those seeds will be effective."

This was a cunning tactic, because whenever she asked for mustard seeds, which were freely offered, she found she must decline them because there had been a death in the house. This was true in every case, so it gradually dawned on her that death is everywhere. No-one escapes it... And that her precious child had died too. With that insight, she had the tiny remains of her son cremated, then returned to the Buddha to thank him, becoming his disciple and follower, remaining faithfully with him until the end of her days.

"We fear death in our western culture," Paul told me. "We conceal it, hide from it, think of it as failure, the failure of modern science and medicine; but that is truly not healthy... And that's why the ancient Greek philosophers were encouraged by their teachers to contemplate their own mortality, to conjure up mental images of their own death, so they could kind of mourn for themselves and get over it."

"Good grief!" I expostulated. "How bloody morbid is that?"

Paul laughed. "*Good* grief is exactly what it is," he said. "Try it! Try thinking of yourself, your dead body, lying in a coffin, the world carrying on without you. Think how you might feel. You have to let go of everything; all your desires, dreams and ambitions, all your pet hates and prejudices, all your friends and loved ones, all your possessions... Everything! You simply have to grieve and let go... It can be wonderfully liberating."

Twenty

Almost a year before she died of Covid, I asked Carol to marry me. The moment occurred after a luxurious Sunday lie-in, following yet another passionate lovemaking session. I was sitting at the kitchen table over a plate of scrambled eggs, with a mug of steaming hot tea in my hand. Carol was standing at the sink, filling it with suds, a wisp of hair plastered to her cheek. The total perfection of this cosy domestic scene suddenly struck me hard, and the earnest hope that we could make it last forever, prompted the obvious question.

When I said it... "Will you marry me, my love?" Carol, caught by surprise, turned slowly. Without at first saying anything, wiping her hands dry on the towel she was already holding, she came and stood beside me, tousled my still damp hair for a second, then sat in a nearby chair, gazing into my eyes, close enough that I could see the tears brimming in hers.

"No... I will not marry you, Freddie," she said then, clearly unhappy, taking my hand. "I love you too much for that."

Sadness enveloped us both, like a mist descending, and I needed an explanation.

"Why not?" she continued, before answering the precise question I was about to utter... "Because I'm twice your age; and, especially, because I can't give you children. You should marry a younger woman one day and have a family. I hope you will. You'd make a fabulous Dad..."

Of course I remonstrated with her, told her I didn't want that, but it was no use.

"You don't know what you want from life yet," she said, softening with her voice what sounded to me a rather harsh comment. "You need to explore all the possibilities before you tie yourself down."

If she hadn't been weeping; if I couldn't see and feel her sorrow; if I hadn't immediately recognised what a sacrifice she was trying to make on my behalf; I would have argued harder. Probably, I would have got angry, but, at the time, I accepted it, and a similar occasion never arose between us again. I wish she had known, though, that I never did marry, and that I've never had kids.

My brother was more the marrying type, it turned out. After getting his Cambridge degree, despite the Professor urging him to take on a lectureship and join his A-team, Paul opted for teacher training. He said he wanted to put the ideas he had been working with to optimum use, educating young hearts and minds. It was on the same course at the college in London, that he met his Mary.

Having studied for a Master's degree after graduating from uni, Paul's wife was a couple of years older than we were. Not ugly exactly, I would say though that she definitely lacked 'pulchritude', to use another of Mr Wright's words (from the Latin, meaning 'beauty'). She was short in stature. Her ears stood out, and her face was sort of pointed, like a little mouse, in a way that was almost comical; but you daren't ever laugh. Except when Paul or the children were around, she always looked tight-lipped and severe.

They found jobs together in a large London comprehensive school, and set about starting a family. Charlie liked Mary from the start, satisfied that her commitment to Paul was total, and her influence on him beneficial; and was naturally in heaven over the grandkids: Hugo, Raphael and Milly.

I liked Hugo too. He was my kind of boy; loved his train sets and soldiers, climbing trees (when his mother wasn't looking), digging holes, rambunctioning around like I used to. A great kid! I remember when he was old enough reading Jules Verne and Kipling stories to him from books like 'Journey to the Centre of the Earth', 'Kim', and (ironically, considering what happened) 'The Man who Would be King', also, an absolute favourite for both of us, Conan Doyle's magical, 'The White Company', which was about the adventures of a company of archers during the Hundred Years War, fighting in France and Northern Spain between the major battles of Crecy and Agincourt. He was a tough little nut. He'd as soon fight as cuddle, but even so, when he was still little and I could grab hold of him, I always called him my Huggie.

Raphael and Milly, though, were different. They were strange. One day, for instance, when he was about three, Raphael kept asking Mary why she called him Raphael when his name was Philip.

"I don't live here," he used to say. "I live in Camden."

Paul and Mary were living in Greenwich at the time, one street back from the river, so I imagine that house will have been under several fathoms of sea-water these past many years, like the rest of central London. Luckily, they moved to the South Downs not far from Torville when Paul shifted over from a state-maintained school to one of the new academies in those parts.

Anyway, the thing is, little Raff had a string of hissie fits, insisting he came from a family called Turpin, who were a line of butchers, and that he wanted to go and see his Mum and Dad, his brothers, sister and cousins, apparently telling Mary about each of them by name. Paul and Mary invited me to Greenwich fairly often for Sunday lunches when I was stationed at Woolwich, and when I first saw the boy go into one of these obsessive tantrums over his origins, the meal almost over, I piped up immediately.

"Let's go over there now," I suggested.

Mary stayed behind with Milly, still a toddler. Paul was reluctant about the expedition, but I was ultra keen to put a stop to this nonsense of Raff's, so the rest of us piled into my Defender and off we went. The first sign that I could have been wrong about the kid was that, once we got through the Blackwall Tunnel, past Mile End and Bethnal Green, our little reincarnation baby seemed to know where he was going. Past Pentonville and he started pointing things out, like King's Cross station (he knew about the Harry Potter platform), and the British Library on Euston Road. It was right weird! Paul tried to make me turn around and head back to Greenwich, but by now it was three against one: Raffa, Huggie and me.

Raphael guided us unerringly to a three-storey terraced house with about eight steps leading up to the front door in Lawford Road. At first we just sat outside, watching and waiting. Even I doubted I had the nerve to go and ring the bell to find out who actually lived there; but, in the event, it wasn't necessary. When a neatly-dressed couple, a man and woman in their fifties, came round the corner, Raff was out of the car in an instant, running towards them as fast as his short legs could go, slamming into the man's right knee and the woman's left as he grabbed each of them by the leg, screaming out "It's Philip! It's Philip!" at the top of his voice, while hugging them as tight as can be. Sheepishly, we others followed and began trying to explain.

Oliver and Mavis Turpin had rarely had such a fright. Paul, I must say, was the diplomat who saved the situation, calming Raffa and with him everyone else, while I simply took care of a somewhat astonished Hugo. Mrs Turpin helped when she suggested we go inside for some tea, Paul holding firmly onto his younger son all the while for fear of him disappearing upstairs in search of what he insisted was still 'his' room.

Once settled round the table in the family parlour, the best bone china in evidence, we waited in silence for the beverage to brew in the kitchen next door. After a while, Mavis called out to her husband through the hatchway.

"You'd better tell them about Philip, Ollie..."

Oliver blew out his shiny red cheeks. "I'd rather it was you, my love," he called back. "Or at least that you were in here with me."

'Alright then! I suppose." We heard, followed by a big sigh, followed by footsteps.

Mavis Turpin bustled back in, told her spouse that for once he must be Mother and pour the tea, apologised for not having either cake or biscuits to offer, plumped herself down rather heavily, and began the extraordinary tale.

Oliver and his brother were indeed butchers, as their father had been before them. She pointed to a photo on the sideboard of the three men taken thirty years earlier. Raffa, who was still trying to cling to the older man's trouser leg, jumped up to look closely, joyfully exclaiming, "Gramps and Uncle Jim..." Whereupon, silenced by this outburst, unable to continue with her narrative, Mavis whispered aloud to herself, and anyone else within earshot, "It must really be him!"

The couple had married in their twenties and had two older sons, one now also a butcher, the other a farmer, raising livestock, both married. The couple went on with their lives until, completely unexpectedly, Mavis realised she was pregnant. Her periods stopping had seemed like a gift; the end of menstruation, she blushed to recount; but little Philip, already well on the way, was born healthy, albeit after a long and exhausting labour, and had lived until the age of four, when he was killed in an accident, drowned in a nearby pond that had frozen over but whose surface gave way as he launched himself across it, away from his doting mother's safe custody, as if fleeing some imaginary fear, to greet his doom. Rescue and resuscitation attempts went on all afternoon, but to no avail. Death had been accomplished in an instant.

"He rushed away as if the Almighty was calling him and the Devil was chasing," she said in a hushed tone, full of awe.

"She was stricken with grief... We both were," her husband joined in. "And now... Can this somehow really be him?"

I didn't know what to make of it, either then or later, after Mary got involved and first invited the Turpin couple to Greenwich, then went to their place one day so that Philip-turned-Raphael could meet almost all his close relatives. It was, by all accounts, a lively reunion, the lad astonishing several folk present by telling them things about themselves a four-year-old couldn't possibly have known. One example concerned his cousin Sandra, who was not by any stretch a gambler, but who had been given a strong tip, won a small fortune on a horse race one day, and never told her husband, Ned, until much later when the money was all spent. Another story was about his older brother, Sidney, the farmer, who had some sheep stolen, then chased after the culprits in the dead of night with a shotgun, was almost convicted for attempted murder but got lucky, receiving only a suspended sentence and a fine for causing 'actual' bodily harm (rather than the more serious 'grievous' variety), by claiming the weapon misfired and had only been intended for the purpose of intimidation;

to which tale he replied that it would be better if no-one ever did discover the actual nature of his thoughts and intentions on that sorry night of distant memory, going on to remind his listeners proudly that thieves had thought twice ever since about trying to rob and bamboozle him out of his precious creatures.

I had to agree with him. Violence is necessary at times. Anyway, these were the kind of tales that emerged; and, it seemed, according to Paul, that it did some good within this alter-family of Raff's, to hear them again and mull them over but strangely; after being fully pre-occupied with all this, going over to Camden, meeting his family, relating these stories and such for something over a year; shortly after his next birthday, he lost interest completely. It was as if now, for him, Philip had never existed... (Although Hugo went on calling him 'Turnip' instead of 'Turpin' for years.) To me, though, Raffa was always and forever strange... As, of course, was his sister; but she was weird in a different way. She used to talk to the dead.

I think Milly was three when it first happened. Mary took her along when she went to visit one of the other teachers at home. It was mainly a social visit, but they did have a seminar to prepare together, so Mary settled her daughter quietly in a corner somewhere with her doll, and maybe some paper and crayons, then, some time later, more than an hour in fact, when they went to fetch her, Milly was nowhere in sight. It was a big old house, with a cellar and an attic, and several flights of stairs; and only as Mary and her friend finally approached the top landing, calling out as they went, did Milly appear from one of the topmost rooms. She was smiling as Mary picked her up to carry her back down the stairs.

"What were you doing in there?" Mary asked.

"I was talking to the old lady," Milly answered, quite unfazed. "She said she was waiting for the boys to come home. Do you know who she meant? They sounded awfully nice."

The 'old lady', it turned out, had been Mary's friend's great-grandmother who had died in the 1930s. Three of her sons had joined the army during the first world war and all three had been killed in the trenches, the last of them in November 1917 only days before the Armistice. Granny Miller, as the old lady was called, had apparently never got over the loss, but that was the first time anyone claimed to have seen her as a ghost. Milly said she was sitting in a high-backed rocking chair, knitting.

"The boys will be cold," she had said. "I'm knitting Alfie a scarf. The other two will want socks."

We passed it off at first as nothing more than an over-active imagination, but after that Milly was always talking to people no-one else could see or hear, especially if she ever went into churches or graveyards. It was weird, and gave me the creeps whenever I heard about it, but curiously she was always so happy with these conversations. To myself, I used to call her 'The Witch'; and I still wonder if she could have been responsible for some of the venom in my heart. Whenever, later on, her father and I were at loggerheads, whenever he challenged my authority and some of the decisions I made, whenever harsh words were spoken, usually by me, I would catch Milly glaring pure hatred at me through those vitriolic violet-tinged eyes she had, striking me to the core like a curse. I heard that among some aboriginal peoples, a man could be killed by a shaman's harsh look or spell. After those encounters with Milly, the vindictive teenage Daddy's girl, I certainly believed such things might be true.

On the whole, though, Paul and Mary were pretty down to earth on these matters, taking their children's eccentricities in their stride, confident they would both outgrow the worst of them. They were not so matter-of-fact on other subjects, however, and we had some highly energetic discussions at times when the children were young.

I remember, for example, one Christmas Eve when I was there helping them celebrate. Hugo, who was still tiny, had a chest infection and with it a high temperature, then started having alarming fits. It was pitiful to watch the little lad first becoming stiff all over, then twitching manically for a couple of minutes. Completely unconscious, his eyes rolled scarily back in their sockets. He also soiled his pants and started foaming at the mouth, but by the time we got him to A & E at the District Hospital a few minutes away, the convulsions were over and he was just enormously drowsy. They wouldn't even let him see a doctor. After waiting for more than two hours, the nurse just said to take him home, give him a cold bath, and keep an eye on him.

"It happens all the time," she said. "He'll be fine."

When Paul complained a bit, she said dismissively that we were welcome to wait for a doctor, but it was Christmas and they were short-staffed, so we could expect it to be a long time before one was available, possibly not before well after dark; so we did leave, and he was fine, but it was a scary twenty-four hours until the fever broke. For some reason this episode restarted the debate about God letting children suffer.

This time it was Mary who took the lead. Fetching a small black book from a shelf near what they called their 'meditation corner', complete with altar, candles, incense, crucifix and Buddha figure, the same items as far as I could tell that Paul had once installed in his bedroom at home, she started to read: *Your joy is your sorrow unmasked. The selfsame well from which your laughter rises was*

126

oftentimes filled with your tears. And how else can it be? The deeper that sorrow carves into your being, the more joy you can contain... Joy and sorrow are inseparable."

She said the book was called 'The Prophet'. It was by Kahlil Gibran, a Persian poet. I said they were fine words, but that still didn't get God off the hook. Paul then took his turn.

"Jesus said the same thing," he began. "It goes like this: 'Blessed are you who weep now, for you will laugh'."

"And Christ suffered," he continued after a pause. "Not only the pain of being whipped and crucified, but also the emotional pain, the humiliation of what we call his passion."

"Remember too, 'the slaughter of the innocents'," Mary added, the pair of them a double-act now, and on a roll, "King Herod had dozens of babies mercilessly killed to try and rid himself of his foretold rival, the 'King of the Jews' that would be heralded as the Messiah."

But that, I thought, was even more evidence of God's inhumane cruelty.

"There are two worlds to consider," said Paul, taking his turn again. ' Two kingdoms... One earthly, one heavenly."

"You don't believe in Heaven and Hell, surely!" I expostulated, unable to stay calm any longer. "You can't believe that the things we do in this life result in everlasting bliss or torment, depending on how a person is judged at the moment of death... What could be more unfair than that?"

"Okay. No... No!" He quickly replied, echoed immediately by Mary shaking her head. "It isn't like that at all. Let me try to explain."

The Buddhist monks had helped him see, he told me, that most things in scripture, including the bible, should be thought of as allegory; as more symbolic, in other words, than a literal, actual or factual presentation of things. Obviously the account of the origins of the earth in Genesis clashed with the findings of science: the universe has been around for billions of years and couldn't possibly have been created in just seven days (or six, if you don't count the rest-day). God, in that sense, is a poetic Creator-figure. The Ten Commandments given by God to Moses on Mount Sinai in the Book of Exodus, Paul was suggesting, is principally a list of the injunctions necessary for *any* group of people trying to live successfully in harmony with each other: rules and recommendations not to kill each other, not to steal or tell lies, to be faithful in marriage; things like that. Obey social conventions, in other words, for your own good, *and* for the good of all. Buddhists have similar rules, it turns out; although they prefer calling them 'precepts'.

"So, when Jesus talks about the kingdom of heaven," Paul

continued, "He is speaking metaphorically, always likening it to something else: a tiny mustard seed, capable of growing into a great tree; yeast, that makes bread rise in the oven; a pearl of unbelievable value. The man from Nazareth knew that the world beyond this world could not faithfully be described in any other way; so heaven is not an actual place, somewhere people go when they die. It's more like a state of mind; but not really that either. It's the pristine state of one's soul when fully in communication and communion with the sacred overarching unity of the Holy Spirit, a state you have to strive for and experience before you can even begin to comprehend what it's like and what it truly means. That's why we do meditation and the other wisdom exercises, to foster spiritual contact. It's also why we teach meditation to the children at school."

"When we die," he continued after a brief pause, "You could think of it as like a raindrop, fallen onto the earth, finally making it downhill, downstream and down-river to join the ocean; our souls rejoin the great totality, the infinite and timeless dimension of being from which we each came. Do you see?"

"Let me get this straight," I said, thinking about little Raffa and the possibility of reincarnation. "Christians believe one thing and Buddhists another. One lot either go to heaven or hell. The other lot get reborn countless times. You can't have it both ways, so, which side are you on?"

They looked blankly at each other for a moment, seeming unable to decide who should try and answer. In the end, it was Paul who spoke next.

"This is difficult," he said, "Because you are asking a binary question; one that requires a 'yes/no', 'right/wrong', type of answer. Wisdom, though, so often lies in unifying 'both/and' concepts, rather than the binary 'either/or' type. It may seem paradoxical, I admit."

You could tell he'd been trained in philosophy.

"You want it both ways, you mean," I replied, feeling pretty disgusted. "That's typical!"

I ended the discussion there, but we came back to it many times over the years. They were a right sanctimonious pair; Mary always clinging to Paul like a limpet, echoing his every word. They wanted me to know about Eckhart-Smith's scheme of personal development through stages towards wisdom and what they called 'spiritual maturity', how more people should become 'wisdom-seekers', and how that was going to make the world cleaner, safer and happier. It was absolute rubbish of course.

"People are basically selfish," I told them, "On the lookout only for themselves, their families and other people like them."

They agreed that was how people started, but insisted they could progress if they got past the binary stages and developed some form of unitary or 'holistic' vision; which is where their famous meditation and other 'wisdom exercises' came in.

I had to insist that it really wouldn't catch on... And who was right in the end?

Twenty-One

Paul and Mary were always harping on about the epidemic of anxiety and depression engulfing the world alongside Covid, resulting from people being bombarded round-the-clock with terrible and terrifying, wall-to-wall news; horror stories of both natural and man-made disasters, air and water pollution, disease, death and decay, famine, floods and fires, hurricanes, whirlwinds and tornadoes, tsunamis and volcanoes, drought and deprivation. The whole boring old story.

No wonder, they complained, that people everywhere were rushing around, madly preoccupied with avoiding distress rather than facing their pain, physical and emotional, with hope and courage, living a life filled with meaning and purpose, searching for wisdom and maturity, and making their suffering count. Pleasure-seeking, they insisted, had led folk into all manner of destructive behaviour, on much of which, according to them, could be blamed the parlous state of the planet. People were unhealthily addicted to so many things: alcohol, gambling and drugs, of course, but eating, sex, shopping, gaming and social media too. None of it was conducive to wellbeing, and much of it could be linked to irresponsible advertising and other highly detrimental practices, foisted on them by greedy, unscrupulous money-makers. Such addictions also promoted organised crime, smuggling, and violence... On it went... Ho hum! I'd soon had enough of their high moral tones, although now I wonder if maybe they had a point.

"What's wrong with people seeking a little pleasure in an otherwise dull and dreary existence?" I countered at the time.

"Their lives are dull because they switch off," Paul responded. "Boredom is the price you pay for indifference to the plight of others, for lacking courage and curiosity, and for switching off compassion."

"But most people," I argued, growing heated, "Have very little choice about how they live."

"That's true," agreed Paul disarmingly. "But isn't that because they're educated that way? Children and teenagers are simply not taught about the options available for maintaining and improving their mental health and wellbeing. They could easily learn better how to be aware of, manage and take responsibility for their destructive thoughts, feelings, words and actions. They could be encouraged to reflect more on their core values... Based on wisdom exercises, surely there could be another way."

Another lengthy discussion followed, linking the production of soap and cosmetics to deforestation, air travel to atmospheric pollution, reckless arms sales to the excesses of war and displacement of countless refugees, all the usual hobby horses; but I'm not going to repeat it, much preferring to move on and talk about joining the army.

*

Big Al and I always kept in touch. He hated farm work, especially in winter. Lonely down there in Herefordshire, he was always ready to meet up for a pint and a pub lunch somewhere. I was preoccupied with Carol in those days, of course, and couldn't get away that often. Also, to be honest, Al was such a misery, his company wasn't the best. I kept saying he should try something different, but he didn't want to upset Ada, who had such high hopes for him. For over a year, then, he was stuck in a real bind. Then, suddenly, the RSPCA closed down the farm, following claims of cruelty to the animals after local people saw cows being mistreated.

"Cruelty to farm hands more like," was Al's comment.

So he went back to West Byfleet, where Ada's next ploy was to usher him in the direction of labouring work on a building site. She hoped he'd become an apprentice bricklayer, chippie, plasterer or something. The money was better than in the dairy business, but Al wasn't happy there either. He didn't like being made fun of by the older men, even though I said they were only teasing him because really they probably liked him; and this was the state of affairs in the September, shortly before I started my final year at Torville.

At much the same time, Paul and I got our annual summons to St John's Wood for the ritual interview and miserable pep talk from Grandpa Ralph. 'Moneybags Manning' was still basically ruling our lives.

Nothing ever seemed to change in that hermetically sealed mausoleum of his, a stone's throw from the cricket ground at Lords. It always had a dusty atmosphere and a faint smell of mothballs. The faithful retainers, silent as ever, were either the selfsame as when we first visited as children, after H died, or their replacements were precisely cloned using the same DNA. The place gave me the creeps; as of course, did Grandpa Ralph.

Paul went first into his forever gloomified office with the carefully placed chairs and the one light shining down on the desk. My twin brother's school reports and mock 'A' level results were exemplary. His plans for Cambridge were backed by simultaneous applications to York, Durham and St Andrews should he not be successful, unlikely though that seemed, so Moneybags of course was delighted. It was not quite the same, though, when my turn for the inquisition arrived.

The first thing I noticed was his age. Even in the darkened room, his exceptionally pale, hairless skin seemed tissue-thin, like some kind of ancient flaking porcelain, the tortuous veins standing out, as if criss-crossing blue tributaries across the floodplains that formed the backs of his hands. For the first time, fleetingly, I wondered what might happen to his fortune when he finally popped his clogs. How old was he, exactly? In truth, I didn't know.

He was already aware from the school that my mock results were no better than average, and all my reports were of the 'could do better' variety. I was successful on the sports field, but my enthusiasm for academic subjects, never strong, had waned significantly since Carol came into the picture. It's hard to concentrate on obscure historical details, for example, when your head and heart are full of sex, wonder, and the image of a beautiful woman, but I wasn't about to explain that to Grandpa. Fortunately, my housemaster, Iain Stewart, a great sportsman in his day, had written that I excelled at boxing, rugby and cross-country running, not to mention table-tennis and snooker, and had proven myself a natural leader among my peers. It was kind of him, given that in one end-of-term escapade, I'd led a few of my comrades over to the Leathern Bottle, a jaunt that ended up with him being called to the Cop Shop to escort some of us back to school, and that only after he had taken Pipkin to the hospital for stitches to an ugly slash above his left cheekbone.

We had encountered a bunch of local miscreants, who objected to our posh manners and free-spending ways, in a pub they considered an integral part of their own private fiefdom. I think the Stewpot was proud of us for defending our honour so well, seeing those thugs on their way; especially as one of the more scurrilous among these dreadful ruffians had brandished a flick-knife in our direction. He was the one that sliced up our Tim.

Dismissing me finally, after a painfully uncomfortable twenty minutes, my pallid grandfather actually did me a favour by insisting, by Christmas, on a summary of my plans for the future, plans that were entirely vague at that point. I left the building perplexed. Although I could have ignored his wishes and refused to comply, he had a point. I was drifting towards 'A' levels in history and geography with no idea what might follow, even assuming I passed. Where should my future lie?

A few days later, with Carol away for a while in Scotland again, Al and I met up near Charing Cross for a few lunchtime beers. The plan was to drink until late afternoon, go for a curry, return to the same pub or a different one, drink some more, and then catch the last train home. However, over the leisurely second beer, we began talking about what we wanted to do with our lives. It happened that I was looking out of the window at the precise moment a big red London bus pulled up blocking the view. Emblazoned along its side, as luck would have it, was an attractive advert for a career in the armed forces. Al spotted it too.

It takes a lot to interrupt a beer session between us two, but that did it immediately. It was like a sign from heaven, if you believe in that kind of thing; so we finished off our pints, and trotted straightaway to Yeomanry House in Handel Street, not far from Euston, right opposite the concrete and glass cathedral to consumerism that is the Brunswick Shopping Centre. There we discovered a broad pavement backed by smartly painted, waist-high black railings, and behind them, running half-way down the narrow street, a three-storey decorated, two-tone brick building with two entrances. The larger, main doorway seemed to be connected with the Army Reserve and the University of London Officers Training Corps, so we made for the other, the one with the great big giveaway sign above marked 'Careers'.

Inside, a small waiting area was kitted out with a few chairs and racks lined with numerous brochures, not only about army service but about the navy and air force as well. There were posters on the walls, and more leaflets displayed on the centrally placed desk, but there was no time for either of us to look through any of these because, behind the desk, all six-foot-six of him, stood the impressively uniformed figure of Warrant Officer Gordon Jameson, bristling and beady-eyed. This, we soon discovered, was a typical indication of his habitual state of readiness to serve Queen and country in whatever brutally efficient manner should happen to come into the none too complex circuitry of the brain inside his head.

"Gentlemen," he greeted us. "How can I help you today?"

Having scanned his name badge, I was expecting a Scottish accent, but this was pure Billericay.

"We want to join the army," we said in unprepared unison.

There's a process you go through to join the forces, and this was the start of it for both of us. The first step, which might have been the toughest, was getting past Jameson. It seemed to be his mission in life to put people off a military career at all costs; but I suppose he saw it differently, that he was ensuring only the keenest and most persistent of applicants, rather than time wasters, got through.

He was nice enough initially, I'll give him that. He even attempted a smile, which I have to say looked rather odd; his lips moved but his eyes stayed stony. Having reasserted that, feet firmly on the ground for preference, it was only the army we wanted, he then listed the available range of job options. There was engineering, human resources and finance, intelligence ("No need for you to bother with that one, Son," he said unkindly to Al). There was IT and communications, logistics and support, medical, music and ceremonial. Only last, finally, did he mention combat. Of course, we both immediately said we wanted to become combat soldiers, whereupon an even more sceptical look came into the Warrant Officer's eyes, and a new brusqueness of manner took over. Maybe he thought it was just the beer talking. Anyway, not prepared to spend a great deal of time with us, he just heaped a load of the ready-to-hand literature into our arms, while telling us to read it and come back only if we remained interested.

"Make an appointment, lads," he added disdainfully. "It'll be a bit more formal next time."

We did go back. Apart from the fact that there was no mention of how, when you weren't being shot at, blown up, badly maimed or even killed, you'd be utterly bored bonkers, the glossy brochures made it plain that an army career could be positive in many ways, even fun. As an infantry soldier, they insisted, you'd train and work alongside highly skilled colleagues, *'who'll become like a kind of family'*.

A point stressed many times over, which appealed particularly, I think, to Al, was that we would make life-long friends in the army. There was a decent level of pay, especially when taking into consideration that there were no charges for either accommodation or food, and much was made of the prospects of promotion through the ranks. In addition, we'd be trained in various skills and gain qualifications that could be useful in civilian life later, after your service career ended; although the military authorities might not have wanted to stress torturing and killing people among them, skills which did naturally become indispensible for those of us who became mercenaries and militia later on.

The brochures also mentioned the possibility of playing sports to international levels if you were good enough, also the promise of travel, for instance on deployment to front line operations, peacekeeping and disaster relief missions, and other such fields of delight. Especially appealing was the prospect of mastering a number of weapons, including the rifle, grenade launcher, machine gun, and light mortar. My mouth started watering at the prospect.

"They might even teach us to parachute!" I said to Al, as we sat in the curry house afterwards, reading through all the bumf. We were really excited.

Back at Yeomanry House a week or so later, Jameson got stuck into Big Al. I was in the waiting room, where a stony-faced woman soldier was this time manning the desk, and they had gone through to an inner office to start filling out the required application form. Al, I knew, was nervous. Later, he told me what happened.

"When he asked my name, I stammered a bit, Freddie," he said. "I was jittery, and it came out, sort of... 'Al, Albert... F...Firkin', you know! So he started taking the mick right away, repeating what I said, but in a completely pathetic tone of voice: 'Al, Albert... F...Firkin. Albert fuckin' Firkin... What kind of name's that?' I couldn't believe it."

I wasn't sure if Al was miserable or angry as he recalled this truly humiliating encounter.

"I couldn't believe he was swearing at me," he went on. "I just said it was my name... *my* name. But he still kept calling me F'Firkin after that. It was horrible."

Somehow my big friend had eventually completed the interview and signed the application. It stood us both in good stead that we had cadet force experience at Torville, and could put Major Northwood and Colonel Parker down for references. When my turn came, I had a different kind of a grilling.

"You're a smart lad," said Jameson, after I'd listed my 'O' levels and told him I was studying for 'A's. "Why don't you carry on and go to the university? Join the army at the same time and they'll pay you while you're a student, then you'll go to Sandhurst and get a commission, become an officer..."

I told him I was fed up with school and wanted to get on with my life; and anyway, I didn't want to be an officer. I wanted to be at the front, at the sharp end, doing the business.

"You've no bloody idea, Son," he said, giving me a withering look. "You've got maths 'O' level, right? So take it from me, you're not going to be wasted in combat. You'll be sent for IT training, logistics, intelligence, or even the pay corps. That's how the army works."

I came away disappointed but defiant. Why should I take it from him? After the way he treated Al, he was nothing but a miserable, sarcastic barrel of khaki shite whose word was not everything; so I decided to carry on and take my chances. Big Al did too. And a good thing for all of us that we did.

Nothing happened for several weeks, until we both got letters calling us to a two-day 'Selection Event' at Pirbright, an army camp in Surrey. As it was getting real, I thought I'd better tell my mother what we were up to; and Carol, of course.

"You're not going to go and get yourself killed, are you?"

That was Charlie's first response.

"I think you should get your 'A' levels first, though, don't you?" was her second.

In the end, she knew I would do just what I wanted, and offered no objection when I showed her the army pamphlet that made it sound as if her majesty's soldiers had the safest job in the world.

Carol, as it turned out, had similar misgivings; but was mainly concerned at the unhappy prospect of separation. I told her that I'd probably be stationed in the south of England throughout training and for my first couple of years of service, because that's what I'd have liked to believe, even if it wasn't the absolute truth.

"Anyway," I said to be reassuring, "I'm not in the army yet. They might not agree to recruit me!"

But, by the time I'd gone through selection, I knew it was a fully done deal.

To avoid missing school and giving the game away, I was able to arrange a date to attend Pirbright during the next half-term break. The two days were a doddle for those like me who'd been to a school such as Torville. There were aptitude tests, mostly multiple choice, which even Al found fairly easy. There was a medical examination and fitness tests; running two kilometres in under eleven minutes, throwing a heavy ball three metres while sitting against a wall, pulling on a fixed weight and other stuff like that. There were literacy and numeracy tests for some, but not those of us with maths and English qualifications already. And there was a more difficult maths paper as part of a 'Technical Selection Test', which I'm sure I could have breezed through, until I discovered that a pass meant joining one of those units I definitely wanted to avoid. The pay corps would have to look elsewhere... Warrant Officer Jameson had cunningly failed to inform us that, with no risk to our overall applications, we could refuse to take the TST, which I did.

We had individual interviews about our families, hobbies, education and so on, including the key question, "Why do you want to join the army?" to which; as I drummed hard into Al at every opportunity beforehand; the reply should include 'serving my country', 'taking advantage of the opportunity to improve my skill set', 'meeting people and making firm friends (for life)', and 'seeing the world', all delivered with bounding enthusiasm ("I really want to do this") and confidence ("I'm sure I will succeed"). As I said, it was pathetically easy.

We were both accepted, but were also both advised to wait until we had passed our eighteenth birthdays. That way we would start basic Phase One training at Catterick in Yorkshire, rather than at the Army Foundation College in Harrogate as 'Junior Soldiers'. I was impatient, but it seemed sensible; and, anyway, they really gave us no choice. Al only had a couple of months to go, but said he'd wait for me, so we could join the same intake, and the army was happy with that.

I finally owned up to Stewpot about it when I got the 'Offer of Employment' letter from army recruitment head office, and we agreed I'd stay on at Torville until the following Easter, if only so I could finish the rugby season. He also thought I was daft not to finish my 'A' levels, but I was totally stubborn about it by then.

As for Grandpa Ralph, I simply sent him a copy of the employment letter and a note saying I would be off to Yorkshire the following May. I wonder what he made of it, but shall never know. I was expecting another summons to the big house, but he died suddenly on Christmas Eve, and not prettily. In his room on Christmas morning, the housekeeper, hoping to finish her work quickly and get home to her family, was pleased to find the bed already made, until she realised that it hadn't been slept in, an unheard-of occurrence, and until she went into the adjacent bathroom where, with Grandpa Ralph's stone-cold corpse lying in the middle of it, the floor was covered in blood.

When the police came, all she could say was, "Why on earth did he not shout for help, or call an ambulance?"

But we would never find out.

Twenty-Two

The coroner kept us waiting. Not on the actual day, although she was fairly tardy then too... No, rather, the inquest into Grandpa Ralph's death was put back many weeks. We were told it was because of a huge backlog. You die and you're still in a queue! I was impatient because the solicitor's letter said he would not call a meeting to discuss the contents of Moneybags' Will until the cause of death verdict was in.

The address of Wells, Goodbody & Wells in Belgravia seemed to indicate that, as ever, Ralph had followed his instincts to retain the most expensive set of lawyers he could find, on the dubious assumption that the costliest must be the best, unaware of life's invariable rule that, in all things, the exceptionally highly priced were usually among the greediest and most self-serving of agencies. If they made you feel good, it was only part of a greater ploy to get you spending more inside their premises (or on their website). The actual service was often surprisingly shoddy. Displays of sympathy for customers were fake news, as they genuinely couldn't actually give a parrot's fart for whatever happened to you.

Finally, in the courtroom, we were treated to an extensive report from the official pathologist, giving his best interpretation of the facts concerning Grandfather's final minutes. All indications were that, late in the evening, he had taken a hot bath, thus dilating all the veins and arteries in his extremities. Out of the tub, the water draining away, he had started drying himself, seated on the toilet-seat lid. Bloody footprints either side of the pedestal revealed that bleeding had started then, probably because he had scratched at one of the more prominent varicose veins, which were probably itching ('pruritus', the pathologist called it) as the paper-thin skin would have been dry, flaking and inflamed, due to his poor circulation. He was taking anti-coagulant medication, having had trouble earlier in the year with blood clots, so that's why the bleeding continued. He must have pressed hard on the open wound, as everyone is told to do, but when the blood continued to flow, he may have got flustered and panicked.

The coroner asked how long it would have taken for death to occur, at which the pathologist replied that it could have been as long as an hour, or even more, but anyway at least thirty minutes.

"The average human body contains five litres, or just over ten pints, of blood," he said. "An elderly man whose circulation to both heart and brain were already compromised, as in this case, would only need to lose about two litres before becoming confused and drowsy. It seems he either lay down, or fell to the floor, where he was found. Eventually his heart simply stopped beating."

That was it. The verdict of 'death by natural causes' soon followed, and I finally found out that he had been eighty-nine.

The company of solicitors favoured by Grandpa occupied smart premises in a small street just west of Grosvenor Square that could easily pass for a billionaire's London pad. Wells, Goodbody & Wells occupied a tastefully squat, white-fronted building, dwarfed by the high-rises around it, with a ramp to the black-painted front door for their frailer, wheelchair-bound clients, with a stylishly opulent interior of polished oak, leather-bound furniture, light-coloured velvet drapery and at least one genuine full-sized old master artwork in the style of Caravaggio, together with several smaller Rembrandt-school prints and etchings. It was impressive... As was the sculpted beauty of the honey-haired receptionist, matched by the perfect diction and dulcet tones of her effortlessly welcoming voice. The seduction had clearly begun.

Once inside Henry Cavil's bright, sunny office, things became less entrancing, more business-like. Charlie, Paul and I were surprised to discover five chairs arrayed carefully in front of his desk, rather than three, but had little time to wonder about them before the door opened again, and in swept an imposing matronly personage of about fifty, surrounded by a cloying cloud of expensive French perfume that made me instantly want to gag. This self-assured lady was elegantly attired in a tidy lilac ensemble with matching mid-heeled shoes and handbag, a floral scarf at her neck. Behind her came, like a lapdog, a gawky younger man with a trim, silly-looking moustache, equally finely dressed in a dark olive coloured suit with flare-trousers that couldn't possibly have been tailored in England, although the stout leather brogues on his feet probably were London made. A terrible sinking feeling took over the pit of my stomach as Cavil began the introductions. This effete male intruder looked astonishingly like a well-groomed version of H.

Madame Céline Montauban, it turned out, had been an *au pair* in the Manning household for six months when nineteen. Patrice, her son, she claimed was fathered not by H, as I feared, but by Ralph himself. Gertrude Manning was apparently entirely reconciled to the arrangement whereby her pretty young companions and helpers were encouraged to take care of those needs of her husband that she no longer desired to even acknowledge, much less to satisfy. They were paid extra, of course, handsomely no doubt, and the usual precautions were taken to avoid all risk of pregnancy.

Mademoiselle Montauban, as she should still have been known, never having married, was a member of the Roman Catholic persuasion, and had secretly reneged on the bargain, refusing to take any pills while happily scooping up the dosh. When the inevitable occurred, and she told Ralph she was 'full' (foolishly translating literally one of the French words for pregnant: *pleine*), he tried to insist on her having an abortion, but this was another step too far for the French miss and her irritating religious conscience, so she was packed off back to Lyon where her baby boy was born and she continued to receive pay to stay quiet.

That was the story we heard in silent wonder that morning, and I had no doubt it was true. DNA tests had confirmed it; but you only had to look at the fellow to see the family likeness, even if he could barely utter a single word of comprehensible English. Here was a new relative: a half-brother to H; a half-uncle to Paul and myself. Given our grandfather's solitary and completely introvert nature, that was almost a very good joke.

Charlie wanted to know the sordid details. For some reason, without shame apparently, Madame was happy to oblige. Every Friday evening, at 8 o'clock precisely, Ralph would come to her room. Wordlessly, and without foreplay, sex would occur, brusquely and briefly, and only in the missionary position, face to face but no kissing. Ten minutes later, often less, Ralph would hurry away. The whole thing sounded ghastly. Even Charlie probably wished she hadn't bothered to ask. Cavil broke the silence that followed.

"Now," he began, "You are all here because you are named in the document I am about to read, 'The Last Will and Testament of William Ralph Manning'."

That, I think, was the first time I heard his first name; but I barely took any notice, being naturally eager to hear of my immediate enrichment. Unfortunately, though, a good deal more patience was called for. It took a long time for the somewhat self-important solicitor to go through the extensive paperwork, and just as long then to explain its obscure contents. In summary, though, Moneybags had kept tight control of the purse-strings even in death. Everything was going to be managed through a trust, with Cavil and two named but (to us) faceless male trustees. It would take months, apparently, to obtain probate, sell off property and liquidate other assets, and longer to settle in stages with Her Majesty's Inland Revenue.

"Don't worry too much," the solicitor said finally, "A financial wizard like Mr Manning naturally ensured that a minimum of death duty would be owing... But some cannot be avoided, for he was worth in excess of eight hundred million pounds..."

"Wowee!" I interjected. Even Paul asked him to repeat the figure, if he would be so kind.

Cavil looked so extremely smug while complying, holding his hands up before him in a gesture almost of prayer, that I thought he would soon start to purr.

Ralph had stashed most of his millions in offshore tax havens, which was great, but there was a problem in getting them back home for us to spend. It had to be done, we were told, very gradually, over a period of years.

Each of us in the room would inherit a share of most of the proceeds. There were a number of minor bequests, to be settled on those faithful retainers and others who had served Grandpa in various ways over the years; but we would still get heaps. Madame Céline and Charlie would each immediately get a generous lump sum of one million, then a yearly allowance of £300k. Children 'of the blood' - Patrice, Paul and myself - were up for an immediate two million, an allowance of half-a-mil annually, and a one-third share of the remainder when it became available. The sting in the tail was that all future handouts would only be at the unanimous discretion of the trustees'. To get our hands on the real money, we had to go cap in hand to the triumvirate that I quickly dubbed 'the three wise monkeys'; and they were not easy to please. When you want to buy helicopters, weaponry, explosives and ammunition, it's hard to make it sound convincing that you're using the money in an acceptable cause for the good of humanity; but all that came later on. For the time being, so to speak, I was happy to take the money and run. Nevertheless, I remained passionately intent on joining the army. Nothing would deflect me from that.

I did buy Carol a new car, an electric one. I offered her a Tesla or a Jag, but she plumped for the more modest Kia Nero. At least, to give it distinction, I could pay for a paint-job in her favourite turquoise with a pink floral trim. I also bought a new, gob-smacking highly priced, top-of-the-range, memory-foam mattress for her bed, as I would clearly benefit too. We went to a Michelin-starred restaurant for a celebratory meal, although came away disappointed as, in six tiny courses, there had not been one properly satisfying mouthful of food, meaning they should have given us side orders of chips. The wines though, I will say, were top class.

Charlie took the opportunity to have a new kitchen installed, and got the bathroom revamped. There was a new settee and matching comfy chairs, new carpets, and redecoration throughout the house. I suspected her of having a brief fling, too, with one of the painters; she seemed so cheerful suddenly; but she said it was just the unaccustomed, most welcome relief from money worries; also no longer having to explain every expense in detail to our despotic dead granddad. She could have retired from work but decided only to reduce to part-time at the accountancy job, giving her enough time for the other activities she wanted to do.

Paul, predictably, banked his money, or rather invested it through a financial advisor, putting him in the ideal position when he later got married to buy the Greenwich house for himself and his Mary. Probably, too, charitable fool that he was, he gave a big bundle away.

Big Al and I celebrated together, naturally, but you can't drink two million pounds worth of alcohol in a short space of time, however hard you try; so, after giving my mate a few grand, I too put a chunk in the bank. I did go mad briefly and buy myself a fast car, a bright red Porsche, but that didn't last long. I was taking it for a drive in the Surrey countryside a few days after collecting it, putting it properly through its paces for the first time, when I took a slight risk and gunned it past a slow-moving tractor as it approached a right-hand curve in the narrow road. Unfortunately, a fast-moving vehicle, just a blur in my line of vision, was approaching at the exact moment, obliging me to divert rapidly out of its path. Sadly, I over-corrected my trajectory and finished up, at speed, in the adjacent ditch. The air-bags deployed instantly, saving me from more than minor harm, but the Porsche was totally kaput. Charlie gave me a talking to after the crash, so then I bought the Defender.

Unsurprisingly, we never saw either fancy-pants Patrice or his fragrant, not-so-saintly, Lyonnais mother again.

I had learned to drive and passed my test soon after leaving Torville, and continued to use that period profitably. Quickly recovered from the bruises and sprained wrist of the accident, determined to be the fittest recruit when I got to Catterick, I spent time every day at the gym, on the track and in the pool, toning my muscles, gaining speed and growing stronger; which I made sure Al did as well, despite his protests. This was recommended by both the hateful Recruiting Officer Jameson and the glossy brochures, so it made sense. I had Charlie teach us both how to iron shirts and trousers as, according to the literature (honestly), this was a key skill for army recruits to master; plus I kept up with my boxing lessons, and even began judo training.

The night before we went north, Al came to stay; which was nice because he doted on Charlie, who was equally fond of him in return. We'd been sent travel warrants to exchange for rail tickets, and I had managed to bump us up to first class by paying extra, also to book us on an earlier train. It only takes two and a half hours from Kings Cross to Darlington, from where we could get a taxi, and I was keen to get to the camp before all the other newbies.

Right on the edge of the Yorkshire Dales, it is the perfect place for army training. The barracks cover a wide area, and Ministry of Defence property extends in a broad semi-circle to the west. No-one seemed particularly surprised that we'd shown up two hours before the time given. Once we'd shown our letters of employment and invitations to Phase One training, and our proofs of identity had been scrutinized, we were given a map of the place, then simply told to go to Hut C, leave our gear, and report to Training Room Eight.

The hut was similar to those I'd seen in Brecon in the army cadet force when we went on camp from school. In the vestibule were notice boards with posters about how to arrange the kit in our lockers, how to do various drills and such; and adjacent was the Section Commander's room and Troop Sergeant's Office, also utility and drying rooms for cleaning kit and storing stuff. Inside there was a row of fifteen beds either side, separated by a fairly wide space, plenty of room for thirty young men to do push-ups, or ironing. Beside each bed was a locker. A door at one end led to the washroom area, toilets and showers. That was it.

I bagged the bed with the door on my immediate right, and told Al to take the one next to me. After the initial briefing, when we'd had the chance to size everyone up, keeping guard on our chosen spots back in the hut, I got Al to quiz people on what kind of soldiers they were aiming to become. We wanted combat troops only at our end. Nerdy types heading for signals, IT or logistics were encouraged to head further down.

This would have worked fine if it wasn't for a rival faction. Mario Spencer, an unpleasantly cocksure fellow, whose father came from Liverpool while his mother hailed from Naples, obviously fancied himself as something of a ringleader too. In the end, we were split north and south. They were the dreaded Capulets; we were the stylish Montagues. They were the Puerto Rican Sharks; we were the New York Jets. It was a toxic mix. Like Shakespeare's Tybalt or Bernstein's Bernardo, someone might get rubbed out.

He spotted me and I spotted him right away, exchanging hostile glances across the briefing room. Somehow by the time we reached the hut, he had attracted a following of five, which was one more than me. As well as Big Al, my team consisted of Mack Cotton, a fisherman's son from Deal in Kent (who sadly found he always got seasick on the ocean), Vijay Patel, who looked Indian but was born and raised in Croydon, and the red-headed Terry Wattis from Hayling Island, whose father had taken his young family to Australia for a couple of years while he worked on an engineering project in Tasmania, and whose son had rejoiced in the perverse Aussie nickname 'Blue' ever since. These four and I were to stay together a long time. As the army predicted, we really did become lifelong mates.

The trouble with Spencer began that first evening, after we'd all had our army haircuts and been kitted out with uniforms and fatigues, when his mob tried muscling in front of others in line at the cookhouse. Al and I wandered over to intervene, but our Section chief, Corporal Dai Morgan from Swansea, who couldn't care less about the north-south divide among us, got there first and made it plain who was really in command.

"I'll put the lot of you on a charge if you're not going to behave," he said imperiously in that sing-song Welsh lilt of his. "That wouldn't be a very good start to your military career, now, would it?"

So any clashes between us would have to take place out of sight.

Spencer was calling me 'Little Man' or 'Mann-*ling*', so I started calling him 'Mary' instead of Mario back. Verbal abuse between the two groups soon escalated to minor pranks. When the shower went ice-cold on me one day, I made sure it went boiling hot on Spencer the next. Another time I got Terry to linger behind and rough up the Italian kid's regimentally tidy bed-locker, so that he failed the inspection after breakfast. In retaliation, soon after, I found 'wanker' carved into the toecaps of my brightly shined army boots ('wan' on one and 'ker' on the other). Luckily, I could easily afford the cost of a new pair, but the battle lines were definitely being drawn.

Of the things we had to do, familiarising ourselves with weapons was by far the most thrilling. Next best was the week of adventure training, when we did rock climbing, abseiling, potholing and kayaking. But most days were just a grind, usually starting with physical fitness exercises for at least an hour; circuit training, for example; often followed by a 6 kilometre march wearing a 20 kilogram backpack and carrying our assault rifles. Then we might be either in a classroom, or out and about learning survival and fieldcraft skills, first aid, stripping, cleaning and reassembling weapons and other complex bits of kit. The only way to deal with it was with determined enthusiasm and a strong degree of self-discipline. If you had a sense of humour, that helped too; as, of course, did the mateship, the camaraderie. We had no weekends off, only evenings and a few hours to ourselves on Sundays, so the fourteen weeks went swiftly by.

Spencer continued to be a pest throughout. The days were tough, and quite often we were too weary to leave the camp in the evenings, but occasionally the five of us went in to town. Mary and his mates could usually be found drinking in the 'Bugle and Drum', which was the nearest pub to the camp but also probably the dreariest, so we went to a much better appointed hostelry, the 'King's Arms', instead. The name reminds me that we all had to sing 'God Save the *King*', and 'Send *him* victorious, happy and glorious...' rather than *her* when it came to the National Anthem.

One day, after I'd upset him somehow, poured salt in his soup or insulted his mother, I can't remember, Spencer and his gang burst into the pub we thought of as our place, and invited the five of us out to the car park for a punch-up. I thought it would be just me and him facing off, but as soon as we were out the door, his cowardly lot jumped us from behind. They outnumbered us by one, of course, and we hadn't done much unarmed combat training yet, so it was a pretty amateurish affair as Blue, Vijay, and Mack gave good accounts of themselves. Al used his size and strength to simply hold onto two of the others, which left me free to best Mario. My boxing training standing me in good stead, I gave him a right thumping, and left him with a peachy black eye to show off on parade the following morning; but he was a sore loser and before we were done, glinting in the street light, I could see a stiletto clasped at the ready in his outstretched hand.

Rather than stepping away, feeling surprisingly cool in the face of danger, I waited for his lunge, instinctively stepped aside, and trapped his right arm under my left shoulder, sweeping his right leg away with my left foot while advancing and leaning my weight against his left shoulder with my right hand. This was a judo move I'd perfected. Down he went, with me following, holding fast to his right sleeve, grasping and twisting his wrist until he dropped the knife, before tugging his hand up the middle of his back in a painful lock, at the same time grinding his head against the tarmac.

Back in the pub, someone must have called the rozzers because we soon heard sirens approaching, and this was the obvious signal for us to scarper back to the base. Letting Mario go, I banged his head once more into the ground before collecting his pointy little dagger from where it had fallen. To his credit, when questioned, he told no-one who had hit him. Neither, to mine, did I betray that he had drawn a lethal weapon on a fellow recruit, but it did make a nice souvenir.

A few days later, we were all on field patrol, an ambush-training exercise over hill sides and in woodland, using live ammunition for possibly the first time outside the range. Suddenly, I was rugby-tackled hard to the ground; and at the same moment a live round struck the trunk of a fir tree above me, exactly where my head had been just a split-second before. Spotting Spencer about to take the shot, Al had just saved my life.

The creep denied it, of course, saying that if he'd meant to hit me he wouldn't have missed. Dai Morgan came over, then told the Sergeant, who spoke to an officer; but when Big Al was asked if he was sure of what he'd seen, he hesitated, and I told him best to leave it, for this was something we would clearly have to deal with on our own. At least I felt sure that my nemesis wouldn't try the same thing again in a hurry. That would have been too suspicious for even him to laugh off.

At least once a week, we ventured out onto the assault course. It was something of a grown-up version of the one we had at school, with a load of obstacles that you had to crawl through or under, wade through, climb or jump over, swing on a rope to get past, and stuff like that; so I hatched a plan to ditch Mad Mario for good.

One of his boys had an unlikely name for a soldier: Cameron Makepeace, whose voice would have told you he was from a long line of Englishmen, until you opened your eyes. In fact, this coffee-coloured youth came from Jamaica at an early age, and was raised on an inner London housing estate. He probably joined up to escape the dismal gangland culture of those parts, with its county lines drug distribution, knife crime, occasional shootings, universal disregard for private property, and contempt for any laws designed to protect shopkeepers and other citizens from theft; but I never got the chance to ask him about it. I did, though, clock that Spencer was giving him almost as bad a time as he was me, calling him the 'N' word and such, constantly teasing him, ordering him about and generally treating him like a slave. No doubt young Cam put up with it because it seemed better to be in with the bully than to cross or oppose him. I almost felt sorry for him.

One night in the canteen on the base, where we sometimes spent the evenings, I overheard Mario, trying to be funny, say to one of his henchmen when he thought Cameron out of earshot, having sent him to fetch more beers, that he liked black people.

"Yes. I do... I like them," he repeated for emphasis, in his distinctive John Lennon accent. "I think everyone should own one!"

It didn't get any laughs, and it was a sorry mistake, because Makepeace was already back, having left his wallet in his jacket on the chair, and I'm sure he heard every word. To my surprise, though, other than aim a deadly glare of pure hatred at the back of the madman's head, he did nothing, simply turned away and left the room. Having caught the venom in that look, I decided to follow.

Outside, in the gloom of the night, a picture of rage when I got to him, I could see how hard the Jamaican was struggling to contain his emotions, tears glinting in his eyes, clenching and unclenching his fists; so I decided to wait a few moments, catching up alongside him

146

only when he was calmer and had started sloping off towards the hut.

"You might be able to help me," I said, deliberately calmly and quietly. "Help me... And you could also be helping yourself."

He was reluctant when I spoke to him that first time, telling me to get lost and leave him alone, but I tackled him again the next day and told him what I was proposing. This time he listened but still rejected the idea, saying it would surely risk ending his military career. I didn't think a court martial likely but let it go for the time being. I knew he would come around to my way of thinking sooner or later, especially as, on the third occasion, I added a five-hundred pound bribe. After all, what was such money to me?

One of the toughest of the assault course obstacles at Catterick was the 3.75 metre wall. No-one could get over it without help, so we always went at it in teams of three. A man stood at the bottom and laced hands, forming a step, then in turn the other two putting a foot in the step were hoisted up until they could reach the top of the wall to pull themselves up and get into position, hanging back downwards, arms outstretched to catch the others, one at a time. The last man, still at the bottom, had to walk a few paces away, turn, hurl himself at the wall and try to sort of run up it, arms held upwards to be caught in the grip of the first two. Cameron's job, I told him, was to make sure he was on the wall first, with Mad Mary coming up last.

In the event, it went like clockwork. Makepeace and his buddy got into position at the top as Spencer approached. When he leapt upward, Cam somehow tugged him sideways, hauling him with great strength out of the other man's grip, dumping him hard and awkwardly back down where he came from, and in such a way that, as I planned and hoped, there was serious damage to his ankle.

Spencer had to be stretchered off. His fracture, we later heard, needed surgery and the insertion of a metal plate. The aggressive fool was permanently removed from our lives, and we were never found out. No repercussions ensued.

Twenty-Three

When we were young, Charlie often took us to 'The Rec', a municipal playground, where she would sit us at either end of the see-saw. I, of course, delighted in kicking myself high in the air, but Raul (as he still was in those far off days) refused sullenly to play the game. Charlie had repeatedly to lean on my side of the tipping-point to keep the mechanics in motion, usually until my uncooperative brother decided to walk off and ride alone on the roundabout or sit on a solitary swing.

The see-saw tipping-point of global catastrophe arrived at around the same time as Al and I joined the army, but it was fairly well hidden. (We didn't *see*... Nobody *saw*..!) The most decisive and irreversible changes took place in Siberia, Alaska and much of Canada's Yukon, where there was tundra, material essentially consisting of vegetation and other organisms that had remained frozen for at least ten thousand years, some of it for a couple of million. Fifteen hundred billion tons of carbon in total were said to have been locked up in the Arctic but, as a result of global warming, with disastrous consequences, this living matter gradually began to awaken.

Climate change, as everybody knew, was driven by rising levels of carbon dioxide, methane, and other 'greenhouse gases' in the earth's atmosphere, trapping energy from the sun. Valiant attempts were made to reduce fossil fuel use, attain 'carbon-neutral' emissions, and so stabilize the planet's temperature. Unfortunately, all those efforts were in vain, firstly because of human selfishness, but mainly because of the tundra. Once it started melting, because of the vast amounts of carbon released, all hell was bound to break loose.

Nature was biding her time, mind you. She took a couple of decades to reveal the full effect of this massive thaw, but eventually all the ice in the world melted; from both polar icecaps, the great Greenland ice-sheet, from all the mountaintops... everywhere! This, in turn, accelerated the process, because the white ice had been a good reflector of solar energy, batting it back into space; but with the ice gone, the darker-coloured Arctic and Antarctic oceans absorbed that energy as heat, warming the globe even more; so the melt speeded up, and sea levels rose beyond all previously predicted levels. Hence the flood. I stayed in the army for the first twelve of those twenty years, which massively helped me prepare for who I needed to become.

When it happened, Paul was still at school, of course, but both Carol and Charlie came to our passing out parade at Catterick. They drove up in Charlie's new petrol-driven Audi saloon, Carol's electric Kia being deemed too risky, the recharging infrastructure still being unreliable for long journeys. Afterwards the three of us drove south, near Nottingham, where we were booked into a hotel. Al had decided to return by train to spend a bit of time with Ada, as we only had nine days before joining the regiment for Phase Two training. If I'd known what was going to happen to Carol within the year, I'd have spent all of it with her. But we don't know when we're going to die, do we, any of us? If there is a God, his design for humanity was flawed in this respect, don't you think? Wouldn't life be much easier if we knew exactly how long we had left?

As it was, Carol and I enjoyed a terrific reunion in that hotel room. She marvelled at my improved physique and stamina.

"You've got muscles on your muscles now, dear heart!" she said. 'And I swear John Thomas has grown... We'll have to call him 'Sir John' from now on."

Lady Jane was as sweet and welcoming as ever.

During the later stages of Phase One, every recruit was interviewed and assessed for allocation to a regiment. Al, Blue, Mack, Vijay and I requested to stay together. Happily, that idea was supported, and we were all recruited into The Princess of Wales Royal Regiment, known as 'The Tigers'. As a flexible fighting infantry regiment, this suited us perfectly, especially as all its recruits were taken from London and the southern counties.

In 1966, the Queen's Regiment was formed by amalgamating the Queen's Royal Surrey Regiment, the Queen's Own Buffs (the Royal Kent Regiment), the Royal Sussex Regiment, and the Middlesex Regiment (Duke of Cambridge's Own). Then, in 1992, the Queen's Regiment was further joined with the Royal Hampshires to form the PWRR, the Tigers. All this meant we had a long and glorious history, holding for example the earliest battle honour in the British Army, from the Tangier campaign of 1662 - 1680. The Princess of Wales is counted the senior English infantry regiment and, to my delight, our forerunners were with Marlborough at Blenheim in 1704 and the three subsequent battles of that illustrious campaign. More recently the Tigers were in Iraq in 2004, where Private Johnson Beharry famously won the Victoria Cross for his heroics, twice saving the lives of his commander and comrades under intense attack, despite suffering a severe head injury on the second occasion. It was a tradition to be proud of.

There are three Tigers battalions of at least 700 men each. The five of us completed Phase Two training with 3rd Battalion stationed in London. We then spent time with 1st Battalion in Germany, a motorised force using Warrior armoured fighting vehicles; an exciting time for us, learning to drive and operate its powerful mounted weaponry. Later, we were deployed to the regiment's 2nd Battalion in Cyprus for a lengthier tour of duty.

The 2nd battalion was pure infantry. When we had to go anywhere, we were usually taken by air; by plane or by helicopter; which occasionally meant an exciting low-level parachute drop. The Tigers had been in Cyprus for a long time, currently alongside the 1st Battalion Duke of Lancaster's regiment, split between the bases at Akrotiri and Dhekelia in the south of the island, one to the west, the other about 100 kilometres away in the east. There was important Navy and Air Force presence on the island too.

The British first leased Cyprus from the Ottoman Empire in 1878. When the Ottoman Turks joined Germany in the First World War, we annexed it; which is a polite way if saying we simply decided it was ours. In 1960 the country became independent and joined the Commonwealth, with the stipulation that the two military encampments remain forever as 'Sovereign Base Areas', rather like Gibraltar and the Falkland Islands. Unfortunately, the Turkish government had other ideas and invaded Cyprus in 1974, occupying the northern part, leaving only the south to the resident Greek population. Given that the island is only about 45 miles from north to south, and 120 miles from west to east, this has continued to make life tough for the locals ever since. Our presence there did at least seem to be keeping things stable.

The real importance for Britain, though, concerned Cyprus's key position at the eastern end of the Mediterranean. It formed a base for vital intelligence gathering and necessary military operations throughout North Africa and the Middle East, playing a considerable part in the Iraq and Afghanistan campaigns, for example, also in Syria against the rebel forces of ISIL.

In a way, me and the boys regretted that nothing of the sort was happening while we were there. We just trained good and hard every day. I became a specialist marksman, a sniper in other words. Vijay followed up our first-aid training and became a combat medic. Mack became a logistician, which means it was his job to make sure we had stuff, essentials like food and ammunition, medical supplies and the like. Al specialised in explosives and demolition. Blue trained in communications, and we were all 'assault pioneers', so we made a competent unit.

A 'Fire Team' in the Tigers was a unit of four men; three Privates led by a Lance Corporal; so we had to be split up when still all Privates. Later, when I was promoted, Mack stayed with his original team leader and the others joined me. It wasn't too bad, because two fire teams make a Section, led by a Corporal, so we stayed close, and it all remained pretty matey.

It was hot in Cyprus for much of the year, and we were there to acclimatize, to be ready for operations in other hot countries in the region. We were also sent to Belize for a lengthy period of training in jungle combat. The army had a school there dedicated to that. I have to say, I loved all the exotic locations and the adventure, which probably saved me from madness.

It was while we were on Cyprus that Covid-2 struck the UK. Within weeks, I learned that Carol was dead. I didn't believe it at first. It was too incredible and I thought it must be a mistake. She and mother had been out to Cyprus for a few days only about six weeks earlier; but when she didn't answer her phone for my weekly call, I rang Charlie, who cried while trying to break the news gently. Ignoring her sobs, I told her it wasn't funny to be making up stories like that, got angry with her and ended the call; but the news of the new epidemic came through and doubts crept into my mind.

I spoke to Vijay about it. As a medic, he had already been briefed, and he too tried to prepare me for the possibility that my darling love was gone; but it was all too much. I remember visiting a bar near the base that evening, but have no idea how I got back to my bunk. I had a skinful, Al said later, picked a fight with a chap from the Lancasters, beat him silly, then took a pasting from a couple of his mates. Al had to carry me home. The corporal took one look at my bruises the next day, before telling me this was unacceptable behaviour for a Tiger, and I was lucky he didn't put me on a charge. Demotion was a real possibility, the risk of which continued during the ensuing few days because my conduct was well below par. Luckily, the lads kept an eye out for me and took up the slack where necessary. When I finally emerged from my slump, though, I remained fiercely angry. The boys said I definitely hardened after that. All I remember is that I was itching for a fight, for some proper military combat. Fortunately, it came pretty soon.

Absolutely typically, the army train you for a hot, dry climate then send you somewhere cold and wet, in our case Estonia, where it seemed to be raining all the time. This is the northernmost of the three Baltic States, all three of which were part of the Soviet Union until it broke up in 1991. It's home to a population of less than one-and-a-half million people; and it's where a battle group from 2nd Battalion was sent after a build-up of Russian aggression on its border.

After what had happened in the Crimea in 2014, NATO had set up its 'Enhanced Forward Presence' in Lithuania, Latvia and Estonia, beefing it up again after the unprovoked Russian invasion of Ukraine in 2022. That situation was still rumbling on, following an uneasy armistice, but the signs were that Russia's ageing dictator, hell bent on overturning democratic independence and regaining control of former Soviet states, had already begun a new campaign further north. There were said to be over a hundred thousand of his troops now massing on the borders of the Baltic States and Poland, having marched unhindered right through Belarus. Now the Russian army was opposed by US forces in Poland, German troops in Lithuania, and Canadians in Latvia. We were to join the Queen's Royal Hussars, a tank regiment, and motorised infantry of the Royal Welsh regiment, both already well-established in Estonia, to make sure that President 'Pukin' stayed where he belonged.

When the time came, we flew to the Estonian capital, Tallinn, and then moved on about sixty miles east to the Tapa Army Base for a week's familiarisation and training in local conditions. Eventually, we took up stations about a hundred and fifty miles further south-east, near the Russian border along the River Narva, just north of the Canadians in Latvia.

The cursed Ruskies, we discovered irritatingly, seldom adhere to any rules. There was no official state of war between Russia and Estonia, and they had not yet attempted invasion, claiming only to be on military exercises and *not* preparing for an assault on another sovereign state; but they said exactly the same in 2022 and then marched right into Ukraine. Furthermore, by the time we got there, the bullies seemed to be trying to soften us up.

Hitting civilian as well as military targets inside Estonia, there were barrages of assault rockets every day. Army intelligence told us that the Ivans had mobile rocket launchers that tended to move around and dart in close to the border to make their strikes, usually in groups of five or six. We were safe enough in our trenches, but this seemed uncalled for and demanded retaliation. They were getting too big for their boots, and couldn't be permitted the leeway to grow confident; but our high-ups had a problem: what form could reprisals take without risking a full-scale war? That's where we came in.

Light infantry; fast, fierce, flexible and deadly; that was the Tigers. We could operate with such secrecy and stealth behind enemy lines in a way that could be completely denied later. At staff headquarters, someone drew up a plan. First, the sappers dug a couple of tunnels under the river, emerging beyond the Russian trenches, big enough for us to run through at a comfortable crouch. Then, accurate GPS mapping of the rocket launcher groups was undertaken from satellite observations, so we had a clear fix on them. Next, we waited for two things: fine weather, and for the Russian rocket-men to make camp close enough to the far end of one of our tunnels. When everything came together, we went in, setting off shortly after midnight.

There were two sections together, four fire teams led by a 2nd Lieutenant, Mick Harry. We liked Mick, and trusted him because he'd been a private soldier once, had risen through the ranks, and had been picked on merit for officer training at Sandhurst. There was no question other than that he would lead us from the front.

Fully camouflaged, we made it through the tunnel without incident, emerging into the darkness of a small forest clearing. There was only a sliver of moon, and scudding clouds ensured that even the dim moonlight barely penetrated through the branches to the ground around us. No matter, for we had night-vision goggles, and the lieutenant had a GPS tracker. It was three miles to the makeshift Russian camp. They, too, had picked a small forest clearing in which to park up and bed down, and must have felt safe there because there were only a couple on guard. Mick took down the first from behind, deftly slitting the booger's throat with his army knife, making barely a sound; then he indicated that I should do likewise to the other guard, forty paces away.

Mack and I went together, working our way as silently as possible around the clearing's perimeter. Did I hesitate at that fatal moment? Perhaps... It is an awesome thing to take a man's life for the first time. But if I did, it was only for a micro-second, for in no time he too was down, a lifeless, scarlet-stained corpse lying crumpled at my feet. A knife is a beautiful thing. Death was clean and swift. The poor fellow was dispatched in an instant, and never knew anything about it. I remember momentarily thinking that was how I'd like to go.

Once the guards were neutralised, the other men sleeping in their bivouacs were similarly put soundlessly to sleep, given their final marching orders, by the rest of the troop. Al and two other demolition experts then set to work on the six rocket launchers standing there, waiting until the rest of us were well clear before blowing them sky high.

The following night, we made another sortie. Unfortunately this time we were not so lucky. The Russians were encamped in another clearing, but this time had four guards posted and seemed much more alert. When Mick tried taking out the first, he resisted and raised the alarm with a cry, the last sound he was to make. Another guard took a shot and caught our brave lieutenant in the calf of his left leg. The fire-fight that followed was soon over, for we were all over them in a hurry, killing most, taking prisoner the two who were slowest getting out of their camp beds. There were no more casualties on our side, and the demolition boys soon had their big explosive bonfire going. But the problem was getting Mick home.

Vijay patched him up, stopped the bleeding with a tourniquet and gave him a injection for the pain; then Al and I took turns to carry him, while our packs and weapons were redistributed among the others. Mick was heavy. Having fainted, he was a deadweight; also, the terrain was awkward so it was slow going, but we made it back to base and he was helicoptered forward to Tapa for immediate surgery. For some reason, I was picked out and got 'Mentioned in Dispatches' for our night's work, which is the army's way of praising a person without actually giving them a medal. You don't even get extra pay. But who was I to complain?

We tried repeating the exercise just once more, three or four nights later, when the skies were again clear. Mick was replaced by Lieutenant Montague 'Monty' Ferguson-Jones, a different kettle of fish altogether, coming from a long line of Generals and Brigadiers, but sadly lacking in hereditary moral fibre. When we went in, he put a Sergeant in the lead with the GPS device, and stayed well to the rear. Naturally, we expected the Russians had got wise by now to our little game, and were taking extra care. It was a great relief that they hadn't yet found our well-hidden tunnel exit, but they had augmented their defences. There must have been thirty heavily-armed infantrymen guarding the rocket launchers when we eventually came across them. With surprise on our side, despite being outnumbered, I still fancied our odds. That's what the Tigers were for. But 'Monty' clearly thought he knew better, and ordered us not to engage. He was probably right. The small gains we might achieve were hardly worth risking any lives for. Nevertheless, as we retreated, it felt like a dismal defeat. At least I later had the opportunity to serve my country and the greater good by using my skills as a sniper. The Russians had started taking random pot-shots at us, so it was only fair and reasonable for us to return the favour with interest. With laser sights and extremely powerful telescopes on our rifles, it was hard to miss, even at considerable distances.

There in the trenches, it all felt strangely like being back in World War I, fighting in the fields of Flanders. Mack Cotton was the first to remark on it, saying his great-grandfather had been injured at Vimy Ridge in 1917, winning the Military Cross for his valiant efforts leading a mule train carrying ammunition repeatedly to the front line under fire. Remarkably, the old feller survived the hostilities and lived to be nearly a hundred.

We had been in Estonia for several months. Winter was drawing on and the temperature dropping uncomfortably, when suddenly it was over. We woke up one day and the Russians had gone, pulled back twenty miles initially, and then eighty percent of their entire force vanishing completely, buggering off back where they came from. We remained cautious, but a few weeks later, Ferguson-Jones broke the good news. "We're on our way back to Cyprus, Men! I thought you might like to know."

Officially, the Russian President had died suddenly of a heart attack. Unofficially, the word was, he'd been assassinated, either in a strike by the Americans; which seemed unlikely, given how well protected he always was; or by his own people, maybe using his favourite nerve poison, Novichok. As reported by the plucky independent Moscow television news channel 'Rain', which had been under a ban, there was a new revolution in Russia, a peaceful one this time. Estonia, Latvia, Lithuania, Ukraine, Europe and everywhere else was at last going to feel safe.

This was great news for us all; for everyone except, that is, those of us who simply wanted to fight. In Estonia, killing Russians, I was happy for the first time since Carol died; so must admit I wanted conflict to continue, not peace. However, people being what they are; hell-bent on taking land and its resources from others, greedy for wealth and possessions, intolerant of those who are different in kind cr hold to opposing beliefs; another chance to practice my deadly skills would surely come along eventually. I simply had to be patient.

Twenty-Four

My nephew, Hugs, when he was about twelve, asked me what's it like to kill a man. At first I prevaricated, supposedly trying to protect him; told him it was hard to know if you had actually been the one responsible in the middle of a gun battle when everyone was shooting at the same targets; or, similarly, to be sure of a hit when firing a sniper rifle from a distance of half-a-mile or more. But I obviously wasn't convincing because he didn't believe me. "But you must know, Uncle Freddie," he kept saying, "If not you, then your buddies will have killed... I want to know what it's like... Please!"

You had to admire his persistence; so, in the end, I told him it wasn't pleasant but that it had to be done. The truth is, I was lucky it was so dark when I cut the throat of that Russian soldier, my first kill. It helped that I didn't get a proper look at his face, nor of any of my sniper victims, which would have made it harder. What I hid from myself for a long time, and certainly never revealed to Huggie, was the disgust I felt. I got cold sweats and literally vomited while in the woods, out of sight of my comrades as they watched those rocket-launchers explode and burn that night, and there was a bitter taste in my mouth as we marched smartly back to the tunnel. But the next day, when we were attacked and the Lieutenant was shot, it was easier, much easier, as it wasn't so damned cold-blooded. On that occasion, it was a them-or-us situation; and it wasn't going to be us.

One day, back on Cyprus and in the barracks with some down time, our conversation turned to much the same subject. We had, of course, had numerous lectures during training from various padres on the so-called 'Just War Theory', always invoked to allow Christians to by-pass the sixth commandment: 'Thou shalt not kill'. According to the religious establishment, any war must be declared by a lawful authority, for a just cause, and with good intention. It should only be embarked on when all other ways of resolving the problem had been tried, and when there was a reasonable chance of success. Obviously, it was fine to wage war in self-defence. In Estonia, we were getting ready for a preventive war against a tyrant about to attack. Some theorists also said it was okay to go to war to punish a guilty enemy; and all of this seemed perfectly fine to me, but Vijay had another slant on it that I found peculiar but interesting.

Although not religious himself, he said he came from a Hindu family. One of their holy books was called the Bhagavad Gita, which translates as 'The Song of God'. I always thought the Hindu people had hundreds of gods, including strange ones with elephant heads, or in the form of a monkey, which they do, but Vijay said above them there is really only one formless, impersonal godhead known as Brahman. All the other gods are Brahman in a different form ('avatars' they're called, like the movie), and the Gita is about one of these god-alikes called 'Krishna'.

I'd heard about the Hare Krishna sect, with their orange robes, shaven heads and topknots; the bunch who used to parade down Oxford Street singing and dancing to flutes and tambourine music that Charlie thought wonderful and H dismissed as ignorant twits; but had no idea that the same Krishna was mixed up in a war, for it turns out that the Gita is part of a much longer epic tale from ancient India called the Mahabharata, which tells of a long period of conflict between two families. 'Maha' means great, and the story is about the great King Bharata and his descendants, notably Dhritarashtra and his son Duryodhana. On the other side are the five sons of Pandu, Dhritarashtra's nephews, the Pandavas, one of whom, the middle brother, is called Arjuna. The Gita is mainly made up of a conversation between Krishna and Arjuna. I didn't really grasp all the long Indian names, so it was good that I only had to remember these two.

So, Vijay tells us, the Gita starts with Arjuna in his chariot set between the two great armies on the eve of a big battle. Krishna has shape-shifted into the guise of Arjuna's charioteer, and Arjuna is saying that because he has many friends and relatives on both sides, he does not want to fight. Krishna has to persuade him. He does not reveal himself as a god at first, which must have put him at a disadvantage. When I pointed out that the idea of a senior officer in our army taking instruction from his driver was pretty laughable, Vijay wasn't deterred. He said that as a story it was an illustrative one, not meant to be literally true, and to emphasize the point he added that, like in many a good fairy tale, for the duration of the protagonists' conversation, time stood completely still. So I let him get to the point; which seemed to be Krishna telling Arjuna he had to fight because he was a warrior by birth and profession and it was his destiny.

"Everything comes from Brahman, which is existence itself, and everything returns to Brahman," Krishna said.

To explain further, Vijay read out the section about 'Atman', the name for the essence of the Godhead that is within every being:

Bodies are said to die, but That which possesses the body is eternal. It cannot be limited or destroyed, therefore you must fight.

Know this Atman, unborn, undying, never ceasing, never beginning, deathless, birth-less, unchanging for ever. How can it die the death of the body?

Knowing It is birth-less, knowing It is deathless, knowing It endless, for ever unchanging, dream not you do the deed of the killer, dream not the power is yours to command it.

Not wounded by weapons, not burned by fire, not dried by the wind, not wetted by water: such is the Atman.

Vijay continued with his explanation, telling us that if you kill someone, or if you are killed, that's just 'karma', which is like payback. Do someone a favour and good fortune will smile on you. Do something wicked and bad luck will equally be yours. At least, that's how I understood it at first; but then Vijay explained that Hindus believed in reincarnation, and that each soul has countless lives in which eventually to become perfect and pure, whereupon they finally achieved 'nirvana'; a bit like the Christian heaven; at which point they are reunited with and reabsorbed into Brahman. Each life gives a person the chance to either make progress or to fall backwards on this lengthy conveyor belt towards bliss; and this meant there could ultimately be no 'bad' karma, as any misfortune could be turned into an opportunity for improved self-mastery, for the development of wisdom, compassion and virtue.

This was all a bit like listening to my brother with his quasi-mystical chit-chat, but for some reason I didn't argue with Vijay. I'm not sure he believed in it anyway, and I was thinking of young Raffa who seemed to remember his previous life, so could not completely discount the elaborate story as total hogwash. Strangely, perhaps, I even found it comforting; and I was not alone. Al, Mack and Blue Wattis were listening too, and each in turn admitted having had qualms about killing. We'd never even spoken on the subject before; had, in fact, felt entirely discouraged from doing so by our army superiors, as if they'd no conscience on the subject and therefore neither should we. But so many soldiers suffered post traumatic stress after seeing combat, or got hooked on drugs and alcohol, and not all of it was about what had happened to their mates getting injured and killed. Some of it, surely, was guilt. The Arjuna story helped to take that away. It wasn't our fault people died. It was God's.

With a slightly shamefaced sort of apology, Al even admitted that the first time he was called on to shoot at the enemy at close quarters, on that second night raid in Estonia, he deliberately aimed over everyone's heads, making certain he took no-one's life. That was common among new recruits, I'd read somewhere, so I said not to worry about it.

"Next time, though, you big oaf," I said, "Bloody well aim to kill!"

We relaxed then, and you could tell everyone felt better, because I

158

remember how we went on affectionately teasing Al and laughing at his discomfort. Vijay began telling us how the story ended, until Blue interrupted by eagerly raising his hand, as he had done once in a classroom to ask the training officer a question.

"What is it, Wattis?" the impatient fellow had replied.

Seeing Blue become flustered and tongue-tied, the rest of us had begun creasing up. Now Vijay was echoing that humourless instructor.

"What is it, Wattis?" he said in an exaggeratedly slow and comical manner, all his 'W's sounding like 'V's.

"Vat-Is-It... Vatt-Is? Vatt-Is. Vat-It-Is...? Speak up! Speak up!"

We could barely stop laughing, and Blue went red in the face.

The battle lasted eighteen days, by the way. Krishna did persuade Arjuna to fight, and he was on the winning side, as Duryodhana perished and it was a complete victory for the Pandavas; a bit of a cheat, if you ask me though, for having a god come down to help them. But it was only a story, and we were shortly once more to encounter real life in all its painful glory, off to a truly hot country this time. And it was hot in every sense, for we lost one of our precious number there, and the rest of us too nearly died.

*

As I still remembered some geography, it fell to me to tell the others about the so-called 'Horn of Africa', which gets its name because that's where the continent juts out sharply eastwards into the Indian Ocean beneath the Gulf of Aden at the southern end of the Red Sea. The territory consists of Eritrea, the Red Sea coast as far as the border with Sudan in the north, the small port city-state of Djibouti to the south, then Somalia which reaches to the tip of the horn and overlaps further southwards to the border with Kenya. Landlocked and nestled inside those three countries, bordered to the west by Sudan and South Sudan and to the south also by Kenya, is Ethiopia, the northernmost province of which is called Tigray.

It was easy enough with maps in front of us to explain the lay of the land, but the history of this deeply unsettled region seemed important too, so I continued my briefing to the lads, telling them that, like Scotland years ago with its clans, like North and South America with their native tribes, like Australia and its Aborigine people, as too in the holy land of the old testament and many other places, Africa was originally populated by fiercely loyal social groupings, each with their own language and customs, each eager to establish, maintain, and extend their homeland territory, ready likewise to defend it at all costs

This land, to which they felt a truly sacred bond, was their teacher in many ways. Managing it sustainably and reverentially gave their lives meaning. The native plants and animals gave them building material, clothing, medicine and food. Landmarks - mountains, valleys, rivers, lakes, plains and forests - often the abodes of their gods, also filled their dreams and symbolised intimate connections with their ancestors. Parent figures were thought of as living pioneers going before them, rather than historical figures that were dead and gone forever, ashes to ashes, and dust to dust.

Periods of peace were often interrupted by occasional large scale wars and more frequent smaller skirmishes. Blood feuds arose between clans or tribes that could only be settled by some more or less equitable form of payback, often negotiated almost dispassionately by the elders on either side. The stealing of young girls for wives was also, of course, commonplace. The weapons in use; bows and arrows, swords, daggers, spears and axes; ensured that the slaughter remained fairly circumscribed. Things began to change, though, when adventurous Europeans got themselves in on the act.

I remembered that the Portuguese discovered Mogadishu, for example, the capital port-city of Somalia, in 1517. They benefitted from the trade in spices arriving from India by sea, as well as gold and ivory brought overland from the African interior. Other nationalities soon followed; Turks from the Ottoman Empire, for instance, bringing with them muskets and cannons. Stone walls were put up as the city had to be fortified, and lethal firepower fell readily into the hands of local tribesmen with destructive results.

"I can see where this is going," Blue piped up at this point.

"Yes," I agreed. "The old formula, 'an eye for an eye and a tooth for a tooth'; taking back no more than has been stolen, a life for a life in other words; helps keep the bloodshed between naturally hostile clan groups within acceptable limits... But it's hard to keep count of the number of lives you're owed by rivals when the killing becomes widespread and indiscriminate. When your kinsman has died from a bullet, who's to say with certainty who pulled the trigger, and who therefore owes you a life. Centuries of stability were undermined quite literally in a gunpowder flash."

Religions, of course, compounded the problem big time. Ethiopians, mentioned in the New Testament, became Christians soon after the crucifixion of Jesus Christ. Islam arrived in Arabia in the 7th century and spread outwards, reaching Africa's horn in no time. Neither religion completely extinguished the spiritual traditions, full of ghosts and ancestor worship, that preceded them. To give an example, Christian missionaries in one African territory were delighted with their success in engaging a local tribe, and welcomed them to regular Sunday worship in the enlarged, open-sided native building they used for a church, but were not so happy when a mother was found grieving after her newly-born twins disappeared. A pre-existing superstition in those parts had it that, when twins were born, one of them would likely be possessed by a wicked demon; the problem being that no-one could tell which was the good twin and which the evil one so, to get round the dilemma, both would be taken at night into nearby forest or scrubland and either killed outright or simply left to die, either from exposure, thirst and starvation, or more likely at the mercy of whatever hungry wild creatures came by. As a twin myself, I found that story quite chilling.

Perpetual tension between Christian and Muslim factions continued to play itself out in the Horn of Africa. Unsurprisingly, things got even more confused, and peace seemed completely elusive throughout the region, once 'civilised' people from the north began settling, drawing their maps and dividing up the continent between the so-called great powers, their arbitrary straight lines either dividing and driving asunder tribal people who had lived happily together for centuries, helping to sustain each other, or forcing together different groups that had been mortal enemies for as long as anyone could remember. This was a recipe for bloodshed and agony, as we found out to our cost.

In preparation for our next deployment, I told the lads how Italy had taken control of Somalia in 1905, and that *Italian* Somaliland' existed until we British took it from them during the Second World War; our governors, with startling originality, then renaming the country *British* Somaliland'. Independence arrived in 1960. The new President was assassinated in 1969. A military coup followed, and an army commander, General Barre, became head of the Somali Democratic Republic.

A real despot, Barre immediately began arresting former civilian government officials, banning political parties, disbanding parliament and the Supreme Court, and suspending the constitution. His repressive measures became increasingly unpopular to the extent that twenty or so years later, the country was being wracked by a brutal civil war.

Part of the problem was poverty. The state was essentially bankrupt, and this because there was no more trade in either spices or ivory. Furthermore, all the gold leaving Africa departed through different channels and by-passed Mogadishu to avoid the taxes, which had become monstrously high. In addition, there was widespread famine, the early effects of climate change causing drought in the region, so the people were poor and unhappy. Worse, of course, in huge numbers, they were dying, thus alerting international aid agencies and the United Nations.

There were several factions involved in the civil conflict. Rather than muskets and cannons, both sides now had the most efficient modern military equipment and weapons. Fighting was often fierce either side of the 'Green Line' that artificially divided Mogadishu into north and south, such that the destruction of the city's infrastructure was massive, worsening the already bleak conditions of its citizens. Schools had to close. Hospitals were badly damaged by shellfire. Medical equipment and supplies were hard to find. Furthermore, the militia bosses on both sides of the internal conflict soon realised that aid agencies brought food and materials they could use; also that the surplus could be sold on for US dollars on the international markets or, better still, traded directly for guns and ammunition. Over time, they took about 80 per cent of what Oxfam, Christian Aid and others brought in, and this was the scenario prompting the United Nations so-called 'peacekeeping' mission of 1991, aimed at providing food and medical assistance to those in need. Unfortunately, overwhelmed by the situation, especially by the interference and total lack of local cooperation, that initiative failed.

The response, two years later, was UNOSOM II - the 2nd United Nations Operation in Somalia - involving 28,000 troops and support personnel, mainly from the USA. Here was a prime example of 'mission-shift', the aim being switched from delivering aid, towards establishing democracy and restoring government, setting a dangerous precedent for the kind of mission we were destined for some years later.

UN forces swiftly took the seaport, the airport and the surrounding area to establish a secure base; but the Somali people did not take kindly to their intervention. Growing hostile, they began showing their mounting displeasure to the extent of killing and injuring UN soldiers and murdering western journalists. Finally, in October of 1993, the fateful 'Battle of Mogadishu' took place, during which two US Sikorsky helicopters were brought down in the city by Al-Qaeda trained men from a rebel militia's camp. Fierce fighting ensued throughout the night, and it took a US armoured convoy to fight their way through to the survivors and effect a rescue. At the end of the abortive operation, there were a total of 19 American dead and 73 wounded. Countless Somali people, naturally, perished as well.

I remember watching the riveting movie 'Black Hawk Down' about all this when I was a teenager. However, by portraying the Americans as gung-ho heroes from start to finish, it may have glossed over some of the reality. In fact, the whole thing was a diabolical catastrophe, soon resulting in the United Nations pulling out altogether. Furthermore, fear of repeating any similar kind of battle also led to US reluctance to get further involved in similar types of conflict, with significant knock-on effects when the Rwandan genocide began about six months later. What happened there had a significant impact, too, on subsequent events throughout the region. We had to sit through a briefing, and watch a film about that, before we got involved with another United Nations peace-keeping mission in Africa's troubled Horn. The Tigers were sending a big detachment; so that's when Al, Mack, Vijay, Terry Wattis and me exchanged khaki helmets and navy berets for the unmistakeable UN light blue.

Twenty-Five

It began with an aircraft accident that was likely to have been deliberate, an assassination. In April 1994 the plane carrying the Presidents of Rwanda and Burundi, both Hutus, crashed, or could have been shot down. During the following twenty-four hours in the Rwandan capital, Kigali, Hutu extremists used the double murder (which they had probably instigated) as an excuse to assassinate the Prime Minister and other moderate politicians and journalists, then ordered the astonishing and unspeakable genocidal events that followed in the next one hundred days. Three-quarters of a million mainly Tutsi tribespeople were violently slaughtered by their former neighbours, the Hutus.

Someone should have seen it coming. Imagine how the head of a European manufacturing company reacted when, as early as 1993, Rwandan authorities ordered half a million machetes and other farm implements. Did he ask why a country of only a few million people had such a great need for tools that could be used as weapons in hand-to-hand combat? How many farmers could there be in Rwanda? Or, did he quietly take the order and tell no-one, delighted at the prospect of so much, such easy profit?

There was already a Kingdom of Rwanda in the year 1700. The Twa were there first; aboriginal pygmy hunter-gatherers whose presence in the region dates back almost 7,000 years. The Hutu and Tutsi, both sub-groups of the Bantu tribe; with, therefore, a common genetic heritage; arrived much later, about a thousand years ago, part of a gradual migration from the Congo region. They mingled easily with the Twa, so that the three groups came in time to share a common language and customs; astonishing, in a way, that their similarities so significantly outweigh their differences, which were mainly social: the Tutsi herded cattle, and the Hutu farmed the land. Clans formed, and by the end of the 19th century when the Europeans came, the Hutu had become subject to forced labour by the more powerful Tutsi.

In 1884 Rwanda was assigned to Germany, who gave the Tutsi even more administrative power and responsibility, a situation reinforced by the Belgian Authorities who took over the country during the First World War. In the 1930s they introduced a system that permanently assigned individuals to rigid, socio-economic, ethnic groups; Hutus making up 84%; the Twa only 1%; the remaining 15% being Tutsi. Everyone had to carry a government identity card, marking indelibly which group they were in, at which point the ruling

Belgians changed their minds, replacing Tutsi leaders with Hutus. At the time of independence in 1962, the country was therefore a Hutu dominated republic. Large numbers of Tutsi fled to neighbouring countries. Pro-Hutu and anti-Tutsi discrimination continued for many years, stirring up resentment. The country was a bubbling cauldron, ready to boil over.

Another marker of impending trouble in the early 1990s concerned about 4,000 self-exiled Tutsi, serving in the Ugandan army, who banded together as the Rwandan Patriotic Front. The RPF then invaded the north of the country, only to be pushed back by the Rwandan army with the help of French military forces, enabling Hutu extremists to use this as a pretext for stirring up fear and hatred against all Tutsi, wherever they were. In due course, it was this that led to the outbreak of genocide with the stated intention of killing every Tutsi in Rwanda. That's the real reason why they ordered machetes.

The Hutu leaders used highly offensive labels for Tutsi people, the most uncompromising - *inyenzi* - meaning 'cockroaches', pests to be exterminated, not human beings at all; and they broadcast for months over state controlled radio that someone should eradicate these vermin, make them disappear for good and be totally wiped from human memory. This hate-filled propaganda prepared the tinder awaiting only a deadly spark to ignite it.

Where was the rest of the world at this time? In October 1993, when UNOSOM II was in retreat from Somalia, UNAMIR (the United Nations Assistance Mission for Rwanda) began its ultimately futile work, aimed originally at enforcing a peace deal between the Tutsi RPF and the Hutu led Rwandan army; but, crucially, the UN rules of engagement did not allow them to intervene to prevent the genocide. For example, on the day of the plane crash, ten Belgian commando troopers with the UN tried to protect the Prime Minister but were all captured, tortured, and killed. Undermanned, and without support among their superiors, the UN role was reduced to assisting aid agencies, themselves also vastly hampered by inadequate protection and poor resources from achieving effectively their humanitarian aims and ambitions.

What can you do when you reach a small town where you're expecting to set up a field hospital to treat the sick and injured, only to find a burned out church building filled with the charred remains of 5,000 people, mostly women and children killed mercilessly by grenades and machetes, alternatively burned while still alive? Or when you aim to set up birth control and maternity clinics in places, but quickly discover that most of the women, some as young as eight, others as old as seventy, have been raped, many of them repeatedly and quite deliberately in front of their husbands, families, and everyone? This is the kind of situation we would be facing in northern Ethiopia, in Tigray Province decades later, a surprisingly similar story.

A few years had passed since the Estonia campaign. I was a Corporal now, and the other four were Lance Jacks with fire teams of their own, so we made a tidy unit. Al, Mack, Vijay, Blue and I practically lived inside each others heads, especially when on patrol. We each knew instinctively what the others were thinking. We had a good Sergeant who trusted our judgement, and were delighted to find ourselves once more deployed into danger.

In years of fighting, Mekele, the main city in Tigray had been taken and retaken several times. When another particularly damaging drought left tens of thousands starving in the region, it brought an urgent need for calm and stability so the humanitarian crews could get to work. That was when the UN stepped in to set up a central ceasefire zone. Our job was to patrol and enforce it.

Designated a 'Peacekeeping Force', like our predecessors elsewhere, we were obliged to follow certain strict rules of engagement, which were drummed into us at briefings for weeks before leaving Cyprus. Basically we were not to take sides in any conflict, and were not allowed to use any form of military force except in self-defence, and then only with authorisation from the UN Security Council based in New York. In other words you had to get Russia, China, the USA, Britain and France to agree to it... so Good Luck with that! These stipulations were always going to cause problems, as they always had in the past.

The first thing we noticed at the heavily fortified Mekele airport, a few miles south-east of the city, was the near-unbearable heat.

"Drink plenty of water, Boys!" Jim Beddow, our Sergeant, immediately called out, mothering us like a hen with chicks as usual.

The next thing of note was the enormous refugee camp across the perimeter fencing. When the plane's engines went off, before we even got into the transport, what hit us particularly was the stillness and the silence. Even the emaciated, rag-attired children, silently lining the fence, seemed frozen in an attitude of helpless despair, their mothers and grandfathers mutely looking on. What kind of hell had we entered?

Two years earlier, the UN had established two bases in Mekele, one at the airport and another in the western suburbs across the city, maintaining a militarised throughway between the two. This was the dividing line between the Tigrayans to the north and Ethiopian army factions to the south. The fact that there were Eritrean forces further

166

north and to the west complicated the matter. Nevertheless, extending their influence as far away as Axum, 150 miles to the north-west, and Lalibela, 200 miles to the south, allowed the UN at least a chance of keeping the fragile ceasefire alive, permitting the various humanitarian NGOs to carry out their challenging work.

Once holding a population of 150,000, Mekele had been decimated by the years of fighting. On a flat plain, at over six thousand feet above sea level, surrounded on three sides by a hilly plateau, it had been defenceless against airstrikes and heavy bombardment from above. Most of the high-rise blocks, raised during the prosperous era when the TPLF were in full control, had been pounded to dust and ruin. Since the UN arrived, a few intrepid, small-scale entrepreneurs had opened up or re-established their businesses, catering mainly to military personnel and the civilians attached to them; so there were plenty of bars, restaurants and a few hotels available for recreational purposes. There were also, of course, brothels ('Aids Stations', Vijay called them), which was just as well, as we had arrived during a quiet period. Apart from manning road blocks, guarding the two bases, and patrolling back and forth along the central Green Line several times a day, there was little to do.

"It's too bloody hot for fighting, that's why," suggested Sergeant Jim, "Even for the locals." We all agreed with him there.

One of the major NGOs at work throughout the region was DWB, the remarkable *'Doctors Without Borders'*, also known by its original French name, *'Médecins Sans Frontières'*. One of our more interesting jobs was to escort and protect them on missions inside the country. Their staff were often threatened, their equipment and supplies regularly looted. The hospitals and clinics they manned were also routinely attacked. After we'd been in Mekele long enough to get fantastically bored, I volunteered us for some of that action, and the sergeant was happy enough to let us go. Even now, given what happened, I'm not sure I truly regret it; the fatal events it led to helping me develop the qualities I would need later on.

As it was not yet the fighting season, we had little trouble taking small DWB convoys of food, medical supplies and personnel from Mekele airport to Lalibela, where they were running a hospital. It was a seven-hour journey over rugged, mountainous terrain with multiple switchback bends to slow us down; and, if the Tigrayans had been so minded, plenty of spots suitable for ambush; but we never saw any sign of them. All the same, we kept vigilant and ready at all times, as per training.

On one trip we escorted a Canadian doctor, high up in the DWB organisation, coming to inspect their operations as Head of Mission in

Ethiopia. A chain-smoker, Jay Robins had a permanently haunted look, which is not surprising for a man who had seen as much as he had of human atrocity, a man who had risked his own skin many times over, narrowly escaping death in a bomb blast in southern Sudan when a DWB base was bombed by the Sudanese government, to give just one example. For the few days he was with us, he was as relaxed though, as he probably ever could be, sharing a few beers and insisting on showing us the sights of Lalibela while we were there.

We were in the habit, on those trips south, of staying over for a couple of nights, bunking down in the fortified hospital grounds while the goods were off-loaded from the trucks into the DWB storerooms, and sometimes re-loaded with empty gas canisters and such for the return trip. There was no hurry to get back to Mekele. This close to the equator, the days were almost exactly twelve hours long, night falling rapidly at 6.00 pm, and it would not have been wise travelling in the dark. Even without risk of attack, the roads were too treacherous for that.

First off, Jay took a few of us on a tour of the hospital. Being on the squeamish side, Big Al didn't want to join in. Neither did Mack, a tall, dark stranger to us, even now after all the years we'd been together and all we'd been through, unknown and almost unknowable because he was forever silent. You could tell what Mack was thinking, but only because he was usually thinking of nothing. Forever alert, his face was so often blank and his mind an empty space. His parents were dead, he once told me, and he'd no-one else in the world to care about. In other words, we were his family.

Most of the patients we saw suffered from malnutrition, possibly also from typhus, tuberculosis, dysentery or Aids, but they were all starving, and most were dying. The refrigerated morgue was permanently full, and there was a pyramid of emaciated bodies about three feet high on open ground beside it, waiting for communal burial. As we walked past, something caught Blue's eye, some slight movement. A tiny child, still alive, was raising an arm in distress, so he went over to see, probably thinking he was about to effect a dramatic rescue, but then a nurse, one of the Ethiopian women hired locally by DWB, called out to prevent him from interfering. She had placed the boy there herself.

"He's going to die," she explained as Blue tried to protest. "We do not have enough beds, and we cannot waste food, liquids or medicine on someone like that. We must save it for those with a chance to get well."

Even I thought that a bit harsh, but when we retraced our steps not fifteen minutes later, utterly still now, the little boy had perished.

"Gone with the wind," said the same nurse, not unkindly. "That's how it is here. They all go with the wind..."

In the maternity ward, there was a heavily-pregnant woman lying groaning on a cot. Beside her, a business-like female French medic was putting up a saline drip.

"She arrived *ce matin*, this morning," the doctor said to Jay. "Walked six miles from her village then collapsed, so her husband carried her the other six. Her baby is due to be born, but has become stuck in the birth canal. She is too weak for an operation, even for the *Ventouse*, the suction machine. I am giving fluids, hoping she will be okay for a C-section later, but I do not think she will make it."

"What about her baby, Florence?" Jay asked.

"The baby is already dead, *fini*," the doctor replied, "But we haven't told her yet, or her husband."

"How do you do this?" It was Blue asking. "How do you live with so much death and destruction?"

"Well," she replied, giving him a steady stare, "Sometimes we do have success," at which point her face lit up with the most glorious smile. Here was a middle-aged woman revealed at that moment as truly content with her calling.

"And how do you do what you do?"

"It's what I'm trained for," was all that Blue could think of to say.

Lalibela had also been taken and retaken numerous times before the current ceasefire; but, smaller than Mekele, with a maximum of twenty thousand population and few high-rise buildings, it had escaped the same kind of wholesale destruction. Designated a World Heritage site since the 1970s, it remained a remarkable place, the most impressive aspect being its twelve churches, all hewn out of the local basalt rock, arranged in two main clusters either side of a small, often dry, river called the River Jordan.

Jay said these extraordinary religious artefacts had been excavated and built over a period of twenty-five years in the 12th or 13th century by a king who wanted to recreate Jerusalem. Over ninety per cent of Tigrayans being Christian, the site had remain in continuous use by the Ethiopian Orthodox Church all those years. Many of the churches are freestanding monoliths, but some share a wall with the mountain from which they are carved. Basalt is usually grey-coloured or black, but here it is rich in iron ore that, on exposure to air, wind and rain, gets oxidised, becoming rust on the surface, turning to a vibrant orange-red hue, overlaid subsequently in exposed places by a rich dark green, almost black, growth of algae, giving these constructions a uniquely variegated appearance. The churches are connected by a system of trenches and tunnels, as we found out on our tour.

The most impressive of these holy edifices, quite remarkable even for a non-believer like me, was the cross-shaped Church of St George, which stands alone a couple of hundred yards or so to the west of the others. As you approach, until you get close, all you can see is a double cross carved from the surface rock, its full majesty concealed until you stand on the precipice above and look down into a huge, square-shaped pit, over sixty feet across and at least fifty feet deep, the perpendicular church rising like a rocket in its silo, ready to head for the heavens. Access was down a long, steep ramp carved into the hillside, but the interior was dark and confined so we did not enter.

On the surface once more, we were met at the north-east cluster by a strange fellow; a small, thin, grey-haired man of about sixty, wearing the kind of uniform that identified him instantly as an official custodian of the place. His cap was khaki with a navy peak, resting on which was a wide band of bright red and yellow fabric in two horizontal stripes, those colours clashing bizarrely with the bright pink scarf round his neck, tucked into a worn, faded and crumpled much lighter-pink tunic a couple of sizes too big. Grey flannel trousers, with a respectable crease at least down one of the legs, brown woollen socks and scuffed leather sandals completed his attire, except to mention, over one arm, his insignia of office, a walking-stick with a highly visible cross carved into the ivory handle, painted in St George's colours. The rock in that place was also pinkish-red. Standing motionless to greet us, it was as if this apparition too had been neatly carved from its surface, an ancient and timeless symbol of the dignity of his people.

Jay said his name was 'Leuel'. Westerners called him 'Louis'. Either way, he took over as our guide, leading us through a low archway into an open space in front of a forty foot high monolith which actually looked like a church.

"Axumite style," Louis intoned. "Axumite... This one 'Church Emanuel'. Built for Royal Family... Private."

Following a custom I wasn't happy about, he made us remove our boots and leave them on the porch beside one of the ornately carved stone pillars. Vijay kindly agreed to stand guard over the footwear, which reduced my discomfort a little. Baring my feet made me feel as defenceless and naked as if Louis had taken my weapon, which, strangely, he did not mention, but there was no time to worry too much about that as we were being greeted by the resident priest, standing before us in the low light, dressed in full ceremonial gear, a pure white turban-style headdress, an equally brilliant chemise, a kind of smock, and over that a shimmering bright green and red cloak. Held high in his right hand was a large silver filigree crucifix, a long red and silver scarf dangling from it to the dusty rugs beneath our feet, spread over the bare rock. We lined up in the enclosed space before him as if on parade as he started chanting mellifluously, hypnotically, in a language I did not understand, waving the cross rhythmically backwards and forwards, no doubt bestowing a blessing upon our sinfully needy souls. Who was I to object?

There were carvings and pictures to admire. When my eyes had finally adjusted to the gloomy conditions and someone held up a torch, one in bright primary colours particularly caught my attention. As if painted by a gifted child, it depicted a man with a halo riding a white horse, angels floating in the air above him as he aimed the lance he was wielding downwards towards a dragon below. I could not see a princess in the background, but this was surely St George. Our St George! St George of England...

And so it proved to be. Jay told me that was why the other big church had been dedicated to St George, a point I'd missed earlier. Apparently, the saint himself appeared to King Lalibela complaining that none of the eleven churches built so far had been dedicated in his name, so an extra one, bigger than the others, was built in his honour.

As far as I knew from my schooldays, George was a Roman soldier martyred for his Christian faith in the year 304 AD, whose popularity in England came from the time of the third Crusade in Palestine in 1137 after King Richard the Lionheart called on him for protection. Thus he first became the patron saint of our soldiers, his red cross on a white field symbol immediately adopted by crusaders as their uniform. Some time later, of course, it became the English national flag. As for the bit about saving the princess and killing the dragon, that was an unlikely tale tacked on much later; but here it was again in Ethiopia. Why was it adopted as such a prominent theme of the local religion? Back in town, taking refuge from the heat and downing one or two thirst-quenchers together with Jay, I asked him about it, but he was no wiser than me, and sadly I never found out.

We returned to Mekele. Eventually, it rained. A few showers here and there, a couple of heavy downpours, enough to mark the onset of a new season, but not enough to guarantee crops sufficient to end the ongoing famine. As the temperature cooled slightly, hostilities were set to resume.

We made a couple of trips to Axum in the west, but had become much more familiar with the route to Lalibela, knowing where it was safe to make our rest stops, where to hit the gas and power our way through, just in case of trouble, and so on; so perhaps it wasn't surprising that Vijay's sixth sense kicked in when we were about two-thirds into our latest trip, accompanying a fairly big DWB convoy this time, carrying more than usual in the way of much needed food and supplies. When my Number Two told me he thought we should stop for a recce, I was ready to heed his advice. There was a small ravine ahead, just the sort of spot I would have picked for an ambush. Taking one man from his team, he quickly dismounted, and the pair went swiftly ahead on foot.

We were in radio contact, but would only have communicated that way if Vijay got into trouble. Silence was better, but it meant an anxious wait. Twenty minutes later he returned with news that a burned-out truck set across the road deep in the narrow pass was blocking our route, and that there were gunmen in the hills; about a dozen, he thought.

We instructed everyone to keep quiet, then I called Al, Blue and Mack to join me and Vijay for a pow-wow. My thoughts favoured a two-pronged assault on foot, but Blue cautioned that we didn't know for certain how many guerrillas there were. It might just be a modest lookout party we had seen, but there could be many more rebel soldiers in the hills higher up.

Vijay said the damaged truck was fairly light and empty, also angled in such a way that he thought would make it easy to ram off the road into the hillside, in which case there would be sufficient room for our trucks to pass. We were in French-made 'Jeanne d'Arc' vehicles; named after their potty, voice-hearing, male-impersonating, stake-roasted heroine, known to us as Joan of Arc; which were just like our Warriors but with sturdy front-shields attached, suitable for ramming other vehicles... So that gave us our plan.

It involved creeping slowly forward until we were about half-a-mile from the ravine's entrance, then revving up to ramming speed. The first hit did most of the job. The second wagon finished it, the obstacle careering into the rock-face, almost disintegrating with the impact. One by one, at speed, with everyone lying as low as possible, the remaining lorries followed by the third Jeanne d'Arc whistled through the danger-point. After a brief breathless delay, several automatic weapons opened up from above, strafing the column while inflicting relatively little damage. Nobody was hit, and apart from two ruined tyres and a good number of bullet holes, the convoy got through unscathed.

We pulled up a mile or two further on. Those wrecked tyres needed changing, also a team would have to stay to protect the drivers doing the work, not to mention the DWB passengers who would all have to wait because it was too dangerous to split up the convoy. But I was already thinking about the return journey. We did not want to risk encountering those bad guys again, so I had another word with Vijay and Al. Leaving Mack in command, backed by Blue and his team, after replenishing fluids and checking our gear, we set off back up the trail.

Did I think we might be breaking the UN's Rules of Engagement? Not for a second. In my book, this was pure self-defence, but there certainly were problematic consequences to follow. Anyway, we forked left and right, making our way wide uphill to outflank the ambushers and secure a good advantage over them, hidden away among the rocks below us. As it happened, they had no hidden reinforcements, and two of them were out in the open by the burned-out, brutally smashed truck, poking and pulling it about, clearly with a view to shoving it somehow back in place across the tarmac. Vijay shot them both on a prearranged signal from me. At the same moment, our men all lobbed grenades among the remaining guerrillas, a move that proved pretty decisive.

In a few seconds, after the noise cleared and the dust settled, one or two shots came vaguely in our direction, but all they did was pinpoint for us the location of the survivors, who we then quickly dispatched. Each of them, we soon discovered, was a painfully-thin, poorly-clad adolescent lad, no older than fifteen or sixteen, except for the final survivor, a bearded individual who came creeping out from his hidey-hole waving some kind of white cloth attached to the barrel of a gun. Bad luck for him, I was not in the mood to take prisoners.

When the fracas was over, taking careful precautions, we checked they were all dead and had a good look around before disposing of the bodies and their kit, which was how we found the other boy, who looked even younger than the others, lying at a distance in the shade of a scraggy bush, his Kalashnikov and half-filled plastic bottle of water beside him in the dust. The poor kid was alive but unconscious. One ragged trouser leg was rolled up and the cause of his prostration became clear. There, by his ankle, was the double-incision of a snake-bite. His foot and leg to the knee were swollen and mottled, the skin an ugly mess of blackberry and damson coloured blotches, and nearby lay the decapitated culprit, a six-foot long serpent with highly distinctive but unfamiliar markings. Vijay came over from the other side of the ravine to take a look.

"The venom must be an anti-coagulant," he said. " He's bleeding under the skin. That's what's causing those blotches. It's the same principle as rat poison, except rats swallow it and bleed to death from their stomachs."

To my surprise, he got his medical kit from his pack and took out a tourniquet and a scalpel. Having stopped the flow of blood and poison mid-thigh, he cut into the boy's flesh around the bite area, threw a chunk of dead muscle into the bush and bent down to suck poison from the gaping wound he had made, spitting out every mouthful. Despite the surgery, the unrousable boy made no sound. Vijay's work looked disgusting, and I'm sure it tasted vile, but he kept at it for several minutes before rinsing his mouth and sitting back on his haunches.

"What do you think, Vij?" I asked.

"We need to get him to town," he replied. "If he's to stand any chance of surviving, he needs the anti-venom quick."

On the radio, I told Blue to bring his Jeanne d'Arc and one of the DWB lorries back pronto as we prepared to carry the comatose boy-soldier back down to the road. Halfway there, Vijay turned and doubled back.

"Where are you off to?" I enquired.

"I'm going to get the snake," he said. "We'll need it to identify the venom."

"Good thinking, Batman!" I said. "Why didn't I think of that?"

The boy survived and that was brilliant, not because I cared the tiniest bit about him, but because he gave us lots of valuable intelligence. Information that definitely helped save our lives.

Twenty-Six

Haile Selassie was Emperor of Ethiopia from 1930 until being deposed and killed in 1974. I never knew much about Rastafarians, except for once or twice seeing in London some of those lively, reggae-loving, ganja-smoking Jamaicans with the green, yellow and red striped beanies covering their matted dreadlocks that Charlie and H used to score marijuana from, but I did recollect a connection they had with Selassie. Rastas take their name from his earlier designation as '*Ras Tafari* Makonen', his given and family names, and for some reason they worshipped him as a personification of the second coming of Jesus.

After his death, life got particularly tough for the people in Tigray under the new communist regime based in the capital, Addis Ababa. The Tigrayans belonged to one of the three largest ethnic groups in the country; nevertheless when, in 1984, they fell victim to a brutal famine, they received little help from central government. In hostile reaction, they formed the Tigray People's Liberation Front (TPLF), and by 1991 this military group was strong enough to take political control.

In 2000, Ethiopia had been the world's second poorest nation, but under the Tigrayan government first stability then prosperity gradually increased. However, although the whole population undoubtedly benefited, the seven million people of Tigray were soon seen as getting preferential treatment, so resentment began brewing among the large Oromo and Amhara ethnic factions, as well as among the country's other eighty ethnic groups, in a country totalling more than one hundred million people.

The TPLF-led government was finally forced out of office in 2018. The new prime-minister cemented his popularity by freeing thousands of political prisoners, and he ended the 20-year stalemate war with Eritrea, earning himself the 2019 Nobel Peace Prize in the process. But then everything changed again. The TPLF remained strong in the north, and when they launched a vigorous assault on an Ethiopian army base in Tigray, on the grounds of fearing an imminent attack from that quarter, the hitherto peace-making prime minister declared a state of emergency and ordered an all-out attack.

Unfortunately, neither side was strong enough to bring about a decisive victory, and a particularly gruesome and protracted conflict in the region has been the result ever since. Despite being at odds for decades, the Eritrean and Ethiopian armies joined forces together against the doughty Tigrayans, but with little success, because the opposing guerrilla force had the uncanny ability to simply disappear, evaporating like the morning mist by retreating into the region's rugged highlands, from which there was no real hope of rooting them out.

It was like a story I knew well from H's telling and retelling when we boys were young (Fidel and Raul in those days, not yet Freddie and Paul), about the Castro brothers with Che Guevara in Cuba's Sierra Maestra mountains in the 1950s, trying in desperate circumstances to overthrow the US-backed dictator, Batista. He romanticised it, of course, my father, aching for the chance to sow revolutionary seeds among the English middle class, unable to see this as useless among such a better-fed, and therefore entirely indifferent, constituency than the downtrodden peasants of Cuba. Were there lessons to learn here about what was happening in Tigray? I'm afraid I couldn't see any.

Be that as it may, the next morning when I went in, theatre staff were preparing the snake-bit boy for surgery. He'd been lucky. One of the nurses in the convoy the day before had known about such things, and even recognised the type of snake. More than that, she had set up an infusion of immunoglobulin from one of the packs on one of the trucks, boosting his defence against the poison. She'd also insisted that the tourniquet remain in place throughout the two-hour onward journey, risking the limb to save the life, then organised the required anti-venom injections once we arrived at the hospital. He lived, but his left leg was removed mid-thigh by the surgeon later that morning.

I did not get the chance to interrogate him before they put him to sleep. We'd been ordered to remain in Lalibela until further notice, so there was plenty of time to question him another day. When I did return, he was propped up in the bed smiling at the nurses, who I heard calling him 'Baby'. He was thirteen, but I thought they might be overdoing it with the nickname, until someone told me his name was in fact 'Abebe'. Apparently, in his language, it means 'fully grown', so that was a joke in itself. Even with two legs he could not have been much over five feet in height. Maybe that was why, despite the amputation, capture, and the loss of his comrades, he was in such good humour that day.

Abebe quickly became popular with the nurses, and I couldn't help liking him too. He treated me as a friend, but I had to keep in mind that he was one of the enemy. Also, we could only communicate through an interpreter, one supplied and vouched for by DWB, I admit, but a Tigrayan man nonetheless; so how much could I trust his translation, especially when the one-legged boy spoke for a minute and all I got was the briefest sentence in English? To make matters more farcical, the fellow's 'B's all sounded like 'P's, and his 'P's were like 'B's. What was I to make of sentences like this? "The women were all *bitifully rabed, putchered*, and stacked u*b* in *biles...* Then they were dum*bed* into *bits*."

But I persisted. In fact I went back many times, and Abebe's story was always the same.

He came from a Tigrayan village near the border with Eritrea. When he was six or seven, soldiers from that country swept in one day and massacred all the men folk, including his father. Next, they violently raped all the women before butchering them also. He only survived, he said, because his mother had made him hide in the communal latrine, from where, up to his eyeballs in human waste, he had seen much of the carnage. Most of the other children his age had also been shot. One baby had simply been held by the legs and bashed hard, head first, against a wall, until its feeble skull crumpled like a battered pumpkin. The older girls were snatched to be sex slaves. Older boys were forcibly abducted as recruits; which was also more or less what happened to Abebe about four years later, only this time the culprits were Tigrayans. After being orphaned, he'd made his way to another village where one of his aunts lived. It was safer because the TPLF forces protected it, but they also took boys as recruits as soon as they were deemed useful. He didn't tell me, but I heard later that they were used as sex objects too.

Abebe told me much else of the hardship he had endured; how one day he had been handed a pistol and made to shoot dead an Eritrean soldier, recently captured. If he refused, it was made clear, the next round would be for him. After that, he was given an AK-47, half-a-day to get used to firing it with live ammunition, then taken out on regular patrol, always hungry, trying to live off meagre TPLF rations, his share often pilfered by bigger boys in his troop, freezing cold at night, burning up during the day, and terrified all the time.

The combination of a lengthy ceasefire, drought and famine had caused the TPLF to rationalise their army. They couldn't feed all their men and boys, so they let the younger ones go to fend for themselves. Abebe and a dozen or so others gravitated towards Eleazer, the cowardly geezer with the beard at the ambush, who fancied himself as their leader. This pathetic gang then stayed close to the bulk of the TPLF in the mountains north-west of Lalibela for a while, scrounging food and essentials from their former comrades, making small-scale raids on local farms and villages for supplies, until Eleazer encouraged them to forage further afield and finally to try holding up our convoy. This tale, like something from the Wild West, revealed what Abebe had been freed from by our assault on his poorly led, poorly trained, poorly equipped bunch of underage mercenaries, which was no doubt the real reason for his rekindled joy. To our advantage, in his delight, thankful for his life, he had no hesitation in telling me everything he could about the TPLF and their intentions, and this helped us take appropriate actions, preparing for their attack.

I filed a brief verbal report on the ravine incident soon after we arrived at Lalibela, describing a single action, without bothering to mention that we'd doubled back to take reprisals with the express aim of ensuring our safety on the return journey. Unfortunately, when Jay Robins heard a different, more detailed and accurate version from his staff, he shared it, not only with UN headquarters in Mekele, but also with higher-ups in New York, seeking an investigation, which, of course, meant trouble for me.

At first, we were to be recalled to Mekele for a preliminary hearing, but then I put in a second, longer report, based on the intelligence gleaned from little Abebe, who consistently assured me that the TPLF would soon be back on the offensive, with Lalibela firmly in their sights. In particular, they were after the food stored in the hospital compound and anything else they could get.

This news earned us a breather. We were instructed to stay put and fortify the hospital, erect wooden gun turret platforms at the two front corners, install sandbags around the main entrance and other vulnerable points, reinforce the metal gates, establish a second guard post at the market-place a mile or so south-west of the hospital, and send out spotters with drone-mounted cameras to make sure we were immediately alerted to any impending threats of attack.

We were almost certainly too few to do any good, especially in a sprawling town riddled with tunnels and trenches leading backwards and forwards between all those cave-like churches, places in which it would be easy to conceal several, possibly dozens, of insurgents, and where the dry river Jordan made a further mockery of our defences; but, fortunately, when I made the point on the radio to Jim Beddow, the Sergeant took it straight to HQ. Having been to the town, he knew what we would be up against, and must have been extremely persuasive on our behalf, because within hours we had back-up by helicopter. Jim arrived with a Captain in tow, no less, as well as what soldiers Mekele could spare.

Now tripled in size, and with Captain Dave Maddocks in charge, we Tigers became an efficient and effective fighting force in Lalibela. Soon, we were put to the test. Although the first night remained quiet, satellite images confirmed that TPLF forces were on the move in our direction. Typical of guerrilla fighters, they moved forward in small scattered bunches over the rugged terrain, rendering air-strikes and artillery useless from our point of view.

Early the following morning, the hospital was a hive of activity. All the ambulant patients were led to one of two brick-built storage barns, as far away from danger as possible at the back of the compound, protected by proximity to the exposed hillside over the wall where attackers would be sitting ducks to be picked off at will by our snipers. The bed-bound, including Abebe, were shifted to the maternity ward, which was deemed the next safest place. Under my charge, Vijay, Al, Mack, Blue and their boys were tasked with defending the compound and protecting these patients and the doctors, nurses, cooks and others, including a large number of local people taking refuge there, while the Captain and about half our men went to secure the market-place guard post. Others, under Sergeant Jim, dug and manned a series of forward trenches left and right of the hospital.

I set up my command post in the heavily-sandbagged foyer of the hospital's main building, opposite and about twenty metres back from the main gate. People were still coming and going during the afternoon as we readied our equipment and ammunition, decided who would man which turret, where else to station people, and generally get prepared for an onslaught. In the late afternoon, almost as dusk fell, we heard the firing start up.

While the guard post guys were taking the first hits, all we could do was listen, watch and wait. I discovered later that, rather than simply dig in and defend, in typical Tiger style they had set up an immediate counter attack with 'Madman' Maddocks leading the way. Fully aware of the awkward topography of the town, he took several men into the tunnels around the south-east cluster of churches and blasted to smithereens anyone who got in their way. The effect of this manoeuvre, though, was to drive the TPLF forces in our direction, so it was no time before Jim Beddow's men came under fire, and soon the hospital itself.

Once a battle starts, you just react according to training. We were tremendously outnumbered and the fighting was fierce. After about half an hour, Jim had lost a few men and decided on retreat, co-ordinating with me by radio the opening of the gates for long enough for his two teams to get back into the compound. This was a dodgy moment. Across the entrance we had parked a Jeanne d'Arc wagon that had to be driven aside as the gates swung inwards. Most of Jim's first team got through, but then the rebels advanced towards us in numbers and a full-on fire-fight ensued.

When one of our men went down, Vijay or another of his team would rush to drag him to safety. With a nurse on triage duty inside the hospital, the indomitable French doctor, Florence, was ready in theatre to treat the wounded, stopping the flow of blood, putting up plasma infusions, administering morphine injections. It was impressive to watch, but I was only present for a moment, having helped transport an injured soldier there, then I was back at my post, watching the ebb and flow of hostilities at close quarters.

We were taking some losses, but the Tigrayans were taking many more. Things seemed finely balanced. More of Jim's men had made it to the compound, with jaunty Jim himself bringing up the rear, and the gates were almost closed. Someone was in the Jeanne d'Arc, ready to drive it back across the entrance when there was a mighty explosion, some kind of rocket-propelled device hitting one of the gates, leaving a gaping hole, Suddenly the Tigrayans rushed in through the opening, maybe a dozen or so.

I had Mack and three of his men with me in the foyer at that moment. It was problematic that firing at the inrushing enemy meant also firing towards those of our men standing between us and them. The difficulty we faced was just dawning on me when there was a terrific crash, a cruel shower of glass shards raining precipitously down on my head from above the level of the sandbags. A live grenade, which had landed near my feet, was the cause of this menace, but I barely had time to realise the danger when Mack heroically threw himself bodily over the device just before it went off. He saved the rest of us; but sadly, of course, he could in no way save himself.

I hope I would have made the same sacrifice for him, but who knows? What man alive knows what he would really do in such a situation? Al, Blue, Vijay and I lost a true friend and comrade that day, a brother, ready and willing to surrender his life for a motley makeshift family of mates. It was humbling, but it made me madder than ever.

The hospital was saved by the brave Captain Maddocks, whose fearless troop of Tigers attacked from the rear the rebels attacking us, catching them by surprise in a classical pincer movement and putting them to rout. It was all over by midnight. Not on the same scale as the famous Battle of Blenheim, but the Duke of Marlborough would I feel sure have been proud nevertheless of what we accomplished that day. Besides Mack, we lost only two men, with another seven Tigers injured, among them Big Al, caught when another grenade exploded atop the turret he was manning, sending shrapnel like a dart into the right side of his chest.

When I got to him, I thought at first he was gone. Barely breathing and already turning blue, he looked to be in a terrible condition. Vijay and I quickly got him to the main building on a stretcher, a heavy dead weight, and went barging into the surgical prep room, where Dr Florence was busy deciding who to start working on next.

Fortunately, she did not argue as we plumped Al's near lifeless body down, clearly able to tell his needs were urgent, also reading correctly from our faces our plain insistence that he should get priority. After cutting his tunic away to reveal the surprisingly small entry wound, she listened to both sides of his chest through a stethoscope, then ordered us to take him through to the operating theatre while she went to scrub up, giving out orders to her nurses as she went. Someone clasped an oxygen mask over his face, while someone else put up a drip. Then we transferred him to the table just as the doctor returned.

"We need a tube down. You can do that, *n'est-ce pas*?" she said to the nurse who was giving the anaesthetic. "If not, say so and I'll do it myself."

Removing the mask, tilting his head right back, the nurse put a bladed instrument down my old friend's massive throat and threaded a curved rubber tube carefully through his vocal cords into the airway, then removed the stainless steel guide, replaced the mask and resumed pumping gas. It all took about twenty seconds.

"Bravo!" said the doc. "There's no time for an X-ray, so I am forced to trust my instincts."

She explained her hunch that Al had what she called a 'tension pneumo-thorax', caused by the metal shard opening up space inside the rib cage but outside the lung. Air was being sucked in with every breath, enlarging the space and putting pressure on the lung, which was then unable to expand. She thought the right lung had collapsed completely, the heart and major blood vessels being forced over to the left side, squashing and thereby severely compromising the function of the left lung also. Little oxygen was getting through, and that's why Al had turned blue. She needed to get the air out from the rib cage and re-inflate the right lung quickly or else he would die.

What happened next was a remarkable lesson in physics. Simply putting a rubber tube into the space where the unwanted air was trapped would not have helped, letting more air in and making things worse; so, ingeniously, the tube's outer end was fed into a cylindrical glass vessel containing water. As one end was threaded between Al's ribs, bubbles started rising from the submerged part. No air could travel back through water to get into the tube and cause further problems. As fresh air was being pumped down his airway with the anaesthetic, the collapsed right lung was now free to expand, the heart and left lung regained their rightful places, and Al was soon pink again, back in the land of the living, all set to stay that way once the doc had cleaned and sewn up his wound, making his rib-cage fully airtight once again.

He had lost blood, and the shrapnel fragment was still in there, embedded in lung tissue, so he would need further surgery; but that could not be done there and then. Once stable, and after a blood transfusion, our friend was evacuated by air the next day, firstly to Mekele, then Cyprus, then London. The army looks after its wounded. Within twenty-four hours, he was operated on in a top teaching hospital. Unfortunately, the damage to his right lung was significant. One lobe had to be removed, and the remainder was scarred irrevocably, cancelling his military career.

If a more senior officer had witnessed it, Captain Maddocks' actions that day would surely have earned him a medal. As it was, only poor Mack got a gong. The Distinguished Service Medal was awarded to him posthumously. No doubt, if he'd been an officer, it would have been the Military Cross, but he was in no position to complain, was he? With no family elsewhere, we buried him there in the hospital grounds with as much in the way of military honours as we could muster in the middle of what was still considered a battle zone. Should we have insisted on the repatriation of his sorry remains, guts and midriff savagely obliterated by that deadly grenade, to let him lie forever in a military grave back in England? I'm not sure it would have made any difference, but I was too tired at the moment of decision to put up much of a fight, and there were other things on my mind.

Serious questions over the ambush and its aftermath had not gone away. Vijay, Blue and I were relieved of our duties three days after the Tigrayan attack, by which time reinforcements had been flown in to replace Jim Beddow and the rest of us. We three were then transferred by air back to Cyprus for a full military hearing, with UN and DWB representatives in attendance. The army does look after its men, but only if they are a squeaky-clean heroes.

It was not yet a Court Martial, we were told, merely a fact-finding enquiry, but I was extremely suspicious. I knew the truth would come out. In fact, the three of us decided we had no choice but to come clean about what happened, except the bit about me shooting dead the weasel waving a white flag, of course. Accordingly, I thought it best to take the precaution of getting legal representation, so put a call through to Henry Cavil, still at Wells, Goodbody & Wells, who turned up trumps, and soon had an ex-army lawyer, who knew all the ropes about this kind of thing, flown out to represent us and offer advice.

We weren't under arrest. However, we didn't have anything to actually do, which was dead boring, but it did give us time to prepare. Monkton, the lawyer, whose first name I never heard, listened carefully to our three separate accounts, then called us together.

"This is no good," he said. "You must be completely consistent."

So we went to work on our story, beefing up how strong a force had attacked us during the ambush, how well armed they were, how apparently disciplined, and therefore how much of a threat they posed to us whenever we were going to return by the same route to Mekele, or to anyone else making the same journey south. To us, as Monkton efficiently and dispassionately summed up for the hearing, this was a clear extended case of self-defence. We were to be commended, he said, rather than subjected to mistrust and humiliation.

There were precedents, he argued; in Somalia, for example, during the first UN mission, when similar proactive assaults on enemy positions came to be almost routine; the very situation, in fact, which led to changing the mission criteria for UNOSOM II. But countering this was the strongly-made point that in each case an officer had made the decision, not a lowly enlisted man, and there was written evidence, in the shape of military records, to prove it. The fact that those records were almost certainly concocted after the events depicted could, of course, never be proven so, in the finish, our hearing ended in stalemate.

Because, by now, the story and exaggerated accusations of international law-breaking were all over the press and the media, the army, the UN and DWB all wanted scapegoats to blame and punish. We, centre-stage and firmly in the frame, on the other hand, had made a decent case for our unorthodox conduct, accepting freely that we should have requested permission to retaliate as we had, but exonerated by not having the time to ask for it and get a satisfactory response. Our actions in defence of Lalibela hospital also counted in our favour.

To break the deadlock, it was eventually put to the three of us that our twelve-year commissions were due to expire fairly soon. Still in our early thirties, definitely wanting to stay with the Tigers, we three had already applied for immediate re-enlistment; but, as Monkton put it none too subtly, the writing was on the wall. This was the deal we were offered: the case would proceed to full Court Martial, unless we agreed to take honourable discharges. I was livid. But, there was no other way out. We three were all back in London in less than a week.

Twenty-Seven

There are advantages to being filthy rich. Henry Cavil, as requested, reserved for us the penthouse suite of a luxury hotel in South Kensington, which I took for a week. The Thames barrier had not yet been overwhelmed by rising sea levels, and this premium apartment had a balcony with good views south and west across the city. There were three bedrooms with en suite facilities, a utility room, a small kitchen, and a large, tastefully-furnished, split-level living-space, housing a well-stocked bar complete with wine cooler. For good measure, I had the hotel people install a proper pool table as well.

Trying to forget, not only what we had been through recently, but also what might or might not lie ahead, we tried throwing ourselves into days of decadent enjoyment. Still weary the first night, I hired a celebrity chef to cook up something special; a 'surf'n'turf' meal, lobster and venison, followed by a cardamom and ginger spiced crème brulée, which was all a bit fussy but delicious nevertheless. After sleeping in and lazing around during the following afternoon, we had a curry and hit the spots in the evening. By midnight we were partying at Abigail's, a fancy nightclub in Mayfair. By 2 o'clock though, I'd had enough and made my way back. Vijay and Blue continued getting matey with the friendly hostesses, three of whom ended up at the penthouse.

"We brought one back for you, Freddie," Blue told me, "But couldn't wake you up so she stayed with me. This is Gloria, Moira and... What's your name, Honey?"

We were together, all having breakfast. Blue didn't know Vijay's girl's name.

"I'm April," she said.

"This is April," said Vij helpfully a couple of seconds later. I don't think he knew her name either.

They were nice girls, well-spoken, and quality lookers; a blonde, brunette and a redhead. As gallantly as possible, I told them I was delighted to meet them, but I wasn't really. Something felt utterly wrong.

There was racing that day at Sandown Park, and the decision was made for everyone to go. The girls all had the day off and seemed excited, but begged for time to go home and change their outfits. Conveniently, they were sharing a flat together in Putney. Blue said we'd pick them up there in an hour, so off they went in a taxi while I phoned Reception to order a people-carrier with a driver for the rest of the day.

I remember asking on the drive down what attracted the girls to joining the stable of hostesses at a place like Abigail's (which was owned by an unlikely businessman called Abe Galsworthy, which must have given him the name). Moira just said it was fun. April added that she liked the lifestyle; getting up late, partying at night, and earning decent money to boot. It was Gloria who admitted that part of the plan was meeting attractive, eligible, preferably rich, men like us.

"Few people do it for long," she admitted. "Only for long enough to find themselves a husband."

I knew I had been forewarned.

When we got to the track, despite the girls trying hard to dissuade me, I excused myself from the party and had myself taken to Al's place in West Byfleet. Not feeling in the least sociable, I wanted to see him much more than watch jockeys and gee-gees going round and round in a circle while losing bets and paying handsomely for the privilege. To sweeten things, though, I did leave the gang with plenty of cash, and remembered to send the driver back for them when they were done.

Al was still recovering from surgery. After a few days, he'd been transferred from London to the local hospital for a period of rehabilitation. He was going to be living alone at the bungalow in Woodlands Avenue, Ada having died and left the property to him in her will while we were still on our first tour in Cyprus. Home now, an ambulance came for him three times a week to take him to the hospital for physio, but when he answered the door, he seemed well. I felt real joy to see his grizzled features once more.

Inside, the place looked as if Ada had not long departed. The furnishings were fading and threadbare in places, but nothing really had changed. The same floral wallpaper was hanging throughout the house. The same fussy china ornaments adorned the mantelpiece in the living room. The same crockery and cutlery could be found in the kitchen.

"You need a decorator in here, Al!" I told him. "Better still, one of those interior designers."

"Not necessary," he replied quickly. "I'm going to sell up."

First he insisted on showing me his scar, a great crescent-shaped affair from back to front circling his rib cage. Then he made coffee which, to avoid the gloomy interior, I suggested we drink in the garden, although when we went out through the kitchen door to the patio, I realised the near-terminal neglect of the place extended out there as well. The lawn, once kept green and trim, George Firkin's pride and joy, was now an overgrown weed patch, the flower-beds indistinguishable from the remainder of the jungle, and no visible evidence of the little fish pond I thought I remembered down the bottom.

"It's my re-wilding project," said Al as a joke, then he had to sit down as laughter turned scarily into a prolonged fit of coughing.

"Oh dear!" he said eventually. "Please don't make me laugh. I always end up like that."

But that's how we coped, isn't it? Making a joke of whatever seemed too awful to contemplate seriously; so we laughed (and he coughed) our way through the afternoon while I told him what had happened to him in Lalibela, how the French doctor had saved his life, how Mad Maddocks' men saved the day, and how Vij, Blue and I were put through the wringer over the ambush and the reprisals we took.

"So, what are you going to do now?" he asked some time later as I was thinking of getting back.

"No idea," I replied. "What about you? What's all this about selling the house?"

"I'm moving to Sussex," he said.

It turned out that someone from the Regiment had already been to see him to discuss future employment options. The army had built relationships with various organisations to help ex-soldiers move on with their lives, including with various police forces. Sussex Police, Al told me, were looking for a new Firearms Officer and he had applied. He would have to get fully fit first, but the quacks had said and certified that he was recovering well; and, he told me, you don't have to be as physically robust to join the police as you do for the army. He would get ten weeks training in Brighton and was promised rapid promotion. They urgently needed his skills. I told him I wished him luck.

"You should go for something like that, Freddie," my old friend recommended, but I was perfectly sure that policing wasn't for me.

Back at the hotel, the penthouse looked like a dress shop. Unembarrassed, cruising around the living space in their underwear, two of the girls were trying on clothes. They had all lost money at the races except Moira, who'd had a fine win.

"I've a system," she insisted on telling me. "I always back the second-favourite in every race, and usually come out on top."

It seemed like an admirable scheme, if a little unoriginal; but, of course, what did I care if I won or lost a few quid. There was no fun in gambling for me, and I was about to say something unkind about small-mindedness, when glamorous Gloria, the brunette, sidled up, her hand as if accidentally brushing against one of mine, to say she thought I could do with a drink, and could she get me a beer.

I didn't like the idea that she was somehow trying to latch on to me, but could hardly object as she fetched a cold bottle from the fridge, opened it with a flourish, and poured its contents out under my nose, before handing me a golden glass full of bubbles. To deflect her attentions, I told the boys about Al.

"He's going to be a rozzer!" said Blue. "Who would have imagined that?"

"Dirty Harry born again..." Vijay raised an imaginary Smith & Wesson Model 29, the famous 'Magnum Force' handgun, took aim at the balcony and pulled its imaginary trigger, miming the powerful recoil while imitating the soundtrack: "Pow! Pow!"

We decided to eat in, taking advantage of room service and the hotel's excellent kitchen. We could order what we liked, they said. Then, finishing off the lager, planning on taking a shower, I started walking slowly across the floor towards my room. Gloria evidently decided to join me, following a couple of paces behind, then closing the door after we'd entered.

This was the moment to put a stop to her little game, to tell her firmly to go, but I hesitated, mesmerised by the frank, friendly but purposeful, look in her eyes. Soon, of course, it was too late. I had spent time with girls, obviously, during my time in the army. We all did. Men must have sex. It's a biological necessity. But not with girls like this one, well-educated, independent-minded, self-assured girls who thought themselves pretty much your equal. Gloria, at that moment, knew exactly what she wanted, and what she wanted was me.

As I was removing my jacket, she came up close to where I stood by the bed, nestled her head against my left shoulder and whispered gently in my ear something about helping me relax. As Gloria began undoing the buttons on my shirt, starting at the top, the warmth of her body through the thin fabric of her dress, and the intoxicating scent of her perfume, contributed greatly to my unbidden arousal. By the time she reached waist level, my trousers were on the floor, and John Thomas was thrusting hard against my underpants, soon to be released as my seducer hooked foraging fingers beneath the elastic.

"Hello, Big Boy!" she exclaimed as my love machine came into view. "Now that's what a girl likes to see!"

With only panties under her dress, she was soon naked too, then led me into the shower.

All lathered up, we kissed under the warm spray pelting forcefully down from the enormous rosette above us; then, slickly, without fuss or foreplay, giving a little hitch as I bent at the knees, she completed full carnal connection. In a trice, I was deep inside her, but it was over just as fast, ended by my near-instantaneous climax, which signalled the release of long pent-up tension, sexual, naturally, but something much deeper. I hoped it went unnoticed that the rushing water swept away more than soap suds and semen. It took away copious tears.

Recovering self-control, I dried and dressed quickly while Gloria lingered to make use of the hair dryer. In the other room, the boys were trying to teach April and Moira to play pool, but not very successfully, it seems, as balls kept flying off the table and had to be retrieved. The food arrived as I was about to find another beer. The starter course, a finely spiced parsnip curry soup with little chapattis on the side, made me reconsider and select a vintage bottle of Pouilly-Fuissé from the cooler instead. They made a great combination.

When we took our places, I sat between the novice pool players with Gloria opposite and the lads filling the gaps. To avoid conversation with my new playmate from the shower, I deliberately got Moira talking about the races, a highly successful gambit, except it was then impossible to get her to stop. When the succulent Beef Wellington arrived (and the sea bream with samphire for fish-lover, April), we were still hearing about the second race. Earlier, I'd opened a couple of bottles of 2005 vintage Chateau Lynch-Bages, a beautifully drinkable claret, and so was able to excuse myself from the incessant chat about horses and riders to walk round the table and pour. The excellence of both food and drink happily then prevented even Moira from speaking.

After successfully tempting the figure-conscious ladies with some raspberry-cream filled profiteroles, we moved across to sit around more comfortably and watch a movie on the large-screen entertainment system. Bringing drinks over to go with the coffee, I had no choice but to plonk myself down next to Gloria on the couch. It was the only spot left.

Blue picked an old western, 'Barbarossa', with the country singer Willie Nelson wearing a full red beard in the title role. There was a romantic sub-plot, so the girls liked it, but I'd seen it before and wasn't that thrilled. In fact, I must have dozed off, because the next thing I'm aware of is Gloria shoving me gently on the shoulder, encouraging me to get up.

"Come on, you!" she said, speaking firmly but quietly. "It's time you went to bed."

Meekly as a lamb did I go, and in bed we made prosaic love until, quite soon, I fell fast asleep again. Waking simultaneously some time later, barely conscious, as if in a dream, we gravitated together in the bed and renewed our lovemaking, but this time it was different. I found myself as if possessed by a great angry force, more of what I had been holding back all those years. What began as gentle turned almost brutal. Thrusting ever more forcefully, like an animal, I was using my cock not as an instrument of love but like a weapon, and Gloria was taking it, enjoying it, I could tell. If the others were still awake, they must surely have heard her crying out, partly in anguish, part ecstasy. This coupling was intense, and could only have happened because we were essentially strangers to one another, each engaged in a private world that happened to coincide with the other's. Without a word, when it was over, we both rolled over and slept.

When I came to again, streaks of light were creeping into the room through narrow gaps between the drapes. Gloria was lying on the other side of the bed, her back towards me, breathing softly. As I was looking on, a sharp pain gripped my heart, the pain of grief, for this was not Carol, and recognition of that simple fact held me viciously in its grip . She was gone. Carol would never lie beside me again. And I was still fiercely angry.

Highly distracted, I got up and went into the bathroom. Next, after pulling on some shorts and a T-shirt, socks and trainers, I made my way down to the lobby, then outside for a mind-numbing run. Making my way past the museums up to Hyde Park, I began a clockwise circuit of the periphery, keeping the Albert Memorial and Kensington Palace to my left, nodding in respect as I passed the Princess Diana Memorial Gardens, remembering the Regiment's allegiance to her memory, continuing on, maintaining a good pace, across to Speakers' Corner, south to Hyde Park Corner, and then west again to my starting point. I'd probably covered about four miles but felt fresh and kept going, fuelled by a deeply-felt, slow-burning rage.

After a second circuit, I cut across to the Serpentine and started running multiple laps around the lake until, finally exhausted, I sat down on a nearby bench. Having, as usual, strapped my phone to my arm to count my steps and measure my heartbeat, it now came in useful for its original purpose, for I had to call Blue and tell him to get rid of the girls. Giving him an hour, I insisted they were not there when I returned, and he knew enough not to argue. Gloria, in particular, I said, must be gone.

The bench was on the lake's west side, near the Peter Pan statue, giving me a fine view north over the Italian water gardens. Ending the call, putting the phone back on my arm, only then did I become properly aware of my surroundings. The sun appeared low on the horizon, above the buildings at a slight angle to my right, bright pink and white chestnut blossom reflecting its light from the trees, some petals fluttering down like confetti to make a carpet of the earth, stirred by the same gentle breeze that was giving a shining rippling effect to the water where moorhens and mallards swam about. Two wagtails flitted here and there near me, and two Peacock butterflies were sunning themselves on the grass adjacent to the path until disturbed by a boy in school uniform rocketing past on a skateboard. If I knew the names of the plants and flowers brightly adorning the beds in that place, I would surely record them as well. The point is, I was uplifted by the scene, and felt like staying there forever, but two things intervened. The first, I was ravenously hungry. The second, I had made a decision.

Few people were about yet as I made my way to the Broadwalk Cafe near the playground area in the park's north-west corner, where eggs and bacon, followed by a plateful of pancakes and maple syrup with several cups of coffee, dealt adequately with my first problem. The second issue, fulfilling the consequences of my fateful decision, would take longer to bring about, but I was confident. I hoped Vijay and Blue would join me, but it didn't seem to matter that much, for I was on a personal mission now. Nothing on the planet could possibly get in my way.

Looking back, it was simple and obvious; but, seated quietly on that bench after my exertions, plus the emotional ruckus of the previous night, it came at me like a cosmic revelation. In fact, it was as if a powerful disembodied voice - not mine, someone else's - spoke directly inside my head: "You are a combat soldier, Freddie. That's what you're trained for... Go somewhere and fight!"

My twin brother would probably have called it the voice of God. Maybe it was, or maybe a Freudian psychologist would say it was my own unconscious mind speaking. None of that really mattered, because what counted was the impossibility I immediately felt of disagreeing with or disobeying that message. Wherever it came from, I had to go along with it; certain, as I felt too, that it came with a promise; that in my attempt to follow its instructions, the universe would conspire to assist me. I could only succeed. More than that, there was important work ahead for me to accomplish as a soldier. I'd been hand-picked for a special, momentous and meaningful role in the fast-approaching history of the world. All that came to me in an instant of insight. Light of heart, I began retracing my steps.

Vijay had accompanied the girls in a taxi back to their flat. At the hotel, Blue was alone, and he was clearly unhappy.

"What's going on, Fred?" he said, a little peevishly I thought.

I felt it impossible to explain the experience I'd just been through in the park. If I'd tried, I knew he would think I was potty, so I simply said I was bunking off for a few days. He and Vijay were welcome to stay put, see the girls if they wanted while I was gone, and put anything they liked on my tab. I'd tell them what was happening later. At that early stage, of course, I hadn't yet worked out the details myself, but I had also decided to visit my mother.

Unsure until then of my future, I hadn't wanted to tell Charlie I was home and out of the army, but now seemed like the most propitious moment. She was living in a pretty, small town in Sussex, not far from Paul, Mary and the kids, having bought herself a sweet, two-bedroom house with a modest garden, and a garage for her new hybrid car. Surrounded by well-meaning neighbours, she was gaining a plethora of new friends throughout the thriving community wherein she soon embedded herself. In her fifties, she had kept a good figure, allowed the grey in her hair to show through, and now sported fetching blue, plastic-framed varifocal glasses; also, as ever, a smile. It was good to see her on this, my first visit in over two years.

No longer working, she nevertheless volunteered to keep the books for a couple of local charities, had taken lessons and joined a ukulele band, was in a book club, played bridge, and had even taken up golf.

"How totally bourgeois is that?" I asked, teasing the one-time Trotsky follower. But she just shrugged and kept smiling.

"Things change," she said. "People change... That's not such a big deal!"

She told me about Paul and Mary, still teaching, and about the three children, all teenagers at school. We went for a walk through woodland and up onto the South Downs, taking in the dramatic views over the stone-age fort at Cissbury Ring to the sea and across to the Isle of Wight, hazy in the distance. I could see she was more than happy. She was deeply contented.

"The only thing missing," she told me, "Is that my other son has yet to settle down."

Of course, that meant me, so I told her I was about to embark on something new, a big project that would make her proud, but I don't think she really believed me.

"You're not like your brother," she said. "You've got something of your father's unsettled temperament, don't you agree?"

I was forced, on reflection, to admit it.

"I only hope it doesn't destroy you like it destroyed him," she added.

I said I had more sense than that.

Twenty-Eight

I needed help getting my new project started so, later that day, I spoke to the smooth-talking, well-connected Henry Cavil by phone. I was looking for someone, but I didn't know exactly who that might be. He called me back the next day.

"Bruce Laycock's your man," Cavil said, giving me the necessary contact details. "Runs a company called 'Blinkers', based on his initials, I suppose. Officially, it's 'BL Incorporated' or 'BL Inc'."

I phoned the number. Someone picked up after three rings and a cultured female voice intoned the simple word "Yes", managing to give it two syllables. When I said I hoped to speak to Mr Laycock, the voice replied laconically, "About?" So I told her I was recently ex-army, and it was about getting some work.

"Come on Monday at 1400 hours," she said, wasting no words and giving the address; so I thanked the lady and told her I would be there. All that followed was a click as the receiver went down.

The house was in a quiet, tree-lined road in Pimlico, between the tube station and the river, a narrow, three-storey building with a faded green door. Ringing the bell, precisely on time, I was expecting to see the receptionist I had spoken to, someone I had been imagining as a no-nonsense, middle-aged female martinet, rather than James Bond's comely Miss Moneypenny, as one might have hoped for in the circumstances; but that was not to be. Standing before me as the door opened silently was a man in an orange T-shirt, blue-jeans and loafers, who reminded me somewhat of the Palestinian leader Yasser Arafat, being corpulent and of only medium height. Topped with wiry grey hair, untamed except by being cut pretty short, his thick-lipped, bulbous-nosed, bushy-eyebrowed, suntanned face, with two or three days of stubble adorning the chin and upper lip, wore the blandest expression, with no discernible hint of a welcome.

Giving nothing away, this apparition, urging me quickly inside his den, was Bruce Laycock, known naturally as 'Cocky' to his friends, of whom though he had very few.

"That's my niece, Deirdre" he intoned in a southern African accent, when I mentioned the minimalist phone conversation setting up the appointment. "She's not here. Lives in Rochester. I get my calls put through to her when I'm away... Funny woman. Very efficient... Spinster, of course!"

Laycock led me into a dark corridor that presumably led to a kitchen at the back, ushering me into the only other room on the ground floor, a kind of study and living-room combined, his lair, which smelled of stale cigarettes and was desperately untidy. A solid-looking swivel chair occupied the space behind a large mahogany desk that was cluttered with papers, a dirty half-filled tumbler of water, or possibly gin, two butt-filled ash trays, some paper clips, a folder or two, a paper knife and sundry other objects, including an old-fashioned dial telephone, most of this detritus covered by a thin layer of dust.

Against the back wall, a sparsely-filled bookcase also needed the attentions of a duster. The paint on the ceiling was flaking. Some strips of wallpaper hung damply down. The carpet in one corner was visibly mouldy, and the rest of it was both faded and patchily stained, except where, between a cheap settee and an ancient reclining chair, beneath the wall-mounted television, a rumpled and threadbare oriental rug lay as if in defeat.

Pointing at the only other chair in the room, an upright one in front of his desk, Laycock urged me to sit. Taking the place opposite, he swivelled back and forth and began lighting the cigarette he had taken from a half-empty packet lying open on the desk. Unimpressed in those first few seconds, I lowered myself gingerly to the seat indicated, which gave a worrying groan, shifted a fraction sideways, but did in the end hold my weight.

Without further ado, it was explained to me that Laycock spent most of his time in Africa, in Zambia near the Victoria Falls to be precise, overseeing a paramilitary training camp, the main centre for BL Inc's activities, visiting London for a few days every couple of months with the aim in particular of recruiting people like me. It was a legitimate business, sanctioned by both the civil and military authorities of that country. In return, 'Blink', as he usually referred to it, trained most of the Zambian army's recruits for a nominal fee. Other African countries making use of a similar service were charged significant amounts, as were groups of stateless combatants that he carefully avoided calling freedom fighters, mercenaries or terrorists. Advanced training, for example in the use of complex and sophisticated weaponry, was also available for a fee.

He asked about my time in the army and seemed satisfied, impressed even, with my account. We spoke for twenty minutes or so. He answered my questions about Blink's location, climate, facilities and so on. Finally, he gave me his verdict.

"You'll do fine. I need people like you. Think of it as a stepping stone. Few people stay with me for long. There's always greener grass somewhere, and that's why I'm always recruiting."

I said nothing, undecided, not actually terribly thrilled.

193

"I can make you a Captain straightaway," he added as a sweetener. "We need the men to respect you, and it's me decides on who gets what ranking. You'll have a nice uniform; and (he paused here deliberately)... you get twice the British Army's rate of pay."

It was his trump card, but he wasn't to know that my investments, managed by another firm recommended by Cavil, continued to do exceptionally well. His financial incentives therefore meant nothing, so I had to tell him bluntly that I didn't want to train people. I mainly wanted to fight.

He responded initially to this intelligence with silence, then asked me to wait a moment before getting up and leaving the room. Surprisingly nimble on his feet, I heard nothing while he swiftly climbed the stairs, until the noise came of a door closing and, soon after that, of a toilet flushing. When he came down, he was carrying a crumpled camouflage jacket. Putting it on, he suggested we go for a walk.

Inside the house, Laycock had been completely matter of fact. Once outside, his demeanour altered. He became more sociable, confiding even.

"I have to be careful," he said conspiratorially, gripping my arm as we walked side by side towards the river. "The house is bugged, I know it."

"Who by?" I asked, worried now that my curious companion was hopelessly deluded and paranoid.

"Everyone!" he exclaimed. "The British Security Services, the CIA, the Russians, the Chinese... It's all because of the Blinders. I need to tell you about them, and it's much safer out here."

"Well," I was thinking, "If GCHQ are set on tracking you, they can, with directional microphones and such, even out and about in the streets of London."

"Most of what I'm going to say, they know already, so it's no problem," he said, as if reading my mind. "Let's sit down over there."

We'd reached the Embankment, across the Thames from Battersea and the remnants of the great power station, where there were a couple of benches.

The 'Blinders' he mentioned were people enrolled in Blink's clandestine (because globally illegal) sister organisation, the BL Independent Defence Force, made up essentially of mercenaries, men soldiering for money, responsive therefore to anyone ready to pay, including Government agencies of all colours, hence the interest taken by the various secret services who would have kept tabs on Blind because it's forces might at any time be employed against them. According to Laycock, although he tried hard to avoid such a situation,

Blinders (as he called his troops) might even be fighting both for and against some particular regime at the same time, depending on whoever hired them.

Laycock made clear that he was an Africa specialist, but he knew for example, he told me, of people who had gone to Ukraine to fight the Russian invaders coming up against the Russian President's more or less permanent mercenary army into which earlier had been recruited some of their onetime army comrades.

"I wouldn't be happy about that if my people were involved," he said. "But you have to be realistic. Soldiers like you, like to fight... Even more so if they're getting well paid. Which side they're on hardly matters."

I'd heard a lot about this kind of thing, and the kind of outfit he was obviously running, but this was the closest I'd come to the reality. We talked for over an hour, as the river on one side and the traffic on the other rolled by. Laycock assured me that after six months training people with the Blinkers he'd be happy to transfer me to Blind. Not all the work was with established regimes, with legitimate, democratically-elected governments or totalitarian dictatorships, much of it was with major international organisations, like mining companies, insuring their assets and protecting (possibly controlling) their workforce. Helping smugglers of various kinds also came into the brief at times: drugs, ivory, diamonds. Depending on your moral standpoint, there was plenty of scope, and on this I was like Arjuna with the god-person Krishna urging him on: "Set your scruples aside, my Boy... Do not delay. Do what you were born to do... Just go for it!"

"Large parts of Africa are like the rugged old Wild West," Laycock continued encouragingly. "We go where asked to supply law and order." He laughed... "Well, order anyway! We don't worry too much about the law."

This was much more appealing. I told him finally that I was thinking positively about his offer, and that I'd give him a decision soon. I couldn't wait to tell Blue and Vijay about Laycock's setup, to try and recruit them as well, but there was a disappointment in store for me. When I called Blue later, he said Vijay had got engaged.

*

"It's April," he reported in a melancholy voice when I got back. "Her father is wealthy, apparently. Those twits think they're in love. The girl has even made her Dad turn colour-blind and offer Vij a job."

"Oh dear!" I said. "I smell disaster. How long do you think it will last?"

"The job or the marriage?" he replied.

"Both," I said. "Surely one goes with the other, doesn't it?"

"Yes... But don't breathe a word of opposition to Vijay," Blue cautioned me wisely. "He's already lost it with me a couple of times when I tried making him see sense... We'll just have to 'Go with Flo' for now on this one, Freddie."

Sadly, I had to agree.

The next day, after another terse phone call to Laycock's impenetrable niece, Deirdre, Blue and I paid a visit to the moribund house in Pimlico to sign up as Blinkers, understanding firmly that, unless we proved ourselves useless, we'd transfer into the Blinders later on. The only condition we stipulated involved being allowed to remain in London long enough for our doomed mate's ill-omened nuptials. Luckily, April was an amazingly forceful and impatient young woman. She too wanted the hitch done and dusted real quick. Blue thought she might be scared that, given long enough, Vijay would renege on his promises about settling down. We both wondered too if perhaps, deliberately or otherwise, she'd got herself pregnant; but surely, as they'd only been lovers for a week, that was not very likely.

"Maybe she was pregnant already when they met," Blue suggested. "Women can be very devious."

I suggested we give her the benefit of the doubt for the time being. Given their racial differences, when it arrived, the baby would surely declare itself as either Vijay's or otherwise if fathered by someone with a paler complexion. We should let the drama unfold.

Arthur Henry Hurtley, April's father, doted on this daughter, his only child. His father, Henry Arthur, had been a humble bricklayer who, with diligence, had established a thriving building firm, which Arthur eventually took over. Now it was a vast construction, demolition and development company whose business involved acquiring property, either modernising old buildings or demolishing them to make way for new ones, with huge opportunities for new building on each site's surplus land.

It was a family tradition to rotate the first names of the firstborn son in every generation, but complications following the birth of their daughter meant that Arthur's wife would not be having any sons, or any more children at all. The child was therefore called Henrietta April, so she had at least the same initials as a son would have enjoyed.

Arthur was not in fact dismayed or disappointed. She was such a pretty sweet infant that, in his heart, he was joyful. When Mrs Hurtley passed away, dying of ovarian cancer when April was not quite twelve, Arthur barely grieved the loss, his daughter providing as much in the way of company and compensation as he could ever want. She was wilful, he admitted; but, to him, that was just her spirit, her character, her boldness; the qualities a son might have had, it occurred to him once. He could not help but indulge her every whim, and often her whim was of iron.

It was her choice to go by her second name, April. Henrietta seemed too stuffy and old-fashioned, while to be called after the first month of spring seemed auspicious, even though her birthday was actually in June. Opposites attract, do they not? So, it was easy to see how, a natural blonde and fair of complexion, she might instantly and fatally be attracted to my strong and handsome Indian chum, Vijay, who was (as my politically incorrect father H might admiringly have said) 'as Black as the Ace of Spades'. It was hard not to imagine them naked, locked in each others arms, yin and yang together, making a perfect whole. Fairy tales are made of such material, but this wasn't Hans Anderson. It wasn't make believe... Unavoidably, this - full of uncertainty and the possibility of suffering - was real life.

Arthur Hurtley was not a racist, but many of his friends and associates were. As the inexperienced new son-in-law, Vijay certainly faced resentment from day one. The colour of his skin made the opposition far worse. It didn't help that all Arthur asked of him was to traipse around in his wake day after day, with no chance to prove his worth at all.

"I'm going to show you how the business works, Lad," he would say. "You'll soon pick it up."

But Arthur's methods relied on his personality, on forging alliances, giving and receiving favours, sniffing out profitable situations on the basis not only of experience but also hereditary intuition. Given that most of his new work colleagues mistrusted and disliked Vijay from the outset, undermining his position at every opportunity, how likely was it that business partners, both existing and those being courted for the future, would take any kind of gamble on his abilities? It wasn't likely at all... But this was only one set of his problems.

Having been christened in church, April was typical of the kind of Church of England person who tended to avoid Sunday services because they were boring and she had better things do to. At the same time, like all would-be princesses, her heart was set on a white wedding in a big church (preferably a cathedral) filled with adoring friends and relatives. The fact that her husband was from a Hindu family was, to her, a minor matter that could not be permitted stand in her way. Vijay had to convert. Surprisingly, maybe, he had no major objection.

"I might as well be a Christian atheist," he explained to me and Blue privately one day, "As a Hindu one, don't you think?"

Only a girl like April, backed by her rich and influential father, could arrange both a baptism and a full-on wedding within six weeks. The only drawback, once the priest, the caterers, the dressmakers, the hairdressers and everyone else necessary, had been handsomely bribed, was that it had to take place on a Friday, all the Saturday booking slots for over a year being already taken.

Vijay had fittings in Savile Row for his suit, and took instruction twice a week from the priest-in-charge, Rev. Anne Deacon, at the church, St. Pauls, in Molesey, near enough to the Hurtley mansion on Hampton Court Road, where the infant April had also been welcomed into the family of Christ. He said the procedure was painless. The woman clearly cared only that he learn the right words to say, also that he understood broadly that Christianity is essentially about peace, love and forgiveness. That was all there was to it.

"She was happy that I'd given up soldiering," he told me.

"Have you really given it up, Vijay?" I asked pointedly.

"Congratulate me, Man!" was his reply, clearly somewhat affronted. "I've done with that now... I'm going to concentrate on being happy, and making my girl happy too."

I wish it had turned out that way.

*

On returning from Sussex, I had moved into the modest convenience apartment in the Barbican I'd owned for a long time, since I came into money. When the week at the penthouse was up, the boys had taken separate rooms on a lower floor in the same hotel. When we met up, I discovered that, just as Vijay's romance with April was blossoming, Blue's with Moira had gone sharply into decline.

"Two redheads together, Freddie," he explained. "What can you expect? It was fiery. She was very strong-willed. We just kept blowing up at each other."

So Blue soon joined me in the apartment, while Vijay went over and shacked up with April in Putney.

In the following weeks, we two got ourselves properly kitted out for Africa. Laycock had given me the details of where to go for our uniforms, and the redoubtable Deirdre made sure we attended the London School of Hygiene and Tropical Medicine for all the necessary jabs, malaria pills, etcetera. To maintain our marksman skills, we joined a shooting club with both indoor and outdoor facilities; also, to keep fit and sharp-minded, we trained at the gym every day, and hired an ex-army martial arts instructor for private sessions twice a week. Vijay might be letting himself go, but we could not afford that; plus, as much as anything, it was a good way of keeping our minds busy. The only relaxations allowed, we agreed, would be at the stag party and the wedding itself. Despite the sorry implications for our mate's future, we were looking forward to those.

Twenty-Nine

Arthur was a fully paid-up member of Pootles, the highly respectable private club for gentlemen in St James's Street, founded in the 1760s and named, rather oddly, after its head waiter, Edgar Pootle, and this was the esteemed venue selected for celebrating the end of poor Vijay's bachelor days, with Arthur, naturally, footing the bill. Blue and I had been in contact with the regiment and about thirty of our former comrades planned to come. Most were currently stationed in the London barracks, but several flew in directly from Cyprus on three days' special leave.

It was a quirky old building. No doubt Hurtley and Sons would have liked to get their hands on it, either to modernise, or quite possibly tear it down for a complete rebuild; but, when I tried asking Arthur about it, he was reticent.

"If I even breathed the suggestion, it would cost me my membership," he averred. But the club had moved before, from The Strand in the 1780s, so I didn't quite see the problem.

A knight of the realm, Sir Augustus Browning, April's Godfather, was an elderly retired admiral who could not help exuding the innate superiority of the Royal Navy, the 'Senior Service', over we poor Army lads. Perhaps it was that we were mostly, or had been, enlisted men, regular soldiers not officers; but, when introduced, I felt the disdain dripping off him like engine oil as he briefly took my hand, not shaking it, barely touching it even, while looking upward, right over my head. Imagine, then, what happened when this genetically racist popinjay first met Vijay. Trying to conceal the utter disgust he evidently felt, growing steadily more upright and stiff, his features turning white with the effort, the effect was almost comical if it hadn't, in a way, been also pathetically tragic.

There were others of colour in our crew, and for us it was like a great big, boozy family reunion. Congregating downstairs in the bar, swallowing copious amounts of ale while barely taking breath, we found ourselves in a separate camp from the mainly civilian group, rounded up by the hapless Arthur, of April's cousins and uncles, his friends and business partners. By the time food was served in the top-floor dining-room, some at least of our number, having met hours beforehand for some serious drinking in a local hostelry, found it a challenge to even climb the long, steep flights of stairs.

Arthur, with the Admiral at his side, was there at the top to greet and guide us, both looking fresh in a way that was remarkable, until I learned that they had ascended the dizzy heights by means of the makeshift elevator from the kitchen, shoe-horned in well after the venerable edifice was first built, enabling waiters to deliver and serve food that was still tolerably warm. The modern versions of those same waiters were now being kept busy replenishing the glasses of thirsty servicemen drinking the champagne like it was lemonade, and the claret like it was grape juice. Before sitting down, one or two had even started throwing bread rolls at each other.

There were six tables of eight place settings, plus one of nine because the chaps from the pub had dragged in a red-faced corporal from the Welsh Guards who happened to be drinking there too. Friends and relatives occupied tables two and three; soldiers four to seven. Blue, Vijay and I were on the top table interspersed between Arthur himself, Browning, two of April's uncles, and a cousin. A gong rang somewhere and everyone took their seats. In no time, the loud hum of masculine chatter filled that low-ceilinged room. Next to me was Uncle Davie, April's mother's older brother, a spry, ancient fellow. Keen to establish a military connection, he mentioned that he'd been in the Navy during the Falklands War of 1982, serving on a ship that was sunk.

Davie was on the main deck when they were attacked by two Argentine fighters dropping bombs, a couple of which hit the vessel low down on the starboard flank, the explosions destroying bulkheads and ripping a great hole in the side, causing immediate uncontrollable flooding. Within twenty minutes, the ship had keeled right over and had to be abandoned. Davie modestly described helping survivors up through the smoke from below-decks, putting them into life-jackets and lowering them to the sea where previously launched life-rafts were waiting. Finally, he was able to simply walk nonchalantly down the side of the ship, listing so badly as to be nearly horizontal, and sit calmly for a while on a blade of the propeller, reflecting on life and death in this otherwise beautiful sunset seascape, before sliding into the water to his rescue. The ship went down later, during the hours of darkness, and lies there still, a war grave, three hundred feet or more beneath the waves.

"I had the reassuring if not specially logical sense that I was going to be okay, you see," Davie continued, eyes twinkling, "I felt amazingly calm."

"What happened then?" I asked.

"Eventually we were taken aboard a Royal Fleet Auxiliary vessel to South Georgia," he replied, "And then home on the QE2... That was it!"

He seemed to think it was a great joke, but then his voice took on a slightly more sober tone.

"We lost about two dozen sailors, and quite a few injured," he said. "I've never forgotten them, nor the awful acrid smoke, the fierce flames and overpowering heat... Above all, too, I can't help recalling the looks of horror and grief on those men's faces; not fear, mind you. None of them showed any fear... War's such a terrible waste."

I wanted to continue the conversation and tell him he was a true hero, but that was the moment Arthur, in a brief preview of his wedding speech, chose to stand up and welcome everyone, raising a glass to Vijay, talking about April for a bit, then saying how sure he was that our friend would make his precious girl deliriously happy; at which exact point, entirely unbidden, the Welshman, Taff Morgan, cheerfully drunk, stood and led the gathered company in three cheers. The only thing we couldn't understand later, Blue and I, was why Arthur kept on about April sadly having to pull out of her career at Guys Hospital. Apparently, all this time, he thought she was a nursing student there, so she must have misled him on purpose. As Blue said, women can be devious at times.

We carried on eating and drinking. Uncle Davie was telling Blue the same remarkable Falklands tale he'd told me. The cousin on my other flank, some kind of private banker, proved himself perfectly boring, so I was delighted when Vijay stood up as the waiters finished clearing away the remnants of sherry trifle.

Winking at me, my fine friend and comrade thanked Arthur for his generous hospitality that evening, and for allowing him to marry his beautiful daughter. How wonderfully fortunate it had been, he said, that her good friend 'Abigail' had introduced them to one-another a few short weeks ago. Trying to stem the laughter, Blue nearly choked on his wine; and, as Vijay was finishing, raising his glass 'To love and beauty', I had to cover my grin by dabbing my face with a napkin.

"Now," the groom-to-be added, "Let's everyone enjoy themselves!" And sat down.

Precious little encouragement was required for we men of the regiment to let down our hair. Cheese soon followed, accompanied by Port and Madeira, then the dinner party broke up to reconvene downstairs in the bar. Arthur, with the stuffy Admiral and Uncle Davie in tow, made his excuses and left, urging us to make full use of his account at the club. At about the same moment Taff Morgan's resounding tenor voice rang throughout those hallowed portals in an impromptu rendition of a heart-breaking Welsh song about a girl called Myfanwy. This was, as it turned out, an amazingly prophetic lament about lost love, which was followed by the much more cheerful and ribald rugby song that began, *'Why was he born so beautiful? Why was he born at all?'* At full volume, many voices joined in the chorus,

'He's no bloody good to anyone. He's no bloody use at all!'

And so it went on for hours, the songs getting increasingly raucous, rude and profane as the night wore on. Someone fell, and there was blood. Someone else failed to make it to the mezzanine toilet, puking copiously outside in the hall. Drink was spilled liberally on the spotless parquet floor. Some went off in search of the famed and fabulous 'Abigail'. The barman called 'Time', and eventually went home after the remaining half-dozen of us refused point-blank to leave and carried on serving ourselves. I would decidedly not have liked to be the one clearing up the mess; or, indeed, paying the bill. Arthur must have been glad next day that his April was getting married only the once. That, at least, I feel sure, is what he fondly believed.

Blue and I both count ourselves manly drinkers, but were each forced to remember the following morning how deadly is the consumption of Port. We felt lousy. Fortunately, the wedding was still a couple of days away, giving us time to recover before the next happy onslaught. We skipped Vijay's christening service, preferring extra karate practice instead that afternoon, but looked forward to the principal ceremony where I was to be the Best Man.

In the event, with ladies present and fewer servicemen, it was a relatively sedate occasion. The reception was comparatively modest and restrained too. The most awkward thing for me and Blue was the haunting presence of both Gloria and Moira, both dolled up and looking a million dollars; but they both had new beaus at their obvious beck and call, and studiously ignored us all day, so the discomfort wasn't so painful. They weren't bridesmaids (that duty being reserved for a couple of pre-teens, Arthur's great-nieces), so at least when my turn came to make a speech and make the toast, I didn't have to praise our former love interests by name. Naturally I took the opportunity to regale the party with a military joke, and was delighted that it went down so well, especially with the men.

It was an old tale of a tall Sergeant-Major, standing ramrod-straight in the full dress uniform of the Royal Scots Dragoon Guards (a fine regiment, sadly long gone, merged with others), tasked with discovering from a town pharmacist in Edinburgh the price of what Americans call 'prophylactics', forced to show at the same time a badly damaged item to ask the (cheaper) cost of repair. In possession of the necessary intelligence, making a sharp about turn, this august figure then departed the busy shop, only to return an hour later. Taking the same torn and worn, tissue-wrapped, heavy-duty rubber johnny from his sporran, its place of concealment, presenting it to the chemist once more, the Sergeant-Major blurts out the punch-line in a rich and resonant Scottish accent, like this... "The Rrr...egiment have decided to have it rrepairrred!"

Uncle Davie was still cackling loudly about that hoary tale when later the dancing began.

I did feel relief, though, when both my speech and the wedding celebrations were over, standing there with Blue as we waved the newly-spliced couple off to Heathrow for the start of their honeymoon. The destination of this well-planned journey was India; April never having been to that great country, and Vijay keenly desirous that she see and experience its many wonders first hand. He couldn't have known that his masterful idea would prove such a costly mistake.

On return, they were to move into a lovely, refurbished townhouse in Twickenham, owned by Arthur; paying, of course, zero rent. April had visited and approved it, and decorators had been working already for a few weeks, getting it ready to her specifications, no holds barred. When a delighted Vijay showed us round one afternoon, I told him he was a lucky man, but I was not totally comfortable. Something felt wrong there, or wrong about us being there. Little did I know that none of us three lads would ever set foot in that building again.

Blue and I set off for Africa ten days later. I made sure we travelled Business-Class, and slept well on the overnight flight to Johannesburg to be as fresh as possible for the next hop to Victoria Falls, where there are in fact two airports: one in Zimbabwe, and the one we wanted across the Zambezi River, a short drive north-west of the Zambian town of Livingstone, quite close to those amazing falls that are twice the height and twice the width of those at Niagara. Emerging from the terminal into bright sunlight, carrying our kitbags, we found a smart, olive-green, four-wheel drive Toyota wagon with a uniformed driver in place, and Bruce Laycock seated beside him, grinning fit to burst.

"There you go!" he said. "Good to see you Boys... Stow your gear and clamber in."

It was so good to be away from London. I only realised then how frustratingly hemmed in I'd been feeling. In this place, I could really breathe easy. The thirty minute drive took us through the quiet town, heading south and then east, climbing for the final minutes through unspoilt bush to Bruce's 'Blinkers' HQ, converted from a luxury safari lodge overlooking the broad plain of the Zambezi River. It was only a couple of miles from *Mosi-oa-Tunya*, which translates as, 'The Smoke that Thunders', the local name for the terrific mile-and-a-half wide waterfall, the clouds of spray from which we could easily see from the terrace of the elegant central building, built in African open-air style with ebony pillars supporting a tightly thatched roof. The purpose it served, according to Laycock, was to provide a reasonable measure of comfort for his officers. There was a good kitchen, managed by a chef of some quality, as evidenced by the inventively-presented 'bush tucker' he served that first evening: thinly-sliced, pan-seared, succulent young crocodile meat with a mango salad as an entree, followed by roasted guinea fowl, sweet potatoes and local grown vegetables cooked *al dente*, followed by a large helping of a tasty, nasturtium seed ice-cream garnished with edible flowers from the same plant. What a treat!

We were billeted individually in small, native-style huts with modern plumbing, and mosquito nets over the firm but comfortable beds. After dumping our kit, the Colonel, as he liked to be called here in Africa, showed us around. What we found was both expected and unexpected. Store-rooms and modern, air-conditioned offices stood close to the main lodge, but there was only a small barracks, serving as accommodation for the men in training. The parade ground was also modest in size, and the firing range surprisingly short. The whole scale of things seemed rather limited and disappointing. However, by way of explanation, Laycock soon led us along a path through trees and scrub to a clearing, the site of a big helipad with open hangars for two helicopters, one of which, with a pilot at the ready, was waiting there standing by.

"Hop aboard," the Colonel instructed. "We're going where the real work gets done."

When we landed, fifteen minutes later, Blue and I were impressed. Here, suitably fenced-off but surrounded on all sides by open country, was a large and properly equipped paramilitary training facility, over which no expense had obviously been spared. It was also, we discovered, home to Blink's clandestine sister operation, 'Blind', and therefore a place we would get to know well. For the next hour or so, we went round inspecting the facilities and meeting some of the men.

Back at the Lodge by dusk, after a refreshing swim in the full-size infinity pool that overlooked the plain, clouds of spray from the falls still visible against the western skyline and the fast-setting orange sun, we gathered for a cold beer before that highly appetising three-course repast. I could not have been happier, and I know Blue felt the same for he couldn't keep a smile off his face. We were in paradise... What could possibly spoil it? A message from Vijay, that's what.

It came in on my mobile the following morning at breakfast; the chef had made a brilliantly appetising kedgeree dish; and it came in the succinct form of a text: *'Marriage kaput... Can I join U?'* When I showed him, Blue looked at it and smiled.

"She was always a selfish little minx, that April," he said, cheekily. "I wonder if she'll go back to nursing?"

Truthfully, we were sorry... Sorry, but not in the slightest surprised; so I sent a text back saying *'Probly... Will ask boss'*, and went to find Laycock in his office.

"I'll get on to Deirdre directly," he responded with alacrity, once I'd put him in the picture. "What's Vijay's number? We can't let a good soldier go to waste!"

So our mate came out to Africa, and we were the three musketeers once more. Blue, jokey as ever, put it succinctly like this, "Every silver lining has a cloud."

That was certainly something to ponder, and it became for us a kind of wry, morale-boosting motto as we faced and weathered numerous storms and vicissitudes during the years that followed. Eventually, the sorry tale of Vijay's marriage failure came out; doomed from the outset, it seems now, by a flawed central character, the common ingredient of so much human tragedy, as Shakespeare knew only too well.

"Thinking about it," Vijay told us one day, "Getting married and having a spectacular wedding was so important to April that she never really looked beyond it. Once it was done, she didn't have any real plan or project to occupy herself with any more. Apart from the house, she had no excuses to bully people into giving her whatever she wanted..."

As he described it, his wife of but an hour or two changed personality by the time they were in the car going to the airport, having stopped briefly at her father's house to shower, change clothes and collect suitcases.

"She wasn't satisfied," he said. "She started complaining about everything. To be honest, I think she was scared... Scared of the future with me; scared of not being in control; scared of the unknown; scared of everything."

Here was Madame Bovary all over again, I was thinking, the spoilt daughter of a doting father, without a mother, flirtatiously wilful and self-centred, who never truly grows up.

Vijay said April complained on that ride first about the temperature in the church; too cold. She complained next about the vicar who had spoken, in her sermon, about April's mother looking down from above to bless the happy couple, unwittingly conjuring up in the bride's mind the only person, in heaven or on earth, who always made her feel guilty. She complained about poor attendance at the ceremony; ignoring that, on a Friday, many would have found it difficult to be there. Then, regarding the reception, she complained about the catering; too much food going to waste. Then, typically, she complained about my speech, that terrible, risqué joke, and about her Uncle Davie for laughing so loudly when I told it. She even complained that the band had been playing too loud for people to enjoy conversation.

"I was only grateful," Vijay said with relief, "That she didn't complain about me."

By the time they got to Heathrow, April had calmed down, happy to be made a fuss of by airline staff as a VIP, escorted swiftly through the normally frustrating departures checks and procedures into the luxury lounge for the short wait until boarding; but problems soon reappeared.

Once on the aircraft, soon after take-off, Vijay suggested they settle down in the very serviceable 'beds' in First Class, pulling on eye shades and following his own advice without delay; but the new bride found it harder to sleep, drank three glasses of the complimentary champagne, chatted to the female cabin crew (who wanted to hear all about the wedding), watched a series of movie trailers, listened to some music, tried and failed to drop off to sleep, then watched a whole movie through, deciding afterwards that she hadn't liked it at all. The flight time to Delhi was almost nine hours, and the time difference an extra four-and-a-half, so the late-night service got them to their destination at around midday local time while their body clocks were only just registering morning. When the lights went up and breakfast was served, April was sure she hadn't slept a wink. Vijay, on the other hand, was totally fresh.

"You were snoring," were the first words he heard when he woke. "It's your fault I couldn't sleep..."

And that exchange set the pattern for the next few days. April was unhappy, and it was always either Vijay's fault or that of some other luckless innocent person. She found the heat oppressive, the streets overcrowded and dirty, the traffic ill-disciplined and dangerous, the inevitable delays exasperating, and the inescapable poverty beyond her capacity to either believe or accept.

"What kind of backward country is this?" she was asking before they'd even reached the cultural oasis of their six star hotel. The venomous feeling that backed this remark obviously did not bode well.

Thirty

Most of Vijay's relatives lived in either Mumbai or Kolkata. For this reason, to avoid the possibility of running into any of them, he organised a personal tour with private guides and a driver that went nowhere near either city. The newlyweds were to spend three days and nights in the capital, Delhi, two in Agra, three at the Wildlife sanctuary, Ranthanbore National Park (in the hope of seeing tigers in the wild), then three more days in the beautiful, historic city of Jaipur in Rajasthan. From there they would return to New Delhi airport directly. He felt sure his darling would enjoy every minute of this tour of enchantment; but of course, in this, he couldn't have been more mistaken.

Jet-lagged and weary, April missed the rest of the first day's sight-seeing, taking immediately to her bed and staying there until Vijay appeared, fresh after a dip in the pool, to escort her to dinner; at which, typically, she decided on roast chicken cooked in European style, then failed to eat much of the meat. She was suspicious that the spicy foreign cuisine would have mysteriously somehow tainted her dish, so she left most of it on the plate while applying herself enthusiastically to drinking the indifferent white wine on offer at stupendous price.

While Vijay once more slept soundly, and snored, she then lay awake half the night, too cold and disturbed by the noise when the air-conditioner was running, too hot and sweaty when it was off. Finally, as dawn broke, she nodded off from exhaustion. Later in the morning, grumpier than ever, she insisted on staying put, so Vijay left her to slumber and made his way, first to breakfast then to the lobby to rendezvous with their guide, Mr Gupta, to discuss options, cutting the day's itinerary in half, preserving only the excursion to Old Delhi for April to enjoy in the afternoon. They could catch up a little the following day.

At about eleven, Vijay returned to their room and offered his wife the new plan. To his delight and surprise, April accepted, ordered an omelette from room service and made herself ready by half-past twelve, but the good mood did not last long.

Mr Karan, the driver, left them on a street near the Great Mosque, the 17th century *Jama Masjid*, built to hold 20,000 Muslims for Friday prayers. Having removed their sandals, according to custom, April, to blend in, was wearing a large shawl covering her head as well as her arms. Possibly because of being barefoot and her eyesight compromised by the headgear, she stumbled in the process of climbing the steep stone stairs to the main courtyard, leaving Vijay to catch her up in his arms and carry her gallantly onto the vast forecourt, where he set her down with great care.

"Thank you, kind Sir," she said before looking around, adding bluntly, "Goodness! Look at this barren place. There's nothing much to it, is there?"

It's true that the mosque is mostly open space. There is no interior to it exactly, only a narrow covered area at the front; but that is all that's required for people to gather, kneel, and pray in extended lines facing Mecca to the west. When one of the multitude of pigeons flying around dive-bombed close to her, its little white-coated package of muck splattering the ground at her bare feet, April called time on the visit in disgust. After a quick look across to the nearby Red Fort, the couple returned to recover their footwear and move on.

If April was little impressed by the mosque, she was even less so as they took a short cycle rickshaw ride through the bustling local bazaar, which she found overcrowded and insufficiently spotless for her fastidious taste. They were besieged, too, by the persistent attentions of raggedy children begging for money, one young girl carrying her baby sister in her arms to make her claim on their wealth deliberately harder to resist. It was a truly pathetic sight.

"If you give them anything," Mr Gupta piped up with a quick caution to curb their enthusiasm, "They will never give up, only multiply... Also, they don't keep it. They have to give the money to the men who look after them. It's a confidence trick... Bring only sweets next time, or ballpoints."

April said to Vijay she thought it was mighty cruel to ignore the plight of these ragamuffins, but closed her purse and took the guide's advice nevertheless, at which point Vijay observed that the scruffy kids soon found other, more hopeful prospects, other victims to besiege with their well-rehearsed displays of distress.

When the narrow streets of the neighbourhood became quieter, under Mr Gupta's patient direction it became possible for the couple to wander on foot for a while. April seemed to enjoy, at first, spying on the many monkeys cavorting around, scavenging for food among the rooftops and awnings above the cramped local shops. As one street vendor, selling little rolled up parcels of food, was having particular difficulty fending off the insistent attentions of these wily creatures, April stood by with Vijay in amused wonder; until, that is, taking advantage of her distraction, one of the bolder thieves stole from off her head the sunglasses that she carried there for convenience.

Crying out in sudden alarm, she shouted loudly at the monkey to give back her precious Sungod Renegades, completely ignoring the fact that, even if it could understand words, they would have to be spoken in Hindi. Fortunately, Mr Gupta, knowing what might work (for this was a common occurrence), stepped in smartly to the rescue. Purchasing a small brown paper bag full of peanuts in their shells from the food man, using them to barter, he held his offering out to the offending beast, sitting on a wall nearby, highly alert to proceedings and still clutching his trophy. Then, swiftly, as soon as the bag came within reach, the animal made a grab for it, at the same time letting go of the glasses, which dropped with a clatter to the pavement as most of the peanuts, the bag fatally torn, also rattled down in a shower, initiating a scramble involving not only the principle offender but a dozen or so of his fellow primates as well, each hell-bent on retrieving as many nuts as they could.

April stepped back in alarm. The trade successful, the hero of the hour, Mr Gupta, casually waving his arms to dismiss the unruly mass of monkeys, already in rapid retreat, in one flowing motion then bent to pick up the discarded prize, handing it back to its owner; but April didn't want the glasses, rejecting them as if the culprit had somehow managed to coat them with nerve-poison; so Vijay was obliged to accept them himself and slip them into his pocket.

April never wore them again, he told us. In high dudgeon, she also firmly insisted on returning straight back to the safety of the hotel, so they never visited the Red Fort, the 12th century victory tower known as the *Qutub Minar*, Humayun's Tomb, a remarkable 16th century mausoleum set in majestic gardens built for the second Mughal Emperor of that name, the India Gate and nearby monumental buildings designed for the government of India by famed British architects, Sir Edward Lutyens and Sir Herbert Baker, or any of the other exciting sights on their original schedule, except one. After another late start due to April again sleeping in, before heading off to Agra the following day, they had time to visit Raj Ghat, the site of Mahatma Gandhi's funeral pyre following his assassination by gunshot in 1948.

There was a beautiful symmetry and simplicity about this monument, with a central flame permanently alight, that Vijay found indescribably and almost unbearably moving. He admitted he was already shedding quiet tears as they walked behind Mr Gupta up the slope to the viewing area. There was nothing much to see, and April was clearly bored, but she was also privately alarmed at the emotional reaction of her husband. She simply could not understand the depth of it, and when she asked about his reaction during the long drive south, he could not explain himself either.

"He was such a wise man! Such a great Indian!" was all he could coherently say. To try and lighten the conversation, he asked if she knew what Gandhi had said on a trip to England when asked what he thought of western civilisation. Of course, she had no idea.

"He said it *would be* a wonderful thing!" Vijay said with a grin; but sadly his attempt at humour fell flat for, even when he tried to explain, his wife proved incapable of grasping the point.

They went to Agra. She loved the *Taj Mahal*, remembering a magazine photo of a sorrowful, lonely Princess Diana in that most enchanting and romantic of places, but she was predictably bored with both Agra's Red Fort and the extensive, barren, dry and dusty palace of *Fatepur Sikri*, which they toured on the way to Bharatpur railway station. From here they took the air-conditioned train to Ranthanbore, while Mr Karan, to their surprise, took the much longer journey by road, their luggage with him in the boot of the car.

"They're just dead places," was April's comment on the many ornate buildings they'd inspected.

"Don't you see? They're beautiful, and full of history," Vijay countered, but she wasn't interested in the Mughal emperors, their conquests, their loves and their fatal in-fighting; she was already thinking about going home. If there's one more unpleasant disappointment, she decided in her own mind, she would call it a day, so the tiger park would have brilliantly to exceed her expectations. Unfortunately, though, it did not.

The relatively small National Park is divided into several sections, and visitors are allocated to a different one each time they enter the sanctuary. A specially adapted jeep, with raised viewing seats behind the driver, collects people in small groups from a series of hotels before travelling to the identified park gate for their designated game drive. For safety, no-one is allowed to step out of the vehicle, a restriction which April naturally found highly frustrating. She was equally unhappy about having to get up at six o'clock for breakfast and an early departure; but the worst thing, she discovered, was the cold air at that hour. Despite the blankets provided, before the sun rose high enough to provide any warmth, she genuinely thought she would freeze, possibly to actual death.

In addition, they were unlucky. No tigers were spotted on their route that morning. Also, to make things worse, another couple spent the ensuing lunch period boasting about driving close to a mother tiger with two playful little cubs, showing anyone interested the photos on their smart phones to prove it. Another group had even briefly caught the rare sight of a leopard on a hilltop in the distance. Even so, April denied any feelings of envy.

In contrast, Vijay had genuinely enjoyed the sightings of various deer, a porcupine, langur monkeys, a mongoose, a couple of diminutive sloth bears, and many varied species of colourful birds pointed out by their naturalist guide, Nitin, a real bird lover and specialist. Vijay was looking forward to the afternoon drive, but April refused to go.

"What's the point?" she said. "It's uncomfortable. The scenery's drab, and you hardly see anything... You go, if you like, but I'm going to the spa for a massage instead."

As it turned out, a common traveller's ailment came suddenly upon her, and she had to remain in the room all afternoon, spending most of the time in the toilet. Predictably, in her absence, Vijay's group that afternoon was exceptionally lucky and saw several tigers; first three sisters with two cubs frolicking at a water hole, and later, in the forest near a watercourse, a huge regal male waking from a nap, rising sleepily, and then making his languid way in a wide semi-circle around the tourist vehicles, summoned rapidly after the first sighting of this prize beast by radio messages between the guides. There might have been fifty people watching that tiger taking a drink at the stream before lolloping off into the undergrowth.

Six tigers was more than anyone had seen in a single outing for a long time. Vijay, making the connection between what he had witnessed and his regiment, the Tigers (to which we all felt such strong and lasting allegiance), despite being an avowed atheist, described feeling incredibly blessed. He said he couldn't wait to share his good fortune with April; but by then, however, she'd made her final decision.

"To buggery with tigers, and to hell with Jaipur and India!" she expostulated when he returned to find her indisposed on the bed. "I've told Gupta to rebook the flight... Tomorrow, we're going home."

This was not the end of the beginning. The relationship had barely enjoyed a beginning. Neither was it the beginning of the end... It *was* the end. April rejected Vijay totally, as if he and India were one. She sensed that both had betrayed her, and both, therefore, were cursed. After further remonstrations on her part, and a good deal of pleading on his to no avail, by the time their plane landed at Heathrow, the marriage was over for good. Two days later, Vijay sent me his text. Soon, he was able to join us.

After all these years of austerity and deprivation, it does my heart good to look back and reflect on the idyllic six months we three spent as 'Blinkers' near Livingstone. For one thing, no-one was trying to kill us; unless you count the time a raw recruit from Senegal, in charge of a loaded rifle for the first time, managed accidentally to discharge a round at close range into the baked red earth precisely half-way between my left and right big toes, giving me a jolt, and earning him both a smart clip to the side of his stupid head, and an immediate return ticket home.

The Colonel made sure we always had one day off from our duties each week, and I never tired of visiting the falls, revelling each time in the sheer energy on display, sometimes sitting near the bank on the upper river, mesmerised by the eddies and flow of the current making its way to the edge of the stupendous cascade, before toppling over on its one hundred metre downward journey to the gorge below. It's hard to say why; a reflection on life and the unrepeatable choices we must occasionally make, I suppose; but there was something totally fascinating about the inevitability of that awesome dive, once the pivotal point of no return had been reached.

At other times, I took great delight in walking into the heavy spray below the falls where, except in the dry season, there was always a brilliant rainbow. The vantage point, about halfway between top and bottom of the immense cataract, was actually on the second gorge, a rocky outcrop that was one of the falls' previous sites. Every few thousand years, the water erodes the basalt layer sufficiently to create a new fall-line. In all, according to geologists, there have been seven of these, forming six separate gorges over a distance of about three and a half miles. You can see them from the air, as I did a few times in a helicopter, and once, memorably, from the passenger seat of a two-man microlite aircraft with a rear-fitted propeller that was like a glorified hang-glider to look at, powered by an engine more suitable for a lawn-mower in my eyes than a reliable flying machine, a trip that came about from a conversation I struck up with a German in a Livingstone bar one evening. Günter was the pilot of one of these dodgy contraptions and said that he had been taking tourists up to fly over the falls several times a day for almost twelve years.

"It is totally safe," he assured me, so I agreed to give it a try.

A few days later, early in the morning, I showed up at the Air Batoka airfield, which consisted of a hangar, a building for reception and admin, and a flat dirt strip carved out of the surrounding bush, about three miles upstream from the falls. Blue came to watch but said he wouldn't fly, adding unhelpfully that he thought I was utterly bonkers. I was made to read some instructions and sign a piece of paper that said I knew I was undertaking an operation that carried risks, including the risk of death. They even filmed me saying I understood how dangerous it could be. Having my confession on permanent record was their belt and braces approach to absolving themselves from any responsibility regarding my fate; covering their backs in case any surviving relatives felt like suing them after my unhappy demise. I then had to empty my pockets of everything, for there would be no preventing stuff falling out once the potentially bumpy flight started; and I was given a helmet.

The affable Günter was pleasantly reassuring, speaking to me calmly through the headset, after I took my place behind him aboard the fragile machine as we taxied away down the strip before turning to face into the wind and start the run up to take off. For the briefest moment, as our flimsy craft rose from the ground, I felt the tiniest sensation of panic; and then it was all just elation. Quickly up above the canopy of trees, with the sun rising fast to dispel the lingering ground mist, I immediately caught sight of the majestic river a few hundred yards westwards as we turned towards it, then followed its journey downstream.

Günter took us first in a high, wide circuit, giving me a splendid overview of the Zambezi's many upstream islands, its banks lined here and there by luxury tourist hotels, each with its central building and swimming pool surrounded by serried ranks of individual lodges; then the hydro-electric plant below the second gorge, all the other gorges linked by the sharp zigzag of the watercourse, and back towards the glorious falls themselves. After about ten minutes, he took us lower, into and through the shimmering spray, back and forth until we were totally soaked but, in my case, almost delirious with joy. There seemed to be rainbows everywhere.

We were buffeted constantly by air currents. It was chilly, and the engine noise was extremely loud, but I took little notice of these minor flaws in the total experience. Nothing I had ever done, not even parachuting, was comparable to the thrill of such a seamless connection to nature in all its raw power. I wanted to stay up there for much longer, but the Teutonic Günter was firm.

"I'm sorry, Freddie," he said, "We have to turn back now... Now, we have to turn back!"

Yet there was more enjoyment for me; first, as my pilot told me to take firm hold of the struts while he let me steer for a while; then, as we flew back upstream, low over the river, catching sight of a great herd of hippos in the shallows off one of the larger islands that some tourist boats were trying to approach. As the great creatures wallowed, some raising their heads and opening their mouths to grunt and wail like only hippos can, I could see right down their throats.

"You must do it, Blue!" I said to my mate soon after landing. "You really must have a go!"

But I failed to persuade him.

"Let's just get some breakfast," he said. "I'm hungry. Aren't you?"

Thirty-One

The local town was, of course, named after the explorer, David Livingstone, the son of a Scottish Sunday school teacher who became a qualified doctor and an ordained minister of the Congregationalist Church. We didn't learn that much about him at school but I soon discovered, in a specially dedicated gallery in the town museum, a number of remarkable facts.

Livingstone learned his medicine in Glasgow, studying theology at the same time. By the age of twenty-five, he was having further training with the London Missionary Society, while also continuing medical studies at the Charing Cross Hospital. Two years later, he set off for Africa where he seems to have spent a lot of time trekking vast distances around much of the southern part of that continent, learning one of the principal local languages, Tswana, and looking for suitable places to set up church missions.

At the age of thirty-one, he was attacked by a lion while helping villagers defend their sheep, his life saved only by the heroic intervention of a friend who was bitten and mauled but also survived. Livingstone's left arm was badly crushed during the incident. The broken bone was then set badly and caused him problems, as well as pain, for the rest of his life. There was even a plaster cast of the shattered humerus, misaligned and badly knitted together, in the museum, leaving me totally surprised that he was still capable of lifting weighty objects with that arm, which could no longer, though, be raised above shoulder-height. Other fascinating exhibits, donated by the Livingstone family, included his surgical instrument case and medical box, many letters in his scratchy, ill-disciplined but legible scrawl, his rather shapeless, heavy-duty, brown jacket and matching, rather ugly, smock-like undergarment, together with his navy-coloured peaked cap adorned by a faded red and gold band reminiscent of Louis's, the church guardian and guide at Lalibela.

Something good did happen to Livingstone, though, at about this time, for he met Mary, the oldest daughter of another Scottish missionary, Robert Moffat, who he married the following year. Eight years David's junior, born and raised in Africa, she was a fluent Tswana speaker. The couple went on to have six children before, aged only forty-one, Mary died of malaria. Unfortunately for those children, too, David, the inveterate traveller, was often wholly absent as a father. Neither was he much good as a missionary. According to legend, he only converted one native African to Christianity, a tribal chief; and even he wavered, reluctant to forego his former practice of polygamy, having five wives, also finding it frustrating that Livingstone's God would not obey commands to bring rain down during a drought.

Surviving a lion attack notwithstanding, Livingstone seems to have been a highly unfortunate character. Beset throughout life by illness as well as injury; recurrent attacks of malaria, a near-fatal bout of pneumonia, episodes of cholera are all recorded; he was also a father estranged from his surviving children, and a man still searching for his grail, the source of the Nile, when he died at the age of sixty.

His best known triumph, the discovery of the falls, came about in 1855 when Livingstone was forty-two, during his long quest not only to establish trade and religious missions throughout central Africa, but also and primarily to put an end to slavery in those parts. He renamed those tremendous examples of nature's raw power after his Queen Emperor; although, of course, they had a perfectly good name already, and his 'discovery' was of something that had never actually been lost. Perhaps that was why; as we found out one day when the Colonel organised a trip to the nearest village, Mokuni; the revered traveller was kept waiting half a day by the tribal chief, having to kick his dusty heels in the shade of a great oak-like tree (still standing to greet us), before being allowed entry to the fenced enclosure surrounding the head man's hut and those of his several wives.

Nothing much seemed to have changed during the many intervening years. The enclosure was still there. (We were not invited in.) The huts in the village were still made and thatched in the traditional way. No tarmac or concrete was in evidence. The paths and compounds were still surfaced by hard-beaten red dirt, but we did see small solar electric panels resting precariously atop a few of the huts, and there was just one water standpipe for the entire village community, numbering a couple of hundred.

One building did stand out from the rest, the words 'Neighbourhood Watch' on a painted sign apparently identifying its purpose. However, built of brick, neatly painted green and white on the exterior, with a corrugated tin roof and a small fenced-in forecourt, each of its two cramped chambers was fronted by a locked wrought-iron gate, for it actually served as a lock-up, being used mainly to incarcerate drunks until they were sober enough and well-enough behaved for release. One sorry such miscreant was even in residence during our visit, begging to be let out. It was hard not to laugh.

The other brick buildings, on the outskirts of the village, housed the primary school and a health centre. Both were too small; the children attending classes in morning and afternoon shifts, two or three to a desk, for example, with teachers at either end of the single schoolroom teaching separate subjects to different groups at the same time. Without exercise books, the kids were writing on slates using chalk. Educational ambition here was obviously, of necessity, rudimentary at best; and health care was similarly deficient.

There were few people about, and we assumed that most worked in town, where the older children also attended school, or in the tourist hotels. Those we did see were either elderly women minding children, or chickens and usually a few goats, or younger folk making artefacts to sell to tourists, like carved traditional face-masks, stringed musical instruments and drums, also wooden animals, notably elephants, hippos and giraffes. Everyone here was leading a rather forlorn existence, it seemed.

Another gift from Cocky Laycock, towards the end of our first six months in Africa, was an exciting three-day safari to a game reserve in Botswana. Like Vijay in Ranthanbore, we were incredibly lucky. The guides warned us that, because of the recent drought in those parts, there may be few decent sightings, so we were delighted on the first day to encounter a couple of rhino, one black and one white, together with the white rhino's three-day old calf. Pinto, one of the guides (who admitted with a toothy grin to having once been an ivory poacher), said he had never seen the two types together before, and that it was rare also to see a baby so young.

As we drove on, entering a more forested area, we saw high in the sky an enormous Martial eagle. As we stopped to watch, it suddenly dived down among the treetops, only to re-emerge a second later with a large snake gripped firmly in its talons. Once again, it was Pinto who told us that none of the guides had ever seen that happen before.

The next day, the wonders continued. We rounded a bend in the track at one point to come suddenly upon a big flock of vultures feeding on the carcase of a giraffe, taking to instant flight in a raucous flurry as we approached, some alighting on nearby branches, others rising high on thermal up-currents.

"The final moments of a feeding frenzy," said Pinto. "We've never seen that before either!"

In the afternoon, the two Land Rovers again travelling along a dusty track at a steady pace, one behind the other, we were met and overtaken by a twenty-strong herd of elephants, running at full speed beside us, charging forward and then stopping to feed not too far ahead. Among the great beasts, we spotted a young calf, possibly only a week or two old.

"Stay perfectly still," Pinto commanded.

The matriarch had returned to approach the vehicles and was looking directly into my eyes, only three feet away, giving me the strangest feeling of a deep personal connection to this awe-inspiring creature, as if she was checking me out and saying Hello. I suppose I must have passed muster, for she soon turned away and led her loyal troop away again into the bush.

"Have you seen that before, Pinto?" I asked before he could speak.

"Never!" he replied. "You men have truly been blessed."

There was one more thing to help make those six months a little bit special. I met someone, a woman called Pamila. She was a black person, a native of those parts, beautiful not only to look at but in her character as well. She was calm and dignified, as if always looking at the world, and whoever she might encounter there, with the eyes and mind of a profound wisdom that rose from an inexhaustible source deep within the inviolable centre of her being. She had a compassionate heart.

We met because of an accident. The recruits were digging a trench under my instruction one day when one stumbled. Trying to maintain his balance, he began flailing around with his shovel, which caught me hard on the rib cage beneath my fortunately up-raised right arm. The force of the strike made me fall sideways into the narrow trench. It was over in a flash, and I had to be taken to the small central hospital in town for wound cleansing and a few stitches. A couple of ribs had been broken, so I was going to have to rest up. In the fall, I had also twisted my ankle, spraining the ligaments badly enough to need crutches to get around. A course of physio was prescribed to help me mend quickly. Pamila would give me the treatment.

I had three, thirty-minute sessions during each of the first couple of weeks, then a few more intermittently after that. We chatted, of course, and got to know each other a little. I was not intentionally seeking either sex or romance, and neither was she, but something was clearly happening between us by the end of week two, so I asked that day if she happened to be free for lunch, which she was.

"But, remember!" she teased. "You are still my patient. There's a code of behaviour, you know."

So we had a meal together, during which she told me she was alone in the world and much preferred it that way. I understood, I told her, because I felt exactly the same. When she asked how come, I started to speak about Carol, about how I could never possibly expect to meet anyone to compare. She said she knew what I meant because her husband, Keni, had been similarly special for her, but he had died rescuing a tourist from the river several years earlier.

Keni was a hero, but a dead one, having been swept right over the falls. The only good outcome, she told me wryly, was that the compensation money from the well-heeled Texans, the parents of the boy he saved, had allowed her to study physiotherapy in the Zambian capital, Lusaka. After hearing the story, I felt genuinely sorry for her. Pamila wasn't angry, like I was, but grieving was still going on.

Having similar unfinished business, I suppose we gravitated together out of sympathy. When we finally shared a bed, we clung together from a common need, not to forget, but to remember. It was as though, when we coupled, I was making love to Carol and she was likewise making love to Keni. We did it, and did it passionately, although cautiously, on account of my still tender ribs, but we made love only five or six times in total. It was not a long affair, partly because I went to England for a visit at that time, also because my six months as a 'Blinker' would soon be over. Those few attempts at intimacy, though, were enough, enough for us to quench the fires of anguish and loneliness burning away all this time. The brief liaison was healthy, healing even. We were sated, and parted happily as friends when the time came. Whether those fires of sorrow and torment would rekindle themselves to wreak further havoc later, only time would eventually tell. In the meantime, I had Vijay to comfort.

Assailed by regret, within days of his arrival in Livingstone, my unlucky friend was already saying he should go back to London, troubled by insistent thoughts of a possible reconciliation with April. Blue and I strongly advised him to delay.

"Perhaps she will have regrets too," I suggested. "Give her time to change her mind."

Meanwhile, I contacted Henry Cavil for advice.

In retrospect, there was never any hope for Vijay. April had latched onto him, not out of genuine mature and heart-felt love, but rather from an adventurous sense of gain, attaching to herself a handsome exotic stranger, taking him as her husband like a trophy, certain she would immediately be the envy of her friends. Back from India, of course, she was seeing the situation differently, thinking of herself as saddled with a spouse no-one else in her circle would contemplate having any kind of relations with. No longer able to think of herself as elevating Vijay to her august status, on the contrary now bearing an unspeakably common Indian name, she could only consider herself as degraded by his altogether baser position in society. So her decision to divorce was irrevocable.

When Henry heard back eventually from April's lawyers, many weeks later, he realised as much, but was too tactful to say so directly to Vijay, suggesting he come to London for a meeting to discuss how the action might be defended. Knowing Henry, I suspected him of planning on my friend's behalf, to screw as much of a settlement as possible out of the Hurtley family, and that Vijay would most probably end up almost as rich as me.

My decision to go home with him followed a call I had from Charlie one evening. Luckily, I had my mobile with me on the veranda of my little lodge. With my still aching ankle resting on a stool, I'd been contemplating the short walk across the tiles to the fridge for a cold beer when it rang. A week or two earlier, I'd suggested that my mother might like to fly out for a visit to the falls, and knew she was considering it.

"You've decided to come then?" I asked, as soon as the connection was made.

"No... It's not about that," she replied.

"What then?"

"I'm going to get married again!"

"Really?"

"No... Only joking!"

This was typical Charlie, but I detected a discrepancy. She didn't sound like she was joking.

"What then?" I repeated, to be met by quite a long silence this time.

"I had a mammogram. They found a lump in my breast... It's cancer. I had the operation yesterday."

She said there'd been a single, pea-sized lesion in one breast, with no sign of spread elsewhere in her body at this stage, but the surgery would be followed, once the wound had healed, by a six-session course of chemotherapy spread over three to four months.

"They've already given me a voucher to buy myself a wig," she said, trying to laugh. "Can you imagine me with no hair?"

I really did not want to try. All I could picture was the many times she used to run around topless on the beach in summer when we were boys, her firm, golden breasts, wet from the sea, shining in flashes of sunlight. It was not a sexual thought. I was having but a momentary general sense of female beauty; and this was not just about *my* mother... It seemed to be about the goddess in every mother who ever lived on this earth. I told her I'd get a flight as soon as I could walk without pain.

Vijay and I flew out ten days later. He stayed in the Barbican apartment and I went straight down to Sussex. Despite her recent ordeal, I thought Charlie looked great.

"It's healing okay," she said. "The surgeon told me he'd removed all the tumour in what they call a 'wide excision', which basically meant they took out a lump bigger than a plum. Chemo starts in two weeks."

I decided to stay that long. My ribs and ankle would be fully healed by then. It would be good to catch up. It was ages since I'd spent any proper time with Paul, Mary and their children. And it would give me a chance to visit another old friend.

Big Al had recovered well from his injury. You can lose half a lung, apparently, without it being much of a setback. He'd already done his preliminary training with Sussex Police, and had started at their Armoury near Lewes. He was billeted in a reasonably liveable two-bedroom house in the northern part of that ancient County Town which, he was proud to be telling me, was established in the 6th century, the name coming from a Saxon word for hills or slopes.

"It's a shambles, Freddie," he said after we'd met at the station and walked uphill towards the solid twelfth century castle. "They don't look after their weapons."

He described how, for example, rifles were issued to a group of say twenty officers for training or operational purposes, and then handed in for storage until needed again.

"It's not like in the army where each soldier has their own weapon to look after, to keep clean and in full working order or else get put on a charge," he said. "It's a complete disgrace here."

Another problem concerned firearms discharged during live operations.

"Even if no-one is actually hit, much less killed," Al told me, "The guns are impounded by Forensics, and often not returned until after a trial, which can take months. So, however many weapons we have on the books, we are always short of that number in practice... It's a real headache."

Another scandal concerned a Police issue handgun that had been implicated in a gangland killing a few months before his arrival.

"No-one knew, or admitted anyway, how it got into the hands of those drug dealers," he said. "There was no record of it being taken out. The senior armourer had no knowledge of it, and the only other person with a key and authority to release firearms, the Chief Superintendent, also said he had nothing to do with it... It's a mystery, and not the kind I like."

I commiserated with my big friend.

"I'm going to have to take proper charge and make some big changes here," he said, shaking his big head. "I can see that already."

Al was clearly despondent, so I let him freely share his misgivings, and I therefore also tried to make Africa sound boring when I told him about 'Blinkers'. I didn't want him feeling he was missing out on the fun. Nevertheless, he could tell I was relatively relaxed and happy so must have thought the life that Blue, Vijay and I had chosen wasn't really too bad.

Naturally, too, I breathed not a word about 'Blinders'.

"Poor old sod!" Al said when I told him what had happened to Vijay. He'd been at the wedding, of course, but had not had much opportunity to form a proper opinion of April, so I gave him a verbal pen-portrait.

"Oh dear!" Al commented. "He's dodged a nasty bullet there then."

Vijay would reject that idea, I thought, but I could only agree.

Thirty-Two

The South of England was basking that year in what would once have been called a Mediterranean climate, although the Med was fully ablaze and far too hot all summer long by then. The Sussex air was pleasantly fresh when my brother and his family came over to Charlie's for lunch on a Sunday. We all sat on the patio under two great umbrellas enjoying the ambient warmth, the shade, and a light breeze wafting through.

It started well. Everyone seemed pleased to see me, Paul whispering thanks in particular for my pitching up to support Charlie at this, as he described it, 'challenging' time. Mary even gave me one of her rare smiles and a quick peck on the cheek, and the teenagers lined up one by one to give me a hug. Hugo, confident, was almost as tall as me now. Raffa was a rather shy boy, nevertheless alert and observant. And Milly was less of a witch, much more of a siren than her younger self. They were like affectionate strangers, but I enjoyed watching the interplay between the three of them until, after the simple meal, they excused themselves and ran off to the nearby playing-field, with which they were obviously familiar, taking a cricket bat and tennis ball to play some kind of game. Charlie and Mary went in to wash dishes, leaving Paul and I sat together.

On that occasion, my twin seemed down-hearted, and I assumed it concerned what was going on with Charlie, the cancer and everything, but he said he was okay with that.

"She's getting good treatment," he volunteered, "And the survival statistics are excellent for what she's got."

"But something's bothering you," I prodded.

"Yes," he agreed. "It's the deteriorating climate. Things are already getting really bad..."

He told me, for instance, that the beach at Shoreham on the nearby coast; where there is a large housing estate, shops, restaurants, a pub and all the hoo-hah of a minor seaside resort; had been ravaged by a series of storms during the preceding winter, resulting in much devastation. Many people had left but, unable to sell their uninsurable homes, many more had been forced to remain. In addition, the Shoreham Harbour authorities had raised the wharf sides by three feet a couple of years before, but this precaution had still failed to prevent inshore flooding, the port being put out of use for several months.

These were obvious effects of global warming locally, but Paul was also highly aware of the massive devastation going on around the world: lengthy droughts and uncontrollable wildfires on one hand, torrential downpours, major floods and vicious hurricanes on the other. In a way it was old news to me, as it was also to him, but this was not what depressed him so much as the denial, ignorance and apathy with which it was consistently being met, especially by those in a position to make a genuine difference.

As Charlie went upstairs to take a nap, Mary returned and joined the conversation in even greater despair.

"It's the children I worry about," she said. "What kind of world are they growing up in? What will it be like in another ten or twenty years?"

Although these two upright citizens made them sound gravely concerning, these were not things I had thought about much.

"We're caught in a greed culture," Paul continued, "A mercenary society that depends on ever-growing consumerism; people buying things they are seduced into wanting, without realising they don't need most of it. It's a kind of relentless treadmill. People don't live a balanced life of rest, work and play. They have to work all hours and fit in what life they can around the grafting... That's all wrong!"

"Not only that," Mary chimed in, "They have to work harder for longer before they can retire... There's simply no joy in any of it, because everyone is competing with everyone else, and the healthy sense people used to have of being part of a thriving community is breaking down. It just isn't there in most places."

"What can anyone do about it?" I asked.

"That's the point," answered Paul, clearly miserable. "We don't know... We thought we did, but we don't."

They went on to say how, in the early days, they'd joined protest groups like 'Friends of the Earth', 'Greenpeace', and 'Extinction Rebellion', going on marches in London and elsewhere, and had even risked getting arrested once by squatting outside an oil refinery to stop the tankers getting in to load fuel, or out again to distribute it. Eventually, though, they found this kind of action unsatisfactory.

"When we looked around," Paul explained, "We realised most of the others were protesting out of either anger or fear, or maybe from a complex mixture of both, and the people we were trying to persuade; politicians, leaders of industry, and so on; responded accordingly, rejecting the angry people, saying they were ill-informed, while pacifying the fearful with empty reassurances."

"Even those of us fully prepared with unassailable scientific truths were ignored," Mary added. "It was all too frustrating, so we decided to just do our bit and raise the kids to be as earth-conscious as possible; prepare for the worst, and hope for the best."

So they installed solar panels on the roof of their house, swapped the gas boiler for one of the new, eco-friendly hydrogen ones that most people couldn't afford, switched to electric vehicles, cut down on eating meat and using dairy products, and recycled everything. But this was by no means sufficient.

"There are lots of people like us," Mary said, "But not enough... The majority simply stick their heads in the sand and carry on as before."

"The politicians are no better," Paul added. "You can understand it. They need votes to get re-elected every five years, so steer clear of unpopular measures, say the right things, sign up to all the proper treaties and such, but routinely fail to deliver."

"Like the promise of nuclear reactors the government made," Mary said, fired up and on a roll. "Remember that, a few years ago? They were going to build seven or eight; and how many have we got so far? Only one! Meanwhile, many developing countries are busily adopting a materialist lifestyle, trying to catch up with the affluent west, and you can hardly blame them. Everyone wants running water and electricity in their homes, quality health care and education, a car to drive, good roads to drive them on, planes to fly about in, and airports for them to land at. I know that... But destroying thousands of hectares of rainforest to furnish land for cattle farming and vast plantations of monoculture cash crops can only bring more destruction. It's got to stop, Freddie. People really must change!"

"One of these days," cautioned Paul, morosely, responding to Mary's distress, "The biggest ice sheets are going to melt. Then things will get terribly bad..."

"There must be a solution," I suggested, faking optimism as best I could. "What do you think it could be?"

Mary's answer was prayer. They seemed to think a wholesale transformation of human psychology was needed, everyone suddenly wising up to being personally connected to the planet; also, like kin, to each other, regardless of obvious differences; and this all sounded familiar. When the children returned, bringing much-needed cheer, they found their parents gloomily resting in silence, and me in search of more beer.

It was hot again the next day. We had the air conditioning running in Charlie's car as I drove her into Hove for an appointment at the wig shop. She'd sensibly decided to go there while still feeling well, even if weeks away from actually losing her hair.

"Plus I shall have the added benefit of my son's opinion on what suits me and what doesn't," she added with more confidence in my fashion choices than seemed reasonable under the circumstances.

In fact, I hated all the wigs she tried on, just couldn't get used to the idea of her needing one. However, fortunately, although she experimented with a few of the more flamboyant creations which just looked silly, there was an attentive young assistant, very practiced in dealing with women in this hideous situation, who guided her towards picking something more modest that was not so different in colour and style from her normal hairdo.

"Most of the ladies I serve talk of this experience as surreal," she said. "It's quite normal to feel awkward, I tell them. Treat it as an adventure... Those who do best are the ones with a good sense of humour."

Sense of the ridiculous, more likely, I was thinking, but I could see Charlie being impressed by her sympathetic approach.

"What's your name, Dear?" she asked.

"Phoebe," came the reply, and forever after Charlie would call her wig by that name. It was a standing joke we shared, one that, I feel sure, helped her get through the coming ordeal.

A few days later, we drove to the hospital for the first treatment. I can't say I enjoyed it, but Charlie seemed to perk up, treating the nurses and reception staff as if they were long lost chums and instantly going about befriending everyone in the waiting area.

"It's my first time," she announced brightly to the small cluster of folk sitting patiently in the sunlight. "What's it going to be like?"

An older woman, dressed in the grey and white habit of a nun, assured her in a soft Irish accent that the whole thing was a piece of cake, but I spotted the opposite message on the haggard face of another, younger woman, who quickly turned away, as if to hide her true thoughts.

Soon it was Charlie's turn, a nurse coming to collect and lead her into the chemotherapy suite, through the door of which I glimpsed five or six separate stations, each with a reclining clinical chair beside which was a drip-stand for the litre bags of pharmaceutical toxins designed to kill cancer without actually killing the patient. It was a case of 'drastic measures for drastic situations'.

I finished the cup of coffee someone had kindly offered me earlier, and was about to set off for a walk in the nearby park to pass the time (Charlie had arranged for the nurses to ring me when she was ready for home), but then there was a surprise: a new arrival, a woman who looked about seventy, thin and pale, shuffling along with the aid of a walking stick, hanging tightly to the arm of a fit-looking forty-year-old, a man I immediately recognized.

This was Tony Marciano, who's mates called him 'Rocky', who I remembered from my early days with the Tigers in Cyprus. I assumed his companion, wearing a bland headscarf and not bothering with a wig at this late stage in the progress of her illness, was his mother. Once she was settled in a chair, as he hadn't yet noticed me, I went over to shake his hand. When he introduced me to the woman beside him, calling her his wife, it was a bit of a shock. Donna was half way through her second course of the dreaded treatment, breast cancer having recurred with a vengeance after she'd been clear of it for over four years. At just thirty-eight, the lacklustre hopeless look in her eyes made her seem done for already.

It's funny what makes you angry, but this encounter, and seeing everything else at the hospital, wondering what fate had in store for my mother, all put me back in a rage. Rocky was allowed to stay with Donna through her treatment session, so I walked around that park alone, fuming away feeling helpless until the phone finally rang. That evening, Rock got some other ex-Tigers together for a drink and a sing song in a pub where he lived near the Brighton Marina. Like him, they were all, with varying degrees of success, trying to make civilian life work. Most were married with kids. Two or three were already divorced. Several admitted having had treatment for stress and PTSD, and felt let down by the Army, hearing about which did nothing to diminish my bad temper, so unsurprisingly I got myself utterly smashed that night trying to drown out not sorrow but fury.

When next I saw him, back in London a few days later, Vijay was not happy either. April had not responded to any calls or messages, having probably changed her contact numbers and such. When he went to the house in Twickenham, he found it rented out already, the tenants entirely unaware of the identity, much less the whereabouts, of the owner or his daughter.

When he called April's father, Arthur invited him to lunch at an attractive riverside restaurant in Molesey. There he said April had gone to the USA for a while, and he didn't know when she'd be back, but Vijay didn't believe him. He was sure as could be that April wouldn't want to travel anywhere again so soon. He did think Arthur meant it, though, when he offered his temporary son-in-law generous severance pay, making it clear that, given his daughter's intransigent opposition, he could no longer employ the poor man, even if he did at any point decide to return to the position which had initially, with great generosity, been kept open for him.

Using his fieldcraft skills, Vijay then set up a camp hidden away in some woodland on a little island diagonally across the river from the Hurtley family home. His powerful binoculars gave him a decent view of the building, and he was fairly certain he caught a glimpse of his quarry at one of the windows on the first day. You could say, as she later claimed, that he was stalking April. From his point of view, he would argue, they were still married and she gave him no other choice.

Once he knew her whereabouts, Vijay switched his vantage point to the south side of the car park of a school to the north of Hampton Court Green, from where, well-hidden behind a screen of trees, he could observe the front entrance of the house. When April emerged, mid-morning on the second day of his stake-out, she was leading a full-grown Rhodesian Ridgeback, and was accompanied by another woman that he instantly recognised as Moira. Quickly breaking cover, he set out to follow them. They were obviously taking the dog for a walk. It was Arthur's pet, known as 'Growler'.

By the time he'd back-tracked across the car park and down the school driveway, the women had advanced towards Hampton Court. When they crossed the main road past the bridge and kept going in a straight line, he knew they were headed for the towpath, rather than the Palace. Keeping pace at a distance for a while, it soon occurred to him that this might not be his best move. He needed to catch April when she was alone, not with a friend, so he did an about-face, returned to his hidey-hole, and resumed his lonely vigil.

About an hour later, he clocked the party returning, and soon afterwards Moira drove away. He thought of going to the gate and ringing the bell but knew there was CCTV and an intercom, and that April would not let him in, so he waited until she ventured out again on her own.

"Lucky dog!" he was thinking when, in the early evening, she emerged with Growler once more by her side. He realised the animal might present a problem, but decided to follow her anyway. Climbing the low fence this time, he sprinted across the green, let her get ahead a little, then caught up when she'd travelled about a hundred yards down the towpath, at the point where she was letting the dog off his lead. Waiting until the few other strollers, joggers and dog-walkers dispersed in various directions, leaving her in sole possession of that short stretch of the path, he resumed his approach.

"April," he called as he reached her, trying to take her arm gently at the elbow from behind.

"What are you doing here?" she immediately cried out in alarm, stepping away. "You can't be here... You mustn't!"

"We *are* still man and wife," he responded, taken aback by her hostility.

"It is a public place, in a free country... April!" he added, trying to make light of her dismissal.

"Go away! Leave me alone!" she said, walking swiftly on as the loyal family beast started snarling.

"April, please... I still love you..." Vijay, growing desperate, started after her. "I only want to talk to you for a few minutes... Please?"

But, sensitive to his mistress's state of alarm, the faithful hound came between them and began barking furiously, making ready to pounce. For a second Vijay considered drawing his army knife and slitting the animal's throat, but just as quickly realised that, however satisfying, it would not do his cause any good. All he could do was back off, listening to the dog carry on barking while he retreated, defeated, all the way back to the bridge.

I tried cheering him up, but it was hard. I think he really did love April. He was so bereft that he lost his appetite for days, even weeks, after this wretched confrontation, and didn't sleep properly for months. I was sure I must quickly get him back to Africa, and fully occupied again once out there. This was especially true after Henry Cavil said, the date set being months away, that there was no point him staying until the divorce proceedings reached court.

In the meantime, shortly before our return flight, I invited Vijay along for a treat I'd organised for my family. I was putting Charlie, Paul, Mary and the children up for a night at The Ritz and taking them all to a show, a fabulous extravaganza at the Albert Hall from the Canadian troupe, Cirque du Soleil: *The Circus of the Sun*. I think even Vijay forgot his woes for a couple of hours, spellbound like the rest of us. And the best thing for me that evening, as we were all finally saying our goodnights, came from young Hugo, seventeen now, when he said he'd be applying to Sandhurst. An officer in the family, I thought. That made me feel really proud.

Thirty-Three

Before departing London, the Colonel called from Africa and asked me to meet Deirdre at the Pimlico house. At last I'd be able to match a face to the sombre voice on the phone. We had, by then, spoken a fair number of times, however I remained unsure what to expect, trying to picture this woman as a Laycock's niece. Could she possibly look anything like him?

When I rang the bell the next morning, at precisely the appointed time, the person who answered the door must have been adopted, for there was no family resemblance whatsoever. Deirdre was tall, taller than her uncle by two or three inches, and thin. She wore a dark grey women's suit with a cream-coloured blouse fastened at the top by a simple mother-of-pearl clasp, and was altogether as 'buttoned-up' as could be.

Following this apparition into the front room, I took the same rickety chair as before, interested to note that Deirdre also sat in front of the Colonel's desk as if he were there with us in the room, a curiously absent presence sitting attentively in his comfortable, padded, maroon-leather swivel chair. Looking round I saw the place was as dusty, dirty and dishevelled as ever. Deirdre noticed my glance.

"He won't let me get it cleaned," she offered. "The one time I did, he gave me hell."

Wondering why I was there, I shrugged but said nothing. Two could play the silence game as well as one. Meanwhile, the enigmatic spectre in the other chair was clearly observing me carefully, taking her merry time getting to whatever the point was going to be. I heard a fly buzzing somewhere, and the faint rumble of buses away down the street outside.

"He wants you to take these back to Livingstone."

Her clipped voice breaking the stillness surprised me at first, because I couldn't see what she meant. In the dark, propped against the desk near the foot of her chair, one with a plastic seat she'd obviously brought in from the kitchen, was a battered old leather briefcase. Only after she'd spoken did she reach down, draw the thing onto her lap, open it and reveal its contents: pages and pages of documents.

"I'm not going to tell you what they are," she added mysteriously. "But of course you must know they are sensitive. Please don't lose them... Preferably don't look at them... Don't show them to anyone... And please deliver them directly to my uncle, only him. Is that clear,

Mr Manning?"

She did not even trouble calling me 'Captain'.

I still don't know what the papers held, and why they were so special that they had to be hand collected and delivered, but I suspect it was all a pretext. Cocky Bruce just wanted me and Deirdre to meet. Furthermore, my suspicions seemed confirmed by what happened after my return to Blinker HQ. His attitude had shifted pleasantly, and it was like the Colonel was now ready to adopt me as his protégé, almost as if I were a son.

He promoted me to Major on the spot, then said I'd finished with Blinkers, that it was time to turn me into a Blinder, and with that he began to initiate me into the dark secrets of mercenary soldiering in Africa. I spent many days with him, firstly in his office at HQ, poring over computer screens, maps, and documents; but never, strangely, those I'd brought back from London, which I thought possibly concerned the evasion of tax. Next, we visited clandestine training camps in different parts of the continent, set up like the one I was familiar with, but mostly smaller and with much more sophisticated weaponry and equipment. Thirdly, we travelled to see live operations going on in various places where Blinders were at work or, occasionally, to check out situations where they might go if Laycock thought it both reasonably safe and exceptionally worthwhile.

Like me, curiously, he was not primarily motivated by money. He had enough of it, and didn't particularly enjoy spending his fortune, except when it was for the betterment of his precious organisations. But he did understand the power of hard currency to motivate people, and in setting high prices for Blinder intervention, he was making clear that he offered nothing less than the best trained and equipped, most efficient military forces that money could buy. In a way, I respected him for that, and made it my watchword later too when I held command of my own little army, until after the flood that is, when money itself lost all value, becoming instantly useless.

We travelled around to Libya, Liberia, to my old stomping grounds of Somalia, Eritrea and Tigray, to Mali and Mozambique. In each of these places and a few more more, I discovered twenty to thirty mainly British and a few other European ex-soldiers, plus a few Yanks, Canucks, Aussies and Kiwis, all under one of Laycock's trusted Field Commanders. In this way I got to meet most of the extraordinary and wonderful crew that, over quite a number of years, the Colonel had somehow put together. And wherever such men were stationed, they led a hundred or more local troops (in one case over five hundred), either mercenaries or government forces, all of them Blinker-trained.

You could really take control of a place and do some damage with those troops, and this was the life Blue, Vijay, and I lived for the next four or five years, for the last two of which, after Laycock's heart attacked him one not-so-fine day, I was more or less in total control. Forced to stay at the Livingstone HQ, taking no further active part in operations, the boss promoted himself to Brigadier. In his place, it was me now, newly appointed as 'Colonel', and life's trajectory changed once again. More 'hands-on' as a leader than Cocky, I was on the move all the time.

Long before all that, news had come through from London that Vijay's divorce was finally completed. Also, Al got in touch to say that poor Donna Marciano, Rocky's wife, had finally died and been put to rest. He had chatted to the Rock at the pub gathering after the cremation, and Al must have judiciously let something slip, because the recently bereaved ex-soldier was asking after military work. Could I help?

As it happened I recruited not only The Rock but also four other ex-Tigers from that get-together in Brighton, put them through six hard weeks of retraining as Blinkers, assessed their strengths and weaknesses (the older ones had become rather slow on the ground), and formed them into a specialist unit of Blinders, with Blue as their Field Commander and Vijay his second-in-command.

It doesn't suit me now, after so many years, to record all the operations, the daring raids, ambushes and other skirmishes, the more tedious security details, the larger-scale battles and what-not, that this group and all the other Blinders were part of throughout the African continent, working for (and sometimes against) a weird and wonderful variety of dictators, terrorists, rebel groups, freedom fighters, governments, opposition parties, legitimate global mining companies, and the even more criminal rapists of our planet's entombed riches (diamonds, gold, silver, rare metals, oil, etcetera), also smugglers of those same treasures, plus ivory, heroin, cocaine, marijuana and other drugs, not forgetting black-market medicines and vaccines. Mostly, though, setting ethical considerations aside, it was all enormous fun.

We were good at what we did... The best. We were feared and respected, and when our foes found out we were coming, such was our reputation that as often as not they simply laid down their arms, or possibly just disappeared. We seldom had casualties, and the only deaths came once when one of the newer recruits drove his vehicle into an unsuspected minefield and blew himself up, then a second time when we lost a helicopter in a sudden sandstorm, but there was nothing I could do about those, except instruct Deirdre to order replacements, a new wagon and another chopper for those that were not only damaged but also marooned, irretrievably buried deep in the shifting African sand.

By now, I was spending some of my own money. The Brigadier in semi-retirement was naturally enough reluctant to expand the enterprise, so he made me a sort of partner, gave me legal licence (regarding the legitimate 'BL Inc.') to buy stuff, write cheques, recruit people, enter agreements, and so on. The same conditions applied as well, between him and me, to 'BL Independent Forces', the Blinders in other words. All we did was shake hands, and this was the preliminary to me getting us involved in nothing less than a minor war in Burkina Faso, a landlocked country bordered by Togo and Ghana to the south, the Ivory Coast to the southwest, Benin to the southeast, Mali to the northwest, and Niger to the northeast. A bloodless change of regime in the capital, Ouagadougou, had suddenly catapulted a surprising new President into office.

Madame Miriam Bogarde, a Christian lady educated at the Sorbonne in Paris, was determined to improve the lot of her people who, during years of military rule, had suffered from widespread corruption in high places and often violent suppression of individual liberties. She wanted to put a stop to famine and poverty, to rebuild the country's basic amenities; its transport, communication, banking, education, healthcare systems and sewage treatment facilities; to get people vaccinated, improve inter-religious harmony, end the practice of female genital mutilation and much else. She told me about her ambitions after inviting me to a meeting in their National Assembly building one day.

"The problem for me," she said, speaking good English with a notable French accent, "Concerns money... We are a poor country, relying mainly on agriculture. We have mines for gemstones and precious metals, but they are still in the hands of thieves and racketeers, and I do not have an army to rely on... Can you help with that?"

I don't know how she heard of me, or Blinders, but she was well-enough informed to know what I was thinking.

"You will, of course, be well paid," she reassured me speedily.

But, obviously, there was a catch. We were going to have to succeed.

"Once the mines are in the possession of the government," Madame President continued, "Your reward will be handsome indeed... Please, don't worry!"

To this day, I suspect she seduced me, as she did everyone, with her winning smile and that innately French *Je ne sais quoi* kind of flirtation that promises much but seldom delivers in full. Possibly, on the other hand, I accepted the challenge because there was little other new work around. Also, after making an inspection of one of the mines still in government hands, and a couple of conferences with her remaining military leaders, I considered there were indeed possibilities. The diamonds, rubies, sapphires and emeralds were certainly real. Above all, it would be exciting, but we were going to need much more kit.

Madame Bogarde owed her providential new position of power to the same events affecting other parts of the globe, the Covid pandemic and climate change. Her immediate predecessor, an army general, together with many other senior officials, and approximately one-in-three members of the original 6,000-strong BF army, had succumbed to a new deadly strain of the virus. Many of the remaining soldiers, together with those of the equally depleted 'People's Militia'; a large supplementary cadre of young men specially trained for both military and civil duties; had subsequently deserted their posts, retreating home to their farms and families to help out in the time of hardship resulting from the uncharacteristic weather patterns. Drought prevented crops from growing in some areas, and flash floods wiped out those that had grown in others. Hands were needed to help with replanting, in the hope of better conditions.

The army had, in any case, been ill-equipped. More importantly, its men had limited experience of combat, apart from those in some units that had seen a little action in Liberia. According to Madame B, about a thousand remaining in uniform would be at my disposal. Another thousand had gone over to the rebels running the mines.

This was the situation, and Vijay was hesitant when I told the lads about it in a conference call. In contrast both Blue and Rocky were enthusiastic.

"We can't just sit around twiddling our thumbs, Vij, you soft bugger," Blue challenged him. "Don't you want a bit of excitement?"

The trouble we foresaw concerned the rebels, thieves and racketeers now having a considerable army of their own. We would train up the residual government troops as per the Blinkers regime, no problem, but we also needed some proper hardware, so I contacted Deirdre and asked her to try and find us a medium-size helicopter, one or two tanks, as many anti-tank rockets and launchers as she could find, a couple of surface-to-air missile launchers with missiles to match, plenty of observation and attack drones, communication systems, automatic rifles and a ton of ammunition. I would have said put it on my tab, but knew I'd need the Trustees to approve such massive expenditure. A call to Henry Cavil was on top of my list as soon as I got back to base.

Inviting Henry and another of the three wise monkeys to

Livingstone was a master-stroke. Sir Peter Bourke, who accompanied him, was an elderly, puffed-up, florid-faced, former Tory grandee who loved being shown a good time; a man insensitive enough, by the way, to keep on referring to African children as 'pickaninnys', entirely unaware of the insultingly inappropriate nature of that decidedly arcane species of colonial terminology. He was, in other words, a self-regarding monster, a throwback, totally devoid of shame. Nevertheless, masking his misgivings, Laycock, in full Brigadier dress uniform, made both men feel welcome, knowing better than most how to give such folk a good time.

He took them to the Falls, of course, then on boat rides and into the bush to view wildlife. Next, he showed them the Livingstone museum, and later even arranged for the pair to enjoy a rare and privileged pow-wow with the nearby village chief and tribal elders (though I suspect he may have bribed some friendly locals to dress up and role-play on that particular occasion). In addition, the visitors sat down on the veranda every evening at The Lodge to a grand feast, washed down with top-grade South African wines. By the time I showed them the sparse-looking Blinker set-up in the bush, deliberately down-graded for the visit, they were ready to eat from the palms of our hands, unquestioningly accepting that investment in the facilities was completely necessary and understandable. Their only question, "Was I sure I'd ordered enough?"

So we went to war in Burkina Faso, routed the bandits without too much trouble, eventually receiving full reimbursement and a handsome reward from the gracious Madame who, in return, kept most of the weaponry for her troops. As a keepsake of the campaign, I still have hidden away hereabouts the diamond cuff-links she presented to me, but have lost the ornate accompanying scroll that honoured me as 'Chevalier (*premier classe*) of the Republic of Burkina Faso'. It was a kind of knighthood, with life citizenship thrown in for good measure.

Not long after the successful conclusion of this affair, D informed us that London's Thames Barrier had been breached for the first time. A tsunami-like wave had overwhelmed the flood defences. Horribly unthinkable though it was for so many, this hitherto failsafe line of protection could no longer be relied on to restrain the damaging waves. Laycock's Pimlico house, so close to the river, could not possibly have avoided the flooding, piles of sandbags notwithstanding, Deirdre told me. Apparently the basement was full of muddy brown liquid, and the tidemark in the hallway reached up over four feet.

"At least I can get the downstairs cleaned up properly," she said, sounding uncharacteristically cheerful. "Uncle can't possibly object to that now."

Government engineers had got to work improving the defences, and the river level went down again, but the global climate's tipping point was clearly at hand, making Deirdre's clean-up fairly futile as the self-same disaster was bound to happen again. However, I thought it best to avoid mention of that little prophecy to her.

The next day, in one of her occasional calls, Charlie confirmed the climate-change news. She told me that torrential rain and violent winds had barely relented throughout the preceding winter, and that Shoreham Beach had been devastated once again by the rising sea in another recent storm. She'd learned from Paul, she said, that there was no ice at all covering the Arctic Ocean now. The Greenland ice-sheet was melting faster than ever, and the same was true in Antarctica.

"The next twelve months will be critical, he says," she continued. "You'd best come and see for yourself."

In fact, global warming was already having a big impact on Blinder operations. People's priorities were changing, such that there were far fewer offers of work. Also, albeit reluctantly, a good proportion of the guys resigned, some powerful kind of homing instinct kicking in as they became increasingly disturbed by tales of woe from their home cities around the world. Sydney and San Francisco, for example, both experienced the double-whammy of multiple inland firestorms and massively rising tides, against all of which they were similarly defenceless. Port cities everywhere, in fact, were struggling to operate normally, which meant, of course, that the flow of goods around the world was regularly being interrupted, delayed, and sometimes prevented altogether. Taking stock of the situation, it really didn't look good.

The reduction in assignments was initially balanced by resignations and departures, which meant that it wasn't immediately necessary for me to lay people off, but that did start happening eventually, and was always a tough call to make. Looking back, I wonder why we didn't dig in our heels and sit out the crisis in Livingstone. At the heart of the continent, it wasn't threatened particularly badly by climate change issues. However, with one exception, we simply didn't consider it. Laycock, alone, decided to stay.

"It's my home now," he explained. "And if things improve later, I'll be on the spot, ready to get Blinkers and Blinders going again."

His faithful native African retainer, Mabvuto, and the star chef, Babyloni, would certainly look after him well. All three waved the last of us off, and even I had a lump in my throat when we parted. I owed that man a great deal.

*

On the plane to England from Johannesburg, some of the recent devastation could be seen below. Passing northwards over the Mediterranean, for example, I could not see much of Malta. Nearing the Channel, the Low Countries of Belgium and Holland appeared almost completely awash, and that situation got me thinking about what would soon be happening at home. Back at the Barbican flat the next day, I shared my ideas with Blue, Vijay and Rocky.

"We need to prepare," I told them. "Things are going to get pretty sticky, so we have to be ready."

Despite improvements to the Thames Barrier, I felt sure the Thames's destiny was to flood permanently. Other major rivers would share a similar fate, which meant that people in their tens of thousands would soon be on the move, retreating to higher ground. The rich, of course, would make for Alpine France or Switzerland, seeking safety among the mountains; but what, I asked my chums, did they think would be happening closer to home?

"Bloody chaos!" offered Blue succinctly.

"Bloody chaos is right," I responded. "And who will be in charge?"

The three of them, their faces blank, stayed silent.

"We will," I said. "Ex-Tigers and Blinders... We need to muster a force... And we're going to need kit."

We also needed a base, substantially above sea-level, so the four of us set to work.

Included in my vision of central London under water was the scene of mainly uninhabitable, barely usable buildings sticking up, Venice-like, with boats (although probably not gondolas) going round between those still habitable and functioning. The Underground would mostly be flooded, and everyone would be trying to leave. There were plans already, it was broadcast publicly, for some government departments to relocate to Birmingham, a city that (unlike most in the provinces) had no major river running through it, a place where canals could (if there was time) be diverted, blocked off or filled in completely.

This disastrous-sounding scenario seemed like a good one to bet on, but other problems compounded the issue. With satellites already in trouble, communications were further hit when the terminals of most of the undersea cables, the majority located at their original points of landfall, became inaccessible and failed. This was called the 'Tonga Effect', after a massive volcanic eruption on that island some years earlier had resulted in a tsunami that destroyed everything. Without reliable communication systems, governments, military organisations, financial institutions and commercial enterprises, basically everyone and everything, would be in dire straits pronto, so I was busting to get ahead of the game. Realising it was older technology that would work best in such conditions, I quickly got Deirdre to source and buy five hundred army surplus radio communications devices, with as powerful a transmitter system as she could find. The same day, I put a call through to Big Al, putting him in the picture.

"Thank goodness!" he said, evidently relieved. "That's great, Freddie! No-one around here has any idea what's going on, or what to do about it. They've all got their stupid heads buried deep under the sand... How do you think I can help?"

Within a week, we were all together down in Sussex. Al had the names of over thirty firearms-trained policemen who could be counted on to join our band when the proverbial hit, when the authorities crumbled, when mob rule and anarchy finally began taking over. Together with all the former soldiers mustered by Rocky, Vijay and Blue, we were going to be in good shape, especially because Al also promised us a truckload of weapons from his armoury.

There were two possibilities for a base. The first was a labyrinthine fortress of a building atop the South Downs at Hollingbury, built back in the 1990s by Sussex Police as a command centre and prison block, but it was still occupied at that stage. The other was Torville House, our old Prep School, which was no longer in use. The new, uncertain circumstances meant few families were prepared to send their younger children far away to boarding establishments for education. The big school, Torville, was still going, albeit with diminished numbers of both pupils and staff, but TH was available, and quickly became our HQ after I did a deal with the bursar of the big school, which had retained financial jurisdiction over the smaller one. He thought the Governing Body would be delighted by the rental income we negotiated. Funnily enough, then, after I chose it, Mr Wright's old classroom became my centre of operations as we began our preparations for the expected cataclysm. What an amusing coincidence.

I first heard the word 'cataclysm' in geography class. Mr Wright later confirmed it as meaning any large-scale and violent event in the natural world, telling us it came from the Greek *kataklusmos*, and originally referred only to flooding, especially to the biblical Flood described in the Book of Genesis, a story I naturally heard about from Miss Warner during scripture lessons in a neighbouring classroom.

Our planning process involved both indoor work, studying maps in particular, and field trips in various directions. We were trying to predict how the cataclysm was going unfold, where would the flooding happen, which places were most likely to stay dry, which roads would be passable and which blocked. We were trying to decide if the railways could be kept functioning, work out the logistics of river transport and so on. The moment to take control was approaching and we had to be fully prepared.

Thirty-Four

As I witnessed myself on several occasions, African states frequently fail. The resulting power vacuum usually leads to widespread civil disobedience, panic, rioting, looting, murder and mayhem; until, at last, someone takes control. In most cases, that would be the army, so I had good insight into what might happen in England. If the Thames basin flooded; and if, as anticipated, the Severn and the Avon followed suit; a horizontal, hotchpotch, wishbone-shaped land mass would remain above the waves. Charlie knew a professor at Sussex University, Neil Fillmore, who could tell us about such things. It was in his office that I understood clearly how my men and I should proceed.

The Prof, a Lancashire-born man in his mid-sixties, who had lived so long in the south that his origins could only barely be detected by the faint trace of a northern accent, was so thin and breathless from chronic lung disease that I thought we might need a nurse, or at least an oxygen cylinder, to help him survive through the morning. He was sprightly enough, though, when you got him warmed up on his subject, full of facts and speculations about the climate emergency, with an "I told you so" gleam in his eye when recounting his researches of decades before, studies that predicted precisely the current unfolding disaster.

"Everyone's going to run," he said as if it were a joke. "But there's nowhere for them to go!"

On a series of large computer screens, he showed me and Blue what he meant. Most Londoners, he thought, would head north-west for the Chiltern Hills, the North Wessex Downs, and possibly the Cotswolds, or south to that precious wishbone formed of the Surrey Hills and North Downs, the South Downs, High Weald, and the Kent Downs. This was the part that interested me, especially when he also told us, with grim certainty, that middle England was doomed. Folk in the west would retreat to Dartmoor and Exmoor, he thought, but in the east there was no high ground to speak of between the North Sea and Birmingham. Essex, the northern Home Counties, East Anglia, Cambridgeshire, Lincolnshire and further afield would be lost. The Humber would flood and take out Sheffield and Leeds. The Ouse would inundate York. People in the north of England would have to head for the North York Moors, the Yorkshire Dales, the North Pennines or the Lake District. Furthermore, in his expert opinion, this was going to happen fairly soon.

"How soon?" I ventured to ask.

"The ice is melting fast now," the canny professor replied. "I think people will either drown or be on the move within six months or a year."

"Skates on then," said Blue.

"Skates on!" I had to agree.

It was Fillmore's topographical and population maps that showed me what was needed, the carving out of some territory for ourselves, a fiefdom we could realistically establish, defend and police. During an initial paper exercise, Big Al, Vijay and Rocky, as well as Blue and I, conferred to draw the lines that became the borders of our new kingdom, South East England, just as we would become its army - SEE Force, later known widely as simply 'Manning's Militia'. It was Al who insisted we think of our territory as a kingdom, also that I should be the King and Commander-in-Chief.

After sending the word out, we soon had a decent-sized fighting force in training at Torville HQ. The plan to secure our borders had to be properly timed, not so soon that the existing authorities would put a stop to it, but not too late, after the meteorological warning signs had provoked the huge, unwieldy expected exodus from the metropolis. The population of London was well over nine million by then.

Anticipating problems, supplying sufficient food and energy in particular, we knew it was essential to keep the southern population at a manageable level, which meant defending our chosen realm against most of the probable invaders. Our northern border was the Thames, obviously, but decisions had to be made about the north-western approaches. The flood would reach Reading and Newbury, Fillmore told us, so the southern ring of the M25 continuing into the M4 motorway corridor across the North Wessex Downs from Theale to Swindon made sense as a defensible boundary, extending on from there towards Chippenham and Bath at the lower end of the Cotswolds. Bristol, the Prof said, would be gone, just like so many other coastal cities, so there was no need to think beyond that.

We acquired uniforms. Regarding insignia, we plumped for the Union Jack with a central tiger's head. Our badges were cut in the well-known shape of southern England, the heel of the Kent coast in the east, the toes of Cornwall to the west. At about the same time, we stockpiled several amphibian transport vessels, and even an ageing hovercraft, to add to the fleet of ferries earmarked for take-over when the time came. The relatively short flooded stretches throughout the new kingdom, between Tonbridge and Sevenoaks, for example, or between Hurstpierpoint and the High Weald north of Haywards Heath, would not pose too much of a problem, particularly as we had drafted experienced sappers into the militia to build pontoon bridges wherever required. It seemed eminently doable, that was what buoyed us up. We were being proactive and our morale was commensurately high.

*

By the time the flood came, Charlie was looking healthy and normal again.

Shortly after chemotherapy, her formerly straight, shiny tresses had grown back dull, tight and curly, making her look like somebody else, an alien, someone who really should never have been. At that stage, she seemed so much a stranger that I found it hard to relate to her properly as a son. The tight-spiralling effect on her hair was, she said, a common side effect of the treatment, but it was still a shock to me. As the anticipated cataclysm approached, though, not only had her hair re-established it's flowing lustre, but the cancer had stayed away. She was feeling perfectly fine, she told me, other than experiencing a tinge of sorrow over the fate of her unfortunate grandson, but it was different for the rest of the family.

Paul and Mary were not coping well with bereavement. Young Raffa had died three or four months earlier, felled by the same illness, Hodgkin's lymphoma, that had carried his great-grandfather off so many years ago. The time from diagnosis to demise had only been a matter of a few weeks, giving them little time to prepare. I considered telling them not to worry, that within a few years Raffa would pop up again in a brand new body with a new name, someone else's child but still intent on clamouring at their door, claiming kinship, just as he had with Oliver and Mavis Turpin in the past. Some cautionary intuition, though, told me that this might not be the ideal moment to share such a challenging thought.

The other children were both away. Hugo was a commissioned officer now, a second lieutenant stationed in Germany with his regiment. Milly, having gone to the University of St Andrew, was remaining in Scotland to be with her boyfriend, Fergus Mackay, who I never met. They were running a hotel in the Highlands, which he had inherited. Perhaps their absence, the empty nest, was what prompted my sibling and his spouse to offer a home to Charlie, who was trying to decide what to do about it when, at my suggestion, we all met to discuss the bad news from Professor Fillmore. His dire predictions may have helped Charlie make up her mind. The couple had a big house, located high on the Downs, so the three of them could stick together and help each other out, which made sense. It would also make it easier for me to ensure their wellbeing and safety throughout the troubled times expected ahead.

The deteriorating situation, I discovered, was giving other people opportunistic ideas as well. Phil Compston, a man with an entrepreneurial flair, could also see what was coming and had decided to do something about it, having managed to acquire from local authorities, through the emergency powers they now exercised, two large slices of open land on which to set up his 'Homestead Enterprises'. The northerly site was on heathland near the top of Box Hill in Surrey. The other was rolling farmland between Chanctonbury and Cissbury Ring in West Sussex. Having called the homesteads, 'Rising Sun' in the north, and 'Rising Moon' in the south, installed the usual campground facilities and a large array of solar panels, he was advertising fifty individual caravan and trailer plots in each location. By the time I heard about it, some folk were already in residence. Al, Rocky and I decided to pay Compston a visit, arranging to meet him at the Rising Moon site.

"Rising Tide, more like it!" offered the Rock, whose old home in Brighton was already lost to the sea.

I calculated the total that purchasing a hundred of his homestead places would amount to at the advertised rate, doubled it, and offered to buy Compston out when we met. After I assured him I'd retain his key staff, especially his manager, Bill Donovan, he was quick to accept. I suspected this was solely because he instantly intended using the money to buy or lease more land for similar projects elsewhere, so I told him I had no problem with that as long as he confined himself to sites north of London. Fortunately, there was no need to make threats, as he already had plans to develop a couple of plots north of Reading.

When the handshakes were done and Compston had left, Donovan joined us in the sales caravan to meet his new bosses, giving me the chance to assess his mettle and try out a few new ideas. A down-to-earth chap in his mid-forties, I took to him immediately, and he seemed to like what I said about expanding both sites to accommodate up to five, even ten, times the number of homes. The demand was going to come, and there was certainly plenty of land. He was sceptical only about the cost, but I soon convinced him that, with a vault full of gold and diamonds, proceeds from my days as a mercenary, on top of my original fortune, I could afford the expense. From then, he was fully committed.

One beneficial side-effect of owning this start-up residential scheme was the information it provided regarding demand for places, reflecting accurately the numbers of people readying themselves to leave low-lying areas, tipping us off about when might be best to put our takeover plans into action. Checking the Homestead website every day for applications, we noticed a surge after a three-week period of relentless heavy rain coinciding with high seasonal tides. All the towns along the South Coast, from Dover to Southampton, were among the first affected while (but only temporarily) the beefed-up Thames Barrier held out. When it finally failed, and Londoners started their move, we put our planned road-blocks in place.

It was surprisingly easy for us simply to station tanks, troops and barricades at all the main junctions on the M25 and M4, turning everyone back, giving out fake news by way of explanation, pretending we were strictly enforcing a quarantine area against another new variant of Covid. We told people, and we also broadcast it on local radio channels that our clever Signals people could interrupt for us when necessary. Long tailbacks obviously deterred others from following the initial set of refugees south. Anyone wanting to head north out of our territory, of course, was swiftly expedited on their way. Only later would we dynamite the northern approaches to the motorways, making it easier to defend that border country.

After the traffic jams led to mighty tailbacks, people naturally started approaching on foot in great straggly lines. It was just like when the people fled Syria or the Ukraine years ago, carrying their few remaining possessions, children clutching soft toys, old folk struggling with sticks and frames, some even being carried on the backs of strong men. It was pathetic, but we could not risk letting them pass. We patrolled the motorways with tanks and armoured cars, backed up by drones in the sky. When the masses reached and tried to breach the barricades, we deterred them with water cannon and tear gas. When they persisted, we used rubber bullets. When that didn't work, we shot a few dead.

Although I dare say precedents had been set in Africa, where collateral damage had been unavoidable, this was the first time in England on my watch that innocent civilians got killed. I ordered the men to avoid targeting women and children, but some of the young teenagers were among the most frenzied in their attacks on our posts and could not therefore be spared. Eventually, the would-be refugees mostly went away and we dug huge pits for the bodies of those who had perished, some regrettably at our hands, and many in the general crush, caught like the French nobles at Agincourt, unable to move forward or retreat, sinking exhausted to the ground, trampled to death and oblivion by those who'd be joining them soon. Victims of panicky insurrection, they were, just as the French warriors had been victims of battle.

We had to be especially careful, I remember, about the Dartford

Crossing. The tunnel was flooded early on, of course, but the massive Queen Elizabeth Bridge, high over the river, remained accessible from both sides. Our strategy involved starting with rows of men and tanks traversing the southern end. In this fashion, we made our way across the structure to the north where, sadly, another fatal confrontation took place.

Not too many came out of London on that eastern side, but people were fleeing Norfolk and Suffolk down the M11 motorway in terrific numbers. I was overseeing the operation, trying to allow lorries laden with produce to pass while stopping all private vehicles, but this was too ambitious. The trucks simply couldn't get through because some cars had turned round and were trying to retrace their steps, while others remained hell-bent on moving towards what they considered must be safety. People in cars, like those doomed soldiers on horseback in 1415, had no exit route whatsoever. It was another drastic situation requiring a drastic solution. Losing patience, I admit, I got the tanks to clear a path, shooting their big guns initially and then simply advancing, pushing aside or crushing everything in their way. The carnage that followed was painful. Nevertheless, in similar circumstances, I would barely hesitate to give that order again.

Once people got to know how ruthless we were prepared to be, Manning's Militia soon commanded near-total respect and obedience, which was important. It made life easier for all, and more than justified that initial ending of life. Later we withdrew our tanks and simply blew up the bridge, on which momentous occasion I made sure I triggered the detonation myself. It was fun, like wrecking those sandcastles on the beach when I was a boy. Vijay clapped, and gave me high fives all the rest of that day. The simplest pleasures are the best, are they not?

I consider myself like a surgeon. Whatever the consequences might be, if something bad is going on, like a cancer, you just have to go ahead and cut it out, and there was plenty going on that was bad in those first days after the flood. Plenty of horror stories emerged later from London too. Despite our best efforts, a few people did make it through to the south, telling their grim tales of widespread 'rape and pillage', as I suppose you might call it, remembering from history the antics of Viking invaders, harrowing accounts of insurrection, anarchy, mob rule, social disintegration, deprivation, desperation, and, naturally, death. What were the politicians, the police, or the army doing to restore order? I do not know, but obviously nothing effective.

Did we have similar problems here in the South? No... Where it surfaced, in the cities and bigger towns mainly, we crushed it, nipped it smartly in the bud and dealt summarily with all ringleaders and many of the perpetrators. Rapists, in particular, got savagely punished. In a rage, I even cut the goolies off one myself, a complete thug who'd been caught on top of a girl of no more than nine, a little fair-haired waif who, thankfully, had already expired by the time he climbed aboard her sorry corpse. I'd seen it in Africa, many times, but this was too close to home. Vijay, taking pity on the creep, later finished him off with his gun, where I would have made him live on and suffer. For months afterwards; while things began settling down, and the new shoreline was being established, half-way up the southern edge of the Downs and those fabulous, famous white cliffs; I was still having visions of that nightmare scene, of that tiny, desecrated, young girl. Some things are simply not right.

Shortly before 'D-Day', as I called it; the day we blocked off all major access roads from beyond our pre-determined borders; we'd taken numerous additional precautions. For example, we annexed supply depots and stores of several retailers, notably supermarket chains. To secure power supplies, we extended Compston's solar energy initiative all over the region, setting up a couple of new onshore wind-farms to boot, the offshore ones due to fail as the sea level rose.

Regarding food, although it seemed that there was plenty of fertile land in our new kingdom for both livestock and arable farming, we commissioned university agriculture specialists to make an informed estimate of the kind of population numbers that could be sustained, requesting figures for now, with plenty of fertiliser available, and for later, when it would all be used up. Learning from African colonial history, we also prepared and distributed identity cards, using people's dates of birth and their NHS numbers; the latter obtained for us by ex-army intelligence operatives hacking into the poorly defended Health Service database; all of which led to some difficult choices.

When all the kerfuffle quietened down and a degree of social stability returned to our little kingdom of South East England, enormous numbers of otherwise homeless people were living on Downland and at other suitable dry places, some in caravans and trailers, but mostly in tents. Because they were squatting on farmland in such numbers, our food calculations proved optimistic. The only way to avoid a devastating famine was to introduce strict rationing, which had to be tightened even further when the supermarket supplies began to expire. In the end, I knew we must cull the population. There were simply too many mouths to realistically feed, but the question was how to go about it without causing new riots. Rocky came up with the answer.

We fixed on a first selection of eighty-year-olds and over. Many were infirm; some were demented; others were simply lonely and helpless; so this would relieve the burden on remaining citizens in a number of ways. The Rock's cunning plan involved inviting the chosen ones to a special voyage on a massive ageing cruise-liner. We put out fake news about one of the Channel Islands accepting such folk with open arms, saying that family members wanting to accompany their elderly kin could go too. Naturally, thousands signed up. The renamed 'Rising Star' set sail from a makeshift jetty that our engineers constructed, and we sunk her five miles out. Obviously, there were no life rafts, so obviously there were no survivors, the hand-picked crew of former criminals included. Everyone left behind was told of the tragedy, but we let out that the cause was an unexplained fire in the engine room, rather than the detonation of pre-set explosives. It seemed kinder that way; and necessary, too, of course, to ensure comparable efficacy and success when we repeated the trick later on.

Another valuable initiative in those early days was to limit people's access to news from outside the kingdom. We closed the airport at Gatwick, of course, having allowed as many aircraft to leave as had pilots that wanted to fly them, but then we blocked off the runways, and there was no other airport in the region under our control usable by any but the smallest of planes. Similarly there were berths available only for small seagoing vessels around the coast and up the flooded rivers, so we had no problem managing who and what arrived from the Continent or anywhere else. Big guns on the cliff tops were helpful too in deterring any larger vessels that approached. Fortuitously, though, we were not a popular destination. It must have been obvious to foreigners that, being a relatively low-lying country, we were going to be crowded enough, and therefore had little to offer flood survivors from elsewhere. A few ex-pats did try to return to their home country, of whom some undoubtedly did evade our patrols, but it did them no good. If they weren't registered and did not hold identity cards, they were simply rounded up and sent back to sea; or, in some cases, shot.

The United Kingdom had comprehensively fallen apart by now. Ireland had long been re-united, north and south, into a republic. Scotland and Wales, both with plenty of high ground, took with alacrity the opportunity to declare themselves independent nations as well, leaving the rest of England ill-defined and ungovernable. Westminster was almost completely submerged, the water mark at its highest reaching almost half-way up Big Ben, all of which rendered the legitimacy and survival of our new kingdom more or less completely secure.

As for what was happening throughout other parts of the world, the news was sparse. I was thankful that, unlike in America, ordinary citizens here did not go about heavily armed. We could only imagine what might be happening in the US as people fought each other tooth and nail over places to live, the means to travel to safety, and daily essentials like food and drinking water. A wholesale, coast to coast massacre seemed likely, with everyone heading for Canada, the Appalachians and the Rockies. In South America, they had the Andes, and in Asia the Himalayas. These would clearly be the main centres of population for the future. Maybe the flood would go down again one day and everyone reunited, but what a different world it would be.

Thirty-Five

We were beginning to work out the logistics of running our new kingdom when, one day, Vijay ran into my office at Torville HQ with a pleasant surprise. Someone had turned up claiming to know me, asking for a private word. This was Timothy Pipkin.

After school, the boy who had cleaned the brass on my cadet uniform and put blanco on my webbing every week, had obtained a degree in business administration, gone to America for a few years, married, got divorced, returned to London, then moved to Winchester where he'd been working high up in National Health Service management. He wanted to ask if he could be useful, so I gave him a job. I also gave him a lot of power and plenty of men to carry out his every instruction, and this was a clever move because he was a genius at organisation. As a direct result of this inspired appointment, things ran efficiently for a good long time.

It is hard now to remember the exact sequence of events as the years went by. I can, though, say that the situation gradually deteriorated as we ran out of fuel and machines failed (including the wind turbines), because few knew how to repair them, and we lacked the spare parts required. Even solar panels, despite having no moving parts, grew increasingly inefficient. In any case, we could never store enough daytime generated electricity to make a difference at night when it was needed. Forced inevitably to rely back on older technology, we even resorted to longbows after firearms ammunition grew scarce.

Despite our talented Quartermaster-in-Chief, Pipkin's heroic efforts, the food situation also got steadily worse. Farms were not able to retain anything like the level of productivity they had achieved initially, so rationing had to get tighter, and I reduced the cull age to seventy; and later to sixty. Trying to make the situation a touch more palatable for people, Pipkin had another brainwave, establishing the principle of exemption certificates: 100 of them for a year's grace; 50 for two years; 20 for three; 5 for four; and just one of these precious lifelines for a full five years. In addition, we said people could trade or pass on remaining years to family members or others, up to a maximum of ten; which meant, for example, that if you were dying of cancer aged fifty-three and agreed to volunteer for the next official cull, you could pass a seven years exemption on to your spouse or one of your children. I was trying to rule with compassion, you see.

The cull reaching sixty was particularly embarrassing for me because Charlie, her once-blonde hair now a rather fetching silver-grey, should have been included, and would have if I hadn't issued a new identity card pushing forward her birth date by ten years. What's the point of having power if you don't use it like that? Paul and Mary, however, didn't agree. They said what I was doing, the way I was using my exalted position, was wrong, which seemed so ungrateful to me, not only as I had just saved our mother, but also because I was seeing to it that both they and Charlie got double rations all the time.

"You can't just play God with people's lives!" Paul exploded one day, still a volatile character despite all the meditation he did.

"Someone has to be in charge," I countered. "Think of Cuba under the Castro brothers that H used to rabbit on about. Our proper names are Fidel and Raul, after all... What about that?"

On reflection, hadn't we set up a Soviet style socialist state, albeit in the guise of a royal kingdom. Some might even have considered that kingdom a dictatorship; but I'm with Shakespeare on that: "A rose by any other name would smell as sweet!" Kingdom or republic... What difference? But I could not get Paul to agree, or Mary, sticking by him, clinging on like a limpet as ever. They were troubled, too, about something else. Using his military connections, Hugo had managed to get in touch. He was now in Scotland, he'd told them, staying at the Aviemore hotel with his sister and brother-in-law (for Milly and Fergus had married), after he and several army comrades had been able to make the place secure from bands of vicious marauders such as were common in those parts. It wasn't a land of plenty, I gather, but in the aftermath of the flood they had enough to survive in reasonable comfort, and plenty of energy from the onshore turbines scattered all around the highlands; at least when the wind blew. Hugo had invited his folks to relocate up there, and they were clearly tempted.

Grandma Charlie had been included in the offer, but to my delight had decided against going. Taking a similarly level-headed approach, I strongly advised my twin against attempting the perilous journey. The stakes were too high. Also, the pair were still much-needed schoolteachers, so for that alone I wanted them to stay. In the event, they were determined, and were not to be deterred, so I did finally agree to them having an amphibious vehicle from our fleet, food for the journey, and enough fuel to travel the 600 miles. The risk of being attacked in cold blood by bandits nevertheless seemed considerable but, peaceniks to the end, neither would carry the firearms I urged them to take. Six weeks later, they set off bravely, full of hope and good cheer; but were never heard of again. Perhaps I should have sent some men with them for protection. However, we were so busy establishing our new country that I couldn't spare any, and was reluctant in any case to risk the lives of my militia in addition to those of my idiot twin brother and his doting wife. No doubt they drowned or were murdered, although Charlie refused to believe it. Nowhere was safe any more.

*

I remember that in the early days there were numerous small-scale insurrections against my regime. These were from young men mostly, fed up with rationing, with little else to do other than farm work and in other tedious unskilled occupations. Limited power supplies, limited communication capacity, and limited transport options, all added up to stagnation. There was little manufacturing, for example, and with the collapse of currency, there was also very little trade. People, increasingly desperate, had to rely on the rations that we controlled tightly. Identity cards and ration books were precious. Living in tents and other makeshift forms of accommodation, cheek by jowl with other unhappy unfortunates, it's no wonder that folk grew increasingly disgruntled and restless. "*Amor fati*", we broadcast repeatedly over the airwaves: "Love your fate, whatever it may be..." But our attempt to instil one of Nietzsche's favourite dictums, (that he'd lifted straight from ancient stoic philosophers), an aphorism once also taught me by the famed Mr Wright, did little to curb the resentment. Young people took up clubs, sticks and farm implements to attack troops guarding food stores, but such aggression was pitifully ineffective against our highly motivated, decently-trained and reasonably well-armed soldiers.

This was different from the frenzied rioting, rape and plunder in the immediate aftermath of the flood, when we'd felt the strongest need to stop all forms of anti-social behaviour in its tracks. Now, to avoid a backlash of escalating violence, I wanted to appear more lenient than had previously been necessary, so for the most part we arrested young rebels and cast them into cells to cool off in Lewes and Winchester prisons, once we had emptied them of their previous inmates, sending the worst of those criminal unfortunates off on *HMS Dynamite* cruises rather than release them to cause further mischief. Those new inmates who misbehaved in custody, or again after release, were also similarly abandoned as quietly as possible to a watery grave. Regrettable, I would call it now, but it was the only form of justice on offer in those difficult days.

Truthfully, there wasn't much opposition to our rule. People are satisfied with relatively little. Give them bread, milk, eggs, fish, meat, vegetables, fruit, clothing, shelter and warmth, and they will be fairly content. Give them, in addition, something to do, something meaningful like the opportunity to make a contribution to society and improve the lives of others, however modestly, and they will even be happy. That's why Pipkin's ingenious plan to get most of them working on flood defences, repair work and building projects, was such a good one.

On the other hand, it's when any or all of those essentials are in short supply that people turn to mischief, start complaining, and work themselves up to rebellion. The ancient Romans knew this; with slaves doing all the work, their citizens had little to occupy them so, to keep everyone calm and under control entertainment was provided: parades, circuses, gladiator fights, lotteries with generous prizes, things to gamble on; 'beer and skittles', in other words. With Tim Pipkin's help once more, I chose to provide something similar.

Reflecting the conditions of former Communist states, I thought of my citizens as belonging to several identifiable categories, each to be treated differently: the *proletariat*, ordinary worker-types, the vast majority; the *military*, essential to treat well and keep on-side at all times; and the *intelligentsia*, academically qualified intellectuals, who could be useful on account of their specialist knowledge and experience, but who could also be dangerous when they started to think for themselves and reject the authority of the state. Sadly, we were forced to remove many such otherwise valuable academics, simply because they opposed the royal regime and would not co-operate with our aims. I wasn't always everyone's popular flavour of the month, but in the early days no-one got near enough to genuinely threaten my life. Some would-be assassins did occasionally try it on, I admit. One of my food tasters even died of poison meant for my stomach, but somehow I survived every time. I was well protected and never in serious danger, but that's not necessarily the case now.

It is almost exactly one hundred years since Charlie gave birth, ushering Paul and me screaming out into the world. Who would have thought I could possibly live so long? Those who truly cared for my existence, and kept constant watch for my safety, have all gone. In recent months I've been having premonitions, and cannot shake the feeling that I will be put to death sometime soon. Like the dinosaur, *Tyrannosaurus Rex*, I am facing extinction as my continued existence is a complete embarrassment to the new ruling hierarchy. For years, totally physically feeble, I have been left in peace, a useless figurehead, hidden away, barely aware of anything going on outside these walls, but I have heard that a new cadre of regents has taken control. Rather than celebrate my longevity, it will surely suit them better simply to do me in, and then likely announce it as being from natural causes.

They're sure to bump off the killer and any other witnesses to my murder, then mock my memory with a glitzy parade and grand funeral, complete with fake honours and eulogies. There won't be another king after me, either. Monarchy, rule by a single head of state, is definitely out of favour.

My own coronation took place in the great stadium at Falmer, already two years into my reign when things had begun to calm down. The army herded thousands of possibly reluctant proles into their seats on a day of brilliant sunshine. Everyone had extra rations, including a rare treat... jam-filled doughnuts, and children in the crowd were each given a small figurine in my image, dressed in the newly-designed royal regalia. There were flags and bunting everywhere. An orchestra kept the people amused with a medley of feel good songs from a much earlier era (chosen by Charlie, as it happens), like 'Things we said Today', 'I'll Follow the Sun', 'Everybody's Talkin', and, 'New World in the Morning'. It was sweet! Then military bands took over as the army, in full dress uniform marched in magnificent formation back and forth, just like at Trooping the Colour when the old Queen was still on the throne and we kids watched on the goggle-box. Each of the three brigades was led by one of my closest comrades; Rocky, Vijay and Blue; while I sat on a raised platform in their midst.

I had wanted Charlie there too, but she declined to appear in public with me; and this was probably a sensible move because someone was sure to have noticed her true age; so it was Big Al beside me who did the honours, raising the newly minted gold crown and placing it on my head as the fanfares rang out and the crowd cheered, spontaneously, I like to think, but possibly prodded as well.

The final rebellion, a few weeks later, was the biggest ever mounted against us. Torville HQ was besieged for more than a day by a fierce group of well organised former fire-fighters who, somehow, had managed to get themselves armed with automatic rifles plus a few hand grenades. The building was hard to defend; a fact which prompted the subsequent move of our base to the former Sussex Police building in Hollingbury, the same labyrinth of a building that I've been living in to this day. Fortunately, we held off the attackers long enough for Blue and Vijay to muster a large enough force to relieve us.

None of the fire-fighters survived, by the way. I saw it as an opportunity. Filling the stadium again, we used it for a Roman gladiator-style form of mob entertainment to make an example of those captured. In pairs, in a spectacle that lasted all afternoon, the traitors were given swords and spears to fight each other to death in front of the crowd (although no children this time). When, finally, there was just one man standing, he was so heavily wounded, cut about the face, arms and torso, that I felt obliged to administer the *coup de grace* myself on the spot with my service revolver. There were boos from among the multitude this time, but I was satisfied. It's what I would have wanted in his place.

*

The years that followed grew increasingly quiet. Successive culls were necessary to keep the population down, so that everyone could be fed, but that was the only excitement. It is possible that terrible things could have happened, uprisings and such that no-one ever mentioned to me, but I was shielded from the worst. For a few years I used to insist on weekly staff meetings with Al, Blue, Vijay, Rocky, and Pipkin, but latterly they tended to deteriorate into extended drinking sessions, at which we did nothing more than regale each other with bold, exaggerated tales from our past lives at school, in the army, and in Africa.

On one occasion, the ever-serious Pipkin tried getting us thinking a little harder about the kingdom's future direction.

"Where are we going?" he asked us.

It was Blue who instantly piped up jokily. "I'd have thought that was obvious," he said. "We're all going to Hell!"

We laughed, of course; but, the only survivor now, I don't accept his prediction. We did, at all times, only what had to be done. Surely there's no blame in that?

Al was the first to go. By the time he was sixty, what remained of his damaged lungs were shot to bits, like old Fillmore's had been. He lost weight; not only spare fat but essential muscle too; and became unsteady, barely able to walk. Proud, though, he insisted he was alright, but he did agree to daily visits from a housekeeper, Mrs Vale, to cook for him, keep the place tidy and make sure he took all his medicines. I used to visit the house in Lewes once a week. Vijay and Blue went there often as well. But we ran into a problem. Like everything by then, medicines were in extremely short supply. Without his bronchodilator, a little blue puffer thingy, Al was struggling to breathe.

"It's hellish when you can't get your breath," he croaked wheezily one day, pausing to inhale forcefully... "I can't take much more of this, Freddie."

And that was the last time I saw my wonderful, life-long friend. Mrs Vale found him dead the next day, lying on his bed, fully kitted out in his best Tiger's uniform, a scrap of paper beside him saying, "Thanks for al` the fun, Mates!"

He'd taken his service revolver and shot a fatal round through the roof of his mouth. Brave man! It can not have been easy.

We gave him a Viking send-off, like in a film I once saw. Pipkin found us a kind of longboat with a single sail, which we packed with kindling and other inflammable stuff, then stretched his corpse out on top of the pile, sending the funeral craft out to sea from the jetty where Vijay, Blue, Rocky and I stood with our longbows. In turn, we quickly lit the petrol-dipped wadding at the tips of our arrows from a brazier then fired towards the departing vessel, already thirty yards out. Mine was the only miss, my eyes too full of tears for me to see clearly, but, it didn't matter. The sun was setting, and the blaze in the western sky was soon matched by the conflagration heading away on the breeze towards the horizon, our friend's seagoing funeral pyre, a truly magnificent cremation.

Charlie was next, my mother, taken in her seventies by a cruel reprise of the cancer which typically she concealed until it was to far advanced to try treating. Another brave soul, in my book. I think about her every day, and dream of her sometimes. Even now, it's hard to think of her as actually gone.

Rocky went quietly too. A heart attack took him in his sleep one day soon after his eightieth birthday. Younger, still in our early seventies at the time, Blue, Vijay and I got together to celebrate the Rock's life and mourn his passing while congratulating ourselves on good health and survival. I remember feeling invincible on that occasion, immortal even; but, of course, we were fooling ourselves.

Vijay had, finally, got himself married again, and much more successfully this time. Claire was as different from April as you could possibly get, dark-skinned (her parents were from Antigua) and as selfless and compassionate for her fellow beings as the other was pale-complexioned and selfish, filled with contempt for people and animals alike (unless you happened to be a Ridgeback called Growler). The new bride was a nurse, fully twenty years his junior, who Vijay met after being inadvertently struck in the bum by an arrow during longbow practice. (Definitely inadvertent. I didn't mean to loose the damn thing at all. Honestly! My ageing, arthritic fingers just happened to slip.) Luckily it wasn't much more than a flesh wound from a glancing blow; but still, he couldn't sit down, and she couldn't stop laughing.

"She was so gentle and kind," he told me the following day. "I think I've fallen in love..."

"Here we go again," I thought. "Another disastrous affair!"

Nevertheless, I was wrong, and they were married on his sixty-first birthday. Astonishingly, nine months later to the day, Claire gave him a son and a daughter.

"Twins," I said on hearing the joyful news. "Just like me and Paul".

I hoped they'd all be supremely happy. Godless creature, though I am, they made me Godfather to both little Mahit (named in honour of Vijay's father) and Bijou, the baby girl; and they had grown into their twenties before their father died at the age of eighty-six, only a week after his grandson, Bijou's child named Vijay in his honour, was born and placed in his arms. A sudden massive stroke carried him silently off in an instant, and this was a definite blessing. He would have known nothing about it.

So that left me and Blue. We tottered pathetically on with declining strength, trying to outdo each other daily at archery, arm wrestling, poker and drinking, until he too finally ran out of steam and expired. His memory had been failing badly. He got mighty confused at times, so perhaps it was best, but I missed him sorely, especially the daily banter we had together. Now, ten years later, I must admit I still do.

I am preoccupied with reminiscences, but I do also wonder about the future; not about my personal future, which will be brief whatever happens, but the future of the planet, and what will become of the people.

Thirty-Six

I cannot remember crying that often since I was a boy, but last night I woke up in tears from a melancholy dream about Carol. It was a strange dream, with H and Granny Gertrude mixed up in it somewhere, lurking around like ghosts. Sitting up in the gloom, I was forced to wipe my damp eyes on the bed sheet.

Laying down again, I could not return to sleep. Something Paul and Mary tried numerous times to explain came back to me, Julian Eckhart-Smith's theory about the process of grieving. I guess it was relevant, something about sadness holding the key to emotional healing, part of a healthy process leading to personal growth. Had my anger prevented me, until now, from grieving properly for Carol, and perhaps even for both Granny and H? Now that my rage was fading, did it mean I could finally feel the underlying sadness, and so prepare to move on? These were my thoughts that dark night.

Just as nature heals flesh wounds, Paul insisted, so - in the right circumstances - does it provide a mechanism for emotional injuries to get better too. Just as large or deeply-damaged areas of skin and flesh, unclean or infected, especially when subject to repeated trauma, fail to heal and require medical intervention, so it is in the face of suffering due to losses and threats.

"Threats are always the threat of loss," Paul told me. "Losses bother us because we get emotionally attached to things. The stronger the attachment, the greater the threat of losing it feels... Aversions work much the same way. We can be equally attached to what we *don't* like, as well as what we do, our prejudices, for example. It's tough to give them up."

He was so earnest about these matters, it was like sitting through a lecture sometimes. To help someone dealing with psychological trauma, Paul once said, "You have to remove the cause of suffering, which means protecting the person from further loss, even to the extent of removing them entirely from the negative situation. You have not only to isolate them and make them safe, but you also have to make them *feel* safe; to feel not just safe but respected, cared for and, if possible, loved."

"Love is the best medicine," Mary often chimed in.

Healing and curing were different. Healing implied 'making someone whole again'. Curing, by contrast, was impersonal, referring only to the suppression or eradication of symptoms. The technical terms both came from Greek. (Mr Wright would have loved this.)

Catharsis involved releasing emotional energy through weeping and wailing etcetera, or sometimes through laughter. *Lysis* means letting go, little by little, the strength of attachment and aversion to people, places, activities, ideas, beliefs and all the rest. It means reducing one's grip on likes and dislikes, in other words.

Paul made it seem sensible to me at the time. So, in what way does a person grow through this process? By no longer harking back with either longing or regrets concerning the past, according to Eckhart-Smith, and by becoming less fearful of the future. We achieve maturity by staying increasingly focused in the present moment, by being less pre-occupied with oneself and better attuned to the plight of others, by engaging more meaningfully, too, with the planet and the natural world.

"Wisdom, maturity, compassion and love," Paul told me. "These are the products of healthy grieving, along with inner peace, contentment, courage, hope, and a great deal more."

I wasn't sure what to think, then or now, but it certainly has some appeal. Charlie seemed to agree with it one time when we were talking about the future of the planet, wondering about who might survive Armageddon. She'd been reading a book from the vast library that my man Pipkin had the intelligent forethought to retrieve and protect, about the wisdom traditions of native people.

In some African cultures, she said (as I'd seen for myself out there, but without appreciating the significance), whenever some beloved person dies there's a widespread outpouring of grief and conspicuous lamentation for two or three days, but then it's done. Everyone gets back to their lives as normal. In western culture, in contrast, a sombre pall lies over those left behind, with deliberate suppression of our emotional reactions, resulting in a prolonged and frequently unresolved healing process. People regularly apologise when they cry in public. Scars remain, and wounds can fester forever.

"Unlike us," Charlie added, "Native people tend not to think of time as linear. For them, it feels more circular."

For North American tribes like the Ojibwe and the Potawatomi, she told me, the arrow of time always curls back on itself, as in the *ouroboros* symbol from ancient Egypt and Greece, the one with a serpent holding its tail in its mouth.

"What goes around, comes around... Is that what you mean?" I asked.

"I'm not sure," she said. "I think one meaning is that people get what they deserve; but it also means that human societies wax and wane. They never last forever."

It put me in mind of a trip to Egypt some of us made when we were stationed in Cyprus. After visiting the pyramids near Cairo, we flew south to tour first the great underground tombs of the Pharaohs, then the temple complexes of Luxor and Karnak, both at least two-and-a-half thousand years old, and both ruins, despite restoration. They were astonishing artefacts of a long-gone civilization; oddities now, which I should perhaps have had the wit to recognise as signs that the buildings and monuments of our own time would eventually suffer a similar fate. People would come as tourists to gawp at the relics we leave behind, shrug their shoulders, then go look for an ice-cream. What they should be, those folk, and we should have been, is pilgrims, wrapt in awe and wonder, seeking portents of what will befall us in our turn. Man-made structures, we would then see, are like all the sandcastles I built on the beaches in Cornwall, destined every one to be swept away by the tides of time.

On the brighter side, though, more than fifty years on from the great flood, there are signs that that massive inundation is finally receding. Weather patterns, so turbulent for so long, seem to be settling. The ice-caps are possibly beginning to re-form at the top and tail of the earth. Dry land is surely re-emerging from beneath the sea.

Charlie's book emphasized that the earth, the land, was the source of all that sustained the native people; sustained them physically, mentally and spiritually. Rather than thinking of land as property, as capital, like we used to do, they revered their territory, took their identity from it, valued its connection to their forebears, acknowledged kinship, too, with the animals they shared it with, felt warm respect as well towards all the trees and plants that offered their generous gifts of food, medicine and raw materials; wood for the fire, for example, and birch bark for building canoes. Those tribespeople felt themselves blessed, reading the land like a library of essential information, with vital news too about the weather and about the seasons, offering valuable details about everything they could possibly need. They felt grateful, those indigenous folk, and devised ceremonies of thanksgiving, took powerful mind-altering medicines to enhance their sense of connection with the great cosmic whole, and lived life to the full until the bad times came, when so-called 'civilization' arrived.

Charlie was convinced that such wise people would return. They would be the only ones to survive the cataclysm; not only American Indians, but other first nation folk also, the aborigines of Australia, for example, the tribespeople of Africa and the Amazon too. As long as they remembered their sacred traditions and cultures, or somehow recovered them by intuition, they would surely endure and eventually thrive.

259

Perhaps that's what's happening already. The meek are inheriting the earth, materially poor and primitive, maybe, but spiritually rich and sophisticated, better connected to the land, more respectful of each other, considerate caretakers of the natural world, frugal, taking only what they need, welcoming the cycles of the seasons, the cycle of life and death. These are the chosen ones who will live on, Charlie thought, those who, alone perhaps, have ever truly lived life to the full. The rest of us, wrapped in our precious little bubbles, the artificial, self-centred, private, comfort-zone cocoons we have constructed, struggling almost to breathe in the fresh, clean air of righteousness, have done little else than pretend, frightened children in a world of make-believe, intolerant of change, of what seems new, different or alien, impatient, immature, foolish... And clearly doomed from the start.

It makes even me want a God to pray to, even if there isn't one. It's like the hymn we used to sing at Torville School sometimes; *"Dear Lord and Father of mankind, forgive our foolish ways..."*

Funny how that just popped into my head. *"Re-clothe us in our rightful mind"*, it continues. What a good idea!

Reflecting on the great catastrophic flood, its antecedents and aftermath, recognising our ultimate powerlessness in the face of it, and forced to confront the inevitability of one's own bleak destiny, extinction; all that does seem to invite a degree of humility, I can see. The bigger picture could easily make a person feel humble; humble with each other, humble towards nature, humble, at last, before some kind of divine being, an Almighty God, Creator, Spirit of unity and Lord of the universe! Personally, I don't honestly think that way. But I understand now how others might, especially people like my brother Paul and his Mary.

Is that why I have lived for so long? To experience and grasp some inkling of all that? Who knows? But, whoever they are, those 'primitive savages', the ones that Charlie considered supremely wise, holy people, hidden saints of past and future, building enlightened communities wherever they are on the globe, I sincerely wish them good luck.

Think of it... The revival of wild life, the rain forests, the coral reefs, the snowfields, the grasslands and the prairies *'where the buffaloes roam'*; the whole, precious, sacred cycle of life restored with no further destructive mechanised interference from witless humanity. What a vision! Perhaps that's how the world will be, how future societies are meant to be. Perhaps that's how things are becoming.

Let's think about this. Destruction, death, rebirth and revival; *"What goes around comes around..."* I wonder if Charlie was right... And what about reincarnation? Will I, too, be reborn like young Raffa all those years ago? I hope it will be elsewhere, if it happens, on another planet out there somewhere in this or some other galaxy, on a world of peace and plenty. I hope, too, with all my heart, to be reunited with Carol in such a place, as I also so devoutly wish she was here with me now. I've missed and longed for that beautiful woman every day of my life.

It would be wonderful to be reunited with Charlie, too; with Granny, with Big Al, Blue, Vijay, Mack and The Rock; with The Colonel and Deirdre; even with Pipkin, with Pamila and her Keni, with George and Ada. What a party we'd have! I might meet David Livingstone, or even the Duke of Marlborough! And, strangely, I'm also looking forward in such a place to meeting up again with H, my troubled father, and with Paul, my contrary twin, his Mary and their kids. We had such tortured relationships, typical of which occurred when I foolishly mentioned my plans for that first cull, sending people to sea then sinking the wretched cruise liner with everybody on board.

"You can't do that," Paul said, deeply shocked. "It's murder! You're a bloody murderer, Freddie!"

"What do you suggest, then?" I countered, surprised to hear him actually swear.

Mary and Charlie were with us, but no-one in the room could think of any other viable options.

"People are going to die anyway," I said. "This way, we get to choose who; and those who've already lived long lives should be sacrificed first, to help save the rest, don't you think?"

Well, they didn't think. Even Charlie expressed misgivings, not seeming to mind so much what was being considered, only that I would be the one giving the orders and taking responsibility.

"Someone must," I said. "Otherwise there will be chaos."

Paul and I argued all the time back then. Usually he stayed calm and it was me who ended up getting angry. We bitterly frustrated each other, so it'd be lovely to share affection, to be like real brothers for once. But I know these are all pipe dreams. It's no use wishing that way, so I'll take the last of my magical whisky, and go sit on the balcony in my favourite comfy armchair. Perhaps I'll let myself fall sleep and make it easy for them by not putting up a fight or making any fuss. I'm too weak to resist anyway, so what would be the point?

"Violence is the last refuge of the incompetent," Mr Wright used to say when breaking up fights in the schoolyard, often flicking us painfully behind the ear with an index finger before sending us off to detention. Well, I am certainly much less competent these days, and there's no real fight left in me. The odd thing is I'm resigned. I scarcely mind it at all.

I was indeed once the *Tyrannosaurus Rex* of this kingdom. Truthfully, I did not set out to become a monster, a bully, a tyrant, or a king. This was my fate, my destiny. Circumstances entirely, rather than any choice or ambition of mine, took me to such heights of power and privilege. It's been a good life, an interesting one, never dull. Admittedly, I may have done some things that *others* would have shrunk away from, regretted, and probably wished otherwise; but me... No! I genuinely do not regret anything. I'm a good, simple fellow at heart, doing only what had to be done. I have always done my best, or tried to...

Perhaps I'll do better next time.

The Death of a Tyrant King

Garrotte in hand, behind the guardroom door, the man is surprised by the woman's voice calling so soon from the corridor, down which she had only recently departed.

'Dave... You'd better come and see this!"

Stuffing the weapon into the folds of his tunic, he approaches the spot where she waits, in the open doorway of the Royal Chamber.

"He's gone," she says.

Hastily pushing past her, and seeing no-one in the darkened room, he jumps immediately to the obvious conclusion.

"Has the old bastard escaped?" he exclaims. "I can't believe it. Where would he go... And how?"

"No... Gone... Dead," she says. "On the balcony... Look!"

With some relief, the man, Dave, goes through to find Manning's corpse where he'd left it, slumped sideways in a battered old beige chair, clutching a small silvery object in his hand, the shattered glass of a whisky tumbler shining like snowflakes in the moonlight at his feet.

"Is it a gun?" asks the man. "He's not gone and shot himself, has he?"

But again his thinking is off; as he soon discovers by unwrapping the stiffening fingers to retrieve the object of interest. Careful not to activate any of the buttons, he holds it close to his face for inspection, unaware that, at precisely the same moment, two characters dressed in black from head to toe, wearing capes with hoods and full facemasks, are silently entering the guardroom; exactly as planned by the ruling hierarchy of the fledgling state that is about to be declared a republic. Finding the space empty, exchanging brief glances, they proceed along the same corridor traversed by the others shortly before. Both men are carrying long, sharp knives; one also has three black hessian body bags rolled-up under one arm.

"He's still warm," Dave observes meanwhile. "Can't have been dead half an hour... What's this contraption, do you suppose?"

"It's an old-fashioned dictation machine, I think," the woman responds helpfully. "A pre-digital one. I noticed a pile of cassette tapes on his desk back inside, each one numbered... Let's see what he's been saying."

The two assassins stealthily take up station outside the door of the chamber, at precisely the same moment as the woman presses 'rewind'. A whirring sound emerges, followed by a click. The four living presences within earshot, still as statues in the deafening hush, instinctively hold their breath as the 'play' button is triggered, releasing into the pregnant stillness the croaky yet unmistakeable voice of their late ruler, reciting a final self-justification.

"I did not set out to become such a monster, a bully, a tyrant, or a king. This was my fate, my destiny. Circumstances entirely, rather than any choice or ambition of mine, took me to such heights of power and privilege."

A brief pause follows, a kind of sigh on the tape and a gulping for breath, as the woman looks across at the man called Dave, whose face betrays nothing, waiting for the monologue to resume.

"It's been a good life; an interesting one, never dull," the dying dictator is wheezily heard to continue. "Admittedly, I may have done some things that *others* would have shrunk away from, regretted, and probably wished otherwise; but me... No! I genuinely do not regret anything. I'm a good, simple fellow at heart, doing only what had to be done..."

In stunned disbelief, the woman can barely stifle a snigger.

"Doing only what had to be done..."

Dave, too, appears shocked.

"A good fellow? No... No way!" he cries out, for he had seen his wife and child butchered at the tyrant's command. "He was a vile, evil man... Evil, power hungry... and mad!"

But the ethereal voice from the machine is not done.

"I have always done my best, or tried to," it intones as if to rebuff these and all accusations. "Perhaps I'll do better next time."

Seconds later, taking the final click from the dictaphone as their cue, the assassins enter the room swiftly to complete their business, and within a minute it is over. Had he been a witness, Freddie Manning, the tyrant king, would surely have admired the brilliance of the combat skills on display.

The End

Printed in Great Britain
by Amazon

29276221R00155